SHE WAS DESTINED TO LOVE HIM . . .

A firm believer in portents and prophecy, Lady Elfrida Rochelle is stunned by a premonition that the Earl of Shields, the man she is meant to love—but has yet to meet—is in terrible peril. Heading for London straightaway, she intends to convince him they belong together . . . though of course they must never wed. For it is written in the stars—if she marries him, he will die. . . .

. . . AND FATED TO REFUSE HIM!

A steadfast bachelor, the Earl of Shields has no intention of taking a bride simply to fill a nursery. Life with the extraordinary Lady Elfrida, however, would be anything but dull. Though he has little faith in her cursed crystal ball, he cannot deny that danger seems to stalk the intrepid black-haired beauty . . . nor can he ignore his own burning desire to possess her. Somehow, he must learn the truth behind the sinister accidents that threaten their future, and convince Elfrida that the safest place for both of them is in each other's arms. . . .

Books by Sara Blayne

PASSION'S LADY

DUEL OF THE HEART

A NOBLEMAN'S BRIDE

AN ELUSIVE GUARDIAN

AN EASTER COURTSHIP

THEODORA

ENTICED

A NOBLE DECEPTION

A NOBLE PURSUIT

A NOBLE RESOLVE

A NOBLE HEART

HIS SCANDALOUS DUCHESS

AN IMPROPER BRIDE

Published by Zebra Books

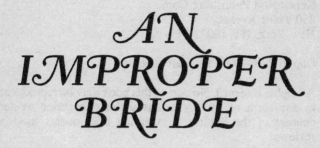

AN IMPROPER BRIDE

Sara Blayne

ZEBRA BOOKS
KENSINGTON PUBLISHING CORP.

http://www.zebrabooks.com

To Steve, for his forbearance and support; to Kathryn, for her encouragement and cheerful optimism; to Morgan, who never stopped asking, "Is your book done yet?" And to Caleb for giving me the idea I needed to forge to the end. I love you all.

Chapter 1

Lady Elfrida Rochelle, the eldest granddaughter of the Duke of Albermarle, slipped quietly away from the family gathered in the withdrawing room. Lost in thought, she wended her way through the castle's maze of twisting corridors and winding stairs to her private quarters. These were called the Crystal Suite because her great-grandmother, Lucasta Albermarle, a noted scryer of her day, had been used to practice her art of divination in the tower room overlooking the plunging river gorge and, beyond the Devon shoreline, the blue stretch of the English Channel. It was widely circulated that the former duchess had foreseen numerous momentous events, such as the emergence of the first cuckoo clocks in the Black Forest and the staging of the very first official cricket match, which, as it happened, had pitted Kent against All England. There was also the adoption of the qua-drille as the dance of fashion in France, not to mention lesser occurrences on the order of the attempted theft of the Albermarle betrothal ring by Genevieve Hayden, the beautiful red-haired adventuress who was fated to become Lucasta's daughter-in-law and the very next Duchess of Albermarle.

A faint smile touched Elfrida's lips at the thought of her great-grandmama Lucasta, with whom she had not the smallest doubt she would have had a great deal in common, and her grandmama Genevieve, who long ago had captured her imagination. How she would like to have known the woman who had tamed Edmond Rochelle, the Duke of Albermarle, her grandfather, who at seventy-four not only exuded an unnerving aura of command, but was at present contemplating—of all things—*matrimony* with a voluptuously endowed widow less than half his age!

The old rogue, she thought with a fond, if rather sardonic, glint in her eyes. There would be talk that Albermarle had at last entered his dotage or at the very least was clearly round the bend. But then, the duke's sun sign was Aquarius with the moon in Leo. How very *like* Albermarle to do precisely what no one would have expected him to do, something wholly outrageous and sure to set everyone off balance! And with predictable complications, she mused, a furrow marring the purity of her lovely brow. He *would* have to arrive at Albermarle Castle unannounced with Estelle, Lady Barstowe, in his entourage—*now*, when Gideon, the Marquis of Vere, Elfrida's brother and the duke's heir apparent, had found it prudent to rusticate in the country until a certain irate husband had been given time to recover from a pistol ball to the arm.

Fortunately, perhaps, Vere was off to Honiton for a day or two ostensibly to view a prizefight, though with Vere one could never be quite sure with what he might be involving himself. But at least he had not been present for the duke's unheralded arrival. Elfrida could only shudder at Albermarle's probable reaction to the discovery that Vere had been involved in yet another duel! Worse, however, was the dire prospect of placing a delectable morsel like Lady Barstowe within Vere's lethal sphere of influence! The inevitable ramifications of such an ill-advised course were tantamount to inviting disaster upon the house of Albermarle and most certainly upon Vere himself, who, without a fortune of his own, depended for his daily existence upon the largesse of his grandfather, the duke! Not that that inescapable fact would make a whit of difference to Vere once he arrived home to discover a beautiful widow had taken up residence in the family pile. Elfrida knew her brother too well to suppose he would be moved to abstinence by the desirability of, if not actually currying his grandfather's favor, then at least avoiding incurring his grace's out and out displeasure. Nor would Vere be deterred by something so insignificant as the circumstance that Lady Barstowe had apparently done the seeming impossible—she had, to all appearances, captured the elusive heart of the Duke of Albermarle, a man who had, for the past twenty-five years, worn the willow for Genevieve, his beloved duchess!

A plague on her brother and the duke! thought Elfrida, who did not require a reading of the Tarot cards to predict the disastrous possibilities inherent in the immediate future of the inhabitants of Albermarle Castle. Even at two and twenty, Elfrida's brother, Gideon, the Marquis of Vere, was a veritable devil with the women. And how not? reflected Elfrida. Vere, after all, was a Scorpio, the most powerful sign of the Zodiac. In Gideon, the Scorpio's inherent grasp of all that pertained to both the primitive and the sublime passions between male and female along with that penetrating insight into the emotional depths of others that was characteristic of Scorpios had been intensified to a frightening degree. Indeed, Vere's cold, hooded stare was enough to curdle one's blood, the devil! Nor was that all. Possessed, furthermore, of the Rochelle legacy of raven-black hair and eyes the mesmeric blue of lapis lazuli, which in turn was coupled in Gideon with a Scorpio's brooding aura of secrecy and a fatal charm, Vere was a deadly and irresistible force where females were concerned. Even fearing him, they simply could not help being fascinated by him. It was like asking a moth to resist the flame—or, worse, the scorpion to resist delivering the fatal sting. No doubt her grandfather had failed utterly to take that potent factor into account when he had determined upon bringing Lady Barstowe to Albermarle in order to make her feel a part of the "Family"—or had he?

One could never be quite certain what was going through the duke's head at any given moment. In his own decidedly unique manner of reasoning, it might very well have seemed a perfectly logical move to unloose the harbinger of chaos among the inhabitants of Albermarle Castle merely to observe the interesting results—rather like conducting an abstract study in the sudden, violent disintegration of a family. It was something Albermarle was perfectly capable of doing, and only Albermarle would overlook the pertinent fact that it was his own family he was intent on wrecking out of a purely academic curiosity. Or perhaps in his typical, absent-minded fashion he had momentarily forgotten that those beings whom he was manipulating for his own ends were his own kith and kin—indeed, that they were, when he was jolted out of his airy contemplations, people for whom he entertained a deep and enduring affection. To some, this mani-

festation of the duke's character must seem uncon-
scionably cold, even inhuman perhaps, but to those
who knew him intimately, as did Elfrida and the
other members of the family, it was simply one
of Albermarle's numerous quirks. No matter how
dispassionately his grace might appear to use his
immediate blood relations, the duke always made
everything right in the end.

And besides, Elfrida reminded herself, it was just
as possible that Albermarle, having fallen victim to
the beautiful young widow's undeniable charms,
had his head too high in the clouds to reckon on
what to Elfrida was all too obvious. He might even
have momentarily misplaced the memory that his
heir apparent was a notorious womanizer who
already had three duels to his dubious credit or
that, loving the duke as Vere did (though Gideon
would rather die than admit to such an affection), her brother would be compelled to exert
his considerable Scorpio powers to test the widow's worthiness to assume the title of the Duchess
of Albermarle.

Elfrida did not doubt that Vere could and *would*
seduce the widow if he chose to carry the thing out
to its logical conclusion. To Elfrida's knowledge the
marquis had never failed in an amorous undertaking. However, if he did take the widow to his bed,
it would be because Lady Barstowe had already
proven unsuited for the honor that Albermarle had
intended to bestow upon her. Elfrida was certain of
that.

It was not, after all, the lady's virtue that was in
question. What she and her ducal cicisbeo might
choose to do behind closed doors was a purely
private affair between herself and the duke and
none of Elfrida's concern or her brother's. Should
the lady choose to take on a younger, more vigor-
ous lover after the marriage vows were spoken, it

might even be overlooked, so long as the affair was conducted with discretion and, of course, it did not involve a member of the duke's immediate family. Those would be matters for the duke to decide and would hardly concern Vere.

Nor would Vere be interested in the lady's motives in marrying the duke. *They*, after all, were utterly transparent and therefore perfectly obvious to everyone. A woman born to nobility, especially one with little or no fortune of her own, must be expected to seek to remedy that deficiency in an advantageous marriage; and everyone knew the profligate Earl of Barstowe had left his widow with hardly a feather to fly with. The question, therefore, was not whether Estelle, Lady Barstowe, was attracted to Albermarle for his title and his fortune, for she undoubtedly was, but whether she possessed those qualities that would make her a worthy wife, one who would strive not only to meet the responsibilities inherent in the elevated position of the Duchess of Albermarle, but one who would satisfy at least the fundamental obligations owed to her husband, the duke.

What Vere would be looking for was some sort of assurance that the lady was not a scheming female with a heart of jade who would not hesitate, once she had achieved her ends, to treat the duke with a sudden, chilly indifference or even disdain. That sort of injury to the duke's pride was naturally not to be tolerated, and Vere was just the one to see through a charming facade to whatever lay behind it. Indeed, Elfrida doubted there was anyone who could pull the wool over Gideon's eyes (save, of course, for their younger sister Violet, who was as utterly elusive of understanding as would be anyone born under the sign of Pisces, which, as everyone knew, was personified by two fish swimming in opposite directions). And there was the rub.

Elfrida herself, after all, entertained no little doubt in the sincerity of the widow, who, a bubbling Gemini, seemed to present all the depth of character of a sparkling glass of champagne. Appearances, however, could be deceiving. She had obviously tickled Albermarle's fancy, not to mention his nose and probably various other parts of his indisputably aged but still-handsome anatomy; and, quick-witted and at least superficially well-read, Lady Barstowe was perfectly capable of retaining the duke's interest, of even proving to be a source of happiness for him in his declining years, *if* she did not suddenly take the urge to launch a career on stage as a diva or embark on a tour of Asia Minor purely for a change of scenery. Albermarle was prone to unpredictable starts, which might lead him to do any number of incomprehensible things, like taking up kite flying from the castle parapets in the dead of winter, as he had done the previous January. Or appearing at breakfast one morning wearing a helmet with a sharp-pointed visor in the style of the pig-faced bascinet worn by the First Duke of Albermarle, his Fourteenth Century forebear. Or taking it into his head at the ripe age of seventy-four to wed a woman less than half his age—but he was exceedingly unlikely to see anything in the least enticing about making any extended stays away from Devon in order that his duchess might pursue a career in the opera. And as for sailing away from England to tour the Orient, why, he would sooner parade down St. James's Street in his natural state as do any such thing. In fact, Elfrida would be less surprised if her grandfather did the latter than if he chose to embark on a voyage to distant parts. Save for the obligatory Grand Tour, Albermarle was and always had been firmly rooted on English soil and saw not the slightest reason why anyone should be enamored of the notion of jaunting willy-nilly about the rest of the world. Unfortunately, Lady Barstowe did not promise to be similarly disposed. As a Gemini, she must almost inevitably grow bored with twiddling her thumbs about the family pile while Albermarle occupied himself with his various unfathomable pursuits, like undertaking to compile a census of all the redheads born in Devon in the past forty years, a project upon which, having engaged the services of a dozen or more chroniclers, he was presently launched.

No, decided Elfrida, letting herself into the airy environs of the Crystal Room. The odds were greatly stacked against the success of such a marriage. Perhaps if Albermarle were twenty years younger or Lady Barstowe ten years older, things might have worked out remarkably well between them. They did, after all, enjoy a 5-9 Sun Sign Pattern, which meant that their natal Suns were trined, Elfrida reflected, determined to give the widow her due. Unless there were some serious negative aspects between their other planets, they were, astrologically speaking, practically meant for one another. Unfortunately, Albermarle, having entered his seventy-fourth year and having been born under a fixed sign as well, was entirely too set in his ways ever to change now. And Lady Barstowe, both young and ruled by a mutable sign, was hardly prepared to assume a sedentary existence. Therefore, while the widow might very well be astrologically attracted to the aging duke, the likelihood that the romance would be able to withstand the test of time was nebulous at best.

But then, perhaps Lady Barstowe had every expectation the marriage would be of an exceedingly short duration; indeed, there was always the distinct possibility she was even counting on that very thing. In which case, she would hardly be motivated to exert herself to extend her husband's life expectancy. She might even be moved to do all in her power to discourage the duke's continued good health. Certainly, that would be Vere's concern, thought Elfrida, her brow puckering in a worried frown.

To say Vere would not take kindly to anyone who had deliberately set out to misuse his grandfather would be to put the matter exceedingly mildly. Her Scorpio brother could be expected to view such an occurrence as grounds for a punitive action of the sort to make the siege of Troy seem like child's play, never mind that Albermarle was perfectly capable of determining his own life for himself or that the duke would undoubtedly cut his grandson off without a farthing for Vere's unwelcome interference.

No, somehow the inevitable must be averted, although Elfrida, for the life of her, could not think how it was to be done. She was far too fond of Gideon ever to wish to see him in the lurch. It had been bad enough when their parents met an untimely demise two years ago in what had been termed a yachting accident, though no one really believed a sailor of the late marquis's remove would be driven onto the rocks in a gale. Gideon had believed it less than anyone, but especially so when it was revealed the marquis and marchioness had had on board a fortune in gold salvaged from France, all of which had presumably been lost to the bottom of the sea. Add to that a sizeable gambling marker presented against Vere's estate by the Earl of Blaidsdale, who had never seen the day when he could beat Vere at Faro or any other game of chance, and Gideon could hardly be blamed for thinking his father had been the victim of a sinister plot to bring the marquis and his progeny to ruin.

That, however, was all water under the bridge now. There had been no proof then that the marker was either forged or the product of chicanery, and there was no proof now that Blaidsdale had been behind the death of the marquis and marchioness. The reality was that, galling as it might be to Vere, her brother, thanks to Blaidsdale's marker and the loss of the *Swallow* with its treasure, was dependent upon his grandfather to sustain him in the manner of living to which he had ever been accustomed, and it behooved Elfrida to discover a way of preventing the marquis from doing something to jeopardize his standing with the duke.

Had that been all to occupy her as she roamed aimlessly about the octagonal confines of the tower room, perhaps Elfrida would soon have come up with an answer to her dilemma. The truth was, however, that Albermarle had arrived with further disturbing news, which served as a powerful distraction from what should, in the norm, have been the main issue at hand.

Viscount Hepplewaite, who, while deep in his cups, had had the temerity only two months past to steal a kiss from Elfrida beneath the grape arbor at Lady Wrotham's house party, only three days ago had had a period put to his existence in a manner that was both horrifying and mysterious. He had, as a matter of fact, to all appearances been brutally stabbed with his own sword and then, a lamp having been knocked to the floor in what was theorized to have been a struggle, the body had been burned beyond recognition. Indeed, his lordship had been identified only by the signet ring on his charred right hand and the brass buttons on his coat. By that and the testimony of the members of the household that their master had been closeted alone in the room in which the fire had begun.

Really, she reflected, things were come to a sad pass when someone could cut the stick of a man like Viscount Hepplewaite in his own home and then come close to burning an entire wing of the house down around his victim. She shivered at the cold-bloodedness of the deed, the news of which had occupied the conversation at tea. It was inconceivable that not a single clue as to the murderer's identity had been uncovered; indeed, it would appear that no one had the slightest notion who might even have wished ill of Lord Hepplewaite. After all, Hepplewaite, aside from a few minor infractions on the order of the kiss he had stolen from Elfrida and a tendency to overindulge himself in those frivolous pursuits common to his contemporaries, had enjoyed the reputation of a charming ne'er-do-well. A member of the Carlton set and an intimate of the Earl of Shields, who was offering a sizeable reward for information leading to the capture of his friend's murderer, Hepplewaite was, in fact, generally well-tolerated among the members of Society. Which very probably meant, no doubt, mused Elfrida, that the murder had been the unfortunate by-product of a burglary or some such thing. Certainly, that was the theory going the rounds of London's best salons and withdrawing rooms; and, if it were a matter of a burglary gone sour, it was exceedingly unlikely the murderer would ever be found, let alone delivered to his just deserts.

A pity, Elfrida thought with a small shake of her dusky curls. While it was true that she, herself, had never particularly warmed to the viscount, she could not but think he deserved better than to have been foully done in and then laid to rest without at least the satisfaction of having his mur-

derer brought to justice. She would be more than
a tad bit surprised if poor Hepplewaite, caught
wholly unprepared to be violently severed from this
life, were finding it utterly impossible to reconcile
himself to the reality of his death. Very likely he
was even now occupied with haunting the scene
of his unhappy demise until such time as the
events of that fatal night were finally brought out.
Only, since it was unlikely that they ever would
be, he would be condemned to an eternity of
unrest, like Thomas Nettleby, her great-great-
great-great-grandfather's lord of the bedchamber, who, having been discovered before his
master's bedroom door one night nearly two hundred years ago with the back of his skull caved in,
had been haunting the corridors of Albermarle
Castle ever since.

At that thought it came to Elfrida to wonder, not
for the first time, if the spirits of her own dearest
mama and papa, too, were roaming the earth in
a state of unrequited wrong. The notion was not
a comforting one; indeed, Elfrida was plagued with
a bitter sense of failure that she had not been given
so much as an inkling beforehand of the events
that had led up to her parents' untimely demise.
Nor did it help to remind herself that no one could
command the mists of seeing. Knowing that dreams
and visions came of their own or not at all did
nothing to ease the ache in her heart that she had
been able to do nothing to prevent the premature
loss of her mother and father.

She *should* have foreseen it, Elfrida told herself,
catching her lip between her teeth. Failing that,
she should at the very least have *sensed* something
was gravely amiss. Instead, her dreams had been
uneventful, disturbed by nothing more momentous than the premonition that Gideon had won
a considerable sum at Newmarket on a dark horse

and had promptly flung it all away on a new team
of perfectly matched blacks. Elfrida derived not
the least satisfaction that her dream had proven at
least partially right: Gideon had won a substantial
purse, only it had not been on a dark horse at
Newmarket, but on a gentlemen's wager concerning something so absurd as the time it took for a
leaf, caught in a spiral of wind, to drift to the
ground. The matched team of blacks, moreover,
had shrunk by the time of his arrival home to
a single Irish stallion of magnificent proportions,
which was rather whimsically, perhaps even pro-
phetically, named Dark Reverie.

Certainly the subsequent arrival of the news of
the marquis and marchioness's ill-fated voyage had
had all the aspects of a "dark reverie," one, moreover, from which there would be no awakening.
Perhaps therein had lain the warning, and she,
caught up in her latest cause, a campaign for the
betterment of the plight of chimney sweeps, had
been too busy to see it for what it really was.

Well, that had been the last campaign, her final
lost cause, she reminded herself. Never mind that
she had been born under the sign of the Ram and
must consequently be fated ever to be drawn to
one crusade or another. She would never be so
remiss again as to follow the beat of another drum
to the detriment of her one, true calling.

She, Elfrida Frederica Rochelle, was a prognosticator and a scryer, one born, like her great-
grandmother Lucasta before her, with the true
gift of divination.

There were times when, really, she wished she
had not been singled out for what she could not
but think was a rather dubious honor. The truth
was there was little to recommend in forever being
visited with dreams and visions of the future, which
must be somehow interpreted and whose meanings

in the end very often proved nebulous at best. And,
after all, what good did it do anyone that she had
glimpses of the future if she could bring no one
to believe in them?

Unfortunately, *she* believed in them; indeed, she
could no more deny them than she could suddenly
make herself stop having them. Not even drugging
herself to sleep with extract of Valerian root combined with the essence of Passion Flower and Kava
Kava root had served to banish them. The dreams
came, as did the visions in the shew stone, whether
she willed them or not. Or they would *not* come,
no matter how hard she tried to summon them.
It was the curse of the seer to be at the mercy of
the gift. And, like a potent drug, the lure, most
especially of the shew stone, to one with the eye
to see was practically irresistible.

Indeed, as if drawn, she found herself standing
over the small round table set in the curve of the
window overlooking the river gorge. Her hand, as
if possessed of a will of its own, was already reaching
to lift the square of silk off the mound at the table's
center.

The cloth removed, the crystal orb into which
Lucasta Albermarle had once gazed was revealed
residing innocuously in its silver cradle. Elfrida,
however, had looked before into its depths to
behold the swirl of mists whence visions came. She
knew what it was to be drawn out of oneself into the
miasma of potentialities, to behold the tantalizing
images of things that were yet to be.

Unfortunately, it would seem thus far to have
proven of remarkably little benefit to anyone,
sighed Elfrida, dropping into the straight-backed
chair set before the table. After all, she reflected
with a wry quirk of her lovely mouth, what use was
it, really, to know beforehand that Sullie Wicks,
the scullery maid, was going to stumble over the

kitchen feline at the precise moment that Henri,
the French chef, was in the process of removing
the *fricassée de poulet* from the skillet to the warmed
platter if, in trying to warn of the impending disaster, Elfrida inadvertently precipitated it? Involuntarily she shuddered at the remembered horror
of events: herself bursting unannounced into the
kitchens, her French heel coming down on the tail
of the cat quietly lapping cream from its saucer,
the blood-chilling yowl from the offended feline
which launched itself across the room straight into
the ankles of Sullie Wicks, who was carrying a bowl
of soapy dish water to be tossed out the kitchen
door. The bowl flying into the air to land with
unerring accuracy upside down on Henri's bald
pate was certainly a never-to-be-forgotten image,
as was the devastation of *fricassée de poulet* marinated
in *eau de vaisselle*. Dishwater, after all, was hardly
to be viewed as an appetizing sauce.

If nothing else, the unfortunate incident had
served to teach Elfrida one important lesson: no
one, not even a scryer given to see glimpses of
future events, had the power to alter that which
was meant to be. It might even be, she reflected
wryly, that one would do better not even to try.

In which case there would seem to be very little
point in having been born a prognosticator and a
scryer. Indeed, perhaps Violet was right, and she,
Elfrida, should occupy herself with other, more
constructive pursuits, like accepting Lord Harry
Wilcox's offer of marriage—never mind that she
entertained only a sisterly affection for him or that
she was quite sure they would make each other's
lives perfectly miserable. Crabs and Rams simply
did not go well together, romantically speaking,
not with a 4-10 vibratory pattern. While he was a
perfectly charming gentleman when he was not
scrabbling away in a veritable peeve of hurt sensibil-

ities and though he had the uncanny knack for
making her laugh at his many little absurdities, she
did not doubt that, as her husband, he would soon
douse her fiery spirits with his Cancerian disap-
proval of her impulsive nature, not to mention his
tendency to give way to a stifling jealousy. Still,
there could be little doubt that, married to Lord
Harry, she would be kept far too busy at butting
her head against her husband's hard Cancerian
crab shell to have time for the frivolous pursuit of
divination. And what did it matter, really, if she
had yet to discover her Twin Soul, the one man
who, joined with her in a state of Oneness, would
make her complete, even as she would make him
physically and mystically whole? Having already
reached the ripe age of five and twenty without
having discerned the identity of her karmically predetermined, astrologically perfect mate, she must
soon be forced to settle for a lesser union if she
intended to experience the joys of motherhood,
not to mention the mysteries of passion. After all,
it was not *impossible* for a Crab and a Ram to achieve
romantic fulfillment if one approached the marriage with an understanding of the astrological
forces in play and a willingness to compromise to
achieve at least a measure of harmony. And at least
in motherhood she would be assured of a true
purpose in life rather than the self-doubts and
seeming futility that her pursuit of divination had
thus far brought her. Surely that must be worth
the sacrifice of karmic perfection.

At that thought, her head came up, her eyes the
clear blue of the sky on a cloudless spring day
flashing in unconscious defiance. Now she was
being utterly absurd, she chided herself. Everything that existed in Nature must surely have a
purpose. Perhaps foreseen future events could not
be altered, but that did not necessarily mean the

outcome of such events was not open to manipulation, did it? If one knew there was going to be a fire, one might not be able to prevent the conflagration, but perhaps it would be possible to stop someone from going into the building about to ignite. Indeed, would not one be morally obligated to do all in one's power to see that everyone was evacuated before it burst into flames? Unless, of course, she groaned silently to herself, in all the confusion of trying to *save* all the poor unfortunates, one knocked over a lamp and actually started the fire!

"Fiddlesticks!" she uttered, propping an elbow on the tabletop and dropping her chin into the palm of her hand. Really, it was all very confusing when one tried to apply reason to something which was, by its very nature, quite beyond the bounds of logic. One found oneself inevitably going round in circles, which was all very disagreeable to an Aries, whose natural inclination, after all, was to ram straight through to the heart of any matter, and logic be bloody well damned.

Well, the heart of the matter was that she, Elfrida, had been, for whatever reason, given the gift of divination. Not to use it would be to deny her essential being, even as settling for less than her karmically predetermined, astrologically perfect mate simply to experience motherhood and the sense of purpose that had hitherto been eluding her would be to bring a negative influence to bear on her karma, and that was not to be thought of. Indeed, despite her spells of doubt, she would be far better served to simply forge ahead in true Aries fashion. No doubt in time she would learn to use her gift as it was meant to be used. She sighed, her eyes drawn to the luminous depths of the crystal. If only she had *some* indication of what that use was!

Hardly had that thought crossed her mind than

it came to her—the one potential good that
might be gotten from a reading of the shew stone.
If it were marriage and the purpose of rearing a
family that were needed to keep her from forever
plunging into deep waters, would she not be
wholly justified in seeking a vision of her karmically predetermined, astrologically perfect mate
in the crystal? And, after all, what harm could
there possibly be in it? At the very least, there
would be nothing to lose and possibly a great
deal to be gained in such a venture.

Deciding that, indeed, there could be no harm
in using the powers bequeathed to her by her great-
grandmama Lucasta to discover the one man she
was meant to love, Elfrida gazed fixedly into the
translucent depths of the shew stone. Her will
quiescent, her mind focused on the erubescent
heart of the crystal, she waited, just as her great-
grandmother must have done all those years before
her. She reminded herself that the crystal's visions
could not be coaxed from the stone. They came
of their own, or they came not at all. She was only
the scryer with the eyes to see if the powers that
be willed it.

Even so, not everyone could do what she did.
True crystal gazers were born, not made, to see
within the crystal transparency to the swirl of mist
from which visions formed. She beheld it now,
the first soft vaporous clouds, the sublimation of
transparency to ether, of will to divination. She
waited, her mind empty of everything but the dis-
tillation of mist into seeing. As the room receded
and faded into shadows, she felt herself drawn into
the crystal's miasma.

It was movement in stillness, a soundless hurtling
without sensation. Clouds rushed past her, parted,
vanished, but she felt nothing, heard nothing. She
only saw: a night sky studded with brilliant stars

above a spreading pall of grey pierced through by church spires, chimney stacks, and the roofs of tall houses; and then the descent through wreaths of fog to a street dimly lit by the shrouded glow of a single street lamp, a house bathed in darkness, a door opening, the eerie shapes of shadows—a man, alone, turning his head to look at her.

He was tall and well built, his eyes the grey-blue of winter mist and yet etched at the corners with laugh wrinkles. The high, wide, intelligent brow, the long, straight nose and wide, sensuous lips, the firm chin and stubborn jaw—all gave the impression of a magnificent arrogance. Indeed, everything about him exuded a golden, masculine pride. And yet there was about him, too, the sense that his manly strength was tempered with a not insignificant capacity for gentleness, that his shining confidence overlay a sympathetic heart.

He was Guy Herrick, the Earl of Shields, and he was, she knew instantly, without a doubt, her Twin Soul—her karmically predetermined, astrologically perfect mate. But more than that, there was, hanging over him, an unmistakable pall of danger!

Chapter 2

Guy Herrick, the Earl of Shields, stared, unseeing, at the leap of flames in the study fireplace. His silent musings could hardly have been said to be of a rewarding nature, as was evidenced by the grim line of his handsome mouth and the bleak hardness of his eyes, just now the opaque grey-blue of slate. He was sprawled in a leather-upholstered armchair, his long legs, crossed at the ankles, stretched out before him, while the slender fingers of one hand held a forgotten glass of brandy. His buff unmentionables were travel-stained, the polished sheen of his brown Hessians marred by a greyish dust. His hair, the color of gold guineas, was tousled, as though he had repeatedly thrust his fingers through it.

That he had not bothered to rectify the imperfections in his appearance upon his arrival some hours ago at his Town House on Grosvenor Square was mute evidence that his lordship was distracted indeed. But then, his thoughts, far from concerning his normally impeccable appearance, were consumed with the memory of the dreadful scene of destruction to which he had been witness little more than a fortnight before.

Good God, it had appeared that Ludgate Hall had been swept by an avenging fury! Indeed, in view of the completeness of the devastation, it was a marvel that only a single wing of the once-great house had been made to succumb to the voracious flames. Nevertheless, it was doubtful the Tudor manor would ever be returned to anything approaching its former glory.

Even more horrific, however, than the sight of the entire west wing of Ludgate Hall reduced to rubble was the knowledge of what those charred remains had been meant to conceal.

James Randall Ludgate, Viscount Hepplewaite, the man who had been one of Shields's closest friends since their school days together at Eton, had been foully impaled on his own sword and then left to burn in the conflagration.

"The devil, Jamey boy," murmured Shields, rubbing a hand hard over his eyes, as if by that he might rid himself of the images evoked by his own haunted fancy. "Pray God you were not left to burn alive!"

Feeling the bile rise to his throat, Shields threw back his head and tossed off his drink in a single swallow. The fiery liquid did little to ease the cold, hard knot in the pit of his belly, any more than had the numerous libations that had preceded it. Nevertheless, he reached for the decanter on the occasional table beside him, only to find the vessel was empty.

"Hellsfire!" he cursed and lurched to his feet with the intention of ringing for a fresh decanter.

His hand went still on the bellpull, his brow knit in a frown. He felt weary to the bone and was aware of a vague disgust at himself. He had neither bathed

nor eaten since his return to London after a fruitless attempt to discover something—*anything*—
that might lead him to the truth surrounding the
tragic events at Ludgate Hall. He hardly knew how
long he had sat brooding in the solitary confines
of his study, sickened to the core by the realization
that, had he been but a day earlier, he might have
averted Jamey's premature death. His hand
clenched about the bellpull. One *day*, he thought.
He gave the bellpull a yank. One bloody damned
day!

Had he been too arrogant? Too bloody sure of
himself? If he had had it to do over again, would he
have chosen to humiliate Hepplewaite by ordering
him from the Faro table before the demmed fool
could drop five thousand in a single evening?
Could he thus have averted the ensuing tragedy?
When the idea had come to Shields, that at last he
had been presented with the opportunity to teach
Hepplewaite a lesson once and for all, he had
hardly thought he would be robbed of the chance
to undo the events of that cursed night.

He had made the journey to Ludgate near Shaftesbury to return Jamey's markers, just as he had
intended to do from the very beginning. After all,
he had meant the entire exercise to be an object
lesson in self-restraint, something of which the viscount had ever been in exceedingly short supply—
which was why Shields had determined to put it
off for that extra day. He had wanted to give Jamey
time enough to stew in his own juices before delivering him from the apparent consequences of his
cursed poor judgment. He had been met with the
sight of Ludgate Hall's still-smoldering ruins.

Hell and the devil confound it! There was no
possible way he could have known the fate that
awaited his friend at Ludgate Hall. Still, he could
not dismiss the fact that, had he sent for Hepple-

waite the morning after the viscount's ill-considered debauchery, there would have been little need for Jamey to depart London for a period of rustication in the country. In which case, the viscount would undoubtedly be alive today.

Damn Hepplewaite and his cursed easy nature! He should have known better than to engage at Faro while in his cups—especially when Shields owned the bank. Jamey had never been a poor gamester. Knowing, however, that he, Shields, was not to blame for Hepplewaite's death any more than he was accountable for the viscount's run of bad luck did nothing to ease the bitter taste of gall in his mouth. He *felt* as if he were at fault. But then, he had felt an odd sense of responsibility for Hepplewaite ever since he had first come upon young Jamey, a boy, then, in the lower forms, suffering harassment at the hands of Shields's own, older contemporaries. Perhaps Shields had seen something of his younger brother in Hepplewaite, a pale reflection of the boy who had looked up to Shields and who had died of fever at the age of seven. Whatever the case, though Shields was eight years Hepplewaite's senior, Shields had taken the boy under his wing, a relationship that had persisted through the succeeding years until fate had intervened.

Who the devil could have put a period to Jamey's existence, and why? pondered the earl, only vaguely aware that Craddock, his very proper London butler, had entered to replace the empty decanter with a full one and then, after a single glance at his master's forbidding aspect, had as quietly withdrawn. Given to indulge in excesses of drink and vice, Hepplewaite had hardly been the sort to endear himself to others. On the other hand, he had never been known to incur deep feelings of hostility or aversion, at least not to the degree that would incite motivation for the heinous crime of murder. He was Hepplewaite, that was all—weak-willed, pleasure-loving, and basically harmless—a featherweight in all respects. It seemed ludicrous to suppose that anyone would be so aroused as to cut his stick for him, especially in a manner that was as brutal as it was deliberately cold-blooded. But then, the theory was that Hepplewaite's murder was the accidental by-product of a burglary gone bad, Shields reminded himself with a sardonic curl of his lip, a postulation that would seem to leave a great deal to be desired.

In truth, everything about the crime was puzzling. Why had the sword been used instead of a knife, which would seem the more logical weapon if it was indeed the work of a sneak thief surprised in the act of robbing the house? And why had the blade been left buried in the victim? Would it not have been instinctive to pull the weapon free, especially if it had been part of the thief's intended booty, as was the theory put forth by the local magistrate? And the bloody fire. What reason would a thief have to burn the house down around his hapless victim? A fire would have attracted a deal of immediate and unwanted attention for a man intent upon escaping while burdened with his ill-gotten loot. The fire, however, would seem to make as little sense if it had been meant to hide the act of an intentional, premeditated murderer. After all, leaving the blade imbedded in the victim would seem a glaring oversight in such an event. Even twisted and warped out of shape, there had been no mistaking the significance of the object protruding from the charred body—a significance that would seem to point, not to murder, but to a self-inflicted death!

And therein lay the source of Shields's unquiet thoughts, for that was the somber possibility that had occurred to him immediately upon being apprised of the circumstances surrounding his friend's untimely demise: Hepplewaite, rather than face the almost certain financial ruin to which his profligate habits had brought him, had taken the honorable way out. Good God! And yet even that all too plausible explanation for the viscount's end did not explain the fire. Nor did it, in the final analysis, resolve all the questions that had plagued Shields the past three days, robbing him of his sleep and driving him to seek some sort of resolution to the puzzle of Hepplewaite's death.

Having known the viscount perhaps better than had anyone else, Shields could not but find it exceedingly difficult to believe Jamey could ever have brought himself to cut his own stick, especially in so medieval a fashion as to fall upon his own sword—egad!

The devil! thought Shields. *Nothing* concerning Hepplewaite's bizarre end made any sense, and least of all his own obsession with what in reality had nothing to do with himself. He had lost a friend, a circumstance that could not but be viewed as unfortunate, but it was, nevertheless, *un fait accompli*. There was nothing he could do for Hepplewaite now beyond offering a sizeable reward for apprehension of the person or persons responsible for the deed and engaging the services of a Bow Street Runner to investigate the crime itself, both of which he had already done days ago. It was little enough in the circumstances, but it would simply have to suffice.

Egad, he was sickened by the whole bloody business, not to mention a surfeit of brandy on an empty stomach. What he needed was a bath, clean clothes, and a tray sent up to his rooms. After which, some sort of diversion to woo him from his black mood would not be amiss. Not White's,

perhaps. Not this night. The gaming tables most
assuredly held no appeal. A woman, then—his mistress, who, despite a shallowness of intellect that
Shields had begun to find trying, nevertheless was
gifted in the art of giving a man pleasure.

A wry glint came to his eyes at the thought of
his mistress. The truth was Sylvia, Lady Loring, had
long since begun to pall on him. The air of helpless
femininity, which she so artfully portrayed and
which he had found charming in the beginning,
was become rather thin of late and wholly transparent. Underneath the facade, he now clearly discerned a calculating female with a grasping nature.

He was hardly surprised to discover the woman
with whom he had shared several weeks of intimacy
cared not a whit for him beyond the size of his
purse. After all, she possessed little beyond her
feminine assets to sustain her in a manner befitting
a woman born to gentility. He was even willing to
accept that theirs was nothing more than a financial arrangement so long as she continued to satisfy
his needs in exchange for his generosity. Those
were, after all, the rules of the game. Still, he found
that he was become increasingly disenamored of
fluff without substance and, specifically in Lady
Loring's case, beauty with demmed little evidence
that she possessed a heart.

Egad, he must be getting old, he thought with
a sardonic curl of the lip. Always before it had been
enough if the wench was well to look upon and
willing—and did not bore him to distraction. Certainly, Lady Loring had fallen into the first two
categories. Her beauty, however, beneath all the
feminine frills was the hard perfection of a gem-
stone, and her wit, while keen, tended to be tipped
with poison. While he was perfectly capable of par-
ing a man, or a woman for that matter, down to
size with the cutting edge of his tongue should the

occasion call for it, Shields entertained a decided
aversion to a steady diet of vituperative badinage.
He had, in fact, had every intention of breaking it
off with the beautiful Sylvia; indeed, had yet. Only
the unlooked-for complications involving Hepplewaite and his subsequent demise had postponed
the inevitable.

Still, he was not averse to a last fling with the
versatile Lady Loring, he decided. He might even
go so far as to present her with a generous parting
gift to tide her over until she found a new patron
to maintain her in the manner to which she had
grown accustomed under his protection. It would
be worth a few hundred pounds to be distracted out
of his demmed brooding thoughts for the evening.

The decanter of brandy forgotten, Shields strode
briskly from the room and made his way up the
curving stairs to his private chambers.

Little more than an hour later, having rid himself
of all his dirt and having fortified himself as well
with a cold collation of roasted duck, cheese, fruit,
and thick slices of bread heavily buttered and
washed down with a tankard of ale, Shields exited
his Town House feeling rather more the thing.
On the other hand, he found that he had cooled
considerably on the prospect of calling on Lady
Loring for the express purpose of indulging himself with a last savoring of her womanly delights
only to inform her afterward that he was severing
the purse strings.

"The devil," he muttered softly to himself as
he stood suddenly and most uncharacteristically
undecided on the walk. He was sardonically aware
of the footman waiting at rigid attention at the
open carriage door and of the team of high-
steppers moving restively in the traces. The last
thing he wished at the moment was to engage in
a contretemps with his soon-to-be former mistress.

Equally distasteful, however, was the notion of turning back into the house to give rein to the dark mood that had laid hold of him the past several days.

It came to him that he was decidedly in need of some new source of diversion, that, indeed, he was grown uncommonly jaded with his usual pursuits. These were not precisely new feelings and only partially owed their roots to the shock of Hepplewaite's horrific demise. The truth was that, for no little time now, he had begun to entertain the vague sense that his life might be just a trifle empty, that he was, in fact, become rather bored of late with the normal run of things. What he needed was something new and completely out of the ordinary to distract him from the cursed malaise that seemed to have fallen over him.

Hardly had that thought crossed his mind than a random breeze carrying the fresh scent of lilacs caressed his cheek. Inexplicably, he shivered, feeling the hairs rise along the nape of his neck.

"The devil," he cursed, and had forcibly to restrain himself from giving in to the sudden urge to glance over his shoulder. Indeed, had he not known better, he might have suspected he was succumbing to something so absurd as a superstitious bent. Egad, he had the distinct sensation that what he had just experienced was a frisson of warning!

Immediately, Reason returned to banish the absurdity. No doubt what he was suffering was a reaction to having imbibed two decanters of brandy. Not that he was in his cups. He had never since his salad days been known to succumb to hard spirits.

At last, smiling in wry amusement at himself, he climbed into the carriage.

"Lady Courtney's," he said to the coachman on a sudden whim.

It had been some time since he had been to see his cousin, who never ceased to urge him to drop by at any time. She, after all, was confined to the house until the time of her fourth lying-in, which was, by Shields's calculations, little more than two or three weeks away. The pregnancy, coming as something of a surprise, had been a difficult one, but, possessed of the Keene obstinacy, she adamantly refused to remain at home at Thorncrest while her dearest Courtney must be in Town for the Sessions. Of all his numerous cousins, who numbered fourteen in all, Nancy and her brother Albert were the only ones whom Shields more than tolerated. No doubt an hour or two spent in the boisterous environs of Nancy's home with her three young hopefuls would serve to cure him of any developing tendencies to the irrational, he told himself sardonically, as, deliberately, he shrugged off the still-lingering prickle of unease that had assailed him.

It was a true vision. Elfrida had known it the moment Shields looked at her out of the depths of the crystal bequeathed to her by her great-grandmother, Lucasta. His eyes seemed to pierce her to her very soul, and when the vision was swallowed up in a swirl of mist, she was left with an ineffable yearning to have it back again, to have *him* back.

Instead, the tower room closed in around her, and the shew stone swam into focus—round, erubescent, and smooth, its visions obscured in transparency.

She was made aware of a delicious languor and that her cheek rested on folded arms on the tabletop as she peered at the crystal orb directly in front of her nose. Then a tentative hand grasped her most inconsiderately by the shoulder and shook her.

"Elfrida. I beg your pardon, but pray do wake up," urged her sister, Violet.

Elfrida blinked up at Violet with a distinctly glazed expression on her lovely features. Indeed, still caught up in the vision that had appeared to her in the shew stone, she was experiencing not a little difficulty in comprehending how her youngest sibling should suddenly have become a part of it.

"Violet?" she queried in bewilderment. "You—here? But how?"

Elfrida was rewarded for those compelling utterances with a doubtful glance from singularly blue-violet eyes. "I hesitate to mention the obvious, Elfrida: I came by way of the stairs. On the other hand, I daresay that is not precisely the question you were asking, is it? I do so hope you have not been imbibing that curious concoction of somniferous herbs again, Elfrida. Not that I should dream of telling you what to drink or what not to drink, any more than I should wish you to dictate to me what I should or should not do." Violet gave vent to a tiny shudder at the merest thought of such an infringement on her freedom. "It is only that I fear you are about to need all your wits about you."

"Dear, am I?" Elfrida countered, lifting her head to study her sister's strikingly beautiful countenance, which was rendered wholly unreadable by its expression of dreamy imperturbability. Indeed, trying to fathom her Pisces sibling's innermost feelings was like trying to plumb the depths of a bottomless pool and to as little avail—although Elfrida was not averse, upon occasion, to ruffling the surface merely to observe the fish's hasty retreat to the secret, untroubled deep. "Do not tell me—Gideon is home."

"I shan't if you don't wish me to," replied Violet, arranging herself with unconscious grace in the windowseat. "Shall I refrain from telling you as well that, when last I saw him, he was on the point of escorting Lady Barstowe on a tour of the topiary garden?"

"No, was he?" Elfrida gave vent to a comical grimace. "I should have expected no less from Vere. Furthermore, I imagine it was Albermarle who suggested it. It would be so very like the duke."

"I believe Grandpapa did mention Lady Barstowe had expressed a desire to see the gardens and that, as he himself was promised to Mr. Gladdings for the next hour or two, he would depend upon Vere to see that Lady Barstowe was kept amused."

"And no doubt she shall be," grimly predicted Elfrida. "Mr. Gladdings indeed! You may be sure Albermarle, rather than closeting himself with his estate agent, is even now taking advantage of the opportunity to avail himself of a nap. His grace is up to something, Violet, I feel it. But then, I daresay you must sense it as surely as I."

"I'm not sure it would be accurate to say I 'sense' any such thing," hedged Violet, slipping with fish-like ease beneath the pertinent question. "Not that I should in any way dispute your judgment in the matter, Elfrida. You may very well be right. After all, Grandpapa never does anything without a reason, does he? And more often than not, that reason is wholly incomprehensible to anyone but himself. In any event, I daresay that you have already devised some countermeasure to save Gideon from Grandpapa's manipulations, have you not—if, of course, his grace is, as you said, 'up to something'? And if you have not, well then, it can hardly matter, can it? I daresay whatever is meant to happen will happen."

For a moment Elfrida stared in mute admiration at her sister's serene aspect. Indeed, she never ceased to be amazed at Piscean logic. But then, Violet was perfectly in the right of it. Things *did* proceed according to cosmic order, and the germ of a plan *had* taken root in her fertile mind.

Elfrida sat bolt upright in the chair, memory flooding back to her. Impulsively, she clasped her sister's hands in her own. "I am glad you are here, Violet. For you must know that I have just been visited with the most marvelous vision. And I simply must share it with someone."

"A vision? Truly?" murmured Violet, her normal aspect of dreamy abstraction giving way to what might be construed as a glimmer of interest. "But naturally you must share it with me—if, of course, that is what you wish to do. Though I have never had a prophetic dream myself, I remain open to the possibility that there may be certain gifted individuals capable of receiving glimpses of future events. Indeed, I am utterly fascinated by the notion."

"Only, you do not really believe I am one of those gifted individuals," interposed Elfrida in exceedingly dry tones.

Violet drew back, hurt disbelief writ plain on her face. "No, how can you say so? Elfrida, you know I should never cast doubt on any of your prognostications," she declared. "Indeed, when have I ever?"

"Whenever I have been brash enough to relate one of them to you, dearest," replied Elfrida. "You simply cannot help yourself. But never mind, I am willing to take the risk this time. It is not every day, after all, that one is given a vision of one's karmically predetermined Twin Soul, the man who is one's astrologically perfect mate."

"And you have?" queried Violet, with the involuntary arch of a dubious eyebrow.

"I have," affirmed Elfrida, coming to her feet with a rapt expression. "And he is glorious, magnificent, a man for whom I should dare any peril, any obstacle, any hardship. I can only wonder how it is that we shall finally be brought together. We *shall* be, you know. It is written in the stars."

"In the stars, naturally," agreed Violet without so much as a quiver of emotion.

"You doubt it, I can see that you do," Elfrida laughed. She was, after all, far too exhilarated by her recent excursion into the realm of the extraordinary to be in the least fazed by her sister's patent disbelief. Besides, she hardly expected Violet to grasp the true significance of the Momentous Event, let alone to lend any credence to it. "Nevertheless," she forged ahead in true Aries fashion, "we *are* destined to meet under astrologically predetermined circumstances. We simply cannot help ourselves. Mere mortals are powerless to change or avoid that which has been determined by the stars."

"But of course they are," agreed Violet with surprising readiness. "It is precisely what I have tried often enough to tell you: Whatever events have been set in motion will proceed to their inevitable conclusions, no matter what we might think to do to alter them. When you think of it, you must see it is all a simple matter of cause and effect. One thing must inevitably lead to another. Perhaps the stars do even have some influence on the outcome of things, since they exist in our universe, and everything contributes in some fashion or another to everything else." She paused, as if made suddenly sensible of the fact that she had been waxing rather eloquent, which was wholly unlike her. "Then it is not someone with whom you are already acquainted?'' she hastened to add in sudden confusion. "I mean, if the two of you have yet to be introduced, after all.''

"I did not say we had not been introduced. We have, you know. But, yes,'' agreed Elfrida, who, having little difficulty in surmising of whom Violet was thinking, smiled in sympathetic understanding. "I'm afraid that I shan't be marrying Lord Harry after all. I am sorry to disappoint you, Violet. However, as fond as I am of him, you must know that Lord Harry and I should never suit. The man who is my Twin Soul, my astrologically perfect mate, is just that. He is everything I should ever wish for in a man.''

Strange that she had never felt that way about him before, mused Elfrida, smiling whimsically to herself. He had always struck her until then, in fact, as hopelessly top-lofty, vain, and odiously insensible of the feelings of others. He was, after all, the Earl of Shields, the man who, upon being presented to her during the second intermission of her coming-out ball eight years before, had proceeded to advise her to undergo some instruction in decorum and, while she was at it, a lesson or two in the minuet—purely for the benefit of her gentlemen partners, who, naturally, must have a care for the shines on the toes of their shoes— egad! Upon which, he had flicked her under the chin with a careless forefinger and, sauntering past her, had asked Lady Madeleine DuBois for the honor of the next dance.

Really, Elfrida marveled, she had thought never to encounter a more disagreeable gentleman!

Eight years ago, however, she had been a gawky seventeen-year-old who had vastly preferred sailing her beloved sloop in a stiff breeze to dancing the night away with a bevy of gentlemen admirers. On retrospect, she could not but think his lordship had, in his own inimitable fashion, been giving her some exceedingly good advice. Certain it was that, before her second Season in London, she had, with a Ram-like determination that had taken her dearest mama quite by surprise, mastered the minuet and learned to comport herself with a decorum that would have done credit to one of the Queen's very own ladies-in-waiting.

Unfortunately, she had never been given the pleasure of flaunting her feminine accomplishments before the arrogant earl. Shields, as it happened, had been abroad during her second Season, and Elfrida, having turned down four eligible offers of marriage, had not returned for a third Season. Indeed, preferring to set up housekeeping in her mama's house in Bath, she had hardly been back to London in the intervening years. It was not until the death of her parents that, knowing her sixteen-year-old sister would have need of her, she had taken up residence once again with her grandfather in the family pile, along with her Aunt Roanna and Elfrida's young cousins, Alexandra, Valentine, and Chloe.

Albermarle had served as a haven of sorts, a place far removed from the rest of the world. At Albermarle, she could let herself grieve, even as she allowed herself to draw on the memories of happier times in order to put things in some sort of balance. That, however, was all come to an end that afternoon as Elfrida gazed into the shew stone and beheld the vision in the transparent depths.

"Well?" Violet finally prodded. "Are you or are you not going to tell me who you saw in your vision? Or how, for that matter, your having seen him is going to save Gideon from his own proclivity for behavior that can only be described as self-destructive?"

"But of course I am going to tell you." Elfrida

came around to gaze at Violet with sparkling eyes. "But first, my dearest, best of little sisters, tell *me:* How quickly can you make yourself ready to go to London?"

"To London? Good God," exclaimed Violet, drawing back with something approaching horror. "Why ever should I wish to do that?"

"Pray do not play the gaby, Violet. You are just turned nineteen, after all, and it *is* the middle of March. It should all be perfectly obvious to you."

Violet's eyes widened in dire enlightenment. "Oh no, Elfrida. We discussed all that ages ago. We agreed it was pointless to bring me out when I haven't a feather to fly with. Besides, I find very little that is appealing in the notion of displaying myself before the *Ton*. You know how I hate to think people might be staring at me."

"Then you must just learn to accept it as an inevitable facet of your existence. Of *course* they will be staring at you, you absurd little peagoose," declared Elfrida, taking in the vision of loveliness that was her younger sister. "How should they not, when you are possessed of the sort of beauty that inspires men to dream of performing great feats and women to rise above feelings of envy. You naturally draw attention wherever you go. I daresay it will do you good to get out into the world for a while. And it will undoubtedly save Gideon from making an utter cake of himself, since I shall insist he must escort us to London to see to our safety. As for the wherewithal to provide you with a new wardrobe, Grandpapa will stand the nonsense."

"Grandpapa!" exclaimed Violet, genuinely alarmed. "He will do no such thing, Elfrida, even if I could bring myself to ask him, which I cannot."

"Pray don't be absurd, Violet. *I* shall ask him. And he will gladly give his consent. After all, you cannot imagine he actually *wants* us underfoot, can you, when he has the delightful Lady Barstowe to keep him company? Naturally, Aunt Roanna and the children will go with us, since it will fall to her to introduce you into all the right circles."

"Aunt Roanna would detest doing any such thing, Elfrida, and you know it," insisted Violet, who felt herself being helplessly swept up into what gave every evidence of being one of her sister's irresistible schemes. "She is far too indolent ever to consent to something which must so obviously tax her meagre store of reserves."

"On the contrary," Elfrida countered, having anticipated that most obvious of arguments. "I believe you will find Aunt Roanna is all eagerness to comply. Obviously, you have failed to take into account the significant motivating factor: Roanna's absolute terror of her father-in-law. Not only will she jump at the opportunity to remove herself from the duke's proximity, but I daresay she will not be able to thank us enough for having provided her with the excuse to do so."

"The devil, Elfrida," groaned Violet, viewing her sister with open dismay. "What must I do to convince you I do not *wish* to go to London? Indeed, that I utterly detest the notion? To have to endure the supplications of any number of adoring suitors, none of whom I could bear to refuse out of the fear of hurting their feelings! Faith, you know what it was like our one small Season in Bath together. I was driven to distraction by my doting admirers!"

"Not one of whom perished or so much as went into a sharp decline upon your precipitate removal to Albermarle," Elfrida did not hesitate to remind her, "no matter how ardently they professed they would do so."

"Nevertheless, they made my life quite impossible," Violet insisted with a shudder. "I shall not go, not even to save Gideon from his own self-destructive nature. Pray do not ask me to do so, Elfrida. I should rather live the rest of my life as a spinster on the shelf than be forced to make my curtsey in Society. And there is nothing you can say that will change my mind."

"But I have no intention of saying anything to change your mind," asserted Elfrida, who had sustained a sharp pang of guilt for having sent Violet into a spin.

Violet, having expected something quite different from her older sister, stared blankly into Elfrida's unruffled countenance. "You—you haven't?"

"Of course I have not." Brushing a stray curl from Violet's cheek, Elfrida smiled reassuringly. "If you are that determined not to go, then that is the end of it. Pray forget that I ever mentioned it."

"But Gideon—?"

"—will just have to take his chances. Naturally, Grandpapa will hardly be pleased to discover his heir apparent has seduced the future Duchess of Albermarle, but it simply cannot be helped, can it?" Elfrida said, thinking out loud. "Of course, I shall find it a trifle more difficult to arrange for an excuse to be in Town, and I suppose I shall have to settle for a room at the Charlton. I daresay, however, since I shall be incognita, I shall not run too great a risk of ruining my reputation by staying in a hotel without benefit of a female companion. It might even be fun. At any rate, I shall have to chance it."

"You will? But, why, Elfrida," queried Violet, taking a deep breath to restore her nerves to their normal equilibrium, "when we have two perfectly good Town Houses, which no one ever uses?"

"But I should have thought it was patently obvious," declared Elfrida with a shrug. "I could hardly go around incognita, now could I, if I stayed in

Albermarle House, not to mention Vere's? Of course, if I had a good excuse for my presence in London, none of these stratagems would be necessary. I should be able to watch over the earl without his even being aware of it.''

"The earl? What earl?" demanded Violet, who could no more resist the allure of a mystery than she could turn away from a loved one in some sort of difficulty.

"The Earl of Shields, of course. The man in my vision. Did I not tell you? He is my Twin Soul, my karmically predetermined, astrologically perfect mate.''

"Shields? Good heavens," declared Violet, a frown of concentration marring the purity of her brow. "Was it not that particular nobleman whom you once vowed you would like to see hoisted on his own petard?''

"The very one. Only, I believe I wished him doused in boiling oil at the time, then fitted on a spit over hot coals, the devil. Fortunately, however, I have matured a great deal since our first and only infelicitous meeting. I realize now that his lordship was only trying in his own way to be kind.''

"*Kind?* Oh, naturally. On the other hand, he also figured largely in the conversation at tea," Violet was typically compelled to point out. "This vision of yours, does it not occur to you that it might be nothing more than a simple dream? After all, you were asleep when I found you. And you will admit that the news of Hepplewaite's untimely demise was uncommonly distressing. It would not be in the least strange if the earl should happen to pop up in your dreams, especially as he is known to have been Hepplewaite's closest intimate.''

"Pooh," asserted Elfrida without the slightest hesitation. "I always succumb to sleep in the wake of a seeing. It does not signify in the least. You may be sure I know the difference between a common dream and a vision—and a dream of prophesy, for that matter. I beheld a vision of Shields in the shew stone, and he *is* my karmically predetermined, astrologically perfect mate, I am sure of it. That was, after all, the question that was uppermost in my mind when I was drawn to look into the crystal. But what is more, I have seen, hanging over him, an unmistakable pall of danger of which he is patently unaware. Which is why it is imperative that I set out for London at once."

Her chin came up in unconscious defiance as she faced Violet with a glint in her eyes—a circumstance that had the effect of causing Violet to experience a sudden sinking sensation in the pit of her stomach. She had, after all, seen that look all too often before and nearly always with dire consequences for someone, most often for Elfrida herself. "I shall leave day after tomorrow at the first light—with or without Gideon to give me countenance. In any event, you need not worry your head over me. I have been used to determining my own existence for no little time now; and, thanks to the competence left to me by Great-aunt Millicent, I shall rub along well enough, you may be sure of it."

"I haven't the smallest doubt of it, Elfrida," agreed Violet, who was sometimes made to wonder if she were the only one in the long line of Rochelles who was not given to bold action and feats of daring, not to mention a marked propensity for eccentric behavior. Indeed, she often felt rather like a cuckoo chick hatched unawares in a falcon's nest. "Indeed, I am sure of it," she had added, giving herself over to what she philosophically viewed as an Inevitable Force, "because I shall be going with you."

"*Shall* you, dearest?" exclaimed Elfrida, clasping Violet's hands and giving them a squeeze.

"I shall, just as you knew I should all along," Violet answered accusingly. "You know very well I can never refuse you or Gideon anything, especially when you seem determined to fling yourselves headlong over one precipice or another. Only, do not expect me to accept every invitation or to exert myself to be a success. I have no intention of allowing myself to be caught up in an endless whirl of social events."

"But of course you do not," Elfrida said with perfect gravity. "Naturally, you will spend most of your time visiting museums and art galleries, not to mention curled up in your sitting room catching up on all the latest books from the lending library. I daresay you will go quite unnoticed."

"Wretch!" declared Violet, giving into an unwitting burble of laughter. "You do not believe any such thing. It does not signify, however, for that is precisely how I intend to go on. You, however, had better be contemplating how you mean to approach Grandpapa, not to mention Aunt Roanna. It is all very well for you to say they will be amenable to doing their part, but it has been my experience one can never be sure of *anything* where a Rochelle is concerned."

"Yes, but then, you have never been given to see a vision of the man you were born to love," returned Elfrida, suddenly sober. "Shields is in danger, Violet. I know it. I really must go to London. There is no one else to warn him."

Chapter 3

Shields was in a thunderous mood. That much had been made evident to the household the instant he stepped across the threshold, a forbidding scowl etched in his handsome brow. Acknowledging Craddock's circumspect words of greeting with a curt nod and the summary announcement that he was not at home to callers, he had proceeded directly to the stairs with the obvious intention of barricading himself in his study. It had been Craddock's unhappy duty to inform his lordship that, as he had failed to anticipate his lordship's wishes in that regard, he had already admitted a—er—gentleman, who was presently ensconced in the downstairs withdrawing room. A Mr. Tuttle, to be precise, who had insisted his lordship would have every wish to see him.

Shields, who, on the contrary, would have liked nothing better than to consign his caller to the devil—indeed, who could think of few things he would least like to attend at the moment than the subject which Mr. Tuttle had come to discuss, paused, one foot on the bottommost stair. "Inform Mr. Tuttle that I shall receive him in my study directly. Oh, and, Craddock. You may tell Gaspard that I shall be dining in this evening."

"As you wish, milord." Craddock bowed, and, turning with stately grace, proceeded to carry out his master's orders.

Shields, mounting the stairs two at a time, made his way to his study. Entering, he shut the door firmly behind him and reached for the decanter of port on the grog tray.

The devil, he thought, pouring a glass. It had been nearly three weeks since Hepplewaite's death—time enough to relegate the matter, if not to oblivion, then most certainly to the back of his mind. Today, of all days, he was in no mood to bring it once more to the fore. Not only had he been forced to endure a wholly unrewarding two hours with his stepmother on the subject of what she had hysterically come to view as her only off-spring's emerging inclination for rebellion, (an aptitude to which his half-sister Lady Julia had no doubt come naturally in response to the smoth-ering influence of her mother, Shields sardonically reflected), but he had once again been given the royal roundaboutation by his mistress.

The lovely Sylvia, it seemed, had been summoned home to Gilcrist Manor in Kent, presumably to attend an ailing relative, and was not expected back in Town before the morrow. The devil she had! thought Shields, who could not but find her week-long series of absences rather too convenient, espe-cially in light of the fact that he had been presented that morning with a reckoning for her quarterly expenditures, which had amounted to a deal more than the liberal sum he had set aside for her use. Clearly, the lady was in hopes of weathering out the storm away from port.

Shields, who had ever had the reputation for treating his barques of frailty with generosity, nevertheless disliked the notion of being bled dry by a female, especially one who gave every indication that she was doing her best to avoid him. If he had entertained any doubts that the affair had run its course, her purchase, at his expense, of an enameled plunge bath inlaid with gold leaf and sporting gilded cherubs for feet—egad!—had rid him of them.

It was time to end it, and the sooner the better. Sardonically lifting his glass in tribute to the severing of ties with the beautiful Lady Loring, he drank.

The arrival of Mr. Elias Tuttle at that juncture served instantly to dispel the lady from his thoughts, but hardly to elevate his mood. An impenetrable mask of ennui descended over the earl's features as soon as Tuttle was announced.

"Mr. Tuttle," he said, taking in the fubsy-faced Bow Street Runner garbed in a rumpled yellow coat of inferior cut, not to mention paisley unmentionables that gave the appearance of having been slept in repeatedly and often. "What brings you so soon back to London? I had not thought to hear from you before the fortnight was out. May I assume you have good news to impart—the identity, perhaps of Hepplewaite's murderer?"

"I'm afraid not, milord," replied Tuttle, who gave every impression of one wholly at ease in the midst of the subdued elegance of his employer's study. His eyes ranged over the leather-upholstered chairs and divans, the great mahogany desk, the globe ensconced in its carved wooden cradle, the ceiling-high bookcases filled with leather bound volumes, and, at last, the thick, claret-colored Ushak carpet underfoot. "Properly fuzzed by it all,

I am, milord. Not a clue who could've done the foul deed or why."

Shields, who did not suppose Tuttle had imposed himself on his presence for the sole purpose of reporting he had uncovered nothing of importance, reserved judgment at that unexpected announcement. The man, after all, had come highly recommended to him. Despite his unprepossessing appearance, Tuttle was, Shields had long since been given to surmise, possessed of a keen, probing intelligence.

"I confess to being disappointed, Mr. Tuttle," said the earl. "You found nothing, then, which might lead to an understanding of the tragic events surrounding the viscount's death."

"I didn't say that, not precisely, milord," Tuttle demurred. "I found plenty that could lead in any number of directions, perhaps even to you, milord. Which is why I came back to London, somewhat precipitately."

"To me?" demanded his lordship, one arrogant eyebrow sweeping upward toward his hairline. "Are you suggesting I had something to do with Hepplewaite's demise?"

"Certainly not, milord. Farthest thing from me mind, assure you. It was something the viscount's gentleman's gentleman let slip. Seems it was low tide with his lordship. Had even gone so far as to have recourse to a cent-per-cent. A Mr. Nicodemus Pickering. Ever heard of him, milord?"

"I believe I may safely say I have never numbered any of his ilk among my acquaintanceship. I must presume you have a reason for asking?"

"I do indeed, milord. Y' see, Mr. Pickering was becoming most insistent on the matter of Lord Hepplewaite's failure to pay up. Seems his lordship put him off with some sort of assurance that you'd stand the nonsense."

"No, did he?" murmured Shields, hardly surprised that Hepplewaite had committed the supreme folly of consulting a cent-per-cent. Jameyboy had ever been the sort to look for the quick solution to his problems without bothering to consider the long-term consequences. Perhaps, for that same reason, it was equally easy to believe Hepplewaite had not hesitated to give the name of the one man who had stood his friend throughout the years as assurance to a common bloodsucker. "And you believe this Pickering will have the temerity to make some claim on me, is that it?"

Tuttle lifted a rumpled shoulder in a shrug. "Cent-per-cents are a queer lot. Just thought you had ought to know, milord. A dangerous man, Mr. Pickering. Might pay to watch your back."

"No doubt I am obliged to you, Mr. Tuttle. On the other hand, I fail to see why I should be in any way concerned. Hepplewaite, most regrettably, is dead, and I have never so much as exchanged a word with Mr. Pickering. What could he possibly think to gain by involving me in his affairs?"

"Mayhap nothing. On the other hand, you should understand, milord. Pickering will not be pleased that the fish got off the hook, so's to speak. First of all there's the blunt. Nothing gets the dander of a cent-per-cent up like losing his investment. And then there's the principle of the thing. A man who makes his living sucking the blood out of folks can't afford word to get out that some'un had got away with it, even if it was by having his stick cut for him. Bad business, that—unless, of course, Pickering was the one who had it done, which I haven't ruled out yet, mind you. In which case, he'll not look kindly on anyone looking to tempt fate, so's to speak, by offering a reward, especially one on the order of what you've put up, milord. And if it wasn't him who did the killing, he'll be wondering if there might be others who'd think to rob him of what he considers his just dues. Mr. Pickering'll be wanting some'un to pay, you can depend on it. And he'll have his ways of seeing to it."

Shields, who found little to amuse in the notion that he might find himself hounded in the near future by a low-life creature whose sole purpose was teaching those beneath his thumb that no one escaped paying the likes of Mr. Pickering, not even the dead, favored Tuttle with a chilling smile. "You may be sure Pickering will catch cold should he attempt anything so patently unwise, Mr. Tuttle. Was there anything else that you wished to report at this time?"

As it happened, the Bow Street Runner had preferred to keep to himself for the time being the tidbits of information he had uncovered, which in Tuttle's words made up a veritable "hodgepodge of twistings and turnings."

"Just you leave it to me, milord," he had said, taking his departure, "to sort out what's pertinent and what's not. That's what you engaged me to do."

Shields, who vastly preferred to delegate the entire matter of Hepplewaite's demise to one who made a living at such things, was contented to leave it at that for the time being. Nevertheless, the interview with Tuttle served to fill him with a distinct feeling of dissatisfaction, which had most to do, he did not doubt, with certain inescapable truths. Not the least of these was the realization that Hepplewaite had behaved toward Shields himself in a manner that violated every gentleman's code of honor.

Shields had never misled himself into believing Hepplewaite was anything but weak. He had, however, credited the viscount with a sense of what it was to be a gentleman. Patently, Hepplewaite had been driven by an overweening sense of desperation to do what he had done.

"The devil, Jamey," Shields declared to the empty room. "Why did you not come to *me?*"

That question, coupled with Shields's growing conviction that he had mishandled the event of Hepplewaite's plunge into deep waters, was hardly conducive to the earl's peace of mind. Certainly it could not have been said his mood was in any way improved when he departed his Town House some hours later and entered his carriage.

"Drury Lane," he announced in a curt voice to his coachman. "The Theatre." Eyes set firmly ahead, he settled back against the velvet squabs as the carriage lurched into motion.

He was to speculate no little time later that it was undoubtedly some bizarre quirk of fate that prompted him to glance out at the closed carriage stopped across the way. Certainly, it was no ordinary feeling that gripped him as he found himself staring briefly into the face of a veritable goddess of beauty with hair the blue-black of ravens' wings. Hellsfire, it was, in fact, curiously reminiscent of receiving a quick jab to the midsection from someone on the order of Gentleman Jackson or Mendoza, perhaps!

The epiphanous event lasted no more than the instant it took for the earl's carriage to sweep past the other conveyance, and yet Shields was left with the curious impression that his life had in some manner been irrevocably altered.

Egad! Clearly he had been affected more than he suspected by his preoccupation with the circumstances surrounding Hepplewaite's demise, not to mention the birth of unfamiliar feelings of guilt coupled with self-doubt. He was not in the norm thrown into a quaver at the sight of a beautiful woman. He was even less prone to thoughts which were not well founded in cold, hard reason. And yet, in the space of the past five days he had been subject to not one, but two exceedingly peculiar notions, neither of which could remotely be ascribed to the realm of the logical.

The devil, he thought, deliberately leaning his head back once more against the squabs. No doubt an evening at the theatre would serve to curb such tendencies, he told himself, and next discovered his thoughts had turned without conscious volition to a contemplation of the woman he had fleetingly glimpsed.

He was not made to feel in the least comforted by the realization that he was laboring under the impulse to order the coach to turn back with the vague excuse of inquiring if the lady were in need of some sort of assistance. It was not his habit to impose himself on females with whom he was unacquainted, especially females of quality no matter how strikingly attractive. Indeed, he did not doubt he would have found on closer inspection that the Goddess of Beauty was a deal less inspiring than his momentary impression had led him to believe. Worse, she very likely was one of the new crop of young beauties who had arrived in London for the Season for the express purpose of snaring a husband.

He reminded himself that green girls just out of the schoolroom held little appeal for him and that, further, he was perfectly content to have the title go one day to his Cousin Albert, especially as he himself entertained a distinct aversion to the notion of being leg-shackled for life to a female who must surely bore him as soon as he had bedded her. That, after all, had been his experience with every one of the numerous women who had briefly captured his attention only to lose it as soon as he became intimately acquainted with them, Lady

Loring being a prime example of the inconstancy of emotional attachments. Not that he had ever been emotionally involved with Sylvia, or any of the other barques of frailty whom he had variously taken under his protection for that matter, for he had not. Indeed, not since a single, regrettable incident in his extreme youth had he made the error of mistaking lust for something other than what it was.

It was patently absurd, then, to fancy that he was suffering anything more than a momentary fascination with a peculiar set of circumstances—a chance encounter which had afforded but a single glimpse of an undeniably enchanting face revealed in the uncertain glow of a street lamp. On the contrary, had he been sufficiently intrigued to wish to learn the lady's name and perhaps even a direction at which she might have been reached, he would not have hesitated to employ whatever means were at his disposal to satisfy his curiosity. He was, after all, a Man of the World who had acquired a deal more than his share of Town Bronze in the past several years. That he had done none of those things was proof enough that he was a victim of nothing more uncanny than his own ruffled temper and a momentary flight of fancy.

At any rate, the opportunity was past, and the chances were that he would not lay eyes on the raven-haired beauty again. It was not his custom to attend the numerous galas designed to provide the plethora of matchmaking mamas with the opportunity to display their single daughters to advantage. He had not deigned to make an appearance at Almack's for the past several years and eschewed the dubious pleasures of Vauxhall Gardens. Unless she proved to be a kinswoman of one of his closely knit circle of intimates, it was doubtful he would formally make her acquaintance.

Unaccountably, he sustained an unwitting pang of regret at that deduction, which perversely served to set him more firmly than ever against the urge to glance back as his carriage turned onto Brook Street and entered the flow of traffic.

Consequently, he failed to see the closed carriage pull away from the curb, and, maintaining a discrete distance, follow in his wake.

The performance of Shakespeare's *Hamlet*, featuring John Kemble in the leading role, did indeed distract Shields from his earlier brooding thoughts, but it hardly served to alleviate his black mood. Fortunately, his cousin Albert, in the company of Oliver Shipley, Viscount Winterbrooke, who had the distinction of being Shields's oldest friend, arrived in the earl's private box during the first intermission with the apparent purpose of rescuing Shields from a dismal evening spent in solitary contemplation.

"Missed you at Whitcombe, old friend," observed Winterbrooke, surveying the earl's impassive features with seeming casualness. "Smashing ride after the hounds. Wished you had been there. As a matter of fact, now that I think of it, haven't seen you anywhere for some little time."

"No doubt I am moved that you noted my brief absence from circulation," drawled Shields with cool imperturbability. "I should have thought you had enough to occupy you. Surely the incomparable Miss Slaton has not so soon begun to pall?"

"Miss Slaton, as it happens," grinned Albert, a youth of three and twenty with the Herrick fair good looks, "has taken herself out of the running. The lady has accepted Hazleton's offer of marriage."

"As you see, my luck continues to hold good as

gold. I daresay the Incomparable was dead set on
having me leg-shackled and domesticated in her
own time. Fortunately, her family is purse-pinched,
and Hazleton's fortune is greater than mine.'' Smiling, Winterbrooke shrugged. ''Saved once again
from the fruits of my own folly. Still, she was a
charming piece. I daresay I shall not soon find
another quite so tempting.''

''Winterbrooke pines,'' Albert lamented, clapping his hands over his heart. ''Who would have
thought it of him?''

''Winterbrooke pines for his lost youth,'' declared the viscount, who, of an age with Shields, was
not above thirty-five. ''Or he pines for something to
relieve the ennui of the moment, but he does not
pine for a woman. There is always another. Are
you set on seeing this tragedy through to the end,
my friend?'' he added, turning his hooded gaze
on the earl. ''Or might I entice you away to some
less weighty environs? Mrs. Blakeley, it is rumored,
provides a more than passable supper at her gaming establishment.''

''And Mrs. Blakeley, I have heard from reliable
sources, is a most fascinating woman,'' interjected
Albert with the elan of youth.

''She is a woman of the world who would think
nothing of preying on the inexperience of a young
coxcomb with no bronze and demmed few brains,''
Shields countered dampeningly. ''On the other
hand, I confess to something less than my customary pleasurable anticipation at viewing the Prince
of Denmark's descent into madness.''

''Splendid,'' applauded Winterbrooke, sweeping
an eloquent arm toward the exit. ''Let us away
from here forthwith!''

Shields saw her at once; indeed, how could he
not, even across the teeming crowd in the foyer?
She was magnificent—tall, for a woman, and pos-

sessed of a willowy slenderness, which her mantle of royal blue trimmed in ermine could not conceal. Neither did the hood, hastily drawn over the regal head, deny him a glimpse of curls the color of ravens' wings.

The next moment she was gone, vanished in the press.

"The devil!" Shields cursed. "Winterbrooke, did you see her? By the saints, Albert, you must have seen her."

"Seen whom?" demanded Winterbrooke, eyeing his friend curiously. "Devilishly close in here, old man. Some beauty strike your fancy?"

Shields, cursing himself for a blithering fool, shook his head. "Never mind. I daresay it was nothing. For a moment I thought I saw someone I knew. She is gone now. Probably slipped out the door."

The elusive Goddess of Beauty, however, was not so easily dismissed from his mind. Shields found himself, moments later, searching the street for a slender figure draped in royal blue. He was conscious of disappointment, tinged with not a little annoyance at his failure to spot her. Worse, he could not quite dismiss the peculiar feeling that she was like to pop up anywhere and at any time, only to disappear at will again, a notion which he viewed as indicative that he must surely be losing command of his senses.

Clearly it was time he took control of himself. After all, there was nothing unusual in the events themselves. Very likely the object of his peculiar obsession either resided on Grosvenor Square or had been waiting in the carriage for someone else, who did, to join her. Certainly, there was nothing strange in the fact that she had attended the theatre or that, coincidentally with himself, she had decided to depart before the performance was finished. Indeed, had she been less striking in her appearance, he doubted not he would have taken little or no notice of his two chance near-encounters with her. And that was all there was to it—a not unnatural masculine attraction to an undeniably beautiful woman. At the very worst, he could congratulate himself on his unerring good taste, he told himself, and with a cold deliberation, well known to his intimates, without remorse relegated the unknown beauty to oblivion.

With the result that, when he awakened the following morning, feeling considerably more himself after a night of disport among friends in pleasurable surrounds, he was not troubled with so much as a thought of the mysterious female who had occasioned him what could only have been described as a momentary abstraction.

On the contrary, having indulged in his morning gallop in Hyde Park and returned home to change and partake of a hearty breakfast, he spent an unremarkable morning closeted with Andrew Norton, his private secretary, in the dispatch of mundane business matters. The afternoon, likewise, was to be devoted to unfinished business—in particular, the unpleasant matter of severing ties with his mistress.

To that end, Shields ordered the carriage brought around shortly after two o'clock.

"Bond Street, Thomas," he declared to the coachman as he briskly mounted into the carriage. "Messers Johnson and Tate."

"Yes, milord," replied Tom Milburn, his wooden-faced expression betraying nothing of his reaction to that significant announcement. So, the rumors flying belowstairs were true. It was to be a parting of the ways between his lordship and the lady, was it? A trinket from the jewelers to soften the blow had ever been his lordship's way. And about time, too, to Milburn's manner of thinking.

Lady Loring was as mean-spirited as she was close-fisted with them what served her. Belike his lordship had finally seen her for what she was. Not at all like the lady what was occupying the house next door for the Season. She had a way about her, *she* did. Treated everyone, even the lowliest, with a fine condescension, unlike some of the quality he could name. But then, not every lady of the quality had a fine woman like Meggie Wheeler for an abigail.

The faintest of smiles softened the set of Tom Milburn's mouth at thought of the trim lady's maid with dancing brown eyes. She could make a man feel top o' the trees with naught but a glance from those eyes, she could.

Shields, who had not a glimmering of the power of Meggie Wheeler's orbs to send a man into a transport, alit from the carriage some fifteen minutes later before the establishment of Messrs. Johnson and Tate. The purchase of the intended trinket took no longer than was required for Mr. Tate to ascertain the purpose of the earl's visit and, subsequently, to bring forth from the back room an exquisite diamond bracelet.

Exiting the shop some moments later, Shields was feeling pleased with himself for having taken the decisive first step in alleviating himself of an association that had grown as tiresome as it was become distasteful, when he was overcome suddenly and inexplicably by what could only be described as a strong premonition.

He *knew* she was there before he saw her.

His rapier glance found her in an instant. Looking stunning in pale lilac and pink, she was, in fact, gazing with studied innocence at an assortment of bonnets displayed in the window of Burbage's Haberdashery directly across the street from him.

The devil, he thought. One sighting could be

attributed to chance, a second to coincidence. A third, however, was something else altogether. Indeed, it came to him that the elusive Goddess of Beauty was stalking him!

A chill smile played about the earl's lips. If the impertinent wench had thought to capture his interest, she had succeeded admirably. On the other hand, if her intent was to lure him into her net, she would soon catch cold at any such attempt. Shields had been hunted before by scheming beauties intent on trapping him into marriage for his title and his fortune.

Her little game of Will-o'-the-Wisp had gone on long enough, he decided, stepping down from the curb. It was time he made the lady's acquaintance. Glancing right and left, he started across the street.

The hackney coach came out of nowhere, bearing down on Shields with uncontrolled fury.

"Shields! LOOK OUT!"

The cry was a woman's scream of horror. That much registered on Shields's consciousness just before he leaped out of the immediate path of destruction; then, with the instinct of the born horseman, he reached up to catch the harness as the carriage horse lunged abreast of him.

It was over in seconds. Shields, vaulting astride, pulled the frightened animal to a plunging halt.

"Easy, lad," he crooned, running a hand down the lathered neck.

" 'E'll be all right now, gov'nor," called the hackney driver, who, having scrambled down from his perch, was already at his horse's head. "It weren't at all like 'im t' bolt thataway, gov. 'E are a good lad. Something must've frightened 'im."

"You may be sure of it," agreed the earl, slipping easily off the animal's back. He felt the flesh quiver beneath his touch, as he ran his hand over the horse's rump. "He has a tender spot. I daresay he was struck a blow by a missile of some sort."

"You means some'un threw something at 'im, gov'nor?" demanded the driver, his tone changing from chagrin to one of dawning outrage.

"Here," replied the earl, stepping back, "see for yourself."

"The devil take me, if you doesn't 'ave the right of it, gov'nor. Some'un spooked old Bob apurpose. I'll cut 'is 'eart out for 'im ifn I finds the cove what done it."

"Quite so," murmured his lordship, who was only partially attending as he swept the gathering crowd a searching glance. Hardly to his surprise, he discerned not so much as a glimpse of a slender beauty with raven curls beneath a pink straw bonnet trimmed in lilac ribbons to match her pelisse.

Shields, ignoring the press of the gathering crowd, not to mention the vociferous admiration of his stunned coachman, mounted briskly into his carriage and ordered Milburn to drive to Holles Street and the home of Lady Loring.

Only when the carriage had lurched into motion did Shields give vent to the cold rage seething in the pit of his stomach.

Egad! Bedazzled by a pretty face, he had allowed himself to be set up like the veriest cull! And he had almost been made to pay the price for it with his life! Patently the chit had lost her nerve at the last moment. In calling out, she had undoubtedly saved him from becoming the victim of what had been meant to appear something so mundane as a street accident. Even so, it had been a deal closer than he could have liked. Had she waited another few seconds, he would undoubtedly have been made to join Hepplewaite in the bloody Hereafter.

At that thought, a hard glitter came to his eyes. It occurred to him that perhaps he had come closer than he thought to Hepplewaite's murderer. Or perhaps Tuttle was right. Perhaps his offer of a reward for the villain's apprehension had sparked this sudden desire to have the Earl of Shields put permanently out of the way. Whatever the case, it would seem exceedingly farfetched to suppose that the curious string of events was not in some manner connected with the one significant anomaly in Shields's previously well-ordered existence—the brutal demise of his friend. Indeed, he could think of no other explanation for the singular incident that had nearly cut his own stick for him.

One thing was clear. There was a deal more at stake than he had previously imagined in making the acquaintance of his mysterious Goddess of Beauty. But then, meeting her should not be too difficult an accomplishment, he reflected grimly. Somehow he had not the slightest doubt that he had yet to see the last of her.

Had he expected to find the damnably elusive beauty lurking outside the Town House occupied by Lady Loring, however, he was soon to be disappointed. When he arrived before the four-story brown brick on Holles Street, there was not a sign of the raven-haired beauty anywhere to be seen. He was not to be so fortunate in the case of his mistress.

The lovely Sylvia was indeed at home to callers. She was, in fact, entertaining visitors. Her brother, Captain Frederick Wilkes of the Life Guards, who had long been a drain on his sister's financial resources, was ensconced in military splendor on the divan before the fireplace. Seated next to him, Mrs. Cora Fedderman, the wife of an East Indian nabob, held forth on the merits of blue lapels versus white as applied to regimentals.

"Nothing complements red so well as a white lapel and cuffs," she was eulogizing. "White is, after all, so distinctive when in its pristine finest. But then, of course, blue is so splendidly subtle. It positively exudes an aura of elegance."

"An elegance, madam," ironically observed Shields from the doorway, "which has served in the past to put to rout more than one enemy of England."

The assembled company, Shields noted with cynical detachment in the sudden, stark silence, appeared as little gratified to find him imposed upon their gathering as was he to realize he would likely be forced to postpone his purpose in coming until a later date. Lady Loring, looking a veritable vision of feminine vulnerability in pale rose, her short blond curls clustering daintily about her face, was the first to summon her wits about her.

"Guy, *darling*," she exclaimed, rising hastily from the dimity sofa with crocodile feet, a monstrosity that Shields abhorred, though he doubted not he had been made to stand the nonsense for it. She crossed to him in a flutter of rose satin and lace, her arms held out to him. "I have missed you dreadfully. Whenever did you arrive back in Town? Why did you not send word you were coming? I fear I am not at all presentable."

"I daresay you could never look anything but charming," Shields replied cynically, well aware that the lady had been actively avoiding him the past several days. Eschewing the opportunity to plant a buss on the rouged cheek held up to him in favor of saluting the knuckles of one dimpled hand, he drawled, "Is that a new gown, my dear? It well becomes you." Releasing her, he turned his attention to his mistress's bosom bow, a plump beauty with improbable red curls and an annoying habit of fluttering equally improbable thick eyelashes without the slightest provocation. "Mrs. Fedderman," he murmured, inclining his head. "An unlooked-for pleasure, no doubt."

"Meaning, my lord, you would gladly consign Captain Wilkes and me to the devil," twittered Mrs. Fedderman, who had not failed to note with keen interest the coolness in Shields's demeanor toward his inamorata or Lady Loring's subsequently heightened color, which had as quickly faded to an intriguing pearly pallor. "And how not? We are decidedly *de trop*, are we not."

"Gammon," interjected Captain Wilkes, a gentleman of five and twenty who, despite a petulance about the handsome face, displayed to striking advantage in crisp regimentals. "Ain't as if his lordship really cared a fig about us, one way or the other. I daresay he would politely send us packing if he did."

"As astute as ever, Wilkes," murmured Shields with only the barest hint of irony in his well-modulated tones. "I had not thought to see you in Town. The last I heard, your regiment was about to be mustered."

The captain gave an airy gesture of one shapely hand. "You know how it is, Shields. One delay after another. I have begun to wonder if I shall ever see any of the fighting. As a matter of fact, I was just talking to Sylvie about selling out. For what that would bring and just a few hundred more, I might have the colors of a lieutenant colonel in the Royal Horse Guards. I daresay I should look smashing in Oxford Blues, what?"

"One's mind is boggled at the prospect," agreed Shields, who could not have cared less what did or did not become the young coxcomb. Further, he had not the slightest doubt whose purse was meant to supply the few hundred additional pounds required to purchase the captain his promotion.

"Nonsense," interjected Lady Loring, awarding

her younger brother a darkling look. "You will do perfectly fine as you are, Freddy. I see no reason to belabor the point. His lordship has not called to hear you extol the virtues of the Royal Horse Guards." Lifting china-blue eyes to Shields, she dimpled prettily. "On the contrary, I believe he came to see me. Guy, darling, pray do come and sit down. I shall ring for a decanter of brandy. As it happens, Freddy and Cora were just on the point of leaving."

"They need not. Certainly not on my account." Slipping his hand beneath Lady Loring's arm, Shields drew her to the door. "I shall not be staying. No doubt your guests will be pleased to grant us a moment."

She was not given the opportunity to voice the protest that rose so plainly to her lips. Shields, inclining his head to the others, led her out into the corridor and shut the door behind him.

"Shields, really," declared Lady Loring, assaying a smile that did not quite banish the watchfulness from her eyes. "Must you go away in a huff? I am well aware how you feel about Freddy and Cora, but I fail to see how I was to know you would call today. After all, it has been well over a fortnight since . . ."

"A fortnight, indeed." Shields, recognizing all the signs that his mistress was on the point of favoring him with a thinly veiled curtain lecture on his various failings, a practice into which she had fallen all too often of late, felt a sudden pall of ennui sweep over him. With chilling deliberation, he moved to cut her off before she could sink her subtle barbs into him. "This has nothing to do with Wilkes or Mrs. Fedderman or how I feel about them. Indeed, you have a poor notion of my character—do you think for one moment I should choose to dictate whom you see?" Shields, in no mood to prolong the inevitable, reached inside his coat for the velvet box snug in the pocket over his chest. "But then, regrettably, my dear, I have been aware for some little time that we are prey to what I can only describe as irreconcilable differences."

Shields, who had played out this scene before with any number of mistresses and always with the expectation that it should be conducted according to the rules of the game—with civility—was not prepared to have the beautiful Sylvia suddenly launch herself at him, though, on retrospect, no doubt he should have done.

"Shields, no!" Flinging her arms about his neck, she clung to him, tears welling up in the beautiful eyes in a manner that might have softened his resolve had he not been made all too privy in the past to similar demonstrations of histrionics from his inamorata. "Guy, darling, say you do not mean that. I could not bear it if I have lost your affections. You know I could not."

"On the contrary," asserted Shields, who had little doubt it was not his affections she could not bear to do without. Clasping her wrists, he pulled her hands down between them. "You will do very well without me—just as you have always done."

The lovely face went pale and, clasping at the front of his coat, she appeared to sag against him. "Oh, how cold and unfeeling you are! Can you not see how you have wounded me? Dearest, I beg you. Pray do not treat me in this cruel fashion."

"It would be cruel to pretend to feel something I do not. There is no sense in enacting a Cheltenham tragedy, Sylvia. You knew from the very beginning that this was bound to come eventually. We have had a pleasant interlude, but we both understood from the beginning that that was all it would ever be."

"How easy that is for you to say!" the countess

declared bitterly. Letting drop the presence, she favored him with a contemptuous look. "Nor does it help that I have been expecting it for some little time now. You are not the lover you fancy yourself, my lord. Did you think I should not feel the coldness in your touch? Faith, how I loathe you and all of your kind. You use me and then think you can dismiss me without a second thought. The devil take you. It means nothing to the wealthy Earl of Shields that Lady Loring will be left without a feather to fly with so long as he has had his pleasure with her."

"A pleasure, madam," Shields answered coldly, "which diminishes with each passing moment. Clearly, we shall do better to part—now, before we are denied even the pretence of civility."

Inclining his head, he turned to take his leave of her.

Consequently, he did not see the look of panic cross her face, or the dawning of cold, hard realization. She flung herself after him.

"Shields, *no!* You do not mean it, any more than I meant any of the dreadful things I said." Her fingers clenched in the fabric of his coat. "Guy, dearest, it is only some terrible misunderstanding." She lifted her face to his, her lips parted invitingly. "Come upstairs with me, darling. I shall make you forget this ever happened."

Shields, weary of the charade, could only marvel that he had ever allowed himself to be enticed into an affair that was proving as distasteful as it was difficult to bring to an end. Still, she was a woman with whom he had shared a certain intimacy, no matter how ill-advised it might have proven in the final analysis. "You may be sure," he said, firmly putting her from him, "that I have already forgotten it. I have instructed Norton to settle your expenses to the end of the next quarter, madam.

You may keep the house until you have made other, more felicitous arrangements.''

"And that is it?" demanded the lady with an air of incredulity. "You think to salve your conscience with a paltry allowance and the house until such time as you decide to put me out on the streets?"

Deliberately, Shields pried her hands loose from his coat front. "If you had bothered to come to know me better, my dear, you would realize how little it would serve you to appeal to my conscience." Coldly, he released her, and, negligently tossing the blue velvet box on the sideboard, he left her.

"Come back, Shields!" she shrieked after him as he made his way down the staircase. "You will not walk away from me! I shall not stand for it. Do you hear me? *Shields!* You will find that I am not so easily discarded, I promise you!"

Shields, who could only wonder that he had ever found anything remotely attractive in the volatile Lady Loring, was left with a sour taste in his mouth as he ordered the coachman to take him to his private club.

A few rubbers of piquet, however, and an excellent supper of mushroom soup, followed by *boeuf bourguignon* with a side dish of buttered asparagus and a dessert of vanilla souffle served most satisfactorily to dispel the unpleasant incident from his mind. He was further abetted in that regard by Winterbrooke's invitation to repair to the viscount's Town House to sample a pipe of exquisite Bordeaux which Winterbrooke had newly purchased.

With the result that Shields, upon arriving home a scant three hours before dawn, had relegated the entire affair to the realm of ancient history where it belonged.

He had not likewise, however, dismissed the incident of his near-fatal encounter with the Goddess of Beauty. It was very much on his mind as, having relieved himself of his coat, his yard-long neckcloth, and his waistcoat, he stood staring down into the fire.

Indeed, it had come to him on more than one occasion throughout the evening to wonder who the devil she was and what possible connection she could have to Hepplewaite's demise and whoever now presumably wished the Earl of Shields out of the way. He recalled the hauntingly lovely face remarkable for its ivory complexion and its finely molded features, the nose long and straight, the lips enticingly full and wide, and the chin, in addition to being delightfully pointed, giving the distinct impression of a strong, stubborn nature. The Goddess of Beauty was no common-born wench, he would stake his reputation on it. Nor did she strike him as being one who would be easily persuaded to do something she had no wish to do.

Why, then, had she apparently lent herself to a plot to put an untimely period to his existence? And, equally provocative, why should she have backed out at the last moment?

Clearly, she was not possessed of a case-hardened nature. No doubt someone had coerced her into an act that was counter to her true character— someone on the order of Nicodemus Pickering, perhaps, came insidiously to his mind. If that were the case, then she must be desperate indeed, he thought, his lips thinning to a grim line as it came to him to ponder to what new lengths she would be persuaded to achieve her machinator's objective. No doubt he might expect to receive in the near future an anonymous invitation for a midnight tryst at some secluded place, or perhaps he might look forward to being lured into some dark alleyway where he could anticipate being set upon by felons. A pity the mysterious Goddess of Beauty had not seen fit to come to him for help out of her dilemma. But then, she was a woman, after all, with all a woman's frailties, he reminded himself. She could hardly be expected to brave the lion in his den.

Hardly had that thought crossed his mind than he went suddenly still, his every sense attuned to the silence around him.

Almost immediately he heard it again—the faintest jiggle of the door handle. Noiselessly, he melted into the shadows on the far side of the door.

The door swung open on silent hinges. Shields, assailed with the subtle scent of lilacs, froze, his eyes on the silhouette of a pistol extended through the opening, followed stealthily by an arm, a shoulder.

The intruder went suddenly still.

Shields tensed, ready to spring.

The next instant, the intruder moved in a flurry of black velvet. Sweeping around, the cloaked figure came face-to-face with the earl, the gun trained at arm's length on a point right between Shields's arrogant eyebrows.

"*YOU!*" pronounced the earl in awful accents.

"*OH!*" gasped the intruder in shocked bestartlement.

With a sharp *pop*, the gun went off—and shot Shields dead-center in the forehead.

"Oh, good God!" exclaimed the Goddess of Beauty, staring in petrified horror at her victim's stunned countenance.

Chapter 4

Elfrida, leaning her chin on her knees pulled up to her chest, peered out the bedroom window down on the stables below. From her position on the seat in the bay window, she should have had an unobstructed view of the mews directly behind and on either side of the house. Unfortunately, a thickening pall of fog was making it increasingly difficult to discern anything more than the vague shapes of buildings. Even the glow of the stable lamp was little more than a pale aura of yellow in the mist.

Through the open window, the nearly constant clatter of carriage wheels on the cobblestoned street out in front vied with the lively strains of a country dance issuing from Lady Braxton's gala four doors down, not to mention what gave every indication of being a musicale going forth across the square and the raucous merriment of a party of gentlemen clearly in their cups. How different from the quiet of the country, thought Elfrida, who had almost forgotten what it was like to be in

London. How strange it was to think she was actually *here* in the City!

Nothing could have kept her away, however, not after the vision that had come to her in the shew stone over a se'ennight ago.

Despite Violet's dire forecast that her sister's plans were doomed to come to naught due to the unpredictability of the principals involved, the cavalcade that had departed Albermarle Castle some forty-eight hours later would seem to give mute testimonial to Elfrida's powers of persuasion.

Gideon, it was true, had proven as difficult as would any Scorpio of Vere's remove who had, in addition, an agenda of his own. His sights having been fixed on immediate prey, he was not made readily to apprehend that the entire female contingent of the Rochelle family was bound and determined upon removing forthwith to London. Furthermore, having finally impressed on him the fact that this was not some sudden flight of feminine fancy, but an inescapable aspect of his younger sister's having passed her nineteenth birthday, Elfrida had still most forcefully to remind him that he could not, in all conscience, allow his sisters, not to mention his aunt by marriage, to proceed on a three-day journey without a male member of the family to serve as escort. Indeed, it simply was not to be thought of.

"I fail to see why," had observed the marquis, favoring Elfrida with his unnerving stare. "You and Violet have been used to jaunt all over the countryside without needing me to tag along—until now. You've some ulterior motive, Elfrida. Out with it."

"You are quite right, Gideon," Elfrida had freely admitted. "As it happens, I have an unnatural dread of being murdered. Is that so very difficult for you to understand? Three women and three children traveling in a manner which can only be described as conspicuous at best are bound to attract a deal of notice. Is it really so farfetched to imagine we might draw the attention of poor Hepplewaite's murderer, especially as we shall pass within a very few miles of Ludgate Hall?"

"I seriously doubt Hepplewaite's murderer has been so witless as to remain in the proximity of his crime," Gideon shrugged. "On the other hand, I suppose it is not unreasonable that so shocking an event might cause even my normally dauntless sister to feel some trepidation. You are right, of course, to remind me of my duty as head of our immediate family. No doubt I can put off my personal plans for a se'nnight or two."

It was Elfrida's most ardent hope that a few *days* away from the enticing Lady Barstowe would suffice to put Gideon's "plans" permanently out of his head. In any case, she was not in the least disappointed to find Albermarle in one of his generous moods when she approached him next. Indeed, she did not doubt he had just benefited greatly from a lengthy tête-à-tête with his new lady love, who, manifesting every sign of one inordinately pleased with herself, smilingly excused herself from the room. But then, she had had every right to be smug, thought Elfrida, who could not but have noted the sparkle of emeralds and diamonds on the widow's left ring finger upon which had resided the Albermarle betrothal ring!

"Violet has determined upon a Season in London? Egad," commented the duke, raising his quizzing glass to one eye the better to observe Elfrida's expression. "What the devil put that bee in her bonnet?"

"I am sure I cannot say, Your Grace," Elfrida did not hesitate to reply. "Doubtless she has benefited from your own illustrious example."

"The devil she has." The duke's arrogant black

eyebrows fairly snapped together over the bridge of his ducal nose as he let drop the quizzing glass. "I doubt not this new start of hers may be laid at your door, little miss malapert. You've some scheme in the making, my girl."

"If you call it a scheme to wish to see my sister brought out in the hopes that she may find a suitable husband, then I stand guilty as accused, Your Grace. Violet, in case you had forgotten, Grandpapa, is just turned nineteen."

"Forgotten?" Albermarle's slender frame, as proudly upright as ever it had been, stiffened, even as the keen blue eyes, which could appear as chill as winter frost, sharpened to steely points. "Unless my memory fails me, *Miss*, you are all of five and twenty and still unwed."

"And you, Your Grace," Elfrida instantly shot back, "are four and seventy and stand eagerly at the threshold of matrimony. Is that not proof enough that miracles can still happen? Perhaps I myself am not beyond all hopes of redemption."

"Impertinent wench! It would need a miracle to find a man capable of putting up with your unruly tongue—a saint or a devil, I know not which. In either case, I should wish him well of you."

"And yourself well rid of me, I doubt not, Your Grace," sweetly observed Elfrida. "Be that as it may, however, I am like to be with you for a very long time, or at least until Violet is happily wed."

The duke's arrogant features, still formidably handsome despite the record of his years etched in lines about the eyes and mouth, gave way to a flicker of sardonic appreciation. "You've a deal of your great-grandmama Lucasta in you, girl. More's the pity. Never was there a more meddlesome woman than my dearest departed mama, or one more out of touch with reality. Take heed that you do not emulate her too far. In her day she was judged an Original or, at worst, a charming eccentric because she had the protection of being the Duchess of Albermarle. In an age in which we have lived to see the madness of a France overrun by the mob, another might not be so fortunate."

"Or one might be seen for what she *really* was— a woman of foresight and vision," Elfrida quietly asserted. "I am sorry it was never given me to know my great-grandmother, Your Grace. I should be proud, nevertheless, if I took after her in some small way."

"Yes, *you* would, would you not," the duke uttered, his gaze enigmatic on Elfrida. Then, quite abruptly he turned the subject back to the original topic of discussion. "As for Violet, it is time the child made her curtsey in Society. If anything, you've left it till too late, Missy. But then, naturally there were extenuating circumstances. It was a bad business, that, losing her mama when she did. Still, there is no sense in adding another spinster to the shelf, is there? Be sure I shall stand the nonsense of a wardrobe and whatever else is needed. You have only to send the accounting to Hammons. And if you find a husband for the chit, I shall likely be persuaded to throw in a reasonable dowry to sweeten the pot. Now be off with you."

"You are all generosity, Your Grace." Elfrida smiled, dropping into a curtsey.

"I am nothing of the kind, I warn you," retorted the duke. "One day you will push me too far, Elfrida."

"Yes, Your Grace." Still smiling to herself, Elfrida had made a hasty retreat—and had nearly collided with her Aunt Roanna, who was waiting anxiously outside the study door.

"Did he *agree* to it? Elfrida, I have hardly been able to contain myself. Tell me, dear. What did he *say?*"

"He said he would likely throw in a dowry if we succeeded in marrying Violet off, the old bugbear." Elfrida laughed, pulling the other woman, a delicate blond beauty of nine and twenty, down the corridor away from the duke's private sanctum. "Of course he agreed to it, dearest aunt. There was never any doubt of it."

"Never perhaps in your mind," declared Roanna, giving vent to a shudder. "You, however, have no notion of what it is to stand in dread of calling the duke's wrath down on your head. He has never liked me, Elfrida. You know he has not. I pray for the day that Richard will be so fortunate as to capture a rich prize ship, that we may at last afford a house of our own in London."

"I daresay Uncle Richard's luck will soon have a turn for the better. And you will admit he has not done too badly. A post captain at thirty in the King's Navy is nothing to quibble about. And as for the duke's lack of affection toward you, I am sure it is all a hum. He enjoys baiting you, Roanna, because you make it so easy for him. If occasionally you could find it in yourself to stand up to him, dearest aunt, I daresay it would do you no harm in his eyes."

"Stand up to him!" Roanna's emerald eyes widened in horror. "I should rather stand up to a raging bull than deliberately invite Albermarle's rancor. You are not taking into consideration my delicate sensibilities, Elfrida, which is only understandable since you are utterly deprived of any yourself."

"Yes, well, be that as it may, dearest Aunt," Elfrida rejoined, perfectly aware that beneath the facade of feminine frailty was a Libran woman perfectly capable of coping with her Aquarian father-in-law, if only she would make up her mind to it, "I suggest you rouse yourself sufficiently to pack.

We shall be leaving Albermarle Castle no later than the day after tomorrow."

Despite her misgivings that any such departure date could actually be accomplished, given the parties involved, Elfrida could only be exceedingly gratified that, not only did the caravan of three coaches and Vere's curricle, in addition to the mounted groom leading three of the Rochelle prime bits of blood, depart the castle grounds by the hour she had specified, but that they had reached, in good order, the posting inn outside of Shaftesbury in time to engage rooms for the night.

Fortunately, whether due to Gideon's protective presence or to some other benevolent circumstance, their repose was not disturbed by the unfortuitous attack of any would-be assassins. And as for Elfrida's less than restful sleep, no doubt the inn's specialty of mutton stew could be blamed, Roanna was given to speculate as, descending the stairs the next morning, Elfrida related to her companions the troubling dream that had visited her in the night.

"Certainly, it did not set at all well with *me*," further confessed Roanna, who was indeed looking somewhat more the wilting violet than she normally did. "Valentine, dear," she added to her seven-year-old son, who was involved in terrorizing his older sister with a silver plated, pearl-handled pop gun. "Pray do stop pointing that dreadful weapon at Alexandra. You know it is not nice to shoot people."

"I was pretending to be Vere, and Alexandra is Lord Ester," piped up Valentine, taking careful aim at his sister.

"Then naturally you must be sure to strike your target," observed Vere with chilling dispassion.

"*Mama!*" shrieked Alexandra, a dainty blond replica of her mother.

"Vere, really!" declared Violet, awarding her brother a comical moué of displeasure.

"Valentine, I warn you," declared his mama.

"I fear it is nothing so simple as a product of dyspepsia," interjected Elfrida with a frown of concentration on her lovely brow. Reaching down to grasp Valentine by the scruff of the neck, she relieved the boy of the pop gun before he could discharge it. Then, giving him a tweak of the ear, she firmly clasped his hand in hers. "Any dream depicting the rising of a phoenix from the flames of its own destruction should be treated with all due seriousness," she continued, slipping the toy pistol in the placket pocket of her carriage dress. "It is nearly always prophetic or at the very least pregnant with meaning."

"But you said you dreamt of an overcooked goose, which Henri, in his usual inimitable fashion, salvaged by transforming it into a thick stew with garlic sauce," Violet did not hesitate to point out. "That would hardly seem the equivalent of a phoenix rising from the flames of its own destruction."

"On the contrary," drawled Gideon with a cynical gleam in his compelling orbs, "it is all very clear, is it not? Elfrida's dream must certainly pertain to poor Hepplewaite's demise from overcooking. Ludgate Hall, after all, or what is left of it, is little more than a league from here. No doubt Hepplewaite was attempting to communicate with our divinating sister from the Other Side."

"But of course!" exclaimed Elfrida as they entered the common room, already occupied by a handful of travelers, a tavern wench, and an elderly gentleman bent over a draft of ale in a corner booth. "I daresay that is it precisely. Considering the nature of Viscount Hepplewaite's demise, I certainly should not dismiss such a possibility out of hand. Indeed, contrary to my original thoughts on the matter, I should not be in the least surprised if Hepplewaite, eager to escape the unpleasantness associated with the scene of the crime, has fled this plane with all due haste. And who could blame him? I daresay he has already donned an entirely new persona in anticipation of a fresh beginning. How strange to think it should have fallen to me to be witness to the event of Hepplewaite's flight and metamorphosis."

"I daresay it would only be strange had it *not* fallen to you," observed Gideon, ushering his kinswomen out the door into the courtyard. "Who else, after all, would think to turn a burnt goose into a gone gosling but you, dearest Elfrida?"

"Wretch!" declared Elfrida, not in the least discomfited at discovering herself the object of a roast. She was, after all, grown used to it. "How dare you make game of me, when it was you who saw immediately to the true meaning of the dream. What a pity you refuse to give credence to the extra-ordinary powers of the mind. Given half the chance, Vere, I daresay you would make an admirable prognosticator yourself."

"I should not count on it too heavily if I were you," drawled Vere, favoring Elfrida with his all too disarming grin. "I daresay I should find it a dead bore, mulling over my dreams in the hopes of discovering some arcane meaning, which no one would believe at any rate. No thank you, Elfrida, dear. I shall gladly leave all that to you."

"How very kind in you, Vere," retorted Elfrida sweetly. Releasing Valentine to his nanny, she allowed herself to be helped into the travel coach she shared with Violet and Roanna. "I daresay *your* dreams, after all, would not bear closer examination at any rate, and certainly not a public airing."

"Quite so, my darling sister," agreed Vere, inclining his head in acknowledgment of a palpable hit. "Indeed, you could not be closer to the truth. Our next stop, if all goes well, will see us within striking distance of London. I trust you will enjoy your journey, ladies."

Some moments later, having seen the children and their nanny safely established in the coach reserved for their use, and the three abigails and the marquis's gentleman's gentleman having boarded the third coach, Vere lightly mounted to the seat of his curricle.

"It looks like a fine day for it, John," Elfrida overheard the marquis remark to his groom as Vere took up the whip and the reins.

"Aye, milord," had agreed John Vickers, who, a retainer of long standing, must have known as well as Elfrida that his master chafed at the necessity of pursuing a pace suited to the travel coaches with their passengers of women and children. "Belike we shall make excellent time, milord."

"Oh, excellent time, indeed," had drawled the marquis, holding the prime bits of blood in as they lunged forward, eager at the bits. "For a funeral procession or a cavalcade of nuns, no doubt."

The caravan of coaches that swept out of the yard, however, must have created a fine stir. Elfrida, glancing out the window, had noted that even the elderly gentleman, who had been savoring his tankard of ale in the common room, had apparently been moved to rise from his corner table. Leaning heavily on his ebony stick, he had doddered out to join the handful of bystanders in the courtyard watching as the procession disappeared from view.

The succeeding leg of the journey had been accomplished with nothing more untoward than three-year-old Chloe's having succumbed to travel sickness—due, no doubt, to the consumption of an excess of marchpane, which her brother Valentine had prevailed upon his overindulgent mama to purchase for the three children—and a second, exceedingly curious dream that night, which Elfrida had forborne from sharing with anyone.

Indeed, even now, just thinking about it was enough to cause Elfrida a sudden wrench in the vicinity of her breast bone. It had been a dream of prophesy. She could not be mistaken in that, she told herself as she hugged her knees more tightly to her chest. The symbolic images had been far too portentously significant for it to have been otherwise.

Shields might be her karmically predetermined, astrologically perfect mate, but he could never be her husband. The dream had been quite clear in that respect.

To marry him would mean his certain death!

Faith, what a coil it was to be sure, she thought. Indeed, it would seem a peculiarly twisted fate to be predestined to find the one man who could make her whole, only to be denied completion with him on this plane of existence. Perhaps, in some past life, she had incurred a karmic debt that could only be erased by setting Shields free of any obligation, she speculated, something on the order of requiring one to forgive and forget in order to clear the way for the two to be eternally joined. Or perhaps, due to some sort of karmic "blindness" induced by events in one of his past lives, he would fail to recognize her as his True Love, his Twin Soul. In which case, it would have to wait until another karmic twining of lives to bring him to a proper realization of who she was and the role she had to play in his search for spiritual perfection.

Faith, it was all very complicated, when one contemplated matters on the cosmic plane, she thought ruefully. But then, mere mortals could hardly be expected to grasp the entirety of the Cosmic Order of things. It was enough to recognize when one had been given a sign and to do one's best to follow it, she told herself.

It did not occur to her to consider the possibility that Shields might not be brought to the point of wanting to marry her. Her dream had centered about the symbols traditionally associated with weddings; therefore, it must be interpreted as a sign that a wedding would be in the offing.

Shields *would* ask her to marry him, she knew it. And she must refuse him! But then, she had sworn she would dare anything, do anything to keep him safe, and she would keep that promise, no matter what might be asked of her. It was her karmic obligation.

A fierce light leaped in Elfrida's eyes at thought of how near she had already come to losing him in Bond Street that very afternoon.

It had not proven an easy task to keep track of her exceedingly elusive quarry. Even with the good fortune of discovering the house immediately next door to Shields belonged to Lord Winston Godfrey, one of Vere's closest intimates, and that, further, he had given Vere leave to make full use of it, as he was off on a walking tour of Scotland (a coincidence she did not doubt could be attributed to karmic fate), Elfrida had had a devil of a time staying up with Shields. Worse, she knew for certain he had spotted her the previous night in her carriage, the devil.

But then, it had been her very first experience in the subtle art of stalking. She had set Ned, the stable lad, on watch to warn when the earl's carriage was being readied for departure while she herself had waited, fully dressed and prepared to run out at a moment's notice. Even so, it had been by only the very slimmest of margins that she had managed to gain her carriage before he had emerged from the house. Surely she could be excused the one little error of being caught peering out at him from the carriage window when she should have known to remain, unseen, in the shadows! It had, after all, been eight years since last she had laid eyes on him in the flesh. Not unnaturally, she had been curious to see what changes time had wrought. She had not thought to find herself staring directly into his face, which, she could not but reflect, was even more compellingly handsome than she had remembered it.

Nevertheless, she had not made *that* mistake again. Indeed, she was quite certain she had eluded further detection while she became more and more adept at blending in with her surroundings. It had been quite unexpected, however, to be caught out in the open that afternoon in Bond Street, and all because of the most exquisite of bonnets in Burbage's Haberdashery window.

Really, she had not known how it was that she had suddenly found herself exiting her carriage parked across the street from Messrs. Johnson and Tate. But then, the bonnet that had caught her eye had had spring flowers clustered about the brim and the most charming blue ribbons. In retrospect, she could not but think it had been most felicitous, perhaps even propitious, since, having failed to see Shields emerge from the shop, she had just turned and stepped off the curb with the intention of reentering her conveyance when she glimpsed the runaway hackney bearing down on him. Had she been inside her closed carriage, hidden from view, it would have been quite impossible for her to have seen anything of Shields's impending fate, let alone to cry out a warning. Shields would undoubtedly have fallen victim to a wholly ignominious end!

Naturally, she could not but feel some measure of guilt for having succumbed to the impulse of the moment, even for a bonnet with spring flowers and blue ribbons. Indeed, even though it was perfectly obvious that it had been all for the better, she could not but think she had demonstrated a sad lack of character. Henceforth, she vowed, she would allow nothing to distract her from her purpose. She would keep Shields safe from harm, even if it meant she had, in the end, to give him up for his own good!

That, however, was a matter that could wait for contemplation at a later date, she reminded herself, stifling a yawn as she forced her attentions once more on the mist outside her window. For now, she had only to stay awake until Meggie came to relieve her shortly after dawn.

Shivering in the chill air, Elfrida pulled her black velvet dressing gown more snugly about her. Having already spent more than half the night huddled in her carriage outside Viscount Winterbrooke's Town House, she had allowed herself, upon gratefully finding herself once more at home, the single luxury of changing out of her evening gown in favor of the warm, loose-flowing velvet wrapper shot through with silver threads. The exquisite dressing gown was designed for receiving callers in her boudoir, although, as an unmarried woman, she had never had occasion to do any such thing. Indeed, she supposed she had ought to don the white lace cap of a spinster on the shelf, something she had been putting off in the firm belief that her single state would one day be altered. That, however, was all changed now.

She gave in to an irrepressible yawn. If she could not wed her Twin Soul, her karmically predetermined, astrologically perfect mate, then she would never marry anyone. Indeed, there would seem little point in settling for something one knew was less than perfect, she reflected as, irresistibly, her eyelids drifted down over her eyes.

Elfrida came awake with a start. Faith, she had been having the strangest dream. It was all fuzzy now, but she remembered something about dancing the minuet and stepping on a gentleman's toes only to discover that, not only was the gentleman Shields, but he was admonishing her to keep her eyes open as one never knew when one might be surprised by a visit from the King. Really, it would seem to make little sense, especially in light of the fact that she had been quite overset at what had amounted to a ridiculous warning. Naturally, she would not be dancing the minuet with her eyes closed and certainly not in the presence of the King. Upon which, it came to her with a sudden wrench in the pit of her belly that she should not have had her eyes closed at all! Faith, she wondered, her heart pounding in alarm, how long had she been asleep?

She was immediately swept with a rising panic. Something had brought her awake. Perhaps she had unconsciously heard something—*someone*—outside in the dark. Perhaps Shields was even now being assailed by would-be assassins as he lay asleep in his bed!

Thinking solely that she must reach Shields before it was too late, Elfrida bolted from the windowseat. Only as she exited her bedroom did it come to her that should she surprise an intruder in Shields's house, she would have need of some sort of a weapon. Snatching up the first thing that came to hand, she fairly flew down the servants' stairs to the service entrance at the back of the house, then out across the small courtyard paved

in flagstones to the wrought-iron gate that opened
on the mews.

The thick shroud of fog confused the senses and
gave the mews an eerie aspect of moving shapes
and shifting shadows. Suddenly she gasped, her
heart leaping to her throat, as she thought she
glimpsed a figure dart across the way before her
only to vanish as instantly as it had appeared. No
doubt her eyes were merely playing tricks on her,
she tried to reassure herself, as she came at last to
Shields's back door. Reaching for the key suspended on a chain about her wrist, she froze. The
door was ajar.

It never occurred to her to suppose that someone
of the household had failed to secure the entrance
through some sort of oversight. She knew Craddock, the earl's exceedingly proper London butler,
by reputation. He would never have forgotten to
check the locks before seeking his bed.

Someone had been there before her!

Picking up her skirts, Elfrida entered and made
her way up the servants' stairs to the third story.
From Meggie Wheeler, who had reconnoitered the
house for her mistress, Elfrida knew Shields's door
was the second on the left.

Her heart pounding beneath her breast, Elfrida
reached for the handle.

She was not certain what she expected to find
beyond that oaken barrier. The spectre of Shields,
lying in his bed—dead by an assassin's hand, filled
her with a terrible dread. She never knew where
she found the courage to ease the door open.
Indeed, she was telling herself that it was all well
and good to frighten oneself with tales of Gothic
horror while curled up in a chair by the fireside,
but it was a matter on quite a different order to
actually steal into a room that might very well be

occupied by a corpse, not to mention a deranged killer!

Her fingers tightened on the handle of the weapon, which, on retrospect, she could not but think was wholly inadequate in the circumstances. Still, she was here, and she really must see for herself what lay beyond that door. Drawing a deep breath, she stole forward, the weapon extended before her.

The sensation that she was not alone touched her like the sharp point of a knife between her shoulder blades. She knew without the smallest doubt that there was someone behind the door, someone waiting for her to step into the room. Swallowing the terror that rose to her throat, she spun about.

And was met with the sight of Shields, powerful and forbidding, his eyes boring holes through her.

"You!" he pronounced.

"Oh!" Elfrida gasped, her finger jerking without conscious volition on the trigger of seven-year-old Valentine's silver-plated pop gun with the pearl handles.

Chapter 5

"Oh, good God," exclaimed Elfrida, staring in stunned fascination at the distinct red circle that had appeared in the center of the earl's aristocratic brow. To her horror, she felt her lips begin spasmodically to twitch. Faith, she was going to laugh. Indeed, she could not stop herself.

Shields, who found little at the moment to amuse in the realization that he had just been struck in the forehead by a cork—from a child's toy gun, no less, egad!—was hardly rendered more cheerful by the observation that his assailant displayed what would appear an utter lack of remorse for her misdeed. She had, in fact, clapped a hand over her mouth in a vain effort to contain what gave every evidence of being a rising, not to mention irrepressible, glee.

"Quite so, madam," he declared in frosty accents. "No doubt you have every reason for merriment. You have, after all, perpetrated a masterful hoax against me, have you not? And now you will have the added pleasure of telling me why the devil you should have done it."

"H-hoax?" quavered Elfrida, dashing tears of mirth from her eyes. "No, no, you do not understand. It was never a hoax. The devil," she gasped, drawing a steadying breath. "I-I do wish you will stop glaring at me in that fashion. Really, it is too much, my lord."

Shields, in the process of reassessing his earlier theories concerning the mysterious Goddess of Beauty, was given to contemplate the distinct possibility that the female was deranged as she went off into another gale of laughter. Certainly, she would seem to be wholly lacking in a proper grasp of her present situation—alone with a man in his bedchamber, a man, moreover, whom she had earlier nearly lured to his death and whose privacy and person she had now dared to violate. A cold glitter hardened his eyes. Even more telling, she was *laughing* at him!

No doubt it was the sensation of having an exceedingly tall and compelling presence loom suddenly over even her generous inches that returned Elfrida to a semblance of sobriety.

"Dear," she gasped unsteadily, "I do beg your pardon for laughing, my lord, b-but, really, I could not help myself. You-you had such a thunderstricken look just now. And, indeed, who could blame you? Still, you must see that it was never my intent to-to shoot you. You should not have startled me the way you did. What if I had been an intruder intent upon putting a period to your existence? You might very well be dead at this moment."

"Instead it would seem I am very much alive," observed Shields, forbearing out of politeness, no doubt, to point out that she was an intruder and that, further, he was not at present a corpse only because her weapon had been inadequate to the task!

"For which, my lord, I am exceedingly grateful," breathed the Goddess of Beauty with what gave every appearance of a heartfelt relief.

"Yes, no doubt," observed his lordship, thinking that either she was a consummate actress or he had been right in his earlier speculations that she was being manipulated against her will by an unconscionable blackguard.

Judiciously relieving her of the child's pistol, he shut the door and turned the key in the lock.

"An excellent precaution, my lord," applauded Elfrida, who, reminded of the door left ajar at the back of the house, could not quite subdue a shudder of apprehension. "One that I suggest you would do well henceforth to make a practice."

Shields frowned. Egad, the wench would seem to display a remarkable lack of concern at finding herself locked in a gentleman's bedchamber. On the contrary, she gave every indication of one pleased at what should have been an unsettling turn of events. But then, perhaps that had been her intent all along, he reflected grimly—to be discovered closeted with the Earl of Shields in what could only be described as compromising circumstances. Or perhaps it suited her purposes to have him alone, with the rest of the household shut out. She had, after all, come near to being the death of him only a few hours earlier.

The devil, he thought, not having failed to note that she had shivered, presumably from the chill in the room. Whatever she was about, she was damnably skilled at portraying the unassuming Innocent.

"You are cold," he pronounced. Taking her by the elbow, he conducted her across the room to the fire.

"You are very kind, my lord." Elfrida smiled, gratefully holding her palms out to the warmth of the flames.

"You are mistaken," replied his lordship dampeningly. "Kindness is the last thing you may expect from me." Pouring her a generous brandy from a grog tray on a side table, he pressed the glass in her hand. "Drink," he ordered. "It will help take the chill from your bones."

"It is like to make me three sheets to the wind, my lord," Elfrida objected, recalled to the fact that she had not had occasion to eat since a hasty afternoon tea, which had been interrupted by his lordship's departure to Bond Street and the shop of Messrs. Johnson and Tate. One glance at the earl's forbidding aspect silenced any further protest. "Still, if you insist," she uttered judiciously. Lifting the glass in a silent toast, she valiantly tossed down the stuff—and erupted ignominiously in a fit of choking and sputtering as the fiery liquid burned her throat.

"Little fool," growled his lordship, vigorously pounding Elfrida on the back. "Brandy is not meant to be gulped, my girl. One savors it a sip at a time."

"No doubt I shall remember that," rasped Elfrida when she had got her wind back again, "the next time I feel the need to indulge in strong spirits. I fear I am a trifle shaken. You have no idea with what dread I approached your door. The thought that I should find you slain in your bed by an assassin's hand was almost more than I could bear. Indeed, in such an event I should never have forgiven myself, even though, really, it was all your fault. For you must know I should never have fallen asleep had you not kept me out all day today and until the wee hours two nights in a row."

"No, did I?" queried his lordship, apparently

much struck at the iniquitousness of his behavior in having deprived her of her beauty rest. Not that she appeared to have suffered by it, he reflected sardonically. She was, in fact, even more beautiful than memory had served.

"You did, my lord," Elfrida unhesitatingly confirmed. "Even so, it was unpardonable of me to have succumbed when I knew you were in grave danger. I am convinced it was only for a very few minutes. Still, you can imagine my consternation when I awoke to find I had fallen asleep."

"I daresay you were quite put out by the discovery," agreed the earl, who was able to garner little from her disjointed utterances save that he had been quite right in his earlier suspicions—the wench had indeed been stalking him. And now he would bloody well know the reason why! "After all, you probably thought you had missed your opportunity to catch me asleep in my bed before the cock crowed. Not that it will benefit you in your little scheme, whatever it is. I suggest you tell me everything, beginning with your name. As it happens, I am not in the habit of entertaining females in my bedchamber, especially those with whom I am unacquainted."

"Unacquainted?" echoed the Goddess of Beauty. Her eyes, which he now saw in the reflection of the firelight were a deep, spellbinding blue, widened in disbelief.

He did not remember her! Good heavens, Elfrida thought, hastily averting her gaze as she wrestled with this new, unexpected turn of events. But then, when one went right to the heart of the matter, there was very little reason ever to have supposed he would recall someone he had met only once eight years before and then only to exchange a fleeting word or two. It was only that somehow she had expected there to be some sort of recognition on an extra-ordinary level of perception, a kind of karmic acknowledgment of kindred spirits. That obviously there was nothing of the sort served to bring a whole new light to bear on events. For the very first time it came to her to realize how exceedingly precarious was the position in which she now found herself.

Shields did not know her from Adam, or Eve, as it were. Faith, what must he think of her! Indeed, how was she ever to make him believe she had come to watch over him because of something she had seen in her great-grandmama Lucasta's shew stone? Or even that there had been an intruder before her, as was evidenced by the service door left ajar? After all, the only intruder he had encountered thus far was herself!

"I believe, my lord, that, in the circumstances, I should prefer to remain nameless. Indeed, I think it were better for everyone concerned if I took my leave of you—now, before anyone is the wiser that I was ever here. You will agree that we presently find ourselves in what could only be described as a compromising situation."

"A situation which, compromising or not, you have brought on yourself," observed Shields, in no mood to humor her sudden change of tactics. She had not been concerned with the proprieties, after all, when she stole into his bedchamber and bounced a cork off his forehead. Nor had she appeared in the least squeamish only moments before upon finding herself locked in the room with her victim. Something had occurred to bring her to an awareness that she presently found herself in a coil of her own making.

He recalled the look of dismay in her compelling eyes, just before she had self-consciously glanced away. Surely she had not thought she could break into his house, assault him, and then be given leave to depart without supplying her name and an explanation for her exceedingly odd behavior! She was obviously not in the usual style of young beauties, but he did not judge her to be demented. It was not his demand for her name, then, that had overset her, but the fact that he had not *known* it.

His eyes narrowed sharply on the exquisite profile of her face, limned against the firelight. He could only conclude that he *was* acquainted with her, but for the life of him he could not recall where or how it was that he had met her. Surely, having once seen her, he could not have failed to remember the occasion.

She possessed the kind of beauty that dazzled the beholder and aroused in a man a plethora of primitive male urges, not the least of which was serving, at that very moment, to cause a distinct and familiar stirring in his loins. Indeed, he was acutely aware that he had been laboring for no little time under the impulse to crush her in his arms and savor the promised sweetness of her lips. The devil, hers was *not* the sort of beauty a man forgot!

A dangerous glint ignited in the heavy-lidded eyes. He would have the truth from her, whether she wished it or not. "You were outside my house the night before last in a carriage, and pray do not deny it. You are well aware that I saw you. And again at the theatre. And it was you who called out the warning that undoubtedly saved my life the following afternoon in Bond Street. No doubt I should thank you for that—were it not for the fact that you lured me into the path of that runaway hack."

Had he meant to win a rise out of her, he was not to be disappointed.

Elfrida, giving vent to a gasp, turned to stare at

him with disbelieving eyes. *"Lured* you? Good God, is that what you think?''

The earl's lip curled mockingly. ''You were there, were you not? And hardly had I stepped off the curb than the hackney bore down on me. Pray what else am I to think, my dear?''

''Pray do not call me that,'' snapped Elfrida, her eyes flashing glorious sparks of unadulterated Arian temper. ''I am not your 'dear,' and I was not trying to lure you anywhere.'' Furiously, she began to pace. *"Oh!* Of all the insensible, thick-headed, *blind* ingrates. Gideon was perfectly in the right of it—I *was* an idiot to believe it was my karmic duty to watch over you. I should never have altered from my initial resolve merely to warn you that you were surrounded by a pall of danger. Only *look* at the mull I have made of it! And to think I dragged poor Violet all the way to London against her will just so that I might have an unexceptional excuse for being here—all for nothing. And after everything I have been through—persuading Gideon to let me stay with him in Lord Winston Godfrey's house, when I might have been far more comfortable with Violet and Roanna and the children in the Dukeries, coming to know your household and your habits, sending Meggie over to familiarize herself with the house interior, obtaining an impression of the key to the service entrance, sitting in a draughty carriage for hours on end when I might have been doing something a deal more interesting—even tatting or needlework, which, if you must know, I abhor, would have been more stimulating. Faith, it is hardly remarkable that I should have been momentarily distracted by something so frivolous as a bonnet. Never mind that it was particularly fetching with spring flowers on the brim and the loveliest blue ribbons that tied under the chin or that it has been all of seven years since

I have had an opportunity to so much as *look* in a shop window on Bond Street. I am perfectly aware that I should have stayed out of sight in the carriage. Unfortunately, it was karmically predetermined that I should instead be in a position to see the hackney coach bearing down on you. I daresay it was just as unavoidable that, in dashing over to save you from being attacked in your bed, I have apparently frightened the real intruder away. Not that you could ever be brought to believe that I found the door ajar or that I am almost positive that I saw someone only moments before running away from the house. Naturally, I am to stand convicted in your eyes of being some despicable creature who would not only plot to steal into your house for the sole purpose of shooting you with a child's pop gun, but that I intentionally set myself up as bait to entice you to your death beneath the wheels of a runaway coach.''

Abruptly, she halted in her agitated pacing. Coming pensively about, she favored Shields with an arrested look. ''But then, surely that must mean that you *do* feel a certain attraction for me, my lord. I mean aside from viewing me in the light of some sort of femme fatale with evil designs on your life? Otherwise you would hardly have been drawn to cross the street to accost me, which I must presume you were in the process of doing when you were almost fatally run down.'' Closing the distance between them, she peered up into his stern, handsome features with probing eyes. ''Do you, my lord? Feel at least somewhat attracted to me?''

Shields, who had found a great deal to enlighten him in his uninvited guest's diatribe, not the least of which was that not only was she highly connected (the ''Dukeries'' of the Campden Hill District, after all, were so named because they housed only the very highest ranks of Society), but she obviously was innocent of participating in anything more sinister than a misguided scheme to protect him from a mysterious pall of danger, whatever *that* meant—egad!—was caught momentarily off guard by this sudden, swift alteration in her demeanor.

The mysterious Goddess of Beauty promised, if nothing else, to become a wholly disruptive influence in his life. Find himself "somewhat attracted" to her? he marveled, assailed at exceedingly close range by the fresh scent of mist, which yet clung to her hair, and by the aroma of bath soap tantalizingly perfumed with lilacs, which emanated from her silken skin. The devil, *attracted to her* did not begin to describe the effect she would seem to have on him! Every instinct of self-preservation cried out to him to usher her immediately out of his house and straight to her door, there to instantly disabuse her of the notion that he wished to have anything more to do with her. Instead, he made the supreme error of looking into her eyes, which, like azure pools of unplumbed mystery, seemed peculiarly designed to rob him of the power of all cogent thought processes. Worse, he was acutely aware that her lips were only an enticing scant few inches from his.

"Attracted to you?" he uttered thickly, feeling himself drawn to those tantalizing lips. "You must be perfectly aware that you are a diamond of the first water. I daresay you do not require me to tell you that."

"No, but then, that is not what I asked you, my lord," Elfrida did not hesitate to point out. Marveling at her own brazenness, she leaned the palms of her hands against his chest. An unwitting thrill shot through her at the hard leap of muscle beneath her touch. Indeed, she experienced a strange, unwonted giddiness at the realization that his white silk shirt was open nearly to the waist.

How strange that the sight of the thick blond mat of hair on his chest should have the effect of igniting an unfamiliar warmth in the vicinity of her nether regions! Obviously *she* was attracted to *him*, but then, she had known that from the moment he had appeared to her in the shew stone. He, unfortunately, would not seem reciprocatively responsive, she noted, observing the hard rigidity of his handsome features. "Pray do not be afraid to open the budget, my lord," she earnestly entreated. "I really must know the truth. A great deal depends on it, you see." Tilting her face up, she ran a pink tongue over suddenly dry lips. "Are you not in the least attracted to me?"

Shields, who had long since come to suspect that his Goddess of Beauty, far from being the designing Circean that he had originally imagined her, was instead a madcap little Innocent—one undoubtedly in need of a lesson in the dangers of giving in to irrational impulse, it was true, but an Innocent nonetheless—had forcibly to restrain himself from demonstrating precisely how attracted he was to her.

He was little comforted by the unnerving realization that, so great was her power to disarm and distract him, he had given in to the impulse to lower his head to hers. In no little bemusement, he beheld the little minx purse her lips in anticipation, even as the luxurious veil of her eyelashes drifted down over her captivating orbs. He froze the instant before his mouth brushed hers!

Good God, he thought, jolted to his senses. She was a beguiling minx who had not the smallest notion of the strength of her spell over him, and he vastly preferred that she remain in ignorance of how close he had come to succumbing. He had never made it a practice to take advantage of untutored innocents. He was bloody well damned if he would start now!

"You, my girl, are in grave peril of discovering a deal more than you bargained for," he rasped, acutely sensible of the fact that her firm, well-rounded bosom was pressed against his chest and that, further, she was wearing next to nothing beneath what he had long since come to realize was an undeniably alluring night dress. Deliberately, he clasped her by the arms and put her at a less disturbing distance from him. "You may take my word that I am not totally indifferent to your feminine attributes. I might even go so far as to say I find you reasonably attractive—for a female who seems peculiarly bent on wreaking havoc on my person, not to mention my peace of mind."

It was soon made evident he had not precisely given the answer for which she had been hoping. Her eyes flew ruefully open, and the tantalizing Goddess of Beauty heaved a shuddering sigh of what would seem to be resignation.

"I suppose I should find a measure of comfort in that much, my lord," breathed Elfrida, willing her heart to cease its unwonted pounding. For the barest instant, she had been so certain he was on the point of kissing her! Indeed, it had come to her that he was not quite so indifferent to her as he would have her believe. But then, surely, he could not appear so insufferably cool if he had been under the sway of powerful emotions. Certainly, if he had felt anything, it could not have been on the order of what *she* had experienced as she waited, her breath suspended, her blood racing in her veins, for the touch of his lips against hers— only to have him draw suddenly away, the devil. "It is, after all," she added, "rather better than the last time we met."

"But then it has been some little time since that

memorable event, has it not?'' ventured his lordship, giving in to the temptation to brush a stray
curl from her cheek. ''Seven years, unless I am
mistaken.''

''Eight,'' Elfrida absently corrected, thinking it
was time she consigned her great-grandmother
Lucasta's shew stone to a trunk in the attic. After
all, what had it ever brought her, really, but one
miserable coil after another.

''*Eight* years. But of course it was,'' agreed the
earl, noting, in the play of firelight over her hair,
the fascinating glint of blue in the raven locks. She
was possessed as well of the creamy perfection of
skin as smooth and lovely as alabaster. Hellsfire,
but she was magnificent—the Goddess of Beauty!
Where the devil had he met her before? he pondered, searching his memory.

Eight years before, he was preparing to accompany his uncle on an excursion into France to find
Albert, who had been on a tour of the Continent
with his tutor when the revolution had broken out.
There had been a French woman, a Mlle. DuBois,
who had had word of Albert from her sister in
France. Mlle. Dubois had been a house guest of
the Marquis of Vere. His wife, Eugenie, was the
French woman's cousin. Yes, it was all coming back
to him now.

Shields had attended a ball at Albermarle House
in order to meet with Vere and the French woman.
Little more than a day or two following that evening, he had departed with Albert's father for the
Continent on a search that was to occupy the better
part of six months. In consequence, he remembered little of the gala, other than it had been
the only social event he had attended that Season.
Certainly, he could not recall having danced with
anyone other than the French woman. Still, it was
worth a try.

"There was a—er—ball, was there not?" suggested the earl, thinking that the Goddess of Beauty could not have been much above the age of a schoolroom miss eight years ago. "I asked you to dance."

"It was my coming-out ball," Elfrida declared, recalled abruptly to the present.

The earl's eyebrows fairly snapped together at that revelation. Her coming-out ball—good God!

"And you did *not* ask me to dance. On the contrary, you advised me to take lessons in decorum and the minuet. Which I subsequently did. Not that you were around to notice during my second Season in London. Nor does it signify." Straightening her shoulders, she looked at him with the full force of her eyes. "Obviously, I have made a terrible mistake, my lord. You were not then, nor, clearly, are you now, consumed with an overwhelming desire to join with me in body and spirit in order to experience the mystical heights of a karmically predetermined passion."

Shields, who was still in the process of assimilating the startling discovery that not only did he presently find himself locked in his bedchamber with Lady Elfrida Rochelle, the daughter of the former Marquis of Vere and the granddaughter of the present Duke of Albermarle, but he could very likely look forward in the near future to being challenged to a duel by the lady's brother, a stripling noted for his cold nerve and his reputation for being dangerous, was hardly prepared for this new revelation from the Goddess of Beauty. Good God, he thought, join with her *how?*

"It would seem I misread the signs," continued Elfrida, wanting only to tell him everything and be done with it. "Not that I am *not* convinced you are in grave peril of your life, my lord, for in that, I daresay I could not be mistaken. Indeed, no doubt

that was the sole purpose for which I was given to
see you in the crystalline mists.''

Drawing a deep breath, she looked Shields
straightly in the eyes. ''You see, my lord, I am a
prognosticator and a scryer. Not, of course, that
you will believe me when I tell you that I am given
to see visions in a crystal ball or that I am frequently
visited with dreams of a prophetic nature. It has
been my misfortune that no one does. But in this,
I was so certain. Faith, I cannot understand what
went awry. I knew, when I beheld you in my great-
grandmama Lucasta's shew stone, that you were
my karmically predetermined, astrologically perfect mate, my Twin Soul—the one man with whom
I was meant to be joined in order to achieve spiritual wholeness. It would seem, however, I am the
only one of us who is sensible of any astrological
magnetism between us. *I* am drawn to you with
my whole heart and soul, but you apparently feel
nothing.''

''Nothing?'' queried Shields, who was at the
moment in the sway of any number of powerful
emotions, not the least of which was a strong sense
of astonishment. He did not doubt there was not
a man alive who could be near the Goddess of
Beauty and feel *nothing!* To join with Lady Elfrida
Rochelle in any manner, let alone in body and
spirit, in order to achieve the mystical heights of
a karmically predetermined passion, however, was
tantamount to madness. But then, he was dealing
with a young, misguided female who believed she
saw visions in a crystal ball—egad! Patently, it was
up to him to bring some sanity to the situation.

''Indeed, my lord, nothing. At least nothing on
the order of a cosmic awakening of primordial
passions,'' asserted Elfrida, beginning to experience the soporific effects of the brandy she had
imbibed, in addition to two days and nights with

little more than occasional brief snatches of sleep. "Really, my lord," she added, smothering a yawn with the fingers of one hand, "I confess to being more than a trifle disappointed. But then, I daresay it is not your fault, never mind that you are a Leo or that I am an Aries, and that, consequently, we enjoy a 5-9 Sun Sign vibratory pattern. Very probably there is some other inhibitive factor that is preventing you from responding in the manner that would normally be indicated."

Shields had not the smallest notion what a Sun Sign vibratory pattern was; indeed, he was only marginally aware that, having been born on the tenth of August, he fell under the Zodiacal sign of Leo. He was acutely cognizant of the fact, however, that in having failed to give full rein to his primitive male instincts, he had not only been found seriously lacking by the impudent Lady Elfrida, but he stood convicted in her eyes of some sort of abnormality!

One arrogant eyebrow fairly shot upwards toward the earl's hairline. "What sort of inhibitive factor did you have in mind, Miss Rochelle?" he inquired in measured tones.

Elfrida, who was longing for nothing more than to be left to go to her bed, failed utterly to note the earl's use of her name. Indeed, she was having a great deal of difficulty even following the threads of their conversation. "I beg your pardon, my lord?" she queried around a second, irresistible yawn. "What inhibitive factor?"

"The inhibitive factor that you have suggested prevents me from taking you right here and now, as you so richly deserve, Miss Rochelle," declared his lordship, advancing a purposeful step toward her. "I beg your pardon, am I boring you?"

"Dear, no," Elfrida replied distractedly, lifting a hand to her forehead. Faith, why the devil had the room to start swimming, she fretted, now, when she sensed she needed all her wits about her! "Though it is true I was expecting something from you quite on a different order, I daresay you could never be boring, my lord. Leos are ruled by the Sun and in consequence may, in the norm, be expected to dazzle all who come in contact with them."

"I, however, am something outside of the norm, is that it?" demanded his lordship, appearing suddenly to tower over her.

"I did not say so, my lord," retorted Elfrida, vaguely irritated at his insistence on submitting her to a Spanish Inquisition when, clearly, she was in no case to respond with any degree of rationality. "If I appear less than bedazzled, then no doubt I beg your pardon, your lordship. The truth is, beyond accusing me of any number of odious things, including plotting to cut your stick for you, and demonstrating a decided disinclination to take me to your bed, you have given me very little upon which to judge."

Shields, who was hardly accustomed to having young women of quality steal into his bedroom, let alone one who claimed to be his Twin Soul with whom he was karmically predetermined to join in order to achieve a cosmically generated primordial passion, only then to intimate his failure to ravish her was due apparently to some flaw in his character—or manhood, good Lord—was not appeased by her less than humble apology for having twice yawned in his face. The little devil! He was sorely tempted to instruct her in the true meaning of primordial passions! But then, it was yet possible that was what the beautiful Miss Rochelle had had in mind when she concocted this highly improbable tale of hers. After all, she was clearly past the first blush of youth and still a spinster. And little wonder, if she publicized the fact that she dabbled in the mystic arts! Few men in search of a wife would wittingly saddle themselves with a female who was, at the very least, delusional and, at the very worst, a calculating vixen willing to go to any lengths to snare herself a husband.

A hard gleam came to his eyes. Whichever was the case, the Goddess of Beauty should be given a taste of what it meant to beard the lion in his den. Lady Elfrida Rochelle was about to learn, once and for all, that the Earl of Shields was not to be taken lightly.

"Come, Miss Rochelle," drawled his lordship, slipping a steely arm behind her waist, "has it not occurred to you that I have been hampered by the dictates of a gentleman's code of honor?" Deliberately drawing her close, he bent his head to touch his lips to her forehead, then to her temple and lower still to the corner of her mouth. "Or did you think," he said between sending little thrills of pleasure down her spine with each brush of his lips, "I make it a practice . . . to take advantage of . . . unmarried females of quality who . . . assault me in my bedchamber?"

"I assure you it never occurred to me, my lord, that you did any such thing," breathlessly asserted Elfrida, who could not but be struck by this previously unconsidered possibility. "The truth is I had not thought at all in those terms—indeed, I did not initially think of anything beyond rushing to your defence." A low gasp burst from her lips as he found the exquisitely tender place below her left earlobe. "I see now, however," she declared, her voice half an octave higher than normal, "that your gentleman's code of honor might indeed be a significant inhibitive factor." With a gusty sigh, she allowed her head to loll to one side to give him greater access for his pleasurable manipulations.

"You may be certain of it," returned his lordship, who was acutely aware of her melting response to his caresses. Whatever else she might be, Miss Rochelle was obviously a woman of strong passions. The devil, he thought. She was a deal more than that. She was a goddess of arousal whose mere proximity was enough to have stimulated a painful bulge at the front of his breeches. Pulling the neck of her dressing gown open, he pressed his lips to the soft swell of flesh above the square decolletage of her chemise. "It is, in fact," he uttered thickly, molding his hand to the rounded perfection of a firm, full breast, "the only thing at the moment that stands between you and ruination."

"Then, I do wish you would relegate it to obscurity, my lord!" gasped Elfrida, experiencing a galvanizing shock of pleasure as his lordship squeezed her nipple, which was most curiously taut, a circumstance that she attributed to a sudden elevation in practically all of her vital functions. Indeed, her heart was pumping with such vigor that it seemed that she could not catch her breath, and she was quite certain that, like the banked coals of a fire stirred to sudden flame, she was in the grips of a mounting fever. Further, she was become aware her knees were on the point of giving way beneath her. Clinging with her arms about his neck, she gasped, "I pray you will not allow it to stop you now, my lord!"

The devil, thought Shields, who was perilously close to the point at which a gentleman's code of honor might very well become a moot question at best. Clearly, the Goddess of Beauty was not in the common run of females. She responded to his lovemaking with a sweet, untutored generosity quite unlike the practiced ardor of his numerous past mistresses. Far more thought-provoking, however, was the effect that *she* would seem to have on *him!*

A single, brief glimpse of her from his carriage window had been sufficient to pique his curiosity, never mind that he had not, since his salad days, fallen error to allowing a pretty face to cloud his judgment. Even less had he indulged in toying with young, inexperienced females, who were, after all, bait for Parson's Mousetrap. Certainly, he had never committed the blatant folly of succumbing to the allure of an unmarried woman of quality, who, in addition to professing to be blessed with the dubious gift of prophecy, was a daughter of one of the most powerful houses in England! To find himself even remotely tempted to take her to his bed would seem to demonstrate how far she had already seduced him from the path of reason. To acknowledge that she had done much more than that, that indeed he was exceedingly close to flinging all caution to the wind, was tantamount to embracing an act of insanity. Hellsfire! She aroused him as no other woman ever had before her!

"Enough!" he uttered between gritted teeth. "You haven't the smallest notion what you are asking." Pulling her arms down from around his neck, he held her from him. "It is time you were leaving, Miss Rochelle, before you become wholly disabused of your girlish fantasies."

Elfrida, in the grips of the first arousal of emotions she had not even known she possessed, but which she was quite certain were not the products of any "girlish fantasies"—good God—blinked up at Shields in no little bewilderment. His lordship, she noted, was breathing heavily, and his eyes, between slitted eyelids, glittered with a feverish intensity that might have been alarming had she not been reasonably certain the phenomena could be attributed to the manifestations of a karmically predetermined passion. Obviously, Shields's highly developed sense of honor was more than just an inhibitive factor. It was, if anything, an impediment to the advancement of destiny!

"Really, my lord," she declared, drawing a deep, steadying breath, "there is nothing to fear in what we are experiencing. It is only the natural expression of the cosmic forces extant between Twin Souls. Naturally you must feel some wariness in the fact that I am unmarried and a member of quality. On the other hand, you are mistaken if you think of me as a girl. I am a woman of five and twenty, and quite beyond indulging in girlish fancies, I assure you." She stepped back and began deliberately to undo the fastenings down the front of her dressing gown. "Would it help if I told you that your sense of honor need not be a consideration? I, after all, am well of the age of determining my own existence. And, since I am firmly resolved never to marry, you need not feel under any obligation to offer for me in the misguided notion of making an honest woman of me." Blushing at her own temerity, she slipped the gown down off her shoulders and arms and allowed it to fall in a velvet heap on the floor about her feet. "I should only refuse in any case."

Shields was presented with the sight of the Goddess of Beauty in naught but her fine white mousseline chemise with the square decolletage, the fabric of which was rendered all but transparent as she stood, limned, against the firelight. Even more telling, the wholly improper Miss Rochelle was reaching up to undo the pearl buttons at the front of the bodice!

"The devil!" he uttered, clasping her wrists in order to put a halt to her madness. The absurd little Innocent had not the first idea what she was risking. At the very least she would be a ruined woman. At the very worst, there might be a child, and he was demmed if he would have it on his head that he had fathered a by-blow on the Duke of Albermarle's granddaughter. Not marry? Good God, there would be no other recourse but to marry, whether she wished it or not. Her grandfather, the duke, not to mention her brother, the marquis, would make certain of that. The last thing Shields could wish was to find himself facing on the field of honor a youth better than a dozen years his junior, especially one who, having already engaged in three duels, was known for hitting his man. Well acquainted with Vere's reputation for sheer, cold-blooded nerve, Shields did not doubt he would have little choice but to shoot to kill in order to avoid his own unwanted early demise, and that was hardly an issue devoutly to be desired.

On the other hand, she was here, and she was damnably desirable. Indeed, he could not recall ever having wanted a woman as much as he wanted at that moment to have Lady Elfrida Rochelle.

Elfrida, upon finding her wrists pinioned in the earl's powerful grip, felt her heart sink. Faith, it would seem not even a karmically predetermined passion was sufficient to override the earl's damnably obdurate adherence to a gentleman's code of honor. Or perhaps she had got it all wrong. Perhaps she had put him off by her unmaidenly display of ardor. The devil, it was a trifle late now to put on missish airs or to adopt the pretense of coy unattainableness. Besides, it was not in her nature to pretend to be something she was not. She and Shields had been born for this moment. She had assumed that her astrologically perfect mate would understand and accept all that she was offering. But then, she had, perhaps, failed to take into account a Leo's overpowering inherent need for self-esteem, not to mention this particular Leo's masculine pride. Naturally, honor was all-important to Shields. He was, after all, a man who, by his very nature, must command the respect of others.

"But of course that is it!" she exclaimed, awarding Shields a look that fairly took his breath away. "Indeed, I cannot imagine why I did not think of it sooner. My poor Shields. Naturally, you could never bring yourself to dishonor a maiden. I do beg your pardon, my lord. I really should never have asked it of you." She smiled reassuringly up at the astonished earl. "You may release me now. I promise you are quite safe."

"No doubt I am relieved you have come to your senses," observed his lordship, obliging her by letting her go, only to be struck by an immediate sense of foreboding at her sudden capitulation, a feeling that was hardly alleviated by the Goddess of Beauty's next observation.

"Yes, I am sure you are," agreed Elfrida, everything quite clear to her now. "And you may be equally certain that I shall not bother you again until I have removed the obstacle that must inevitably stand between us."

"An object no doubt to be devoutly desired," observed the earl, who, manfully ignoring the damnable ache in his groin, forced himself to speculate what new scheme she was hatching. "And that obstacle is, of course . . ." Enlightenment struck him with blinding force. "Good God! You *wouldn't!*"

"Dear," said Elfrida, giving Shields a pitying look. "You need not take it so to heart, my lord. Naturally, I should have preferred a more straightforward means of achieving our karmic destiny, but it simply cannot be helped, can it? I daresay it will not be all that easy to find someone willing to relieve me of my maidenhead without any strings attached. I should not think Lord Harry Wilcox would look kindly on my asking him to perform this little service for me, especially since he has repeatedly asked me to marry him. And you may be sure that while Sir Wilfred Knowles would not hesitate to take me up on such a proposition, I daresay, short of fortifying myself with strong spirits, I could not bear to have him put his hands on me. Besides being an incorrigible roue, he is, after all, nearly three times my age. A pity there are not male Cyprians for hire for this sort of thing. It would make things so much less complicated. Not that I am complaining, mind you. After all, it is a small matter when taken in light of—''

Whatever it was to be taken in light of, Elfrida was not given the opportunity to say. Shields, uttering what sounded very like a growl, crushed her to his chest and covered her mouth with his.

Chapter 6

Next to her precious shew stone, Elfrida's most treasured possession, since she had first discovered the wooden trunk in its secret cupboard behind the Crystal Room's fireplace, had been the written account of her great-grandmama's prognostications, which the former duchess had taken care to record in great detail in her numerous journals. Spanning a period of sixty-one years, they began with Lucasta's very first seeing at the age of eleven, when the child scryer had beheld, reflected in a dewdrop, a vision of her governess, Miss Pettigrew, in the arms of Lucasta's Uncle Nicholas. It was to be noted that Uncle Nickie, with some artful machinations on the part of a certain precocious young seer, had subsequently been prevailed upon to overcome false pride to wed Miss Pettigrew, who was, after all, the true love of his heart. The accounts concluded with a prognostication, made on Lucasta's deathbed, of a future in which the House of Albermarle would be enshrouded in a dark veil of mist. The vision, Elfrida had since come to believe, must have been a forewarning of the tragic deaths of the marquis and marchioness, though one could not be entirely certain in such cases. Veils of mist, after all, tended, by their very nature to be open to interpretation. More significantly to Elfrida in the immediate present, however, the journals had included innumerable accounts over the years of those who had come to the duchess in search of their hearts' desires and of the very few for whom Lucasta had envisioned an enduring love on the order of an all-consuming karmic passion.

Nothing her great-grandmother Lucasta had ever recorded, however, could compare with the actuality of Elfrida's first kiss from her karmically predetermined, astrologically perfect mate. After all, who could have predicted that at the very moment Shields covered her mouth with his, she would experience the most peculiar sensation of bells chiming and birds singing, not to mention comets lighting up the sky in a most spectacular fashion?

It was hardly any wonder that she felt a trifle dazed when, some little time later, Shields released her to press his lips to her cheek and then her hair. His voice impinged on her reeling consciousness, low-voiced and compelling. However, having just been given to experience a floodtide of emotions well up at her very core to spread outward, like molten lava, to her extremities, she was having no little difficulty ordering her thoughts sufficiently to make sense of his words amid all the cacophony of tweeting and chirping.

"Wha-at did you say?" she asked, her eyes fluttering open to behold Shields smiling bemusedly down into her face.

"I said that, as much as I should like to continue our explorations of karmically predetermined pri-

mordial passions, the clock has just chimed six.
The sun has come up, Miss Rochelle. If we are to
have you safely home without being seen, we shall
have to postpone these pleasantries until a later
date.''

It was only then that Elfrida was given to realize
that there *were* birds singing and that she stood
in a strengthening spill of sunlight through the
bedchamber window. ''Oh, good God!'' she exclaimed. ''It is morning!''

''Very astute of you, Miss Rochelle,'' observed
Shields, reaching down to retrieve her dressing
gown from the floor. ''You may be certain the
kitchen staff have long since been about their
morning tasks, and in a very few moments the rest
of the household will be up and stirring.''

''How very inconsiderate of them,'' declared
Elfrida, reluctantly slipping her arms into the
sleeves of her dressing gown, which Shields was
holding up for her. ''Just when we were on the
point of dispelling the inhibitive circumstance that
stands in the way of our karmic destiny. Really, my
lord, it is too bad of them.''

''No doubt I shall read them a curtain lecture
on their shocking display of conscientious adherence to duty,'' said Shields, who, having come as
near as he had ever done in his life to abandoning
his gentleman's code of honor as regarded the
deflowering of an Innocent, could only view the
breaking of day in the light of a timely, if painful,
return to reality. Indeed, he was ruefully aware that
the reward for his forbearance would amount to
at least an hour, perhaps two, of no little physical
discomfort. Closing the front of his shirt and shrugging on his earlier discarded coat, he conducted
Elfrida to the door and unlocked it. ''As for the
inhibitive circumstance that stands in the way of
our karmic destiny, Miss Rochelle,'' added the earl,

recalled to the cause of his near-seduction by an untutored miss, "I shall have your word you will do nothing on your own to remove it."

"Shall you, my lord?" queried Elfrida, willing her respiration, as well as her heartbeat, to return to normalcy as his lordship took the precaution of glancing up and down the corridor. A hand on her elbow, he ushered her through the door and down the hall to the stairway. "Or you will do what?" Elfrida queried with a profound air of innocence.

Shields, who did not doubt he would be brought to throttle the impudent Goddess of Beauty before all was said and done, answered her with a smile that had chilled the hearts of many a lesser being. "I believe, Miss Rochelle, that you will not wish to find out what I might do should you choose to disregard my wishes in this particular." Having reached the second-story landing, he caught her hand and led her along the open gallery to the curving staircase, which descended to the foyer. "Suffice it to say that I am perfectly capable of carting you off to your grandfather's castle in Devon, there to suggest the wisdom of locking you up in a dungeon."

"I'm afraid Albermarle would not be in the least gratified if you did any such thing, my lord," Elfrida responded with perfect candor as they came to the bottom of the stairs and proceeded to the back of the house by way of a short hallway, which gave access to a ground story withdrawing room with French windows overlooking a small, enclosed rose garden. "As it happens, he could not have been more pleased to see me out of the castle and on my way to London. Very likely, he would only demand you take me immediately back where you found me."

"With good reason, no doubt," dryly observed

Shields, who could not but entertain a certain empathy for Albermarle's reluctance to have his eldest granddaughter returned to his protection. On the other hand, he reflected, ushering Elfrida out the French doors into the garden, he was demmed if he would be made the cause of the lady's getting herself deflowered in order to overcome his own resistance to bedding her. Good God!

He had never encountered a female with a greater proclivity for self-destructive thinking. It was unsettling enough that she was apparently willing to go to any lengths in order to experience a karmically predetermined passion with a man she had met only once, and exceedingly briefly, eight years in the past. It was far worse to realize she had set herself up to serve as his guardian angel!

His blood chilled at the very thought of the risks she had been willing to take under the absurd notion that he required her protection. Good God, she had believed there was an intruder attempting to break into his house for the purpose of cutting his stick for him! And the indomitable Goddess of Beauty had thought to fend the culprit off with a bloody pop gun? Hellsfire, for that alone she should be locked away for her own protection! But then, obviously, Lady Elfrida Rochelle was as fearless as she was impulsive, not to mention determined, headstrong, passionate, and delectably generous—aspects of her character that promised fair to wreak havoc on the previously even tenor of his life.

If there was, indeed, someone out to put a period to his existence, the last thing he needed was to have the Duke of Albermarle's granddaughter impetuously flinging herself in the way of some real or imagined peril with the thought of saving the Earl of Shields from annihilation.

It did not help Shields's frame of mind to realize the danger might very well have been real enough this time. He did not doubt that Miss Rochelle had seen *something* she had taken to be an intruder bolting from the back of the house. In light of his near-fatal mishap in Bond Street, he could not dismiss out of hand the possibility that his would-be assassin might be so brash as to assault him in his own home. Perhaps it was not even so very farfetched to speculate that, having gone so far as to pick the lock, the culprit could be frightened off by the unexpected arrival of a female armed with what, in the dark, might easily be mistaken for something other than a relatively harmless toy. He, after all, had been similarly misled. Nor did he doubt for a moment that she had actually found the door ajar. Whatever else she might be, Lady Elfrida Rochelle had demonstrated that she was not given to prevarication. Hellsfire! She was, if anything, unnervingly forthright!

All of which led Shields to the less than comforting prognostication, based on empirical evidence, that he was faced with a future in which he must ever be concerned with what new stunt Lady Elfrida Rochelle might undertake either to protect him from danger or to alleviate him of any qualms in bedding her. The latter prospect, strangely, had the unsettling effect of eliciting a hot stab of something very like rage through his chest, an emotion that he cynically attributed to jealousy at the mere thought of any man who might take the irrepressible Goddess of Beauty up on her request to please rid her of her maidenhead. Good God, he was moved wryly to reflect, he could not recall ever having suffered the throes of the green-eyed monster before his fateful meeting with the divinating Goddess of Beauty. But then, nothing in his previous experience had prepared him for Lady Elfrida

Rochelle, a female who was as startlingly unique as she was breathtakingly desirable.

The devil, he thought. In spite of the fact that every instinct cried out that he have nothing further to do with the divinating spinster, he was ruefully aware that he was not prepared to have his unlooked-for adventure come so soon to an end. Clearly, he had abandoned all sense of rationality.

Still, he mused with a wry twist of the lips, it was doubtful that *anyone*, short of wringing her lovely neck for her, could deter Lady Elfrida Rochelle from a course upon which she had set herself. It would seem that, until he could discover who was behind the attempt on his life, he had little choice but to maintain a close watch on his self-appointed guardian angel, if only to keep her out of trouble. Unfortunately, while having her a good deal under his watchful eye would seem the only viable solution to the problem of preserving her from an untimely end, it would undoubtedly exacerbate that other, perhaps greater, difficulty of resisting the temptation to succumb to a karmic predetermined passion to bed her.

Somehow he found the challenge rather more appealing than daunting. If nothing else, his association with the Goddess of Beauty promised to be stimulating.

For the present, however, he reminded himself, his main concern must be to see her safely inside Lord Winston Godfrey's house without anyone's being the wiser that she had ever left it.

"I believe, my lord," observed Elfrida, reaching out a hand to stop Shields from following her through the iron gate that led from the mews into the flagstoned courtyard, "that I shall do very well the rest of the way by myself. No doubt I should thank you for seeing me home." She glanced up at her tall companion with speculative eyes. "I do not suppose you would care to save me a deal of trouble by simply telling me your plans for the day. Though in the norm I should like nothing better than an early morning gallop in Hyde Park, right now I cannot but hope you intend to go straight home to bed, there to sleep at least until noon.''

"As it happens, I shall undoubtedly be occupied most of the day with mundane business matters," replied Shields, his gaze narrowing sharply on Elfrida. Good God, even on his morning rides, she had been there. How the devil, he wondered, had he failed to see her? Ignoring her protest, he entered the courtyard after her. "Not that it signifies. You have done your part in warning me that you have foreseen the threat of danger hanging over me, and now you may leave the rest to me. As difficult as you may find it to believe, Miss Rochelle, I am well able to look after myself."

"Yes, of course you are, my lord," Elfrida, judiciously reminded of a Leo's pride, hastened to assure the earl. "Indeed, I never doubted it for a moment. On the other hand, perhaps you have failed to consider the advantage of having a prognosticator to aid you in your endeavor. While it is true I was not given to see the exact nature of the danger surrounding you, it is probable I shall continue to receive premonitory visions. It never hurts to be prepared, my lord. To be forewarned, after all, is to be forearmed, and I—"

"*You*, Miss Rochelle," Shields firmly interjected, "will go in to your bed without further thought for my safety. You will take your beauty rest until well into the afternoon. When you awaken, you will have breakfast in bed, followed by a leisurely toilette. After that—"

"But that is not in the least fair, my lord!" exclaimed Elfrida, who could not but feel a rending pang of disappointment in the earl. How dared he

so easily dismiss her after she had trusted him with
the truth! She should have known better than to
think he might actually give some credence to her
gift of divination. Why should he, after all, when no
one else ever had? But then, he was her karmically
predetermined Twin Soul. She had hoped he
would, at the very least, give her the benefit of the
doubt. That, instead, he apparently meant to sever
all ties and have nothing more to do with her was
really too bad of him. Worse, he obviously intended
to forbid her any part in helping to dispel the
darkness that she had sensed pressing in around
him, and *that* she simply could not allow. It was,
after all, her karmic obligation to do all in her
power to preserve her Twin Soul from any preconceived harm. Furthermore, having twice saved his
life, surely she had earned the right to see the
matter through to its conclusion, she thought with
a rising sense of unmitigated Arian moral indigna-
tion. It was time his lordship was made to realize
that she would allow nothing to keep her from her
preconceived duty.

"I must protest, my lord," she said, girding herself to do battle. "Indeed, I cannot but—"

"*After* which," Shields persisted before she
could voice any of the numerous objections that
had leaped immediately to mind, "you will go
for a drive with me in Hyde Park. I shall call for
you at a quarter till five."

Elfrida, the wind knocked from her sails, came to
a sudden standstill. "I will?" she queried, coming
around to face him. "I-I mean, you will?"

Shields, finding himself staring into eyes that had
the peculiar effect of making him feel somehow
taller, smiled wryly. "You *are* interested in discovering who tried to cut my stick for me, are you
not? And, while I confess there is a certain appeal
to convening in my bedchamber in the dead of

night, you will agree it is not the most practical arrangement. A drive in Hyde Park at the fashionable hour of five will undoubtedly cause some comment, but it will hardly be construed as grounds for a meeting at dawn.''

"A meeting at dawn?" echoed Elfrida, who was still coming to grips with the fact that Shields, far from ordering her to cease and desist in her efforts to aid him in his time of danger, was offering to make her his ally! And then it came to her—the significance of his final utterance. "Oh, good God. You mean Vere!"

"Vere, indeed," Shields agreed in exceedingly dry tones. "As it happens, I have a distinct aversion to the notion of having to shoot the duke's heir apparent, especially as I enjoyed a particular friendship with the young devil's sire."

"No, did you?" murmured a soft, thrilling voice at Elfrida's back. Shields's glance lifted with rapier swiftness. "Odd that I never heard mention of it. Still, I suppose it is kind of you to wish to spare me a bullet."

"*Gideon!*" exclaimed Elfrida, coming about, a hand over her palpitating heart. "How dare you sneak up on us in that manner! Faith, you nearly startled me out of half a year's growth."

Vere, his slender form gracefully elegant in a bottle-green riding coat, buff unmentionables, and brown Military Long Boots, his hair fashionably dishevelled in the Wind Swept, smiled ever so gently. "Then, no doubt I must beg your pardon, dearest Elfrida. It was never my intention to frighten you. As it happens, Dark Reverie picked up a stone on our morning ride and has gone lame." His eyes flicked to Shields and lingered. "I was just on my way from the stables when, curiously enough, I heard my name."

Shields, finding himself the object of a compellingly blue, penetrating gaze, could not but be struck by the family resemblance between brother and sister. It would seem, however, that, whereas Lady Elfrida was sweet fire and passion, Vere was steel and ice.

"That is hardly surprising, Gideon," replied Elfrida, who could not but wish her brother at Jericho. How very like Vere to show up just when she could least wish for a disruptive influence. "We were just talking about you."

"So I gathered. His lordship was just expressing his reluctance to shoot me. A sentiment for which I should no doubt be grateful. The Earl of Shields is well known for his unerring marksmanship." A curious gleam flickered behind the cold intensity of Vere's hooded eyes. "Still, it would perhaps be interesting—"

"It would be nothing of the sort, Gideon," interrupted Elfrida, as close to being out of all patience with her Scorpio sibling as she had ever been. "It is, in fact, outside of enough. You know very well you have no intention of challenging Shields to a duel. Certainly not over me. You are far too perceptive not to realize he is a man of honor and that, further, nothing untoward has happened between us."

"Nothing, Elfrida? How very disappointing that must be," observed Vere with only the faintest hint of irony. "I congratulate you, my lord. In the norm, people tend to find my sister—shall we say—something of an irresistible force."

"No, do they?" murmured Shields, well aware of the warning contained in that gently uttered speech. Hellsfire! The young devil's cub was deliberately baiting him! He deserved to have someone take him down a peg.

Elfrida, who could not have agreed more with the earl, drew breath to remind Gideon that, as a

woman of five and twenty, she was beyond being
guided by her younger brother, head of the family
or not, and that, further, she would appreciate it
if he would stop making a cake of himself in front
of a man he hardly knew.

Shields, however, was before her. "But then, Miss
Rochelle," he drawled, dangerously cool, "is a
woman of strong convictions, not to mention extra-
ordinary perception. I should be exceedingly surprised if those fortunate enough to count themselves among her acquaintances did not appreciate
her unique qualities, would not you, my lord?"

Elfrida stared, stunned into momentary speech-
lessness by that unexpected championship from a
man whom she had only recently shot with a pop
gun.

The same could hardly be said of Vere, however,
who, if anything, appeared to grow more impene-
trably subtle. "You are right, of course," Vere conceded, his hooded gaze never wavering from
Shields's. "I should hope, as well, that, in appreciat-
ing that uniqueness, they would take every precaution that no harm should come to her because of
it."

Elfrida, observing a mask of ennui descend ominously over the earl's handsome features, stifled a
groan.

"No less than do I, I assure you," Shields returned in velvet-edged tones. "On the other hand,
I fear I should have to take exception were anyone
to suggest the Earl of Shields would intentionally
do anything to harm a woman."

Vere arched a single black, arrogant eyebrow.
"A woman, my lord," he said, "who is my sister."

"Which is why I have been disposed to be toler-
ant," Shields rejoined steadily. "I suggest, my lord,
that you see your sister inside. You will agree this

is hardly the time or the place to discuss what should be a private matter between gentlemen."

"Oh, good God! It is nothing of the kind," declared Elfrida, who did not need a crystal ball to perceive when two powerful forces had come into contention and who, further, was in no mood to be made the object of an absurd contest of masculine wills, especially between Pluto-ruled Scorpio and Sun-ruled Leo. There was very little chance of *anyone's* coming out unscathed! "And I shall thank you both to cease to discuss me as if I were not even present. I am a prognosticator and a scryer, not a child or an idiot. Really, Shields, I might have looked for such nonsense from Gideon, who is, after all, a Scorpio and therefore acting according to his nature. It is hardly the sort of thing I should have expected from you, however."

To Elfrida's mortification, her voice cracked at the end, no doubt from the strain of deflecting a multitudinous array of cosmic vibrations generated between two forceful personalities.

Instantly, a frown darkened the earl's brow.

"There, you see?" Shields said meaningfully to Vere. "This is what comes of disregarding a female's more delicate sensibilities. Take her inside at once, Vere. Miss Rochelle is clearly in need of her bed. I promise I shall be available to you should you wish to carry on this discussion further."

"Devil," declared Elfrida, awarding the earl a comical moue of displeasure. "It is not my delicate sensibilities which need concern you, my lord, I assure you. I have been repeatedly informed that I haven't any. Come, Vere." Turning on her heel, she made a strategic retreat toward the house. "Take me inside before I forget Shields is my karmically predetermined, astrologically perfect mate and do something I shall surely regret."

Vere, Shields noted with a hardening of his jaw, showed no discernible signs of following after the retreating Goddess of Beauty. Hell and the devil confound it. Vere might be young in years, but there was that about him which had seemed to suggest he was not the sort given to brash and irrational acts. Still, if it was a duel he wanted, Shields would oblige him. Not with guns or swords, perhaps, (as the one challenged, after all, he, Shields, would have the choice of weapons), but with fists. No doubt a bout in the ring would suffice to teach the young devil's spawn a much-needed lesson in respect for his elders; and, if fight he must, then Shields vastly preferred an arena that would not require him to cut the marquis's bloody stick for him.

"Your sister is a remarkable woman," observed Shields, his gaze, speculative, on the younger man. "As was her mother. I was deeply affected when I heard of the loss of the marquis and marchioness. I held them both in the warmest esteem. You may believe me when I say I should never willingly do anything to harm their daughter."

"As it happens, I do believe you, my lord," murmured Vere with his gently mocking smile. "On the other hand, while I am certain your intentions, at least, are honorable, I confess to entertaining no little doubt in your continued success in resisting what looms to me as inevitable. Indeed, you have my sympathies, sir. Elfrida believes you are the one man she was born to love. You may be certain that conviction has assumed all the proportions of a crusade which she will pursue with a single-minded determination. The truth to tell, my lord, I know not whether to pity or to envy you."

Inclining his head, Vere strode negligently after Elfrida, leaving Shields to stare pensively after him.

* * *

Shields, descending the stairs from his bedchamber some little time later, was even less certain than Vere as to how he should view having been made the object of Lady Elfrida's karmic affections. Not that he placed any credence in the misty concept of Twin Souls. He was a man who put his trust in that which could be demonstrated with factual evidence.

The fact was, he was extraordinarily attracted to Lady Elfrida Rochelle; indeed, he could not recall ever having been more powerfully attracted to any other woman before her, a circumstance, he told himself, that could be attributed to any number of causes other than karmic predetermination. Lady Elfrida, after all, was not only possessed of a face and form that aroused a man's lustier emotions, but she was quick-witted, straightforward, and determinedly independent. Add to that a fresh, unassuming innocence and originality of thought that quite set her apart from every other woman he had ever met, and it was hardly any wonder that he found himself in the demmed peculiar position of scheming how to preserve her from her own impulsive nature. He was ironically aware that, in spite of all her bright courageousness, she was possessed of a vulnerability of which she was wholly unaware, but which must inevitably arouse a man's primitive male instinct to possess and protect the female of the species. More ironic yet was the realization that quite possibly the greatest threat to her well-being was he, himself!

Good God, it was a dilemma to drive a saint to ruin, and he was no bloody saint. Clearly, his first course of action must be to dispose of the annoyance of his would-be assassin with as great despatch as possible. Once that was accomplished, he would be free to explore the singular effects that Miss Rochelle would seem capable of generating in him, emotions that no other woman before her had ever produced with such potency. A whimsical smile played about the earl's lips at the prospect of conducting a factual inquiry into the scientific basis of a karmically-generated primordial passion. If nothing else, he had the distinct feeling he was about to become exceedingly well-acquainted with the Goddess of Beauty in the coming days. No doubt subsequent exposure, he told himself, would cure him of his peculiar obsession with Lady Elfrida Rochelle.

At least it would seem that he was to be spared the added complication of any interference from the lady's brother, Shields reflected with a sardonic smile of appreciation. Vere had, in his own inimitable fashion, made it plain that, having satisfied himself that Shields was a gentleman of honor, he was content to allow his sister to pursue her own course.

In no little bemusement, it came to Shields to wonder what Vere would do were he made aware that Lady Elfrida had determined on ridding herself of her maidenhead in order to overcome the inhibitive circumstance that stood in the way of her achieving her karmic destiny. Hellsfire! he thought. The cold-blooded young cub might decide the simplest solution to that equation was to rid himself of the common denominator—Shields, the man who was the inadvertent cause of his current problems!

Shields found little to amuse in such a scenario. Despite what had seemed an instinctive sense of antipathy between himself and Vere, the earl had yet found that he could not but like the cheeky young devil. If nothing else, Vere could be depended upon to behave in the manner of a gentleman born, and that was a great deal more than could be said for the man whose death Shields did not doubt was at the heart of the sudden disruption of his previously tranquil existence.

Hepplewaite and his untimely demise were the key to the puzzle. Of that much, Shields was certain. The question was what possible bearing did the events at Ludgate Hall have on the two (providing, of course, that Miss Rochelle had indeed frightened off an intruder) apparent attempts on his own life? Shields had developed an acute curiosity concerning the mysterious Mr. Nicodemus Pickering, who would seem to be the only prospect available for consideration at the present.

Entering his study, Shields rang for the butler with the intention of summoning Norton, his private secretary, directly to him. At least he could be relatively at ease with the young beauty tucked safely away in her bed for the next several hours, a circumstance for which he could be exceedingly grateful. He had a great deal to do before he called on Miss Rochelle for their ride in Hyde Park and very little time in which to do it.

No doubt Shields would have been rather less sanguine had it been given to him to realize that Elfrida, having indeed climbed gratefully into bed, was even then in the throes of a dream.

It was always rather strange to find oneself dreaming dreams that seemed to pass before one in the manner of a play in which one had no part save for that of an observer and yet, curiously, to be able to move among the players, unperceived and yet perceiving. It was even more curious to be perfectly aware all the while that one was dreaming and to know that one had only to awaken to bring the dream-play to an end.

Elfrida, for whom such experiences were a frequent occurrence, had never, since her extreme youth, deliberately terminated one of them. Dreams, after all, she reasoned, no matter how disturbing some might be, could not actually harm anyone. Quite the contrary, they were creations of the psyche. As such, they very often provided windows into the mystic unconscious and could be tools meant to heal a wounded soul or relieve a burdened one. Further, properly interpreted, they gave insight into realms beyond the bounds of pure reason, glimpses of the Unknowable Essence, the Universal Self, to which all souls, knowingly or unknowingly, longed to be joined. Still, she reflected, observing the dreamscape passing before her, one could wish the medium of communication could be rather less prone to obscurity.

It would seem to make little sense, after all, for Shields to be acting in the role of a farrier, never mind that he appeared to be performing his tasks with consummate skill. Certainly he displayed to magnificent advantage bared to the waist, his smooth skin, wet and glistening with sweat, his powerful torso and arms seeming to ripple and bulge in all the right places with muscle, as he pounded the glowing iron into shape with a hammer. Faith, but it was all marvelously unsettling.

Elfrida, caught up in the dream, heaved a gusty sigh and clasped a pillow to her breast, only to have the dream, to her dismay, change. Where before she had seemed to stand in a village green with the blacksmith at work over his anvil, she now found herself at home in Devon, and, instead of Shields, she beheld Vere on the point of aiming Valentine's pearl-handled pop gun at one of Albermarle's prized studs, a magnificent chestnut with a flaxen mane and tail, while Violet stood by, eying the marquis with a doubtful frown.

"Really, Vere," Violet declared, "can you be so certain he is not what he appears to be? To me he seems perfectly charming, and you will admit he *is* fair to look upon."

"So you think now." Vere smiled cold-bloodedly. "I daresay, once in the saddle, you would soon discover you little cared for the ride he intends for you. He has the heart of a rogue, my trusting little sister."

"And naturally it is up to you to sound the warning, never mind that Albermarle will undoubtedly be put into a perfect flame to learn the prize stud he meant for me is in reality a high-stepper."

"It is not Albermarle who should concern you," Vere rejoined, thumbing back the hammer of the pop gun. "It is the gift horse one should look in the mouth." Then Vere pulled the trigger.

Elfrida bolted awake to the crash of splintering glass and Meggie Wheeler, staring in mortification at the remains of a crystal toiletry bottle lying in shattered ruins on the floor.

"Dear, I do beg your pardon, m'lady," exclaimed the abigail. "The wretched thing just seemed to jump out'n me hand, it did. I never meant to wake you, m'lady."

"Pray do not be absurd, Meggie. I never thought that you did. I daresay it is time I was awake at any rate." Sitting up in bed, Elfrida drew her knees to her chest. "Faith, how long have I been asleep?"

"The hall clock only just struck three, m'lady," replied Meggie Wheeler, occupied with cleaning up the shards of glass. "You were sleeping that peacefully, you never so much as stirred."

"*Three!* Good heavens, you cannot mean it!" Elfrida, flinging back the counterpane, fairly flew from the bed. "I must have a bath at once. And lay out my blue sarcenet round gown, the one with the embroidered cuffs. Pray, hurry, Meggie. His lordship is to call for me at a quarter till five. Faith, I shall never be able to make it on time.''

"Now don't you fret, m'lady. I ordered your bath water to be prepared half an hour ago. I expect it's just about ready for you. I'll go and make certain while you eat what's on that tray I brought up for you.''

"Meggie, you dear,'' exclaimed Elfrida, who did indeed discover, at sight of the cold collation of paper-thin ham, fruit, and cheese, that she was quite famished. "What should I ever do without you?''

Hardly had the abigail made her departure, however, than Elfrida found her thoughts turning to a contemplation of the dream from which she had been so rudely awakened. It had been a portentous dream, fraught with warning; she was sure of it. The question was, whom was it meant to warn and of what?

Chapter 7

Meggie Wheeler, stepping back to view the results of her handiwork, could not but think her mistress had never looked finer than she did at that moment, dressed to the nines in an Empire frock of peacock-blue sarcenet with a square neck and long sleeves that puffed at the top then tapered to embroidered cuffs. M'lady's ebony tresses caught up in curls high at the back of the head with ringlets around the face and forehead served to accentuate the high-boned cheeks, while softening the determined jut of her delectably pointed chin. Tall and willowy, with a waist hardly bigger than the span of a man's hands, Lady Elfrida, unlike so many of her feminine contemporaries, had no need of long stays to achieve the Classical form. Indeed, the simple, unadorned lines of the frock, falling gracefully from its high waist, seemed to have been expressly designed for her slender frame.

Her mistress had ought to've been pleased at her appearance, reflected the abigail with a small shake of her head. Anyone with eyes to see, how-

ever, could tell that, far from admiring her image
in the ormolu looking glass, m'lady was leagues
away, lost in thought. Belike she had been visited
with yet another of her seeings, speculated Meggie,
who had long since come to accept that her mistress
was not in the usual style. But then, which of the
Rochelles were? thought the abigail, rolling her
eyes ceilingward. Even for the quality, the
Rochelles had more than their fair share of queer
fish. On the other hand, they didn't come much
higher up on the aristocratic ladder than the
Rochelles, she conceded with a sparkle of pride.
And Lady Elfrida was the best of the lot. The truth
was, there was no one else nor ever could be anyone
whom Meggie would rather serve than Lady
Elfrida. Those who scoffed at m'lady's peculiar gifts
didn't know Lady Elfrida Rochelle the way Meggie
Wheeler did. She was a lady of quality in the true
sense of the word, Lady Elfrida was, even if she was
a trifle pixilated.

A frown knit the abigail's brow. Something was
troubling her ladyship. That much was certain. And
Meggie little doubted it was worry for someone
other than Lady Elfrida herself.

"Meggie."

The abigail, jarred out of her reverie, sharpened
to attention. "Yes, m'lady?"

"You have been a part of the Rochelle household
since your mama first came into our service shortly
after you were born," Elfrida observed reflectively.
"I daresay you know us about as well as anyone
could."

"Yes, m'lady," Meggie replied carefully, wondering, as a chill coursed down her spine, if her mistress could now read minds as well as her great-
grandmama's shew stone. "I expect I do know the
Rochelles tolerably well."

"Yes, of course you do," Elfrida said encouragingly. "Tell me—and pray do not be afraid to speak your mind freely—can you think Lady Violet would ever be so remiss as to fall victim to a fortune hunter?"

"Lady Violet? Lord, no, m'lady," replied Meggie, who could not but wonder what should have put such a queer notion in her mistress's head. "Lady Violet'd never be taken in by a fortune hunter's flummery. Not unless some'un was to knock her alongside the head and carry her off, and that's a mite farfetched, isn't it? I mean, what would be the use in it, after all? Lady Violet, begging your pardon, m'lady, doesn't rightly have a fortune of her own, now does she?"

"My thoughts, exactly!" declared Elfrida, turning toward the abigail with an air of triumph. "It could never be Violet who is in danger of being fooled by a handsome scoundrel with nefarious designs."

"No, m'lady," agreed Meggie, carefully settling the straw Gypsy hat over Elfrida's curls and tying the rose-colored ribbons beneath m'lady's chin. "I shouldn't think it was likely, would you?"

"No. Not likely at all," murmured Elfrida, slipping her arms into the sleeves of the ivory sarcenet pelisse trimmed in embroidered rosebuds which Meggie held up for her. But if it was not Violet, then who? she thought, recalling with vivid detail the dream in which Violet had seemed to play the significant role. But then, dreams of prophesy were seldom, if ever, what they would seem to be on the surface.

Really, it was little wonder that oracles and seers had fallen into disrepute, when the messages they were given to perceive were clouded in ambiguity. Still, she could not but believe that certain aspects of the dream were crystal clear. The anvil, for example, could hardly be anything but a symbol either of an elopement or an abduction, now could it, she told herself. And certainly there had been little doubt that the rogue stud was representative of the sort of gentleman of which her mama had warned her often enough—the handsome ne'er-do-well out to get himself an heiress by *any* sort of means— honorable or otherwise. Indeed, she did not doubt that the essence of the dream was a forewarning of just such an event. The question was, who was in peril from whom?

Although she had not seen or spoken to Violet or Aunt Roanna in the se'nnight since their arrival in London, she was reasonably certain the danger did not lie in that quarter. Even if Violet had been a temptation to a fortune hunter, it was doubtful Aunt Roanna had recovered her energies sufficiently after the three-day journey to London to take her protégée out to meet anyone. As for Violet, herself, *she* very likely was content to remain in Albermarle's library consuming any number of books. The fish was happiest, after all, lurking in the serene, undisturbed quiet—unless, of course, that other, upstream, fish were suddenly to gain ascendancy, in which case, there would be no telling what Violet might be capable of doing.

The latter possibility, however, was exceedingly unlikely, Elfrida told herself, firmly quelling the momentary sinking sensation in the pit of her stomach at the mere thought of her younger sister's suddenly taking it into her head to strike out on her own. There was no one more independent than a Pisces at the best of times and no one more intractable than a Pisces determined to pursue a quirkish course upstream against the current. It came to Elfrida that, though there would seem little reason for Violet to take a sudden start, she, Elfrida, would not rest easy until she had made a call at Albermarle House to make certain all was as it should be with her sister.

Resolutely quelling a pang of guilt for having grossly neglected Violet and Aunt Roanna, Elfrida turned to a consideration of an alternate interpretation of the dream—that Violet had been a substitute for herself in the context of the dream-play. Immediately, Elfrida dismissed that possibility as being absurd at best. After all, she was karmically predetermined to love only one man, and Shields was hardly a rogue intent on carrying her off to Gretna Green. On the contrary, he thus far had demonstrated a determined resistance to her every attempt to arouse his cosmic primordial passions. Furthermore, he was reputed to be as rich as Croesus and consequently could hardly be relegated to the category of fortune hunter. A pity, really, she reflected, feeling a slow heat steal along her veins as the dream image of Shields, stripped to the waist, his lean, powerful torso glistening with sweat, leaped disturbingly to mind. Were she not of necessity firmly resolved not to marry him, she could think of nothing she would have liked better than to have Shields whisk her off to Gretna Green for the purpose of forcing her to wed him over the anvil, which was only one more reason to discount herself and Shields as the principal players. In such a scenario *she*, after all, would hardly be the one in danger.

There were, of course, any number of reasons why Shields should have appeared in her dream, the obvious one being her own predetermined karmic attachment to the earl, not to mention the singular events of the early morning hours. A hot blush stained her cheeks at the memory of her own wanton display of amorous intent. Not that she need be ashamed of her actions. After all, her motives in stealing into Shields's room had been altruistic and above reproach. Everything that had come after had been merely the natural product of curiosity coupled with opportunity. She had found herself alone with her karmically predetermined, astrologically perfect mate. Inevitably, she must wonder if he felt so much as a spark of the passion that, by all rights, should have ignited between them. That he apparently had not, she had attributed to her own failure to correctly interpret the vision in the shew stone or to something either in his karmic past or his astrological charts, when she should have known all along that his Leo's pride and sense of honor must stand in the way of his joining with her in the manner of karmically predetermined lovers. Certainly, that same pride must make him an unlikely candidate for abducting her and carrying her off to Gretna Green. Besides, she had not visualized him in the role of the rogue, but as the blacksmith, which led her to believe he was there purely as a representation of a woman's primordial desires which must inevitably be aroused by a magnificent example of the male revealed in all of his exquisite masculine perfection.

Still, she could be mistaken. Shields's presence could easily have some other significance of which she was as yet unaware. As for Vere, she did not doubt her brother had served as the vehicle of warning. Or perhaps she was deluding herself, and the dream was a parcel of nonsense, conjured up out of her own fantasies about Shields and the kiss that had awakened her to emotions on the order of an all-consuming passion.

Certainly, that was what Violet's interpretation would have been, she acknowledged ironically to herself, and anyone else's, if she were ever foolish enough to reveal the contents of her dream. Indeed, she dared not contemplate what Shields would think of it, never mind his seeming accolade concerning her deep convictions and extra-ordinary perception. She did not doubt that, far from believing in her prognosticative abilities, he was only being gracious. In which case, it would clearly behoove her to keep the dream to herself. After all, it would not seem to have any relevance to the main issue at hand—to keep Shields safe from harm—and there would seem to be little advantage in testing the earl's indulgence too far. She might be a seer and a prognosticator, but she was hardly a fool. She knew all too well that, presented with a surfeit of divinations, Shields might be brought to change his mind about making her his ally in his search for the villain behind the plot to cut his stick for him.

A martial light leaped in Elfrida's beautiful eyes. Nothing, she told herself, not even a seer's moral obligation to those about to enter a building in imminent peril of conflagration, must give Shields an excuse to terminate their fragile pact. Indeed, she was quite determined on that. Unfortunately, she was acutely aware that, as an Aries, not only was she temperamentally ill-suited for any sort of subterfuge, but she was cursed to find it exceedingly difficult, when presented with a cause, not to immediately espouse it.

She had ever, in short, found it a sore trial to try to keep anything secret for very long. And how not, when her ruling instinct was to immediately blurt out whatever happened to be on her mind, she reflected with a wry twist of her lips, especially if her temper should happen to be aroused. Really, it was not all honey and roses being born an Aries!

It was, however, undeniably stimulating, she was to reflect some little time later, to be an Aries in the company of a Leo, especially if that Leo happened to be the Earl of Shields. She was ruefully aware that, despite her mature five and twenty years, she felt as giddy as a schoolroom miss when, upon entering the downstairs withdrawing room, she found herself once again in Shields's compelling presence. Really, it would not seem in the least fair that while she, at the mere sight of his tall, imposing figure garbed in a claret-colored, double-breasted cutaway coat, superbly tailored to accentuate his broad shoulders and narrow-waisted torso, and dove-grey, skin-tight unmentionables that must inevitably draw attention to the intoxicating muscularity of masculine thighs, should find herself resisting the karmically predetermined urge to fling herself into his arms and demand that he kiss her at once, *he* appeared maddeningly unmoved.

"My lord." Marveling that her voice should sound cool and collected when her heart, as well as her stomach, were behaving in a most reprehensible manner, she crossed the room to him, one hand graciously extended in greeting.

His eyes, the steel-blue of rapiers, lifted to pierce her through in a single, swift glance. Her breath caught. Then his strong, supple fingers closed about her hand, sending a small shock wave shooting disconcertingly up her arm.

"You came!" she blurted.

An almost imperceptible twitch at the corners of the earl's handsome lips would seem to belie the gravity of his expression. "As you see," he acknowledged and was made wryly aware of the stirring of his blood at sight of the breathtaking vision of beauty.

"Devil," gasped Elfrida, unable to suppress a wry grimace at having stated the obvious. "Really, my lord, you would seem to have a wholly unsettling effect on me. I am not usually gauche. But then, the truth to tell, I was not at all certain you would not change your mind. After all, I did shoot you with Valentine's pop gun.''

"An unfortunate accident henceforth better left forgotten." Shields's compelling orbs studied her from beneath drooping eyelids. Obviously, she had rested, he noted, observing with satisfaction the absence of shadows beneath her lovely eyes. Why, then, had he the uneasy sensation that all was not quite what it should be with his Goddess of Beauty? The devil, he cursed. The divinating spinster was working her spell on him. He was not in the norm prone to feelings of the preternatural sort. He had, in fact, always prided himself on being a man of cold, hard reason. That he should suddenly be given to experience the uncanny perception that something unexpected and potentially disagreeable loomed on his horizon was hardly conducive to his peace of mind. But then, he had never before known anyone remotely like Lady Elfrida Rochelle. It came to him, not for the first time since his initial, fateful encounter with the Goddess of Beauty, that association with a female with the self-professed powers of prognostication must inevitably lead to a wide assortment of complications in his life, not the least of which was not knowing if or when Miss Rochelle had been subject to a vision of portent which might lead her at any moment to dash off headlong into peril.

At that all too conceivable possibility, Shields's glance narrowed sharply on Elfrida's face. "Is that what is troubling you, my girl, the incident with that ridiculous pop gun?"

Elfrida, who was occupied with a plethora of unruly thoughts and emotions, not any of which remotely pertained to the ignominious moment when she had shot his lordship in the forehead with her nephew's toy pistol, awarded Shields a startled look. "I beg your pardon, my lord?"

"You appear distracted, Miss Rochelle," Shields observed, headily aware of the mingled aromas of lilacs and lavender water, not to mention the subtle woman's scent that was uniquely Elfrida's own, that were tantalizingly assailing his nostrils.

"I cannot think why I should, my lord," replied Elfrida, acutely sensible of the fact that her hand still resided in his. Distracted? Good heavens, she wondered, did he feel *nothing* of the astrological magnetic force that was generated between them whenever they were in the merest proximity of one another, never mind in actual contact? "I assure you that nothing is troubling me—save, of course, concern for the fact that someone is trying to put a period to your existence." Gently, she tugged at her hand in his grasp. "Should we not be going, my lord? I cannot think it is at all wise to leave your cattle standing for too long."

"My cattle, Miss Rochelle, need not concern you." To her consternation, Shields's fingers tightened their grip on hers. "And neither, I might add, should the state of my existence. I am perfectly capable of defending myself against any would-be assassins." A shadow of something resembling bafflement flickered behind his hooded gaze. "You, on the other hand, are a different prospect altogether. Are you certain you have not experienced another of your prognosticative dreams or visions, Miss Rochelle? I should like to think you would tell me if you had."

"Should you, my lord?" breathed Elfrida, feeling herself sway toward him, no doubt as a result of the astrological magnetism inherent in the 5-9 Sun Sign vibratory pattern between them. With an effort, she got a grip on her unruly emotions. Faith, she groaned silently to herself. It was going to be a deal harder than she had previously imagined to restrain herself from giving in to her cosmically generated impulses, not to mention her Arian need for instant gratification. Still, she ruefully reminded herself, she had given her promise not to put temptation in his way so long as her virtue remained a deterrent to the completion of their karmic destiny. "You may be sure I shall, my lord," replied Elfrida, forcing herself to meet his gaze unflinchingly, "whenever I am certain I have envisioned something of pertinence to your continued well-being. That is, after all, the ostensible reason for our alliance, is it not?"

The devil, thought Shields, who could not but be acutely aware that his provocative Goddess of Beauty had not provided him quite the assurance that he might have wished from her. Indeed, there was a vagueness about her reply that left him little doubt she was keeping something from him. On the other hand, she had promised to tell him the prognostications that would seem to have relevance to the pall of danger she had perceived hanging over him. Perhaps that was all that mattered. After all, it was not as if he actually believed in her demmed delusions, he reminded himself. He had only wished to be apprised ahead of time if the unpredictable Miss Rochelle were about to launch herself on some harebrained scheme to protect him from something she had conjured up in her undeniably pretty head. Besides, he strongly suspected that he would fail in any endeavor to win a more definite promise from her. Miss Rochelle had amply demonstrated she was possessed of a strong, stubborn nature and a wholly independent mind. For the present, he would be better served, no doubt, not to rush his fences.

"Splendid, Miss Rochelle," he said, releasing her hand and offering her his arm. "You may be sure

I shall hold you to that. And, now, if you are ready, I daresay we have indeed left my cattle standing long enough."

He was still vaguely displeased with himself, however, when some few moments later he clasped strong hands about her waist and lifted her to the seat of his curricle drawn by a matched pair of bays. Climbing lightly up beside her, he took up the ribbons and the whip and, setting the team in motion, waited until he had entered the flow of traffic before glancing speculatively down at his companion.

"You are uncommonly quiet, Miss Rochelle," he observed, neatly weaving a path through the press of carriages and carts.

"I was thinking, my lord," replied Elfrida, a frown puckering her brow.

"Something I suspect you are all too prone to do, Miss Rochelle," commented the earl, when it seemed she did not intend to go on. "Would it be presumptuous of me to suppose you might tell me what you are thinking?"

Elfrida, who had been searching for a delicate way to broach what must certainly be a sensitive subject for the earl, awarded Shields a wry grimace. "I have been trying to think *how* to tell you, my lord. Dear, I'm afraid I am not at all good at beating about the bush."

"As it happens, that is one of the things I find most refreshing about you, Miss Rochelle," his lordship replied dryly.

"It is?" queried Elfrida, who had not thought he had found anything to like in her. "I mean, you do?"

"It is, and I do," Shields assured her with a glint of amusement in his eyes. "As it happens, I prefer to deal in plain pounds. Pray do not be afraid to open the budget. I promise I am not given to delicate sensibilities.''

''No, I did not suppose that you were,'' Elfrida said with a wry smile. ''On the other hand, I am reluctant to bring up something that might evoke painful memories.''

''By which I must presume you are alluding to the unfortunate demise of my friend Hepplewaite. Naturally I must regret his loss, Miss Rochelle, even as I abhor the manner of his passing. I am not, however, of a morbid disposition. You need not fear for my feelings.''

''Very well, then, my lord, if you are quite certain I am not encroaching on a matter of great sensitivity, I suppose I should just say it straight out. Has it occurred to you that the pall of danger hanging over you might possibly have some connection with Lord Hepplewaite's untimely passing? After all, you were intimates, and you have offered a generous reward for the apprehension of the fiend who put a period to his existence. It would seem rather too coincidental that, hard upon the heels of the events at Ludgate Hall, someone should try to cut your stick for you.''

''And you do not believe in coincidences, is that it, Miss Rochelle?'' queried the earl, who had long since come to a similar conclusion concerning recent events.

''I am a scryer and a prognosticator, my lord,'' Elfrida did not hesitate to remind him.

''Yes, Miss Rochelle,'' agreed his lordship with only the barest hint of irony. ''That much we have already established.''

''Devil,'' said Elfrida, wrinkling her nose at him. ''I am perfectly aware that you do not believe I am any such thing.''

''Then you would be mistaken, my girl,'' Shields instantly countered with a strange sort of gravity that brought a blush to Elfrida's cheek. "As it happens, I am perfectly willing to entertain the possibility you are precisely what you claim to be. That having been said, you have still not answered my question."

"Have I not? But I should have thought it must be patently clear, my lord," said Elfrida, more moved than she could have anticipated that she was not to be made the object of ridicule for her belief in the realm of the extra-ordinary. "As one who practices the art of divination, I am naturally of the opinion that coincidences are, in reality, events whose karmic connections have yet to be determined. It has occurred to me that the negative forces which culminated in Hepplewaite's end may not have been restored to balance with his death. In which case, I think it is exceedingly likely that, until they are brought to light, they will continue to wreak havoc on those whose karma is somehow intertwined with Hepplewaite and his fate."

"Meaning mine, Miss Rochelle?" drawled his lordship, tooling his team through Grosvenor Gate into Hyde Park.

"You, unfortunately, might very well have been drawn into the unfolding of cosmic events, my lord," Elfrida speculated, "merely by virtue of your friendship with the viscount. It would, of course, be helpful if we knew why poor Hepplewaite should have met the end he did. Then perhaps we could trace events backward to the point at which your karma might have become inextricably bound up with his, with the result that you would now appear to be in the same sort of peril in which Hepplewaite found himself."

"An intriguing theory, Miss Rochelle," remarked Shields, slowing his cattle to a sedate pace in keeping with the parade of fashionables proceeding along the Carriage Drive to the Ring. "It is, how-

ever, patently unnecessary to speculate when I
became drawn into the events leading to Hepplewaite's demise. I know precisely when and how I
became involved. You might say it was because of
a failure in judgment on my part that Hepplewaite
is dead at all.''

"I beg your pardon, my lord?" said Elfrida, who
could not but be struck by the harshness in the
earl's declaration.

"It was my arrogance in believing I should have
some positive influence on poor Jamey, which led
to the events at Ludgate Hall. I allowed Hepplewaite to lose a considerable sum at my Faro table
in the mistaken notion that I should teach him a
much-needed lesson in restraint.''

"With the result that he decided it was prudent
to leave Town for a period of rustication in the
country, which was why he happened to be at Ludgate Hall. You blame yourself for Hepplewaite's
death! But you could not be more wrong, my lord.''

"I was a fool, Miss Rochelle, to believe I might
have made a difference. Subsequent events have
made me realize the futility of my efforts. Worse, I
must live with the knowledge that my error directly
contributed to Hepplewaite's demise.'' Shields,
glancing down into Elfrida's startled eyes, grimly
smiled. "You are shocked, Miss Rochelle," he said.
"Apparently, you were not given to see that in your
crystal ball.''

"No, but then, I do not need to have resort to
the shew stone to know that you cannot be blamed
for what happened at Ludgate Hall, my lord.''
Impulsively, Elfrida laid her hand on Shields's arm.
"We are each of us responsible for our own karmic
destinies. Whatever led up to that terrible night,
Hepplewaite made his own choices along the way.
You did not kill Hepplewaite, my lord.''

"No," agreed Shields, acutely aware of the earnest face turned up to his, "but that does not alter the fact that, had *I* chosen differently, Hepplewaite would be alive today."

Elfrida's head came up, a sparkle in her beautiful eyes. "On the contrary, my lord," she said steadily. "Without knowing who, not to mention what, contributed to the events at Ludgate Hall, you can be certain of no such thing. It is entirely possible nothing would have served to change Hepplewaite's destiny."

"I'm afraid you will never convince me of that, Miss Rochelle," replied Shields, who could not but be struck by her determined leap to his defense, behavior sharply at variance with what he had come to expect from the females of his acquaintance. *They* had ever demonstrated a ready concern for his title or his fortune, but hardly for himself or his well-being. She was all sweet fire and generosity, was the Goddess of Beauty. Suddenly, he was swept with impatience to have done with the matter of Hepplewaite that he might turn his attentions to the more pertinent matter of becoming more intimately acquainted with the intriguing Lady Elfrida Rochelle. "You and I agree on one thing, however. The event of the runaway hack in Bond Street must be connected in some manner to Hepplewaite's demise. I, too, am skeptical of coincidences."

"I thought perhaps you might be, my lord," smiled Elfrida, judiciously returning her hand to her lap before it could betray her by stealing of its own accord to his clean-shaven cheek. Immediately, she sobered. "Can you think of anyone who might have wished ill of Hepplewaite? Someone, perhaps even this unsavory cent-per-cent you mentioned, for whom you and Hepplewaite both shared a disaffection?"

"You may be certain that I have never had need for recourse to the likes of Mr. Nicodemus Pickering," replied the earl dampeningly. "And if you are asking if Hepplewaite and I had any common enemies, then, no, Miss Rochelle, we had none that come readily to mind. In spite of the popular view that Jamey and I were intimates, the truth is we did not run in the same circles. Our association was not of the usual order. It more resembled the sort of relationship found between brothers of widely disparate ages."

"You were his mentor and protector in other words, my lord? Someone whom Hepplewaite might look up to as a model of manhood?" queried Elfrida, who had wondered what should have drawn two men of such differing natures to become friends.

"Hardly the latter, Miss Rochelle," Shields replied dryly. "Jamey was far too self-centered to emulate anyone, least of all someone who was wont to read him curtain-lectures on the vagaries of his character. I believe it is safe to say Jamey was used to view me in the light of a convenience, someone to whom he might turn when he found himself in a coil, which, now that I have been brought to think back on it, was all too often in the years that I knew him."

"I should not refine overmuch on it, if I were you, my lord," said Elfrida, who could not but feel that, while Hepplewaite might not have deserved to be impaled on his own sword and then incinerated, he had ought to have been given a swift kick in the posterior for all the grief he had caused Shields, a man who had ever stood his friend. "As a Leo, you are prone to help those less fortunate than you. It is in your nature to seek to influence others for the better—just as the Sun sheds light to dispel the darkness. I daresay you simply cannot help yourself, any more than I, as an Aries, can keep from tending to be impetuous, single-minded, and rammishly independent."

"No doubt I am comforted, Miss Rochelle, by the knowledge that I may attribute all my failings to the mere happenstance of my having been born on the tenth of August," commented Shields with only the barest hint of irony. "Thankfully, it will save me the trouble henceforth of having to exercise my faculties of reason in governing my daily existence."

"Pooh," declared Elfrida, giving vent to a burble of laughter at such an absurdity. "Now you are roasting me, my lord. I did not say you had not a mind and a will of your own or that you should not be required to exercise them. Our astrological planets and signs provide a source of insight into how and why we are the way we are. They do not take the place of thinking logically or responsibly. But then, I daresay you were never in any danger of abandoning Reason. You are possessed of far too powerful an intellect not to use it."

"And you, Miss Rochelle, are not the henwit you would have others take you for," observed Shields, glancing down at her with a peculiar glint in his eye. "I begin to believe there is some method to your madness."

"But you do not believe I am really possessed of extra-ordinary powers of perception or that we are karmically predetermined Twin Souls. In which case, I daresay you will not credit me when I tell you I have the strangest feeling we are about to be accosted by a lady and a gentleman riding in a barouche drawn by a handsome team of greys."

Startled, Shields shot her a penetrating glance. "Another of your prognosticative visions, Miss Rochelle?" he queried.

"Actually, no, my lord," Elfrida returned sweetly. "As it happens, I have been observing the reflection of just such a barouche in that brass carriage knob," she confessed, pointing to the knob in question, which, in the shape of an orb polished to a high sheen, was mounted on the dash. "I believe they have been trying for some few minutes to overtake us."

"No, have they?" uttered Shields, glancing back at the carriage, which did indeed appear to be making a concentrated effort to come up with his curricle. Now what the devil, he thought, pulling out of the parade to the side of the drive to await the arrival of the pursuing vehicle. "Minx," he murmured, taking in Miss Rochelle's demure aspect. "You are enjoying yourself immensely at my expense, are you not?"

"It is one of my enduring faults, I'm afraid, my lord," replied Elfrida, smiling up at him. "I am possessed of a lamentable tendency to levity, especially with gentlemen who openly question my sanity. Are you familiar with the barouche and its occupants?"

"Exceedingly familiar, Miss Rochelle," admitted his lordship as the barouche drew abreast of the curricle and pulled to a stop. He reached up to touch the brim of his hat in acknowledgment of the elegantly appareled woman in her early forties who gave every appearance of one on the verge of giving into a fit of the vapors. "Madam," he drawled, a mask of ennui descending over his handsome features. "A pleasant surprise, no doubt. And Cousin Albert. One cannot but marvel what should bring the two of you out together for a drive in Hyde Park."

"You might well ask, Shields," replied the aging beauty, dabbing at her nose with a dainty wisp of lace, which served as a lady's handkerchief. "Not that you care that I am fairly distraught with worry or that you have so far neglected your duties as

head of the family as to refuse to oversee the come-
out of your sole surviving sibling. It is only what I
have come to expect of you. And now see what has
come of it. You are out riding with one of your
barques of frailty when, by all rights, you should
have been supporting me in this, my greatest hour
of need."

"Excellently well expressed, Madam," applauded
his lordship with a sardonic curl of the lip. "On
that note, perhaps you will allow me to make you
known to my companion. Miss Rochelle, I have the
honor of presenting to you Mr. Albert Herrick, my
cousin, and Helen, the Countess of Shields, my
esteemed stepmama. Countess, Albert—Lady Elfrida
Rochelle."

"By Jove," blurted Albert with a grin of irrepressible glee. "The Duke of Albermarle's granddaughter!"

The dowager countess, giving a good imitation
of one who has just had her toe caught in a
mousetrap, blanched, then went a dusky red.

"Mr. Herrick. Lady Shields," murmured Elfrida,
inclining her head so that the brim of her Gypsy
hat concealed the telltale glimmer of mirth in her
eyes. Shields, she did not doubt, had derived a
deal of perverse satisfaction at having caught his
stepmother out on the wrong foot. And little wonder if it was Lady Shields's usual practice to enact
a Cheltenham tragedy in his presence. Shields was
hardly the sort to tolerate with equanimity a female
who was forever flying into high fidgets.

"Charmed, I am sure, Miss Rochelle," Lady
Shields managed with a smile that appeared to
stick to her teeth.

"Likewise, Miss Rochelle," Albert burst forth,
his youthful face expressive of unadulterated admiration. "I say, Shields, you might have given us

some inkling of what you were about. Shouldn't keep so enchanting a lady all to yourself.''

"Really, Albert," scolded the countess, her features assuming what would seem their customary aspect of petulance. "Pray strive to contain yourself. As for you, my lord, it would seem you are to be congratulated for having finally come to an awareness of what is owed to your title. Not that you care a whit what I or anyone else might think of whatever you might choose to do. Nevertheless, the granddaughter of the Duke of Albermarle must naturally be seen as a vast improvement over your usual choice in feminine companions."

"As it happens, Madam," said the earl, giving Elfrida a look that brought a warm rush of blood to her cheeks, "I could not agree with you more. It was not, however, my choice of companions that you wished to discuss with me."

"Good heavens, no. It is Julia, as you must have known all along it was. I am at my wit's end with that child, Shields, as I have told you often enough. Not that you have ever taken a proper interest in her, never mind that she is your own sister—or rather *half-*sister, as you are so fond of reminding me. I daresay she will be the death of me, which I daresay would suit you very well if it were not for the fact that then you would be solely responsible for her. Although, in such an issue you would undoubtedly send her off to a nunnery, which, were it not for me, is where I daresay she would be now instead of in London. I had been in hopes she would attract any number of eligible suitors, which, thanks to my unflagging efforts on her behalf, she has done, as well as at least half a dozen whom I should gladly consign to the devil and one who, despite your timely interference, has proven uncommonly persistent and who I daresay is at the heart of this plot to absent her from the bosom of her loving parent. After all I have tried to do for her and just when that enormously wealthy Russian prince—Vladomovsky or Vladimirov or Vladiminsky or whatever the devil his name is—was on the point of offering for her, this is how she repays me. You must do something, Shields. Whatever you think of *me*, surely Julia should be able to look to you as the head of the family."

"What I *think*, Madam," said Shields in tones of chilly dispassion, "is that, until you see fit to apprise me of what new coil Julia has got herself in, I am regrettably powerless to do anything to help you."

"But she told you, my lord," declared Elfrida, who was prey to a sudden sinking sensation in the pit of her stomach. "Lady Julia is missing. It is apparent Lady Shields and your cousin have been out searching for her, but I'm afraid they have been seeking her in all the wrong places."

Shields looked at her. "The wrong places?" he repeated evenly, his eyes seeming to bore holes through her.

Swallowing, Elfrida returned his gaze steadily. "Indeed, my lord. Lady Julia, I fear, is not to be found in London."

"Not in London, but that is preposterous," asserted the countess, shredding her lace handkerchief in her agitation. "She was upset because I told her she could not accept Miss Emberly's invitation to attend the balloon ascension in Kensington Gardens. She has undoubtedly stolen from the house in order to keep her assignation with her friends."

"Unfortunately, you did not find Julia there," said Shields, never taking his eyes from Elfrida.

"Not so you would notice," confessed Albert, his boyish face filled with curiosity as he gazed from Shields to Elfrida and back again. "Or any of the dozen or so other places we have tried. We were just on our way back to the gardens to look again when we spotted you.''

''And now that you have found me, you will leave it to me to discover where Julia has taken herself.'' Turning his gaze from Elfrida, he looked to the countess. ''It occurs to me, Madam, that Julia might very well have grown tired of her lark and returned home, which is where you should be to receive her.''

''But, Shields, I cannot bear it to wait and do nothing. You know I cannot. I am quite beside myself with not knowing what has happened to her.''

''Nothing has happened to her. Go home, Madam. You have done enough. Albert will stay with you. You may rest assured she will be returned to you, safe and unharmed.''

''Very well,'' sighed the countess after a moment. Having grown visibly more calm beneath Shields's steady regard, she assayed a trembling smile. ''If you think that is best. Home an' you please, Creighton,'' she said to the coachman. Then, as the barouche lurched into motion, she anxiously called, ''You *will* find her, Shields? You will bring her back to me?''

''I have said I should,'' Shields unhesitatingly called back to her. ''You have my word, Madam.''

Only when the barouche was swallowed up in the flow of traffic did he at last turn to Elfrida.

''And now, Miss Rochelle,'' he said in deadly earnest, ''you will kindly explain to me what the *devil* you know about my troublesome sister's disappearance.''

Chapter 8

Not for the first time in her life, Elfrida found herself heartily wishing she had not been the inheritor of her great-grandmama Lucasta's powers of prognostication. It was one thing to be given glimpses of minor future events of a domestic nature, like the vision that her dearest papa's favorite mare would give birth to twins or the dream that her bosom bow, Lady Catherine Welles, was to meet and fall head over ears in love with the dashing Captain Steven Quatrain and subsequently become his bride. It was quite another to take upon herself the responsibility of informing the Earl of Shields that she believed his sister Julia had very likely been abducted and carried off to Gretna Green.

"Elfrida." Shields's voice impinged on her consciousness. "Was it one of your dreams?"

Acutely aware of the earl's gimlet eyes probing her face while he waited for an answer to his question, Elfrida caught her bottom lip between her teeth. What if she had misread the dream images?

Worse, what if she was right about the meaning of the dream and, out of selfish motives, failed to tell Shields his sister was in grave peril, when every instinct cried out to Elfrida that she had been given a true dream of prognostication? Surely, she could not be such a coward. She was an Aries, ruled by the planet Mars, the sign of the warrior. To do other than her heart bid her would be to disavow everything she was. It simply did not bear thinking on, she told herself, unconsciously lifting her head. Indeed, it was quite out of the question.

"Yes, my lord," Elfrida declared, meeting Shields's gaze with a martial light, "it was a dream. And, no, I did not tell you before because I was not certain what the dream elements were meant to convey. I have come to see, however, that it was not *my* sister who was in danger of falling to the machinations of a fortune hunter, but yours. Indeed, it would all seem to make perfect sense to me now."

"Perfect sense?" demanded Shields, who was damnably afraid he understood all too well what the divining Miss Rochelle was trying to tell him. Worse, it would seem he was about to find himself in the devil of a coil. When he undertook to protect the Goddess of Beauty from her own propensity for impulsive behavior, he had hardly thought to be put in the position of having to decide the fate of his troublesome eighteen-year-old sister based on some sort of blind faith in one of Miss Rochelle's demmed prophetic dreams! Hell and the devil confound it, it was asking a deal too much. "On the other hand," he said, "purely for my benefit, perhaps you would care to be more explicit. You dreamed that a fortune hunter had set his sights on my sister?"

"Not precisely, my lord," Elfrida demurred, steeling herself for his scorn, which she did not doubt was soon to be forthcoming. "Dreams of prophecy are seldom that straightforward."

"No, of course they are not. That *would* be too much to ask, would it not?" said Shields, recalled ironically to the fact that he was dealing with the mystic arts, which, by their very definition, were outside the perception of the physical senses and therefore enigmatic to the intellect.

"I'm afraid so, my lord," agreed Elfrida with a grimace. "It is the singlemost frustrating aspect of prognostication that one must rely wholly on subjective reasoning to discover the reality beyond the purely mundane." Resolutely, she forged to the heart of the matter. "In my dream, for example, you were a blacksmith working over his anvil, and Vere was on the point of shooting a rogue stallion with Valentine's pop gun despite my sister Violet's objections that Albermarle would not be at all pleased to discover the stud he had picked out for her was in fact a high-stepper. The elements, you see, were all there."

"The elements," carefully repeated Shields, who could not but perceive the possibility for an entirely different explanation for Miss Rochelle's dream, one that, far from having anything to do with prognostication, reflected a jumbled reenactment of actual earlier events. Events, he thought with a peculiar satisfaction, which would seem to have had a significant effect on her. On the other hand, somewhat to his annoyance, he recognized all too readily the "elements" to which Miss Rochelle must be referring. "You mean the anvil, of course, whose symbolic connotation has long since passed into the realm of the banal. And the—er—stud horse, which, I must presume, is—"

"A symbolic representation of the sort of gentleman who, despite his charming facade, is at heart an unprincipled ne'er-do-well intent on getting himself an heiress by any means, honorable or otherwise," Elfrida supplied all in a single breath, her lovely eyes compelling on his.

"A fortune hunter, in short," Shields concluded with a wry twist of the lips. "As it happens, I am not unacquainted with that particular breed of gentlemen."

"No, of course you are not," replied Elfrida, who could not but be exceedingly gratified at the ease with which she had cleared the first hurdle. "Which is why, at first, the dream would seem to make little sense."

"Only at first, however," Shields extrapolated dryly as he waited to be enlightened.

"Indeed, it could not be otherwise, my lord," Elfrida agreed intently, her face alight with her newfound understanding. "Before Lady Shields provided the essential missing piece of the puzzle, I was able to perceive only the essence of the dream."

"But not its relevance," Shields offered, recalling the vague nature of Miss Rochelle's earlier promise to him. "Which is why you kept it from me."

"You *do* understand, my lord," affirmed Elfrida, fairly beaming at him in approval. "Somehow I hoped you would. While Vere was clearly the vehicle of warning, I was not at all certain what your part in the dream was. I was unaware that you even had a sister, which meant that particular relationship could only be portrayed by Gideon and Violet. Nevertheless, I should have *known* the warning was meant for you, since you would seem to have no other purpose in the context of the dream. Violet, after all, was hardly the likely victim. Due to unfortunate circumstances attending my parents' demise, my sister, unlike yours, is not blessed with a fortune of her own."

"The loss of the *Swallow* and Blaidesdale's marker against your father are not unknown to me, Miss Rochelle," the earl stated quietly. "You have my sympathies, ma'am. On the other hand, Lady Violet *is* the granddaughter of the Duke of Albermarle," observed Shields, who, listening to himself, could not but wonder if he had abandoned all sense of rationale. Had anyone told him only twenty-four hours earlier that he would actually find himself debating the merits of a self-professed seer's dream of prognostication, let alone one that allegedly foretold that his sister would fall into the hands of an abductor intent on marrying her across the anvil for her fortune, he would clearly have thought that person mad. Miss Rochelle, however, would seem to wield a singular influence over him. The devil, he thought. He had the strangest feeling she had somehow irretrievably altered the fabric of his existence while his back was turned. "That kinship," he continued, "might in itself be temptation enough for some."

"It might, my lord," agreed Elfrida, who had herself previously been troubled by that very possibility. "Violet, however, has barely been a se'ennight in London. That would hardly seem time enough for her to attract the notice of a fortune hunter, let alone for him to set his sights for her. And then there is one additional factor that you would hardly be likely to take into account, my lord. Violet is a Pisces and, as such, is exceedingly wary of anyone who might in any way threaten her independence. I cannot see her falling to the machinations of a smooth-talking rogue, certainly not in so short a time frame."

"But you would ask me to believe *my* sister not only is gullible enough to fall for the flummery of an out-and-out bounder," ventured Shields, inexplicably feeling a cold vise clamp down on his vitals, "but she is presently on her way to Gretna Green in his company."

"In truth, I do not know, my lord," Elfrida admitted honestly. "There is every possibility matters have yet to progress so far. Lady Shields did say Lady Julia had wished to attend the balloon ascensions. Perhaps that was all that your sister intended. Such a scenario, however, would not necessarily rule out an abduction. Lady Julia might very well be in Kensington Gardens at this very moment wholly unaware that she is walking into danger."

"Splendid, Miss Rochelle," pronounced Shields, setting the bays into motion. "Then it would seem *that*, at least, should be the start of our search."

As the curricle pulled once more into the parade of carriages along the Ring, Elfrida cast a sidelong glance at Shields's grim aspect. "My lord," she ventured, clasping her hands firmly in her lap. "About Lady Shields. I was wondering—"

"Yes, I daresay you were, Miss Rochelle," said the earl, who did not choose, in the norm, to discuss the subject of his stepmother with anyone, let alone with a female with whom he could claim an acquaintance of less than twenty-four hours. Inexplicably, he found himself compelled to make an exception in Miss Rochelle's case. "Despite what must have been your impression, Lady Shields *was* my late father's wife and, as such, I have ever accorded her the distinction due the Countess of Shields. I have allowed her, in fact, to lead her own life without any interference from me. As for Julia, far from the scorned half-sibling my esteemed stepmama would have you believe her, she, you may be certain, has ever been assured of my affection as well as the mantle of my protection."

"But I *am* certain of it, my lord," Elfrida firmly asserted. "Indeed, I never doubted it for a moment. Leos, after all, may generally be counted upon to be fiercely loyal, not to mention warm and lovingly kind to those in their protection. Lady Shields, on the other hand, is clearly given to find fault with everyone around her. I daresay she was born in late August or September."

"*Do* you, Miss Rochelle," said Shields, flashing her a sidelong glance. "As it happens, you could not be closer to the truth. Lady Shields was born on the fifteenth of September."

"But of course she was," Elfrida answered with perfect equanimity. "I could not be mistaken in thinking Lady Shields is a Virgo. Naturally, she would seem a trifle waspish at times. It cannot but be distressing to be forever looking for perfection in others, not to mention in oneself and one's surroundings, and especially so when one is, by nature, desirous of being helpful to others. There is nothing so difficult to tolerate as people who will not heed one's advice on how to improve themselves."

"Save, perhaps," Shields interjected cynically, "having to listen to someone forever harping on what is perceived to be one's imperfections."

"Quite so, my lord," agreed Elfrida, her eyes brimful of understanding. "On the other hand, I daresay there is no one better equipped to help you resolve a difficult problem or organize your household for you or make all the preparations for a gala involving any number of guests than Lady Shields, were you to ask her."

"You would not think so, were you to hear her tell how greatly she feels she has been imposed upon by everyone around her," observed Shields, who could not conceive of any extenuating circumstance that might lead him to petition his stepmother's assistance in anything—good God!

"And you, most in particularly, I do not doubt, my lord," replied Elfrida, who had a very good idea how galling it must be for the proud Leo to be subjected to the nitpicking of an unhappy Virgo. It was a pity, really, she decided, observing his lordship's chiseled profile. In different circumstances, it was quite possible the earl and his stepmama might have found a great deal to complement one another in their disparate personalities. Lady Shields, when she was not feeling the unappreciated martyr subjected to the arrogant airs of a stepson, who must clearly have been nearly full-grown upon the event of her marriage to his father and consequently beyond requiring the affections of a mama, especially one little more than five or six years his senior, was very likely prone to be engaging, self-effacing, and quite disarmingly feminine. Those attributes, combined with her natural appreciation for an obviously superior being, might easily have lent themselves to a compatible relationship with the earl, who, besides being a magnificent representative of the noble Leo shining with majestic self-confidence, was at heart as generous as he was proud. "Still, it occurs to me that it cannot have been all that easy for Lady Shields, losing her husband when she was yet quite young. Virgos are exceedingly exacting in the mates they choose. I daresay your father must have been a most remarkable man. In which case, it is doubtful she will ever find another to fill the void left by his passing. It is all too bad, really, since Virgos, despite their appearance of self-sufficiency, actually do much better with someone around to provide them with a sense of security."

"Meaning me, I suppose," said the earl, a dangerous glint leaping in his eyes at what would seem the young beauty's bloody demmed impertinence. "You may be certain the countess does not want for anything, Miss Rochelle. Even had my father failed to provide for her handsomely—and he did not—I should have seen that she was well able to live in the style to which she has been accustomed."

"Of course you would, my lord," exclaimed Elfrida, who, made suddenly and acutely aware of the chill in Shields's tone, could not but wish she would learn to keep her tongue between her teeth. It was something she had sworn to master often enough in her life, but to exceedingly little avail. Indeed, she knew from past experience that she could no more stop herself from speaking her mind than she could cease to breathe. "I was not referring to Lady Shields's financial security, however, but to the sense of well-being that comes from feeling needed by someone. And now I clearly have said enough on a topic which, besides being none of my affair, was never my intention to broach in the first place."

"You did ask, Miss Rochelle," Shields drawled acerbically.

"On the contrary, my lord," Elfrida retorted, clenching her hands tightly in her lap. "I should never have been so remiss. What I was on the point of asking, when I was interrupted, was on something of quite a different order."

The devil, thought Shields, experiencing an unwonted pang of guilt at his boorish leap to conclusions. A man of keen perception, he could hardly fail to note the stiffness in the slender frame next to his. Nor could he be mistaken in thinking he had hurt his Goddess of Beauty. It came to him with uncomfortable clarity that his deliberate attempt to put her in her place for thinking to instruct him in his familial duty had been misguided. After all, he had been the one to break his own rule, which dictated he never discuss the dowager countess with anyone.

Shields neatly feather-edged the turn through the gate into Kensington Gardens before glancing down at Elfrida. "Yes, of course it was," he said quietly, observing the Goddess of Beauty's flushed cheeks. "Naturally, you would never be so coming as to inquire into what must be considered a private matter. What was it that you wished to know, my girl?"

Had he thought by that rather oblique admission of culpability to appease his Goddess of Beauty, he was immediately to be disappointed.

Glorious eyes of a spellbinding blue flashed up to meet his. "I am *not* 'your girl,' my lord," said Elfrida with chilly dignity. "I do wish you will cease to think of me in terms of some silly young thing with more hair than wit. I may have been born under the first sign of the Zodiac, that I might be allowed to experience this life in the manner of an untutored soul, but I am, nevertheless, a woman, fully grown, a fact that has apparently escaped your notice."

Shields, finding himself staring into dazzling orbs, was laboring under the peculiar notion that he had just been landed a facer. Twistedly, he smiled. "You may be sure, Miss Rochelle, that, while I may be guilty of any number of sins of omission, overlooking your womanly attributes has not been one of them. What was it you were going to ask me when I so rudely interrupted you?"

Elfrida, caught off guard by what was the closest thing to an apology that might be expected from a proud lion, awarded Shields a wry grimace. "Oh, good God," she exclaimed, thinking that, really, it was too bad of him. "I suppose now I must beg your pardon, my lord, for flying up in the boughs. The truth is I have a devilish temper. I suppose it is better that you find that out now rather than later. Not that I had any hopes of keeping it from you. It has been the bane of my existence that I cannot stop myself from blurting out practically anything that comes to my mind. Nevertheless, I should not have vented my anger at myself on you."

"Splendid, Miss Rochelle," said the earl with a glint of amusement. "And now that we have cleared the air, perhaps you would tell me what you had wished to know about my esteemed stepmama."

"Only that I could not but note something Lady Shields mentioned in passing. Something about a gentleman who she might wish had not been attracted to your sister. Someone, in fact, whom you have apparently seen fit to warn off, but who would seem to show a stubborn disinclination to abandon his suit. It occurred to me, my lord, to wonder who that gentleman might be."

"His name is Marston, Miss Rochelle. Mr. Niles Marston. And you are quite right. He has proven to be either remarkably obtuse or foolish in the extreme if he is still in pursuit of my sister."

"I daresay that, if it is the Mr. Niles Marston with whom I am acquainted, he is more likely to be exceedingly desperate," said Elfrida, frowning.

"You may be sure of it, Miss Rochelle. He has the distinction, after all, of being the eldest son of the late Admiral, Sir Nigel Marston, who amassed a fortune in the New World during the War of the Rebellion. He is also, however, an inveterate gambler. Having tossed most of his inheritance down the River Tick, Mr. Marston is well known to be on the lookout for an heiress to replenish his depleted coffers."

"Good heavens, is he yet?" exclaimed Elfrida, recalling to mind an image of a slender, well-knit gentleman who, despite his four and twenty years, had already manifested the first, unmistakable signs of dissipation in his handsome features. "He thought to send lures out to me a few years ago when I was still residing in Bath."

"If that is the case, then it would seem pertinent

to know if he met with any success, Miss Rochelle,"
drawled his lordship, a gleam of humor in the look
he bent upon her.

The devil, thought Elfrida, stifling a burble of
laughter. He was deliberately baiting her. It was
not in the least fair that he could be so irresistibly
attractive whenever he chose to disarm her. "Mr.
Marston was both well to look upon and charming,
my lord," Elfrida replied archly. "I, however, was
never in any danger of mistaking Spanish coin for
plain brass. It was soon made clear to me that Mr.
Marston, in spite of his engaging exterior, could
not see beyond himself. Worse, he has no appreciation of the absurd."

"Mr. Marston, in other words, Miss Rochelle,"
said Shields with perfect gravity, "is a crushing
bore."

"Indeed, my lord," smiled Elfrida, feeling a curious warmth steal over her as she exchanged an
understanding glance with Shields, "he is precisely
that. Although he might not seem so to a green
girl only just out of the schoolroom. I believe he
is thought to be quite dashing by any number of
young ladies. Furthermore, he may just be blinded
enough by his own overweening arrogance to
believe you would stay your hand if he succeeded
in marrying your sister over the anvil. There is,
after all, no denying the scandal of an annulment
would very likely ruin Lady Julia."

"There will be no need of an annulment, Miss
Rochelle," replied the earl in a voice that sent little
shivers down Elfrida's spine. "And you may be sure
not so much as a breath of scandal will ever touch
Julia. But then, we would seem to be getting ahead
of ourselves," he added, pulling the team to a halt
a short distance off the drive. "After all, we have
yet to discover if Mr. Marston has done anything
to warrant our suspicions."

It occurred to Elfrida that it might prove difficult to do so much as discover if Mr. Marston, or Lady Julia, for that matter, was even in the crowd gathered on the green, let alone if he was intending an abduction of the young heiress. The lure of ha'penny captive balloon rides, not to mention an open-air concert by the Royal Fusiliers Military Band, had attracted an impressive gathering eager to experience the thrill of aerial flight for themselves, even if it was for only the few moments it took to reach the end of the anchor rope, feel the balloon strain against its moorings, and then descend once more to less exalted environs. It was little wonder if Albert and Lady Shields had failed in their own endeavor to find the elusive young beauty among so many.

It was also clear why Lady Shields had looked with disfavor on such an outing for her daughter. The vulgar press, composed of a wide assortment of people from a variety of walks of life, was hardly the sort of milieu Lady Shields would have thought proper for a young girl of the higher ranks of society. Certainly, the marked display of gaiety and high spirits which prevailed would not have been in keeping with the countess's notions of gentility. Even the balloon itself, a spectacular monstrosity of red, gold, and purple stripes hovering, like some enormous aberration of nature, above the crowd, must have filled Lady Shields with abhorrence.

Faith, thought Elfrida, smiling to herself, it would have been marvelous if Lady Julia had *not* set her mind on coming!

"I am afraid, Miss Rochelle, that our outing is not quite what I had intended it to be," remarked Shields, grimly surveying the spectacle before him. "Had I known beforehand what lay before me, I should have arranged to have a groom accompany us."

"On the contrary, my lord," Elfrida could not keep from replying, "you would undoubtedly have cried off from bringing me along. I do see your dilemma, however. Obviously, you cannot leave your cattle unattended, which is why I shall remain here while you go and look for Lady Julia."

"I shall do no such thing, Miss Rochelle," objected the earl, who was soundly berating himself for not having anticipated the difficulties that lay before him. The last thing he could wish at any time was to leave a lady in his care unattended, but to do so in a crowd of strangers was wholly unacceptable. It was even more so when that lady happened to be the unpredictable Goddess of Beauty. "I was going to suggest hiring a hackney to take you home, Miss Rochelle."

"That would not do at all, however, since then you would have no one to see to your cattle. Pray do be sensible, my lord. You are wasting precious time. Your cattle will be perfectly safe with me, I promise."

"No doubt, Miss Rochelle," replied Shields, who could not be more pleased to espy a familiar figure approaching along Rotten Row. "Fortunately, I believe I shall not be forced to impose on your good nature." He was somewhat less gratified a scant few seconds later to note the newcomer's swift change of expression from one of easy recognition of Shields to unabashed admiration as his glance alit on the vision of beauty seated next to the earl.

"Damme, if it isn't Shields," exclaimed Viscount Winterbrooke, trotting his prime bit of blood up to the earl's curricle. "I shouldn't have thought to see you here today, of all days. Not your usual style of entertainment, is it?"

"I shouldn't have thought it was yours either, Winterbrooke," noted Shields in tones heavily

laced with irony. "What the devil brings you out
to rub shoulders with the skaff and raff?"

"As it happens, I ran into the countess and
Albert." The viscount smiled reflectively. "The lad
was positively effusive in his praise of your lady
companion, Shields. Even so, I daresay he did not
come even close to the truth of the matter. Miss
Rochelle, I believe," he added, elegantly inclining
his head to Elfrida.

"Viscount Winterbrooke," said Elfrida, dim-
pling prettily. "I am pleased to make your acquaintance."

"No more than am I," the viscount returned,
his hazel eyes lit with an appreciative gleam. "In
truth, I felt compelled to see the paragon of beauty
for myself. And now that I have, I fear I shall never
be the same, fair lady."

"Shall you not? How odd," said Elfrida, her face
expressive of mirth, "for you are just as my mother
once described you, my lord—some years ago."

"Your mother, was it?" said Winterbrooke, assuming a pained expression. "And just what, may
I ask, did the esteemed marchioness have to say
about me?"

"Only that you were a charming rogue and, had
my father not won her heart long before, even she
might have been in danger of having her head
turned by your fustian."

" 'Fustian!' Good God, Shields, do you hear her?
The lady has accused me of fustian."

"Miss Rochelle has, with her usual perspicacity,
managed to penetrate to the heart of the matter,"
dryly commented Shields, inexplicably nettled by
what gave every evidence of being an immediate
rapport between his oldest intimate and the Goddess of Beauty. "Perhaps I should have warned
you, old friend. The lady is possessed of extra-
ordinary powers of perception. You haven't a chance

of pulling the wool over her eyes. Not that that will deter you from doing your best to win the inside track with her.''

A curious gleam flickered behind the viscount's languid gaze. "Who would know better than you, old man?" he drawled, his lips curving ever so slightly.

The devil, Shields silently cursed. Winterbrooke's damnably amused smirk, far from assuaging Shields's uncertain temper, had more the effect of waving a red flag in his face—which was just what Winterbrooke had intended, no doubt. It was, after all, an old game between them, one which Shields, never having lost a round to his old friend and rival, in the norm might have thought diverting. That he failed to do so on this particular occasion Shields attributed to the peculiar circumstances in which he found himself. He could hardly be expected to view with equanimity a rivalry with his closest intimate for the affections of a female who was fully determined to enlist the services of a willing gentleman to divest her of the impediment that stood in the way of her karmic destiny! Good God, he had little doubt as to Winterbrooke's answer should the Goddess of Beauty present him with such a proposition.

"No one," agreed Shields, with singular directness. "Which is why I do not hesitate to tell you that, in this instance, you are barking up the wrong tree. You have only to ask Miss Rochelle. She and I, as fate would have it, were brought together by cosmic forces quite outside the control of mere mortals. It was, in fact, recorded in the stars that we should meet. In which case it is obvious that anyone desirous of disrupting the karmic unraveling of events, which, after all, were predetermined in one or more previous existences, would undoubtedly be doomed to failure.''

"Oh, doomed, indeed," agreed Winterbrooke, who had not taken his eyes off Shields during the entirety of that intriguing exposition, who, indeed, continued to regard his friend with an air of absorption for some four or five seconds after the earl had finished. Upon which, he drew a sudden breath. "Unless, of course," he added, abruptly switching his gaze to Elfrida, "the threads of that someone's karmic being were an inextricable part of the fabric of destiny being unfolded. Can anyone truly say that is categorically not the case in this, or any other, instance involving the ineffable nature of cosmic events?"

"I believe that is just what I have said," Shields asserted, well aware of the devilry behind Winterbrooke's apparently innocent inquiry.

Miss Rochelle, unfortunately, would not seem to be similarly sensible of the game Winterbrooke was playing.

"Well, no, not precisely, my lord," said the Goddess of Beauty, regarding Winterbrooke with a thoughtful air, which had the curious effect of eliciting something resembling a groan from her karmically predetermined, astrologically perfect mate. "While it is true no one really has the power to alter the fabric of destiny, the other side of the coin, so to speak, must certainly be that whoever influences, even in the most minuscule way, the cosmic texture of events must surely be a predetermined part of it. In which case, Viscount Winterbrooke would seem to have a viable point to make, would he not?"

"Viscount Winterbrooke has indubitably *achieved* his point," Shields pronounced in velvet-edged tones, which were not lost on either of his two companions. "In the process of which, however, it would seem that the more cogent point of the missing heiress has been overlooked. As it happens,

old friend, Miss Rochelle and I require a favor of
you."

It had fully been Shields's intention to ask
Winterbrooke to serve as Miss Rochelle's companion while he, himself, went in search of Lady Julia.
Though it gave him a measure of grim satisfaction
at having deprived Winterbrooke of the pleasure
of having the young beauty to his own devices, the
earl was less than pleased with himself when, some
moments later, he found himself conducting Elfrida through a gradually thinning crowd. While
in other circumstances he might have derived no
little enjoyment from having Lady Elfrida on his
arm in such surrounds, he could not dismiss their
ostensible purpose in coming there was to prevent
the abduction of his sister by a fortune hunter. If
by some bizarre quirk of fate, Miss Rochelle had
indeed hit upon the truth of the matter, the last
thing Shields could wish was to have the Duke of
Albermarle's granddaughter at his side when he
came upon the culprit. It would be bad enough
that Julia would be witness to what must inevitably
be an unpleasant, not to mention potentially dangerous, confrontation. The addition of a second
gently bred female to such a scene as that must be
was hardly a felicitous prospect. Especially a female
on the order of Miss Rochelle, reflected the earl
dourly. Rather than be content to remain at a safe
distance, he did not doubt that his dauntless Goddess of Beauty, in the interest of preserving her
Twin Soul from danger, was quite capable of thrusting herself into the thick of things.

It was soon made apparent that, with the sun
well down on the horizon, the balloon rides had
been terminated for the day, with the result that

a not insignificant number of disappointed would-be aviators had been turned away.

"If Julia has indeed stolen out to be with Marston at the balloon ascensions and if she is yet within the confines of the gardens, I daresay it has occurred to her that her afternoon of forbidden pleasures is about to come precipitously to an end," Shields remarked ironically as he led Elfrida through the press in the direction of the balloon with its backdrop formed by the breeze-rippled surface of the Long Water. "I wonder what Mr. Marston will reply to her when she demands to be taken home."

Elfrida, who had been searching the sea of faces for the handsome features of Niles Marston, glanced quizzically up at Shields. "You do not believe, then, that she has any notion of what Mr. Marston intends?"

"Julia has ever been possessed of high spirits and an adventuresome nature, Miss Rochelle," replied the earl, drawing Elfrida out of the way of a pair of sergeants in the blue-and-red regimentals of the Coldstream Guards who, passing a flask back and forth between them, gave every appearance of being three sheets to the wind. "Facets of her character that have occasioned her over-protective mama to fret not a little. She is not, however, devoid of all sense of who she is and what she owes her name and position." Shields smiled mirthlessly. "I do not doubt that my mettlesome little sister, far from desiring to run away to Gretna Green with an out-and-out bounder, no matter how seemingly charming, is even now plotting nothing more sinister than a scheme to win her way back into her mama's good graces. And therein lies the danger—if, indeed, she has been so foolish as to trust a man like Niles Marston to abet her in what she, in her innocence, must surely view as nothing worse than an afternoon frolic." Pausing, he peered intently

across the way at the stream of conveyances leaving
the gardens by way of the Carriage Drive. At last
he glanced down at Elfrida. "You may be sure of
one thing, Miss Rochelle. My sister will not quietly
submit to an elopement against her will."

Elfrida, greatly struck by the significance of the
earl's final observation, suffered a sudden wrench
in the vicinity of her breastbone. Faith, if only she
had trusted the earl sooner with her dream of
prognostication! Had she not promised him that
forewarned was to be forearmed? And what had
she done but behave like a silly lamb and give in
to her own feelings of doubt! Really, she should
have had greater faith in the karmic ties that bound
them! There was every possibility that had Shields
been alerted to the danger earlier, he might have
been able to prevent his sister from ever embarking
on her ill-chosen course. After all, even if he had
not been brought to believe in Elfrida's peculiar
gift of divination, he might yet have been persuaded to seek out his sister, if only to talk to her.
With his natural gift of penetrating insight, Elfrida
did not doubt he would soon have been made to
see that Lady Julia was up to something. Indeed,
the more Elfrida dwelt on her failure to understand
at once the significance of the dream she had been
given, the more she blamed herself for the dangerous coil into which Lady Julia must surely have
blundered.

A martial light leaped to her eyes. It was time
she ceased to behave in a manner that was wholly
uncharacteristic of her. She was a Ram, not a lamb,
though one would not have known it whenever
she found herself in Shields's disturbing leonine
presence. She was also a scryer, she proudly
reminded herself, born with the true gift of divination. Whether anyone else believed in her or not,
she knew what it was to gaze into the shew stone

Take **4 FREE** Books!

Zebra created its convenient Home Subscription Service so you'll be sure to get the hottest new romances delivered each month right to your doorstep — usually before they are available in book stores. Just to show you how convenient Zebra Home Subscription Service is, we would like to send you 4 Zebra Historical Romances as a FREE gift. You receive a gift worth up to $24.96 — absolutely FREE. There's no extra charge for shipping and handling. There's no obligation to buy anything - ever!

Save Even More with Free Home Delivery!

Accept your FREE gift and each month we'll deliver 4 brand new titles as soon as they are published. They'll be yours to examine FREE for 10 days. Then if you decide to keep the books, you'll pay the preferred subscriber's price of just $4.20 per title. That's $16.80 for all 4 books for a savings of up to 32% off the publisher's price! Just add $1.50 to offset the cost of shipping and handling. Remember, you are under no obligation to buy any of these books at any time! If you are not delighted with them, simply return them and owe nothing. But if you enjoy Zebra Historical Romances as much as we think you will, pay the special preferred subscriber rate of only $16.80 each month and save over $8.00 off the bookstore price!

Check out our website at www.kensingtonbooks.com.

We have 4 FREE BOOKS for you as your introduction to KENSINGTON CHOICE!

To get your FREE BOOKS,
worth up to $24.96, mail the card below.
or call TOLL-FREE 1-888-345-BOOK

Take 4 Zebra Historical Romances FREE!

MAIL TO: ZEBRA HOME SUBSCRIPTION SERVICE, INC.
120 BRIGHTON ROAD, P.O. BOX 5214,
CLIFTON, NEW JERSEY 07015-5214

YES! Please send me my 4 FREE ZEBRA HISTORICAL ROMANCES (without obligation to purchase other books). Unless you hear from me after I receive my 4 FREE BOOKS, you may send me 4 new novels - as soon as they are published - to preview each month FREE for 10 days. If I am not satisfied, I may return them and owe nothing. Otherwise, I will pay the money-saving preferred subscriber's price of just $4.20 each... a total of $16.80 plus $1.50 for shipping and handling. That's a savings of over $8.00 each month. I may return any shipment within 10 days and owe nothing, and I may cancel any time I wish. In any case the 4 FREE books will be mine to keep.

Name _____

Address _____ Apt No _____

City _____ State _____ Zip _____

Telephone ( ) _____

Signature _____

(If under 18, parent or guardian must sign)

Terms, offer, and price subject to change. Orders subject to acceptance.
Offer valid in the U.S. only.

KN030A

and behold the visions form out of the translucent mists. She had dreamed dreams of things that were yet to be. Every fiber of her being cried out to her that this dream had been a true dream. Lady Julia was in peril, and somehow she must be found before it was too late to preserve her from almost certain ruination.

Hardly had that thought crossed her mind than a harshly uttered curse drew her attention to a tall figure, styled after the manner of one of the Unfashionables in a periwinkle blue cutaway coat, ribbed kerseymere vermilion tights with gaping short slits at the ankles, and white gaiters over patent leather shoes. Elfrida's fleeting glance registered hair so fair as to appear flaxen in the failing sunlight and familiar features that, while handsome, were marred at the moment by a singularly ugly sneer.

Elfrida knew him at once. It was Niles Marston, and he was bent over a slender girl with blond hair the color of gold guineas and blue eyes that blazed up at him in angry defiance.

"I was a fool to believe you were a gentleman. How dare you lay hands on me! You are hurting me!" declared the young beauty, jerking her wrist free of Marston's grasp. "I never said I would marry you, and I most certainly have no intention of going anywhere with you. Indeed, I wish never to lay eyes on you again. Miss Emberly will see me home."

"The hell she will," Elfrida heard Marston growl. "You two-faced little baggage. I shall take pleasure in teaching you the error of toying with me—once you are my wife."

"My lord!" Even as Elfrida reached for Shields to alert him to the scene being enacted within a few feet of them, Marston lunged for the girl.

"Yes, I see them." Shields closed strong fingers on Elfrida's arm. "*Stay close behind me.*"

"Yes, yes. But pray do hurry, my lord. Lady Julia has broken away!"

It was true, Shields saw, as, releasing Elfrida, he strode forward in long, purposeful strides. Lady Julia, an avid equestrian, was a deal stronger and far more agile than Marston must have realized. Ripping the sleeve of her pelisse, she twisted out of his grasp. For the barest moment, she froze, her eyes meeting Shields's over Marston's shoulder. Then, flashing her brother a grin, she turned and darted between the pair of army sergeants partaking of strong spirits in celebration of the balloon festivities. Lilting a hurried, "I beg your pardon," she fled across the down toward a barouche occupied by a colorful bevy of young beauties and an older woman who was obviously acting as their gooseberry.

Marston, recovering his balance, flung himself furiously after her—and was abruptly halted by a hard hand on his shoulder.

"Let her go," ordered the earl, soft-voiced and dangerous. "I believe you have been dismissed."

"The devil I have." Marston came around, his face contorted with anger. His handsome features froze in awful recognition. "Shields, I—! Good God, man, it's not what you think. Lady Julia and I had a lov—a—a spat. You know how it is with females. She ran off half-cocked. I could hardly allow her to-to—"

"No," agreed the earl, a chilling light in his eyes, "of course you could not." Drawing his arm back, he drove his fist into Marston's stunned visage. "Any more than could I," finished his lordship with no little satisfaction as Marston, carried backward by the earl's blow, blundered into one of the two besotted soldiers. Colliding with the man's flask-filled hand, Marston sent the contents flying into the face of his victim's friend.

"The devil, man! Just look what you've done," gasped the victim of Marston's ill-fated assault, a strapping representative of that breed of enlisted man who was the backbone of His Majesty's army. "I've a mind to teach yer some manners, I have."

"Aye, teach 'im a lesson!" roared a disgruntled bystander of beefy proportions who was glad enough for any sort of diversion in lieu of his missed opportunity at a balloon ride.

Marston staggered erect, the back of one hand swiping at the blood from his battered lips. "You and your manners be damned," he growled, his hate-filled eyes seeking Shields, who stood poised, ready and waiting.

"*Damned* is it," declared the greatly offended soldier, his face, dripping gin, going livid. "Why, you bandy-legged little coxcomb." Spinning Marston around, he let loose with a roundhouse swing. "I'll show you 'damned.' "

Uttering an oath, Marston ducked. The sergeant's fist landed with a sickening crunch—square on the bystander's chin. The hapless gentleman was sent careening through a press of cheering onlookers straight into a buxom middle-aged matron remarkable for her tall silk hat bedecked with ribbons and plumes and for her canary yellow pagoda parasol, which, boasting cord edging and tassels, was built in the style of a *marquise* with a hinged stick.

Outraged by the intrusion of arms clasping her to an unfamiliar masculine chest, the matron gave vent to a bloodcurdling shriek.

"S-softly, s-softly, Madam," sputtered the gentleman, hastily removing himself from the matron's person. "Never meant nothing by it, I promise."

"*Beast!*" she screamed upon finding herself summarily released. Snapping the parasol shut, she proceeded to wield it in punitive blows over the

poor fellow's head even as the soldier who had had
his flask knocked from his hand, leaped to the aid
of his fellow sergeant, who was caught up in a
growing melee incited by an hysterical cry of "*It's
the bloody French! Every man for 'imself!*"

"Here, you!" rasped the first sergeant, observing
the instigator of chaos, who, apparently choosing
wisdom over valor, was on the point of slinking
away in the midst of all the uproar. "Not so bloody
fast." He dove at Marston's back, one arm grasping
him hard about the waist.

The momentum of the soldier's attack carried
them both headlong past the Earl of Shields, who,
neatly sidestepping the onrush, turned to observe
their ignominious crash into the fife and drum
sections of the Royal Fusiliers Military Band, which
was just on the point of marching past.

Satisfied, upon being given to see his sister's
would-be abductor vanish in a press of outraged
fife and drum players, that Marston had been given
a cogent message, Shields turned to look for the
divining Goddess of Beauty.

Only Lady Elfrida was not behind him. Lady
Elfrida was nowhere in sight.

"The devil!" Shields cursed, shoving and weaving his way past heaving bodies and flailing arms
in the direction in which he had last seen Miss
Rochelle. It was with a mounting sense of futility
that, breaking free at last of the melee, he found
himself on the banks of the Long Water. Hellfire
and damnation! He should never have taken his
eyes off Elfrida. Better yet, he should have en-
trusted her to Winterbrooke's care rather than risk
losing her in the midst of chaos, never mind that
he could hardly have foreseen the bizarre twist of
fate that would send the crowd into a panic. He
had taken her under his protection, and he had

lost her. Aware of a growing pressure in his chest, he searched in vain for Elfrida among the press.

He was to reflect no little time later that he was no doubt influenced by some sort of cosmically generated impulse to make his way toward the gay red, gold, and purple stripes of the balloon, which had yet to be deflated—indeed, which, firmly anchored little more than forty paces from where he stood, yet rode in hulking grandeur above its earthbound wicker gondola.

A fierce stab of relief, startling in its intensity, shot through Shields as his eyes alit on the Goddess of Beauty little more than a yard or two from the gondola. She had lost her hat, and her hair had come loose from its pins, but she was safe and, to all appearances, unharmed.

It was a relief which was to be exceedingly short-lived. Hardly was he given time to recognize the tall, willowy form trying ineffectually to push her way past the wall of panic-stricken people, intent, it would seem, on fleeing the melee going forth behind them, than he realized she was in dire peril of being trampled—if, that was, she were not first forced backward into the chill waters of the lake!

Feeling his fear like a sharp blade in his heart, Shields broke into a run along the grassy shoreline.

The blade wedged deeper as he saw Elfrida flung off her balance. She was falling when he reached her. His arms going out to snatch her bodily to his chest, he dragged her backward to the safety of the gondola.

Anticipating a measure of gratitude for having saved her from a trampling, Shields loosed his hold on her. He was hardly prepared to have his unpredictable Goddess of Beauty erupt immediately into a frenzied struggle.

"Let—me—*go*, you brute!" Twisting in his grasp, she landed a punishing kick to his right shinbone.

"Hell and the devil confound it, Elfrida!" rasped Shields, clamping strong hands on her shoulders and putting her at a safe distance from him. "You've a fine notion of how to treat a man who has just rescued you from being trodden under by a mob."

Had he thought by that to bring her to an awareness of the extreme peril that she had narrowly escaped, he was to be instantly gratified by his success.

"*Shields!*" Elfrida, her features changing from fierce determination to a radiant glow of recognition, fairly threw herself into his arms. "Thank heavens, my lord. You are unharmed!"

Acutely aware of the delectably feminine form molded to his, Shields wryly smiled. "Not altogether unharmed, it would seem. I congratulate you on your method of defending yourself. You've a punishing kick, Miss Rochelle."

"Dear, I do beg your pardon, my lord," exclaimed Elfrida, nearly shouting to be heard above the din. "You have no idea the indignities to my person I have been made to endure since I was swept away from you in the crowd's sudden exodus. I'm afraid I mistook you for a ruffian."

"A *what?*" Shields shouted back.

"A *ruffian*, my lord. I am almost certain one of that ilk had the temerity to put his hands on me in a most unseemly manner just before you came to my rescue. If I am not mistaken, he even went so far as to push me."

"The devil he did!" thundered Shields, who, laboring still under a fierce pressure within his chest in the wake of Elfrida's near mishap, was acutely aware that she was not out of the briers yet. It came to him with chilling clarity how close she had come to serious harm because of him. Without stopping to think that he had never before felt anything remotely similar to the sickening sensation in the pit of his stomach over any female, let alone one he had known little more than twenty-four hours, he vowed that, when he had her safe from the crowd, he would be sorely tempted to ring her bloody neck for her for having caused him to live such a moment as the one he had suffered when he had looked for her and found she was gone.

"Dear, perhaps it was more in the nature of a jostle," Elfrida judiciously emended, noting the earl's suddenly grim expression.

Shields, however, was not attending. He had little need to look to know that his carriage was, for all practical purposes, inaccessible for the time being and that, further, even if he had wished to make the effort to reach it, it would be no little time before he could work free of the press of traffic. The devil, he was in no bloody mood to wait. He could not recall ever before having wanted anything with the urgency that he wanted at that moment to be alone with the Goddess of Beauty.

"Beggin' your pardon, gov'nor," obtruded a voice on his consciousness, "but I've got to ask you and the missus to stand away, if you will. Mr. Carmodie and meself'd loike to close things down before sunset."

"Would you, indeed," said Shields, his glance coming to rest on the plain, honest face of the fellow standing, hat in hand, before him. On a sudden impulse, Shields reached to extract a handful of notes from his purse. "As it happens, the 'missus' and I are desirous of hiring your balloon for a ride."

Thrusting the bills in the fellow's hand before he could voice any objections, Shields clasped strong hands about Elfrida's waist and lifted her into the gondola. Lightly, he vaulted in after her. "You may expect a similar sum if you make it worth our while," he added to Mr. Carmodie, who, apparently recognizing a golden opportunity when it was presented to him, began immediately to stoke the fire.

"Shields?" queried Elfrida as the balloon, released from its moorings, began to rise. "What—?"

"Hush, my impossible girl," growled Shields, and, peremptorily clasping her to him, lowered his head to hers.

She came to him willingly, her lips parted to meet his. With a groan he crushed her to him, his tongue, thrusting between her teeth, hungry to taste of her sweetness. A low sigh breathed through her lips, and, wrapping her arms about his waist, she melted against him. Never before had he known a woman who surrendered so completely to his caresses. She was all sweet fire and innocence was the divine Goddess of Beauty!

He released her to gaze with a sense of bafflement into eyes that shone, dark with dazed wonderment, up at him. How beautiful she was! he thought, running his hands over the luxurious mass of her hair. It came to him with grim humor that there might be a deal to be said for karmically predetermined passions, never mind that he had always believed a man forged his own destiny. He had the curious feeling that, his life having been irrevocably altered by a divining spinster with the power to make a believer of him, he was poised on the brink of cosmic events that would defy even his considerable talents for controlling his own fate.

It was at that moment that Shields, chiding himself for a sentimental fool, felt the gondola give a sudden lurch beneath his feet. Instinctively, he clasped a sustaining arm about Elfrida.

"The saints preserve us!" uttered Mr. Carmodie in horrified disbelief at Shields's back. "The bloody cable's been cut!"

The balloon, like some great winged creature loosed from its fetters, took to flight.

Chapter 9

When Elfrida had found herself swept away from Shields in the crush of fleeing bodies, she had hardly thought little more than ten minutes later to be borne aloft with him in a wicker basket suspended beneath a monstrous balloon. How much less had she anticipated the look in his eyes that, while rendering her speechless, had seemed to freeze time and events so that while some part of her had been aware that she was rising steadily into the air, she had felt peculiarly divorced from it—indeed, from everything except Shields and the piercing intensity of his gaze.

Really, it was all too utterly fantastic.

And then what had he done, but kiss her! Not with the savage fury of that first time in his bed-chamber, but with a strange melting urgency that had banished the last cold grip of fear from her heart. And, faith, she *had* been afraid—more afraid than she could ever remember being. And how not, when separated from Shields in the midst of sudden chaos, she had been left to imagine any number of dire fates to which her Twin Soul might have fallen!

Nothing she could ever have conjured up in her over-fertile imagination, however, could compare with the reality of the plight in which she and the earl had suddenly found themselves.

Cut adrift from its earthly bonds, the balloon had carried them steadily skyward, leaving the familiar comfort of solid ground far behind them. In short order, the figures below had taken on the bizarre aspect of minuscule creatures no larger than glass figurines. In moments, Elfrida had not doubted they would be shrunken to the size of insects, after which they would be doomed to vanish like infinitesimal dots in a painted landscape. Really, it was a most humbling experience to be made suddenly to feel so exceedingly small and insignificant, not to mention most disconcertingly helpless.

Still, perhaps if that had been all or the worst of it, Elfrida might have surrendered herself to the novelty of being given to view the rapidly receding City, laid out like a map below her. Unfortunately, the attendant discomfort of the bone-chilling cold, which, despite the addition of Shields's greatcoat over her pelisse, had grown more acute with every passing moment, had overshadowed any possible enjoyment in their predicament. Faith, thought Elfrida with an involuntary shudder, they must surely have perished of exposure had they continued much longer as they were!

Hard upon that thought arose the spectre of the more dire possibility that they must soon have exhausted their supply of combustibles to maintain the fire upon which their flight depended. Even Elfrida, whose knowledge of the science of ballooning was of the most rudimentary, had had little difficulty in grasping the adversities that prevented Mr. Carmodie from simply setting them down.

Most immediate had been the breeze sweeping them out of the confines of the park, which had rendered an altitude sufficient to carry them over the treetops, not to mention the roofs of four- and five-story houses, of the greatest priority.

Hastily discarding several of the numerous sandbags attached to the sides of the gondola for ballast had accelerated their speed of ascent sufficiently to prevent an immediate disaster. The concern of the moment had then become the necessity of reaching an open area large enough to allow for a safe landing while they yet had the advantage of a measure of sunlight left to guide them in their descent.

Elfrida, viewing the rustic environs of the cow-byre before her, could not but think that, at the moment, it possessed all the charm of a fine country inn.

They had come to ground. They were alive; and, save for a few bumps and bruises, they were unharmed. That in itself, taking into account the harrowing nature of their descent through a spinney of trees, was a miracle indeed.

Thanks to Mr. Carmodie's skill, in combination with Shields's cool nerve, they had weathered the landing itself, which could hardly have been described as picture-perfect. Indeed, looking back on it, she could not but think finding themselves precariously suspended from the sturdy branches of a great oak tree had more the flavor of one of the cartoon drawings that appeared regularly in the *Gazette*. As for the science of balloon-flying, she could not deny being borne willy-nilly through the air at heights few birds enjoyed not only served to excite the senses to a point of near-hysteria, but engendered as well a positive reawakening of one's earliest religious upbringing, which could only be reinforced by the physical sensation of falling earthward at what had seemed a dizzying rate, although Mr. Carmodie, upon pulling the flap to release measured amounts of hot air from the balloon, had firmly assured her that everything was quite as it should be.

For the sake of politeness, Elfrida told herself she would try and forget Mr. Carmodie's lapse into profane language when it had first become unavoidably apparent that, instead of the wide-open grassy lea on the edge of the spinney, they were going to crash into the trees. As for herself, she had seen little of the actual landing, clutched, as she was, to Shields's reassuringly hard chest, her eyes clenched shut.

It was only with the greatest attempt at self-control that she had refrained, upon being lowered from the treetops by means of a rope to *terra firma*, from dropping to her knees and kissing the ground. Indeed, she was sure she owed it to what remained of her tattered dignity that she had not disgraced herself with a wholly feminine burst of tears at finding herself where she did not doubt Nature had intended.

Shields, on the other hand, apart from a grim sense of how they had come to be in a position that placed their lives in jeopardy, had to all appearances thrived on the experience.

And, indeed, if there had not been Elfrida's safety to concern him, Shields did not doubt he would have given in wholly to the exhilaration of their unlooked-for adventure. As it was, he had been all too keenly aware of the young beauty's effort to mask her fear and extreme discomfort behind a determined reliance on a sustaining optimism and the unshakable belief that they should somehow be delivered from their predicament.

It was undoubtedly that shining display of courage in the face of extreme adversity that opened the earl's eyes to the impossibility of continuing on the course he had chosen for himself. There was not a man alive who could long have remained immune to the allure of the Goddess of Beauty, much less held steadfast to the resolve not to bed her. Things could not go on as they had. It was time, he vowed, watching Elfrida lowered safely to the ground, that he took matters into his own hands.

Sliding down the rope to drop lightly to the ground beside Mr. Carmodie, the earl clapped an invigorating hand to the sagging balloonist's back. "Well done, Carmodie," he said, his eyes alight with an inner fire that had the effect of bringing the other man erect, his shoulders squared. "I daresay it was rather a close thing, there at the end. It is a shame about your balloon," he added, his gaze lifting to the shredded remains of varnished silk and tangled lines draped in disabandon among the branches.

"Aye, she'll not fly again, I'm thinkin'," agreed Carmodie, somberly shaking his head. "Still, it was a grand last adventure. You've the makings of a fine balloonist, if you don't mind my saying so, gov'nor. And the missus, here. She's game as a pebble."

"On the contrary, Mr. Carmodie," confessed Elfrida with a grimace, "I do not hesitate to admit I was terrified the entire time. Furthermore, I am not a mi—"

"Missish sort of female," smoothly interjected Shields, wrapping an arm around Elfrida's shoulders with a casually possessive air. Even huddled for warmth in Shields's greatcoat, Elfrida was not so numb as to fail to sustain a startled leap of nerve endings at that unexpected gesture from the earl. "You are quite right, Mr. Carmodie," the earl continued easily, as if, Elfrida noted hysterically, he

were not perfectly aware of the unsettling effect
he was having on her usual calm self-possession.
"The lady is pluck to the backbone. You were not
the only one who was afraid, my dearest," he said,
next, to Elfrida, who could only gaze back at him
in the manner of one demented. "I daresay we all
were. But then, how one manages one's fear is the
measure of one's courage, is it not, Mr. Carmodie?"

"That it is, gov'nor," agreed the balloonist,
thinking he had seldom seen a couple more
devoted to one another than these two. It was easy
to see they had been wedded more than just a
few years the way the gov'nor was able to finish
whatever his missus had begun to say. It took awhile
to get that familiar with someone so as to know
what the other was thinking. Belike the young
beauty had married the gov'nor only just out of
the schoolroom, and yet, from the way they carried
on together, they might have been taken for newlyweds. Bloody well couldn't keep their hands off
one another, he thought with a pang of envy. Then,
suddenly, it came to him, the reason the gov'nor
had been so insistent on having that last balloon
ride. "It's your wedding anniversary! That's it, isn't
it, gov'nor?" he declared with smiling certainty.
"You took the missus up to give her something
special to remember it by."

"You are a sly one, Mr. Carmodie. Is he not a
sly one, my dearest?" demanded Shields, awarding
Elfrida a look, no less meaningful for all its elo-
quently suppressed humor.

Tired as she was, Elfrida almost choked on an
unwitting burble of laughter. "Sly indeed, my lor—
lord of my—my heart," she answered, hastening
to cover her slip of the tongue, which had earned
her a quelling glance from his lordship.

"There, you see? You have found me out, Mr.
Carmodie," said Shields expansively. "And cer-

tainly there is no gainsaying this day's events have made for a truly memorable occasion. On the other hand, it is not quite over yet, is it, Mr. Carmodie?''

"Gov'nor?'' Carmodie, clearly bewildered at what his lordship would seem to be implying, gazed uncertainly from one to the other.

No doubt Elfrida's sudden aspect of what must have seemed to the man a demure self-consciousness, but which Shields did not doubt was his irrepressible Elfrida's valiant efforts not to blurt out the truth, provided Carmodie the clue he needed. His eyes widened with comprehension, and, had there been ample light to see, Shields strongly suspected it would have revealed a dusky tinge of red pervading Carmodie's cheeks.

"*Ahem.* Quite right, you are, gov'nor,'' blustered Carmodie. "We're a far piece from London Town and with night upon us. I expect you and the missus'll be needin' a conveyance of some sort to carry you. If I may be so bold, might I suggest it were better for you and the missus to rest here while I go and see what I can find?''

"An excellent suggestion,'' Shields applauded, placing a hand on the balloonist's shoulder and leading him a few paces away from Elfrida. "As it happens, I believe we have alit on the outskirts of Islington. I am certain I espied from the air a posting inn not more than half a league from here.'' Pulling out his purse, Shields pressed some pound notes into Carmodie's hand. "This should be sufficient to see to your supper, a room, and the hiring of a post chaise. When you have eaten and are fully refreshed will be time enough for you to return for us. Indeed, I shall not look for you much before dawn.''

"I understand, gov'nor,'' Carmodie all but winked at his lordship. "You've a fine night for it, that's for certain. And belike your missus'll be needin' something to distract her from any lingering effects of our recent adventures."

"My thoughts exactly, Mr. Carmodie," smiled Shields, who, impatient to have Elfrida alone to himself, was heartily wishing Carmodie at that moment to the devil.

He was to be made instantly to suffer an unwonted pang of guilt for his uncharitable thoughts.

"Beggin' your pardon, gov'nor." Sheepishly, the man produced a small knapsack, which he proffered to his lordship. "It isn't much, and I daresay it's not what you're used to, but belike you and your missus'd not find it amiss to share a spot of wine and a bite of cheese for your supper."

"I daresay we shall be greatly restored by it. Thank you, Carmodie. A safe journey to you now."

"Faith, what a hum you fed poor Carmodie," chided Elfrida a few moments later when Shields had rejoined her. " 'Missus,' indeed. And all to save my silly reputation, when you know perfectly well I am quite determined to be rid of it. Really, my lord, I begin to have my doubts about you. Admit it, Shields. You have no intention of making my task any easier for me, have you?"

"As a matter of fact, my dearest Elfrida," said Shields, taking her arm and leading her purposefully toward the byre, "I am become quite as determined as you to overcome any impediment which might stand in the way of achieving our karmic destiny. On the other hand, you may be certain I am just as committed to ensuring not so much as a blemish will ever stain your reputation. You, my girl, haven't the smallest notion what it would mean to be a Fallen Woman."

"It would mean, my lord," declared Elfrida, gazing about the interior of the byre, made to appear almost cozy in the fading light of dusk through the open door, "that you would feel little compunction in taking me to be your mistress."

"Oh, practically none at all," agreed Shields, as if he were perfectly in the habit of requiring any number of young beauties to go out and get themselves deflowered as a prerequisite for assuming the role of his inamorata. "On the other hand, I fear you have failed to consider the drawbacks." Leading her with apparent casualness down the aisle between the driving pens through which the milch cows filed for the morning and evening milking, he stopped at the foot of a ladder that gave access to the loft above. "You must realize, of course, that you could no longer expect to be invited to all of the best houses," he pointed out. "Furthermore, you could look forward to being shunned by those whom you once numbered among your intimates." Scaling the ladder, he disappeared from view.

"Buried, as I have been, at Albermarle the past few years," Elfrida called up after him, "I can hardly lay claim, my lord, to enjoying a large number of invitations as it is. I cannot think I shall miss that to which I have already grown unaccustomed. In which case, I daresay it cannot signify," she observed, pulling Shields's borrowed greatcoat more snugly around her against the growing chill of encroaching night. "And as for my intimates, I can do very well without them. I shall, after all, always have Violet and Aunt Roanna, to whom it would never occur to abandon me." Peering up at the square of darkness, she wondered what the devil could be keeping Shields so long—and was nearly startled into a gasp at the sudden thrust of his head through the opening.

"Yes, I believe this will do nicely until Mr. Carmodie's return," Shields commented with apparent satisfaction. "Perhaps you would care to join me, Miss Rochelle."

Elfrida, who was quite certain she had detected the scutter of a rat somewhere in the near vicinity, was not loath to oblige him. Gathering up her skirts in one hand, she made her way awkwardly up the ladder on feet that felt encased in lead.

"Softly, *enfant*," warned Shields, finding her hand in the dark. A frown creased his brow at the icy grip of that firm, small member in his. Hellfire! he thought, feeling something clamp down like a vise on his vitals. What the devil was *this*? "The accommodations are not precisely what you are accustomed to enjoying," he said with forced lightness. "There is, however, a not altogether unappealing view of the lea to be had a few short paces from here."

"So long as it is snug and confined to this earthly plane, I shall be happy with almost anything, my lord," Elfrida assured him with a wry twist of her lovely lips. "After today's adventures, I want nothing more at the moment than to sit down for a time in peaceful surrounds. Balloon-flying, while curiously reminiscent of the mystical flight of consciousness experienced when one is drawn by a vision into the shew stone's translucent depths, is far more trying on the nerves. At least in the latter, one is spared physical sensations on the order of slowly freezing to death or of finding oneself suspended hundreds of feet in the air from something so insubstantial as a bubble of varnished silk." Involuntarily, Elfrida shuddered.

"My poor Elfrida." Sliding an arm about her shoulders, Shields drew her into the comforting warmth of his side. "How do you suppose it is, Miss Rochelle," his lordship queried with a grim glint in his eye, "that you should be given a dream of the attempted abduction of my sister by a fortune hunter, but you failed utterly to perceive something so momentous as our inadvertent excursion into the realm of balloon flight?''

"Do not think I have not been wondering that very thing, my lord," confessed Elfrida in rueful tones. "Just as I have asked myself time and again why I had not so much as the tiniest premonition of what awaited my mother and father at the end of their ill-fated voyage. I am reminded of something my mother once said as my brother Gideon lay badly injured from a carriage accident. It is God's wisdom that we do not truly foresee what it is to love a child, for then who among us would have the courage to bring children into the world?''

"A child begins by stepping on our toes and ends by stepping on our hearts?" queried the earl whimsically.

"Something like that," Elfrida said, smiling faintly in the dark. "The thing is, perhaps it is a blessing that even a seer is not given to perceive everything with perfect clarity, else who would have the courage to embrace one's fate?''

"I suspect that *you* would, Miss Rochelle," replied Shields, coming to a halt before the twin hay doors, opened to frame a rising full moon beyond the spinney. A hand on either of her shoulders, he turned Elfrida to face him. "I believe I have not thanked you yet for your help in preserving my sister from falling prey to Marston's ill intentions.''

"You have nothing for which to thank me, my lord," demurred Elfrida, wondering why she should feel strangely cut off from all sensation, save for a heavy curtain of lethargy falling over her and an icy knot in the pit of her stomach. "I cannot help but feel a measure of culpability in all that subsequently happened. After all, if I had only thought to trust you earlier with the tangled threads of my dream, perhaps, together, we should have done something to stop Lady Julia before ever she left the house.''

''And interfered with the unraveling of karmic fate?'' demanded Shields, struck anew at his Goddess of Beauty's sweet generosity. Good God, she blamed herself for his sister's folly—Elfrida, who had never willingly done anything in her life to harm anyone! ''If nothing else, I daresay Julia will think twice before she commits the error of placing herself at the mercy of a man like Niles Marston. You may be sure she was told long ago about the sort of man he is. Even Albert, who demonstrates a deplorable lack of common sense and who promises fair to emulate the profligacy practiced by his maternal grandfather, has not hesitated to warn her away from Marston. Little good that it has done.''

''I pray you will not be too hard on her, my lord,'' said Elfrida, feeling an absurd mist start to her eyes. She could not but be grateful to have found someone who, while he might not share her belief in the mystic arts, was at least willing to allow her to believe what she would. In truth, she had not realized how much she had yearned to have someone merely accept her for who and what she was with no thought of trying to change her. ''I daresay she is of an impetuous nature,'' continued Elfrida, who, for the life of her, could not keep the thickness from her voice, ''rather on the order of a Sagittarius, and requires not a little understanding from those who wish only to keep her safe from her own need for adventure.''

''For once you are quite off the mark, my girl,'' declared Shields, who could not at the moment have cared less what punishment might be meted out to his troublesome little sister. ''Lady Julia, as it happens, shares your own particular sign. She is an Aries, born on the twenty-fifth of March. Fur-

ther, you may be sure she will have a great deal
for which to answer from her doting mother, who
will not scruple to use Julia's indiscretion to advantage for a long time to come. That is punishment
enough, surely, without my adding to it. In any
case," he said, bending over to peer at Elfrida in
the pale gleam of the moonlight, "I have had a
surfeit of my family for one day. You look worn to
the nub, Miss Rochelle."

"How very kind of you to bring it to my attention," retorted Elfrida with a wry grimace. "I am
perfectly aware I must look a fright. Strangely, however, I cannot bring myself to care at the moment."

"No, of course you cannot," agreed Shields,
who, far from thinking her an antidote with her
luxurious tresses cascading in an ebony mass down
her back and about her shoulders, was acutely
aware that she had never looked more desirable
than she did at that moment. Indeed, he was swept
with the nearly overpowering urge to crush her to
his chest and rain a multitude of kisses on her
wholly enticing lips. He was restrained only by the
growing conviction that his Goddess of Beauty was
soon to be in dire straits.

Stemming his more primitive impulses, Shields
deliberately set himself to the task of unwrapping
her from the voluminous folds of his many-caped
greatcoat. After which, he relieved her of her
pelisse.

"I regret that I cannot offer you silk sheets or a
warming pan to take the chill from your bed, Miss
Rochelle," he said, indicating a hollow in the straw
over which he had spread burlap sacking to create
a cozy nest. To this, he added her sarcenet pelisse.
"Still, it is a couch of sorts, and, thanks to Mr.
Carmodie, who gives every evidence of having
formed a *tendre* for you, we shall not go hungry to
bed this night."

"How *kind* of Mr. Carmodie." Elfrida smiled, espying, laid out on the top of a wooden barrel, a repast of cheese and a hunk of bread, along with half a bottle of wine, all of which she did not doubt had been intended as the balloonist's frugal supper. "I fear, however, that I have little appetite at the moment."

Gratefully, Elfrida sank down on the bed Shields had prepared for her. Really, it was too much, she thought ruefully as Shields bent to cover her with his greatcoat, that the earl's obdurate sense of honor should prevent him from even so much as snuggling down beside her. She was so cold— indeed, had been for so long she was begun to think she would never be warm again.

She was soon to discover to her bestartlement, that the impediment to their destiny was not sufficient to keep Shields from kneeling to take her feet in his hands, first one and then the other, in order to relieve her of her shoes.

"Hellfire. Your feet are like ice," growled his lordship, vigorously chafing those slim, shapely members.

His growing sense of alarm was not alleviated to discover his Goddess of Beauty was shivering beneath the heavy fabric of his greatcoat. Silently, he cursed the prevailing fashion of thin dresses worn with demmed little beneath them, never mind that, in the norm, he had found a great deal that was appealing about them. Being allowed to admire the seductive beauty of the feminine body scantily clad in gossamer gowns was fine in the withdrawing room or on the dance floor. That particular style of feminine attire, however, left a great deal to be desired in a cowbyre in the wake of an unplanned-for adventure in balloon flight. Certainly, her absurdly insubstantial satin slippers worn over rose silk stockings had done exceedingly little to ward off the chill of the rarefied air at extreme heights.

It was clear she was suffering the aftereffects of exposure, coupled with the threatened onset of shock.

"The devil, Elfrida, why did you not say something?"

"What sh-should I have s-said, my lord?" Elfrida demanded, suddenly unable to keep her teeth from chattering. "We were all of us a-at the m-mercy of the c-cold. There w-was n-nothing you could h-have d-done."

"Perhaps not *then*, Miss Rochelle," grimly conceded his lordship. Shrugging out of his coat, followed soon after by his waistcoat, he reached to undo the yard-long length of cloth at his neck.

Elfrida, however, was no longer attending. Lying curled up on her side, she was willing herself to cease her ridiculous shudders. Really, it was not in the least fair that she should disgrace herself in such a manner before his lordship. Indeed, she must try and get a hold on herself. In vain, she concentrated on unclenching her muscles, most particularly in the vicinity of her midsection, only to be seized anew with the tremors. Faith, what a mull she had made of everything! Far from the role of protector she had envisioned for herself, she was become some abject shuddering creature. Miserably, she wished the floor might open up and swallow her rather than that she be made a burden to his lordship. He must be heartily wishing her, along with her meddling, at Jericho.

Clinging with tight fists to the woolen folds of the greatcoat, she was hardly prepared to have strong hands pry open her fingers, much less to have the heavy fabric forcibly removed from her.

In a daze of disbelief, she cried out in protest and tried to rise. "Softly, infant." A strength greater than her own pressed her down again, reached to undo the fastenings of her gown.

"Stop. What are you doing?"

Shields's voice, quietly commanding, reached through to her reeling consciousness. "Yes, I am a heartless brute, am I not? Now, lie still. We must have these things off you if we are to have you warm again."

"I c-can-not th-think th-this is at all pr-proper, m-my lord," objected Elfrida, ceasing to struggle in spite of the persistent voice in the back of her mind that reminded her of her karmic duty not to do anything to test a Leo's honor.

"We shall worry about the proprieties later, Miss Rochelle. I promise," said Shields, occupied with working the hem of Elfrida's gown up over her hips. "For now, it is only required that you trust me."

"B-but I d-do trust you, my lord," declared Elfrida, her eyes clenched shut against the chills sweeping over her from head to foot. "Indeed, h-how not? We a-are T-twin S-souls, a-after all."

"Quite so, and, as such, you must know I should never willingly do anything to harm you," Shields reminded her, as he rid her of her chemise, followed soon after by her stockings and her drawers. "It would be the same as seeking to deliberately harm myself."

"I d-daresay you c-could never h-harm any woman, m-my lord," loyally submitted Elfrida, who, bared to the chill of the air, rolled over on her side and curled immediately into a ball. "As a L-leo, it w-would h-hardly be i-in your nature to behave i-in a m-manner contrary to your s-sense of ho-honor. That m-much we have already e-established."

Shields, quickly lowering himself down beside Elfrida, reached to draw the greatcoat over them. It was only then, as Elfrida was made to experience for the first time in her life the shock of coming into contact with a hard, masculine body molding itself deliberately to her backside, that she realized *he* was as unclothed as was she!

"M-my lord?" she exclaimed. Her eyes fairly flying open, she went suddenly rigid in the darkness.

"My poor Elfrida," murmured Shields, slipping an arm over her waist and drawing her firmly against the lean, muscular length of him. "I have startled you. I assure you there is nothing to fear in what I am doing."

"I b-beg your p-pardon, my lord," replied Elfrida in a muffled voice, "but I sh-shouldn't think it is f-fear I am f-feeling."

Shields was awakened suddenly to an awareness of the cold touch of Elfrida's foot sliding experimentally down the front of his leg, as she unfolded herself against him. "Faith," she breathed, seemingly unable to get close enough to him, "you are s-so splendidly warm!"

"I believe that is the point of the exercise," observed Shields, experiencing an involuntary hardening of a particular part of his anatomy. Grimly, he smiled. He promised to become a great deal warmer than she could possibly imagine before the night was over. But then, he had taken that inescapable circumstance into account when he embarked on his present course. No doubt it was the price he would have to pay for having been born on the tenth of August to an unavoidable, karmically predetermined fate.

No matter what happened in the next few hours, he would marry Lady Elfrida Rochelle by special license with as great despatch as was possible. He really had no other choice in the matter. In the meantime, he had other, more pressing concerns.

Purposefully, he ran his hand over the silken curve of her hip.

Elfrida, clenched against the persistent chill that seemed to have saturated to her very bones, was yet gratefully aware of what could only be considered Shields's selfless, not to mention tender, ministrations. Indeed, she could not but be greatly moved at the lengths to which his lordship was apparently willing to go to bring her comfort. He must be perfectly aware that, while his motives were irreproachable, the world could not be depended upon to so view them. It could not have been easy for him to set aside his unimpeachable sense of honor in order to succor a female whom he hardly knew and whom he was not even sure he liked very much. Worse, he must surely come to despise her for having placed him in what could only be viewed as an untenable situation. After all, as a Leo and a man of noble generosity, he could hardly have brought himself to do less than his all to help a female in distress even if he had to ruin her reputation to do it.

It came to her that, really, she should not accept the earl's sacrifice. Indeed, she could not but think to do so might very well have a negative effect on their karma that could require several lifetimes to redress. There was no telling, after all, if they did not get things right in this worldly existence how soon they might be brought together again. Some souls spent countless turns around the wheel of life in pursuit of their karmically predetermined, astrologically perfect mates without ever finding them. She, Elfrida, had perceived hers in a vision, which, she did not doubt, had been a manifestation of knowledge possessed and passed on to her by her higher consciousness, which was itself attuned to the ineffable Essence. It was a gift that came to one perhaps only once in a multiplicity of turnings. She told herself she must not allow it all to be flung away now, when she had only just discovered her

Twin Soul. Indeed, it came to her through the delicious fog of contentment in which she seemed to be adrift that she had really ought to arouse herself to do something to stop him.

Unfortunately, the permeating warmth of Shields's body against hers, not to mention the mesmerizing influence of his hand moving over her in slow, soothing strokes, would seem to possess a curative power that was not only having its beneficial effect on her, but had robbed her of all volition. She hardly knew when she had ceased to be wracked by shudders, let alone when she had unclenched her muscles to lie, totally relaxed on her stomach, her entire body wondrously attuned to the pleasurable sensations evoked by Shields's strong, sensitive fingers caressing and massaging the nape of her neck and her shoulders. A long sigh seemed drawn from her depths as the palm of his hand slid down her back and over the firm mound of her buttocks, then back again, slowly, steadily, until she thought her entire being must surely turn to liquid and ooze in blissful surrender through the bed of straw beneath her.

"Shields," she murmured, her voice coming from deep in her throat and sounding absurdly thick, rather like the guttural purr of a satiated cat. "My lord, I—"

"Hush, Elfrida," commanded the earl. "Go to sleep. There will be time enough for talk in the morning."

"I'm afraid the morning will be too late for it, my lord," persisted Elfrida, struggling against the seductive weight of her own languor. Perhaps it was already too late, whispered an insidious voice in her head. In which case, it would be the height of absurdity, would it not, to spoil everything in a silly attempt to avert the inevitable. How much easier simply to allow things to run their natural course.

Perversely, that thought, along with a faint sounding of an alarm somewhere in her brain, served to shatter the spell that bound her. It came to her all in a swift, blinding flash of insight that it *was* already too late—indeed, had been from the moment they were carried away by that ridiculous balloon. Faith, she had been born a prognosticator and a scryer. Why the devil had she not seen it as Shields must have done? It was hardly conceivable, after all, that the sudden and conspicuous flight of a red, gold, and purple striped balloon of monstrous proportions would go unnoticed. How difficult would it be for Winterbrooke, not to mention Albert Herrick and any number of others, to perform the simple arithmetic that would equate the missing earl and Albermarle's eldest granddaughter with the man and woman glimpsed in the gondola? There would be no wrapping such an event in clean linen; indeed, Elfrida did not doubt the tale of their misadventure would very likely appear on the front pages of the morning papers. They must certainly be the talk of the Town.

Shields must surely have realized it from the very first, which was why he had not caviled at sending poor Carmodie off on what amounted to little more than a bootless errand to have him out of the way while the earl—did what?

An acutely queasy sensation in the pit of her stomach, she turned on to her back to peer up at Shields with accusing eyes.

"I think, my lord," she said with rammish directness, "I really must ask. What the devil are your intentions?"

It came to Shields that, if nothing else, he would never be bored with the unpredictable Goddess of Beauty. He could not think of another woman of his acquaintance who, finding herself in similar circumstances, would pose such a question.

He did not pretend to misunderstand what she was asking. "You may be certain, Miss Rochelle," he said, relieved that she would appear to have recovered without sustaining any lasting ill effects from her recent adventures, "that, whatever they are, they do not include taking you to be my mistress."

"Dear," groaned Elfrida, thinking that it was not easy to be a seer possessed with the power to dream dreams of portent, "I was afraid that would be your answer. Really, it is too bad of you, my lord, never mind that I should hardly have expected anything different from you. And now I suppose it will little avail me to beseech Winterbrooke's aid in ridding me of the impediment that stands in the way of our achieving our karmic destiny. You will insist that you have already ruined me, when, in actuality, you have done no such thing. You intend to make an honest woman of me, Shields, and I will not have it. Do you hear? There is nothing you can do to make me marry you."

If Elfrida had deliberately set out to pierce the earl's maddeningly cool exterior, she could have found no more certain way of doing it than to bring up the one haunting possibility that had served to bring them to their present predicament. Shields, well aware that he had erred in not leaving Elfrida in the viscount's care and that, as a result of it, had come closer than he could ever wish to bringing them both to an untimely end, was in no frame of mind to entertain the prospect of a future of similar entanglements.

A fierce light leaped in his eyes. It was time his impossible Goddess of Beauty learned what it was for the Lamb to lie down with the Lion.

"You, my girl, haven't the least notion of what

I am capable of doing," he said in a voice that more resembled a growl. "You goad me too far, Elfrida." Leaning over her, he planted a hand on either side of her shoulders. "And now I think you are about to find out precisely with whom you are dealing."

Chapter 10

It came immediately to Elfrida that her Arian inclination for impulsive plain speaking was going to make for a tempestuous relationship with the lordly Lion, who was behaving, at the moment, as if he had got a thorn in his side.

"My lord," she exclaimed, finding herself suddenly pinned beneath the earl and staring up into eyes that appeared to glow with a ferocious intensity—rather as if she were an exceedingly plump mouse and he were a very large, hungry cat. "Shields, I pray you will take a moment to consider. I never meant for this to happen; indeed, I swore I should do nothing to test your sense of honor. I see now that I should never have brought up the subject of Winterbrooke, and in truth I cannot blame you for-for—but I never dreamed you would-would—"

"Would what, Miss Rochelle?" grimly demanded the earl, lowering his head to torment her with merciless, slow-burning kisses in all the most exquisitely sensitive places—up the side of her neck,

behind her left earlobe, and down again along
the soft curve of her shoulder. "Give in to the
astrological magnetism generated by a 5-9 Sun Sign
vibratory pattern?" Propping himself on one
elbow, Shields fairly thrust the greatcoat aside. "I
am, as you are so fond of reminding me, a Leo,
and you are an Aries." His breath caught at the
sight of Elfrida's womanly perfection, revealed in
the silvery sheen of moonlight. Hellfire, she was
even more beautiful than he had allowed himself
to imagine! She was a goddess of loveliness, all
silken slenderness and womanly curves and valleys.
Egad, but she inflamed his senses! "No doubt,"
he uttered thickly, pressing his lips to the rounded
perfection of one of her breasts, even as he slid
his hand down over the flat firmness of her belly
toward the silken triangle at the end of his journey,
"I am prey to nothing more at the moment than
the cosmic awakening of my primordial passions."
Elfrida breathed a gasp as his fingers slipped
between her thighs. "Which is just as you once
prophesied I must."

"It was not a prophecy, but a vision of karmic
predisposition, my lord," objected Elfrida, who
was, herself, in the first throes of what promised
to be an experience of truly transcendental proportions. Indeed, feeling herself on the verge of cosmic
events, she felt compelled to make one last plea
for the sake of his lordship's honor. "I should never
forgive myself if I have inadvertently precipitated
something that you will later regret, my lord. There
is, after all, the matter of the Impediment between
us."

"An impediment that ceased to exist the
moment we were thrust here together," observed
Shields, marveling to find his Goddess of Beauty
already flowing with the sweet nectar of arousal.
She was all sweet fire and passion, was his divining

spinster, and he wanted her more at that moment than he could recall ever having wanted any other woman before her. A faint smile, distinctly ironic, twisted at his handsome lips. The devil, he thought; with Elfrida, he was given to see how empty his life had been before she dropped into it and totally disrupted it. He was made to envision a future in which he would be kept far too busy indulging himself in providing for Elfrida's happiness ever to feel bored. But, most of all, with Elfrida at his side, he would never feel alone. "Rest assured, *enfant,* I shall not be bothered with regret for this night's karmic pleasures." He ran his tongue over the peaked bud of her nipple. "Tell me, my sweet Elfrida, that you want me."

Elfrida, rendered powerless to avert what her unruly tongue had unleashed, was quite certain that she had never wanted anything so much as she wanted Shields to love her. How strange that, now, when she found herself at the threshold of their predetermined karmic passion, she should suddenly discover she could not see beyond the impediment of his thwarted honor. He was a Leo with all of a Leo's pride. If he took her in passion, his pride would demand that, in all honor, he must wed her. And that she must never do, not even if it had meant he would swear to love her. She would not be the death of him. Faith, it was a riddle to baffle the stars, and she was only a seer with the gift to see glimpses of what might lie before her, and even those were too often obscured in shadows. The only thing she knew for certain was that Shields wanted her, now, this night, and whatever else might lie beyond, she could no more deny him than she could deny herself.

"I do want you, Shields," she breathed, telling herself that to be melded even once in body and spirit to achieve the mystical heights of a karmically predetermined passion with one's Twin Soul must surely be asking enough without demanding love from the fates as well. She cradled her dearest lord's face in her hands. "I have wanted you ever since I first saw you in my great-grandmother Lucasta's shew stone and realized our destinies were meant to be joined."

Shields drew in a swift, sharp breath at sight of the shimmery look in her eyes filled with tenderness and a sweet generosity, and yet he could not fail to note a shadow of something behind her tremulous smile. She was keeping something from him—Elfrida, who, by her own admission, could not keep secrets from anyone. An unfamiliar sense of foreboding stole over him, followed swiftly by the thought that he was a brute to use her so.

"The devil, *enfant*," he rasped, smoothing the hair from her brow, "this was not the way I would have wished to take you." Like a drunken squire, he thought, intent on a roll in the hay! Hell and the devil confound it, he had not meant to take her at all.

"My poor Shields, of course it is not," said Elfrida, who did not doubt his lordship would in the norm have wooed her in an elegant setting resplendent with fine wine and candlelight, not to mention a real bed with sheets and a mattress. Leos were romantics by nature. "I pray you will disregard it." Amazed at her own temerity, she ran her fingers through the thick mat of hair on his chest. "We are lovers. We have need of nothing else."

Lovers! Good God, he thought. She was an Innocent, and he was a man who had taken it upon himself to protect her. He had had many lovers before, but none like Elfrida, who asked for nothing in return. It was the devil's own irony that he would take her *because* he had sworn to protect her. At least, he grimly vowed, she should have the one

and only thing that she had ever asked of him—
she would learn what it was to experience the power
of her own body to transport her to a cosmic rap-
ture.

With something resembling a groan, he lowered
his head to kiss her brow, her cheek, and at last
her mouth—deeply, his tongue thrusting between
her teeth to taste of her sweetness.

Awakened to emotions she had never known
before, Elfrida arched against him. That, however,
was as nothing compared to the sensations aroused
by Shields's hands and lips, teasing and tormenting
her, learning the most intimate secrets of her body.
She opened to him, her fingers clutching at his
shoulders, as he found and parted the swollen pet-
als of her body.

"My lord!" she gasped, her eyes flying open in
startled wonder, as he addressed himself to the tiny
gem nestled therein.

"Softly, Elfrida," uttered Shields, his voice
hoarse with his own primordial passion to possess
her. "This is only one step on the way to our final
destination. You need not be afraid."

"No, no, you don't understand," breathed Elfrida, in the throes of a rising ecstasy of emotions.
"I am a seer and a prognosticator."

"Quite so, my dove," groaned Shields, who,
though he laid no claims to the powers of prognostication, had little difficulty forecasting the imminent necessity of bringing his own torment to a
sudden and climactic end. Hellfire, he felt ready
to explode with his need for her!

"I feel myself on the threshold of a cosmic
vision." Elfrida writhed beneath him, reaching for
something just beyond her comprehension.

Egad, it was too much for him. "No more so
than do I," Shields growled, spreading wide her
thighs and inserting himself between them. Fitting

the head of his shaft in the lips of Elfrida's body, he held himself over her, the muscles of his arms and shoulders standing out in ridges. "I fear— however," he ground out between clenched teeth, "that you are—about to be brought—to a painful revelation."

Elfrida, in a transport of blissful discovery on the order of a transcendence of the mundane to a higher cosmic plane of awareness, gazed up at him with eyes that fairly took his breath away. "We are Twin Souls, my dearest lord. Pray do not be afraid of that which lies before us. It is, after all, our karma to be united."

Shields, dropping his head between his shoulders, uttered a laugh that had more the sound of a groan. Good God, she had not the smallest notion of what lay immediately before her. Still, there would seem to be little point in putting off the inevitable moment of enlightenment.

"Then so be it." Covering her mouth with his, he drove himself relentlessly into her.

His mouth over hers stifled her cry of pain and surprise. Shields went instantly still inside her, the sweat pouring over him as he contained his over-powering need to finish what he had started. Care-fully, he drew in a shuddering breath.

"My poor Elfrida," he rasped, pressing his lips to her temple. "You will no doubt be relieved to know that the worst is over."

Elfrida, feeling herself replete with him, could only stare in mute wonder into the darkness, trans-lucent with moonglow. Indeed, she had never dreamed that his lordship would be built on such magnificent proportions. Stranger still would seem her own ability to contain him. Truly, it was a marvel.

She remained silent and rigidly unmoving so

long beneath him that Shields began to grow alarmed.

"Elfrida." Cursing himself for a heartless blackguard, he lifted himself to look at her.

She lay with her legs clamped about his waist, her eyes opened wide and staring into whatever plane seers gazed. Shields suffered a swift pang in the vicinity of his heart. Egad, this was what came of bedding virgins.

"Elfrida, my dear girl," he said, fighting against the agony of his swollen need. "I daresay you must despise me at this moment." Carefully, he began to move inside her, slow, gentle forays that cost him no little effort at control. "Trust me, Elfrida— to carry us both through."

Elfrida, brought once more to an awareness of her present circumstances, blinked up at him with the realization of reawakened sensations.

"Faith, my lord," she breathed, her eyes wide and questioning on his. "There is more?"

Shields, who had been expecting something quite different from his unpredictable Goddess of Beauty, was driven close to the edge of his breaking point. "Much more, my dearest Elfrida," he rasped, feeling the clamp of cold fingers about his heart give way to unutterable relief at discovering his Elfrida was unharmed by her experience. He began to thrust himself more deeply into her. "We have yet . . . to reach the . . . mystical heights . . . of our . . . karmically . . . predetermined . . . *passion*."

Elfrida, who had thought it was miracle enough to have had him inside her at all, was soon brought to realize that, indeed, that had only been the beginning of something beyond anything she could previously have imagined. She felt herself borne on the pinnacle of the earl's driving passion to the very threshold of the ineffable Essence, the Unknowable Knowing, where many lives before, at the very beginning of the endless Cycle of Being, it had been determined that she and Shields should be as One.

With all of her womanly strength, she reached for the thing that hovered just beyond her grasp.

Shields, feeling her reach, drew up and back.

"My lord?" Elfrida gasped, suddenly bereft when she most needed him.

In answer, Shields plunged himself into her. It was too much. Uttering a keening sigh, she erupted in a pulsating explosion of release at the very instant Shields spilled his seed into her.

At last, utterly spent, they collapsed together to their makeshift bed, their bodies yet entwined.

For what seemed a blissful eternity of pure contentment, but which could not have been more than a few minutes, Elfrida lay, savoring the feel of him still inside her. Faith, nothing she had ever read in her extensive studies of karmically predetermined passion had prepared her for the reality of Twin Souls brought into a confluence of primordial emotions. Truly it was a wonder beyond the descriptive power of words. She wished that they might remain there forever, cut off from the rest of the world. There was the simplicity of truth here that was certain to become muddled with all sorts of extraneous incidentals once they returned to take up their lives in London. Not the least of these would undoubtedly be Shields's insistence on making an honest woman of her.

As if there were anything in the least dishonest in what they had just been given to experience, she thought, suffering a pang of tenderness as she felt Shields lightly press his lips to the side of her neck. Each lifetime on this plane of existence was a precious gift which should be lived to the fullest, else how was one to achieve spiritual awareness? And what greater awareness was there to be had than that of being given to join in body and spirit with the one who was one's predetermined other? Everything else must surely be superfluous, she told herself firmly, even as she quelled the small, persistent ache in her heart that they could never be made one in the eyes of the world as they already were one on a higher plane of existence. Firmly, she reminded herself that while her happiness might be fleeting in this turning of the wheel, she and Shields would find one another again in some future existence.

Somehow it seemed a rather cold comfort at that moment as Shields, bestirring himself, carefully eased himself out of her. Sustaining a pang of loss, she steeled herself for the battle she knew was coming. Shields must never know she was compelled to refuse him because of a dream that portended the death of the man she wed. She knew him too well to suppose he would accept that as sufficient reason not to do the honorable thing. He was a Leo, after all. Even if he believed in the dream and its message of warning, he would rather brave death than loss of honor. Really, it was too bad of him, when they might have rubbed along well enough just as they were. Still, if he would be true to his lionish nature, then, she vowed, she could do no less than meet his pride with the courage of the Ram.

Shields, lifting himself to gaze down at Elfrida, was met with the fierce aspect of a warrior goddess who quickly turned her face away.

Good God, he thought, suffering a swift stab of apprehension. What the devil was this? Lying, sated beyond imagining in her arms, he had never questioned that she must have derived as much pleasure from their lovemaking as had he. Surely she was not regretting the loss of her maidenhead. Hellfire! *Not* after having blithely assured him on more than

one occasion of her determination to find someone, indeed, anyone—even a male Cyprian for hire
or Winterbrooke, for God's sake—to relieve her
of it simply because it had stood in the way of their
fulfilling their karmic destiny—egad! The devil, he
could not be mistaken in thinking she had been
a more than willing participant in the unleashing
of their primordial passions! He would wager his
bloody fortune it was not regret she was feeling.

Still, something had engendered that fierce look
of the Amazon girding up for battle. If it was not
anger or loathing that had sparked it, then it must
be anticipation of what should come after their
having realized their karmically predetermined
destiny of passion. The devil! His impossibly stubborn Goddess of Beauty was preparing herself to
refuse his offer of marriage. It could hardly be anything else, he told himself, and yet, he would not
feel easy until he had got it out of her.

"Elfrida," he said, kissing the tip of her nose,
then her cheek, and finally the corner of her lips.

"Yes, my lord? murmured Elfrida, her eyes
closed, her senses quivering to his touch.

Shields pressed his lips to the valley between her
breasts. "Elfrida, you would tell me if there was
something bothering you, would you not?"

"Bothering me?" she echoed, clearly evading
the question.

Shields smiled grimly. He wished she would look
at him. "I should like to believe, *enfant,* you do
not regret what has happened between us."

At that her eyes did fly open to meet his with a
tender blaze that quite took his breath away.
"Never, my lord," she exclaimed, startled that he
could ever think such a thing. "It was the most
splendid experience of my entire life, and I shall
not have you demeaning it with misplaced feelings
of guilt, do you hear me?"

"Elfrida," Shields began, only to have Elfrida silence him with a fingertip placed to his lips.

"No, my lord, I am in earnest," she insisted, determined to bring him to her way of thinking. "Between Twin Souls, there is a karmic obligation to do all in one's power to banish the barriers that stand in the way of complete understanding."

It was a mistake. She knew it as soon as ever the words were out.

"If that is true, Elfrida," Shields said quietly, "then you will marry me. You are, in fact, obligated to do so."

Hastily, Elfrida averted her face. The devil, she thought in mortification at where her unruly tongue had led her. Shields had trapped her. And she, like a fool, had blundered into his snare. Almost immediately she had herself in hand again.

"I cannot regret that which has given me my greatest moment of enlightenment," she said steadily, meeting his gaze unflinchingly. "I do, however, most humbly regret that I must refuse your generous offer. I cannot marry you, my lord. Pray do not ask me why. Rather than lie to you, I should simply decline to give you an answer."

The devil she would, thought the earl, who had not failed to see the swift blur of dismay in her eyes before she had looked away. With an effort he quelled his impatience. Elfrida would be brought to marry him if he had to carry her off to Gretna Green to do it. He vastly preferred, however, that she learn to trust him with the truth. In the meantime, it would seem he found himself in a devil of a coil. Somehow this day's adventures had to be wrapped in clean linen. He knew, if she did not, what it would mean for her name to be bandied about. He would not have Elfrida hurt because of his own failure to protect her.

"You must know I shall not accept that as your

final answer, *enfant*. Furthermore, while I am not disposed at the moment to press you, I strongly suggest you do not try my patience too far. I will have my way in this.''

"I daresay you are used to having your way in everything, my lord,'' retorted Elfrida, her Arian temper pricked by his arrogance. "I predict this time, however, that you are doomed to disappointment.''

Shields, far from being deterred by her prognostication, had the unmitigated gall to laugh, a deep-throated chuckle that had the perverse effect of sending a soft thrill through Elfrida's center. "You need not have recourse to a crystal ball to see how this will end, my dearest Elfrida. You will marry me. In time you will see you really haven't any other choice in the matter.'' Rising to his feet with an easy, supple grace, he reached for their clothes. "For now, I think it is time we dressed if we wish to avoid being caught in our vulnerable state. I see a well down in the yard. No doubt you will want water with which to refresh yourself. Wait here, Elfrida, while I go and fetch you some.''

Elfrida, however, was not listening. Given to see him for the first time limned against the moonlight in all of his glory, she was brought to utter a stifled gasp. Faith, but he was beautiful! A veritable god of perfection, with broad, powerful shoulders and a magnificently muscled chest, not to mention a long, lean torso rippled thrillingly in all the right places. It was little wonder that he moved with the lithe, controlled strength of an athlete, she mused as she took in his lower half, which seemed wrought by a master artist to represent masculine beauty and a supple power. She was aware of a slow rush of heat through her veins at sight of the stark maleness of him. Even with his male member flaccid with spent passion, he presented a magnificent, perhaps even awe-inspiring, example of his gender. Certainly, the mere sight of him was enough to arouse her to feelings of wantonness and a sharp regret that this moment in time was finite, she thought, watching him pull on his breeches, followed soon after by his shirt.

At last, fully dressed, he called that he shouldn't be gone long and vanished into the gloom of the loft in the direction of the ladder. The spell was broken.

With a sigh, Elfrida slipped on her stockings and her drawers, then reached for her white lawn chemise. Really, she reflected ruefully, sliding her arms through the armholes and pulling the undergarment over her head, it was not in the least fair that she should have been given to find her karmically predetermined, astrologically perfect mate only to have to lose him again. On the other hand, as difficult as it was to comprehend the inexplicable twistings and turnings of a karmically predetermined fate, being Elfrida, she could not but believe there must be some purpose behind everything that had happened to her since she had set out to London. But then, she had known *that* the moment she beheld Shields in her great-grandmama's shew stone and perceived the pall of danger hanging over him.

Suddenly, she paused in her dressing, the gown hugged to her breast, as everything became quite clear to her. If she were to be denied a home and family with Shields, at least she had been granted a part in helping to keep him from danger. Indeed, it came to her that that must certainly be why she had been given the Sight. Surely it was no coincidence that, until she had seen Shields in the shew stone, her gift of prognostication had served little purpose beyond landing her in one ridiculous coil after another. She, after all, did not believe in coincidences. No doubt her earlier, awkward attempts at scrying had been on the order of a learning process to prepare her for this, her one true mission in this life.

It would be enough, she told herself, her eyes drawn to a spider web across the corner of the hay door, glistening with moonlit dewdrops like some lovely, incredibly intricate, glass-beaded thing, to know that she had preserved him from his enemies. And when it was done and she must leave him, she would still have her memories. Growing still, she stared, drawn into the transparent depths of a dewdrop.

It came to Shields, as he lowered the pail into the depths of the well, that a life with Miss Rochelle promised, if nothing else, to be an intriguing affair fraught with titillating uncertainties. He had never known a woman quite like Elfrida, who, in demonstrating a wholly beguiling artlessness, yet had the unsettling knack for keeping him off his balance. Certainly she had surprised him with her sweet, unbridled passion. Egad, he had never known a woman to respond so readily to his lovemaking! How different from the game of seduction at which he played with his various barques of frailty! No doubt it was the game and its rules that had so utterly begun to pall on him. With Elfrida, it would never be a game, and therein lay the vast potential for a delectable unpredictability.

He doubted not he faced a future in which he would never know what to expect next from his enchanting Goddess of Beauty, and yet he would never be brought to doubt in the one thing that mattered most—her absolute and incorruptible fidelity. Lady Elfrida Rochelle was one of those rarities—an unaffected female with a penchant for

honesty. It was not that he believed her incapable
of telling a lie. It was just that he knew as well as
she did that she would be positively wretched at
it. Rather than deceit, she would employ a strategy
of evasion or obdurate silence, which would in its
own way be wholly revealing. Wryly, he acknowledged that there would undoubtedly be times in
which he would be sorely tempted to throttle his
headstrong, utterly impossible love for refusing to
trust him with the truth, but at least he would *know*
she was hiding something from him. Elfrida was
as transparent as her precious shew stone and certainly far more easily deciphered.

She was also maddeningly prone to a single-
minded dedication to whatever cause she had set
for herself—in this case her determination to play
the part of his guardian angel. He could only suppose that in some obscure way her adamant refusal
to wed him was connected to her desire to protect
him, though for the life of him he could not conceive of how she had come to believe that marrying
him would prove deleterious to his continued sur-
vival. The devil of it was it seemed that nothing
short of preserving his life at the expense of what
he had come to believe was his future happiness
would serve Miss Rochelle. It was an irony that
he could well appreciate. It was not, however, a
sacrifice that he was willing to tolerate.

Miss Rochelle, in spite of all her glowing self-
confidence and indomitable courage, was sadly in
need of a man to guide her. Fortunately, Shields
was not averse to taking on the task. He was, in
fact, grimly determined on it, especially in light of
recent events.

Whoever had deliberately cut Mr. Carmodie's
balloon adrift had done so with malicious intent.
That much was self-evident, as was the inevitable
conclusion that it had been done in the hopes that

the mishap would prove fatal to some or all of those on board. If the afternoon's event had demonstrated nothing else, it had shown that whoever wanted the Earl of Shields dead was not averse to cutting the stick of anyone who had the misfortune to be in his company.

Shields's lips thinned to a hard line. It was equally certain that his would-be assassins would not hesitate to use any means to achieve their purpose. Whoever had cut the balloon cable had seen Elfrida with him in the gondola. It was not beyond the realm of possibility that she would be seen as a pawn to use against him. Certainly, those behind the most recent attempt on Shields's life would not scruple to put a period to her existence should she present herself as a threat to their evil intentions.

Shields uttered a blistering oath. Barring shutting Elfrida away in a nunnery under lock and key, he could not conceive of a means of preventing her from thrusting herself into danger on his behalf. He strongly suspected that, were he to order her back to Albermarle, she, far from submitting sensibly, would take to stalking him once more, and that he could not allow. It would be far easier on his peace of mind to have her with him than lurking in the shadows somewhere behind him—egad!

Drawing water from the well, he filled an empty milk pail; then, picking it up, he retraced his steps inside.

It was a pity, he thought cynically, that his troublesome love could not simply look into her crystal ball for the identities of those plotting against him. It would have facilitated matters considerably were he simply to know whose enmity he had incurred. For the life of him, he could not conceive of anyone who had sufficient motive against him to go to the

lengths of trying to kill him. He was swept with a
sudden impatience to be back in London and
about the business of finding his would-be murderer. It was time, he decided, to call in Mr. Elias
Tuttle in order to demand an accounting of what
the Bow Street Runner had uncovered. In the
meantime, he thought, his gaze lifting to the darkened square above him, he must see to more immediate matters.

Whatever else came from this night's events, he
must make certain Elfrida was brought to no harm
by them. The whole must be wrapped in clean
linen, and for that, he would need the help of
someone whom he could trust to keep mum about
it. Odd that only one person should come immediately to mind, he mused with a sardonic twist of
his lips. But then, no doubt he owed that to his
divining Goddess of Beauty. Elfrida, after all, was
the one who had told him there could be no one
better if he needed help in resolving a difficult
problem. Then so be it, he thought. No doubt
there was at least a distant possibility he would not
live to regret it.

Dangling the pail from one hand, he ascended
the ladder.

It was a part of London Elfrida had never seen
before. Indeed, in view of the seedy environs of
soot-blackened, brown-brick houses crowded along
narrow, filthy streets, she was hardly surprised that
she had never had occasion to visit there. Amid
the press of murky shops, rag merchants, and gin
houses, one establishment appeared to stand out
from all the rest—not for its unprepossessing front
of dingy, dirt-encrusted windows, she decided, but
because she felt herself irresistibly drawn to it.

And, truly, hardly had that thought crossed her

mind than she had seemingly melted through the closed door over which swung a weathered sign bearing the inscription, NICODEMUS PICKERING. It was, of course, the counting firm of the man who had sucked the last dregs of hope out of Hepplewaite, she knew, just as she knew that the spidery, sallow-faced creature dressed in a dingy cutaway coat and nondescript small clothes and remarkable for his stooped shoulders, the product no doubt of sitting hunched over his greasy ledgers assessing his ill-gotten worth, must be Pickering himself. Of less certainty was the slender, well-knit form attired in the manner of a gentleman born, who sat in a straight-backed chair, his head held in his hands in an attitude of utter dejection in sharp contrast to the smirk of satisfaction with which Pickering was regarding him. And yet somehow she knew before he lifted his head in a last effort at defiance that it was Albert Herrick who had been drawn into the spider's lair.

"Elfrida. Elfrida, wake up!"

Like a scene caught in a soap bubble, the vision shimmered and shook, then burst. Elfrida blinked and looked up at the earl kneeling before her.

"Shields, thank God!" she cried, flinging her arms around his lordship's neck. "I saw him. He is a dreadful creature. And now he is after Albert. We must stop him. At once, my lord. Before it is too late!"

Chapter 11

Shields, at five and thirty, was cynically aware that he enjoyed the reputation of a man who had been favored with more than his fair share of beautiful women. And who was he to deny it? Certainly, there was no gainsaying the long line of barques of frailty whom he had variously taken under the wing of his protection over the years. He had never been averse to setting up flirtations with females of worldly experience. Indeed, why should he? He was a man with a man's needs, and they were women who had no illusions as to what they might expect from him. As a gentleman, however, he had only contempt for any man who dallied with the affections of innocents. Long considered the Catch of the Marriage Mart, he had maintained his bachelorhood with a chilling determination that had earned him the distinction of being dangerous to single females on the lookout for a title and a fortune. He had been known to dash the hopes of those foolish enough to cast lures in his direction with a despatch surpassed only by the brutal expedition with which he quashed the pretensions of their matchmaking mamas. And how not, he thought, when to do otherwise was to take advantage of their innocence and lead them on with false expectations.

He was the Earl of Shields. He had been born to wealth and privilege—and to duty. The last was something he never forgot. Logic alone demanded that he maintain his estates with the same practicality with which he conducted his daily existence, and, because he was a man of honor, to treat his retainers with fairness. Duty required that he ensure the succession. He had been willing to allow all that he held in trust to go one day to Albert, the next in line; and, thus, with the succession assured, his estates maintained in a manner to secure his continued prosperity, along with that of his tenants, he had been content to live his life unfettered by thoughts of marriage.

All that, however, was before a karmically predetermined fate had dropped Lady Elfrida Rochelle into his life.

When it had first come to him, the impossibility of retaining his objectivity, not to mention his sanity, while seeking to prevent the enterprising Goddess of Beauty from her two-fold mission of preserving his safety and ridding herself of the impediment to their karmic destiny, he had not thought to go so far as to actually bed her before he had taken the necessary steps to ensure her reputation. Indeed, it was not until she raised the spectre of a liaison with Winterbrooke that he had seen with dire clarity the only road open to him.

If she was set on being deflowered, then it would bloody well be done by the man who was to be her husband!

Then, even if she remained obdurate in her refusal to become his wife—and he had not doubted

his infuriatingly headstrong Goddess of Beauty
would put up a determined fight—at least he would
have dispensed with the insupportable distraction
of having to guard her virtue like some bloody
damned duenna. He would have bought himself
the time he needed to bring her to her senses.

Now he was not so sure.

Elfrida was proving that, when she set her mind
on a thing, she could be as fixed in her course as
the bloody Thames. Worse, she had somehow done
what he would have thought was the impossible:
She had won the Countess of Shields to her cause,
along with his sister Julia. Hellfire! He did not
doubt next she would have Prinnie himself lined
up against him.

It was not that Julia and Helen, his stepmother,
were in league to prevent him from wedding
Elfrida, he conceded. No doubt either of the two
would have been overjoyed to have Elfrida consent
to become his wife. What Elfrida had done was to
enlist their friendship. The three of them, in fact,
promised to become as thick as thieves, thus creat-
ing an impregnable feminine barrier behind which
Elfrida might retreat should he so much as broach
the subject of marriage.

It was not what he had anticipated when he sent
word to Helen requesting her immediate presence
at the Ram's Head Inn on the outskirts of Islington.

Naturally, she had heard of events at Kensington
Gardens. Everyone was talking about it. No one, it
seemed, however, had known who was in the gondola upon the balloon's release. She must surely
have had her suspicions upon receiving Shields's
most peculiar summons; indeed, enjoining her to
the strictest secrecy had undoubtedly piqued her
curiosity sufficiently to bring her *ventre à terre* to
the appointed meeting place. He should have
known she would not come without dragging Julia

along. Naturally, she could not bring herself to entrust her wayward daughter to any of her several acquaintances with grown girls making their curtsies in Society, not in the wake of Julia's most recent transgressions. But then, as it happened, it had hardly mattered, since Elfrida had cast her spell over both mother and daughter almost from the moment the two had been ushered into her presence in the sitting room Shields had engaged for their tête-à-tête.

The countess, upon espying Shields's companion, had swiftly put two and two together, or in this instance Shields, Miss Rochelle, and the singular events at Kensington Gardens.

"Good God, Shields, you have gone too far this time. Pray do not tell me it was *you* in that ridiculous runaway balloon!"

"Dear, it *is* absurd, is it not?" Elfrida, smiling wryly, rose from her seat beside the fire. "And yet it did not seem in the least amusing when the cable was severed and we found ourselves in dire circumstances. Strange, is it not, how adventures tend not to be at all enjoyable when one is in the midst of one?"

Lady Shields and Elfrida exchanged a long look.

"Yes," agreed the countess after a moment. "I expect they require some little time and distance to give them any sort of an air of appeal."

Elfrida crossed the room to the countess then, her hand graciously extended in greeting. "Lady Shields," she said simply. "How good of you to come. And you have brought Lady Julia. I am so pleased to meet you at last. Please, won't you both come and sit down. Shields has ordered a tray sent up so that we may all be cozy while we discuss what is to be done. I cannot tell you how relieved I was when his lordship said he had enlisted your aid on my behalf. Shields was quite positive that, if anyone could come up with a solution to the absurd dilemma in which, through no fault of our own, we have found ourselves, it would be you, Lady Shields.''

It had been a masterful stroke, one which might have done credit to Pitt, the Younger, reflected Shields, oblivious to the scenery passing by outside the window of his hired post chaise.

His stepmama, who had been fully prepared to read him a curtain lecture on his deplorable behavior in taking flight in a balloon with the Duke of Albermarle's granddaughter, had been immediately disarmed, even going so far as to positively bridle with pleasure.

"Shields said—?'' The countess's startled gaze went to the arrogant figure of the earl. "*You* said that I—?''

"Can you doubt it, Madam?'' said Shields smoothly, reaching to help the countess out of her pelisse. "Pray whom else should I look to for help in a predicament of this proportion? You, naturally, were the first person who came to mind.''

It was only the truth, never mind that he undoubtedly owed it to Elfrida that he had in this instance thought immediately of the countess, who previously would not even have made the list of possible candidates. Ironically, nevertheless, it seemed for the barest instant that he had overplayed his hand. His stepmama looked to be struggling between disbelief and the tendency for her knees to give way beneath her.

Judiciously, Shields escorted her to a seat in the chair recently vacated by Elfrida.

"Yes, well, Shields was quite right to send for me,'' declared Lady Shields, recovering sufficiently to remove her Venetian bonnet with a businesslike air, thereupon to set it firmly aside on the occasional table near her elbow. "I daresay if we put

our heads together, we shall contrive to wrap the
whole in clean linen. We shall begin first by analyz-
ing the damage that may already have been done.
For example, we can be certain that any number
of people witnessed the balloon's unfortunate
flight."

"*I* saw it," declared Lady Julia, who, seated next
to Elfrida on the sofa, was clearly in envy of her
brother and Miss Rochelle for their unlooked-for
treat. "It seemed suddenly to just leap into the sky.
It was a simply splendid sight! And to think all
along it was you up there."

"I suggest, Julia," remarked her mama in quelling tones, "you would do better not to remind me
of your part in all of this."

"Nevertheless," insisted Julia with stubborn
determination, "it *was* splendid, and so were you,
Shields. I was never so glad to see anyone as I was
to see you. I wanted to shriek when I looked back
and saw you land Marston a facer. It was just what
he deserved for tagging after me when I distinctly
told him I wished nothing more to do with him."

"You would do well to remember that the next
time you think to steal out against your mama's
wishes, brat," admonished Shields with a gleam
of a smile. "Another time, Miss Rochelle's extra-
ordinary powers of perception might not be so
obliging as to guide us to you."

"But whatever do you mean?" demanded Miss
Herrick, fairly bursting with aroused curiosity.

"Nothing, save for Shields's reprehensible levity," interjected her mama dampeningly. "Now, as
I was saying. Any number of people witnessed the
events in Kensington Gardens, including, as it happens, Viscount Winterbrooke, who was kind
enough to call to inquire about Julia's health last
evening."

"How enterprising of Winterbrooke," drawled

Shields, who did not doubt the viscount's visit to the countess was more in the nature of a fishing expedition.

"He was exceedingly courteous," insisted the countess, awarding the earl a censorious look. "Indeed, I am not at all certain he did not come out of a genuine interest in Julia. Your sister, in case you have failed to notice, is far from being an antidote."

"My sister is a green girl, only just out of the schoolroom, and Winterbrooke is seventeen years her senior," pronounced Shields with chilling certainty. "You may be certain, Madam, Winterbrooke has not developed a sudden interest in robbing the cradle."

"Nevertheless," Elfrida judiciously intervened, "he was good enough to inquire after Lady Julia. Did he, I wonder, happen to mention the fate of Shields's curricle and pair while he was there? I cannot imagine what he must have thought when we never came back for them."

"As it happens," replied the countess, "when you failed to return, he sent to Shields's groom to fetch them home. Fortunately, it did not seem to occur to him to connect your disappearance with the flight of the balloon, never mind that everyone is speculating who it was and what happened to them. I believe he assumed you were barred by the mob from reaching the carriage and that Shields chose to hire a hackney to take you home. It would seem, in fact, that there is no one who has guessed it was you and Shields who were carried away. Nevertheless, we shall not be out of the woods until we can be certain if anyone saw you come to ground."

"Fortunately, the evening milking had already been completed," observed Elfrida. "And, as dusk was well upon us, we were not readily visible from the ground. I believe we may safely say the only

witness was the balloonist, Mr. Carmodie, who was
with us, and he, as it happens, was pleased to know
us as Mr. and Mrs. Hogbotham.''

"Hogbotham. Good heavens, Shields," exclaimed Lady Julia, her voice shaking with barely
suppressed glee. "Was that the best you could contrive?"

"Oh, but it was exceedingly clever," interjected
Elfrida. Her gaze, going to Shields, was brimful
with remembered mirth. "As it happened, he was
inspired only just in the nick of time by the sight
of a particularly fine hog."

A faint, sardonic smile touched Shields's lips at
the recollection. It had been a perfectly disreputa-
ble porcine specimen, which he had spotted rut-
ting in the inn's refuse just when he himself was
presented with the need of providing some sort of
response to Carmodie's observation that he did
not even know the names of his comrades in peril.
"Hog—botham. George Hogbotham. And Elvinia,"
Shields had added magnanimously, drawing Elfrida
to his side with an apparently fond arm about her
shoulders. "It seems we find ourselves something
in your debt, Carmodie," he had added, giving
Elfrida's shoulder a warning squeeze to quell what
he strongly suspected was a gurgle of her irrepressible laughter about to bubble forth. "Where, by
the way, are you putting up in London?"

"The Bull and Horn, gov'nor," replied Carmodie, who was preparing to board the mail coach to
London. "I expect my associate, Mr. Jakes, will
have collected enough of the blunt to keep us there
for a few days. At least until we can decide what
we're to do with ourselves now that our balloon
enterprise has come to an end."

"I am so sorry you have lost your balloon, Mr.
Carmodie," had exclaimed Elfrida in earnest sym-

pathy. "Would it cost so very much to start over again?"

"I'm afraid so, Mrs. Hogbotham," Carmodie replied with a philosophical shrug. "It took every penny we'd saved up over the years working the fishing boats off Portland Bill to set up in business for ourselves. I got the idea from a monsoor we picked up off a shipwreck in the Channel. He was full of tales about the Montgolfier brothers' balloon and those two that crossed the channel— Blanchard, it was, and Jeffries. Jakes and me, we were going to do it ourselves once we'd enough of the blunt. Now, I don't know. Start all over again? Beggin' your pardon, ma'am, but I don't think I have the heart for it."

"Perhaps it is too soon to lose heart, Carmodie," Shields had replied, as the order was given to board the coach. "One never knows what might turn up."

"Right you are, gov'nor," Carmodie had agreed, smiling a trifle lopsidedly. "Belike a golden egg'll drop in my lap."

Carmodie had not understood what Shields had been suggesting, but Elfrida had. It was obvious from the way she had looked up at him, her eyes mist-filled and shining. She had worn that same look hours later as she related the story of the Hogbothams to Lady Julia and the countess. The devil, he thought, smiling crookedly to himself. Elfrida could melt icecaps with that look.

She had been right about the countess, too. Lady Shields had taken command of the Unfortunate Situation like a member of the Lords of the Admiralty drawing up invasion plans for the coast of France.

Practically the first item of business had been to order Shields's immediate return to London, where he was to make his regular round of appearances.

"If you are asked, you will say just as Winter-brooke has already suggested—that you and Miss Rochelle were caught up in the mob with no hope of regaining your carriage. By the time you reached home after delivering Miss Rochelle safely to—to . . ."

"Albermarle's Town House in the Campden Hill District," Elfrida hastily supplied.

"Precisely," agreed the countess. "The Camp-den Hill District, where you were graciously invited to join Miss Rochelle and her—er—"

"Sister Violet and Aunt Roanna—" Elfrida prompted.

"For dinner."

"And cards, as it happens," Elfrida suggested.

"I'm afraid, Miss Rochelle," interjected his lord-ship dryly, "you were in no case for cards."

"Shields is quite right," the countess confirmed, eliciting a sharply elevated, arrogant eyebrow from the earl. Shields did not doubt that was the first and only time he had ever been right about anything in his esteemed stepmama's eyes. "Your nerves were quite shattered, as would be those of any delicately bred female exposed to the violence of a mob."

"You went straight to bed," declared Lady Julia, no doubt speaking from vast experience with her exceedingly proper mama, "leaving your sister and your aunt to entertain Shields—who, naturally, was prevailed upon to supply all the gory details of the afternoon's misadventures."

"Julia, really," the countess said quellingly. "No lady of refinement would wish to hear 'gory' de-tails."

"Like hob they wouldn't," said Julia to Elfrida in a whisper, which had earned her the gleam of a conspiratorial smile from the duke's granddaugh-ter. Indeed, Shields did not doubt his indomitable Goddess of Beauty must have found it more than a trifle galling that she was to be cast in the role of a wilting violet who must be sent to bed to nurse her shattered sensibilities.

How much less must she have savored being forced to remain behind with Julia and the countess while Shields set out alone for London to pave the way for her smooth return to Society!

Shields could not but sympathize with the young beauty, who faced the drive to the duke's Town House all the way to Kensington in the company of his stepmother. He himself could tolerate the countess's proclivity for reading curtain lectures only in exceedingly limited doses. How much worse must it be for Elfrida, who would be chafing all the while with the knowledge that Shields was without his self-appointed guardian angel! When it had come to him that the only recourse he had for preventing his enterprising Elfrida from dashing into danger in his defense was to lock her in a cell somewhere, he could not possibly have anticipated that his stepmama would, in all practicality, achieve his purposes by the simple expedient of confining Elfrida to her grandfather's Town House for at least forty-eight hours—the prescribed time, presumably, for a traumatized delicately bred female to recover from fractured nerves.

It was to be hoped, he reflected, as, arriving at his Town House, he stepped down, dispensed with the services of the post chaise, and strode briskly past his studiously stone-faced butler to the stairs, that forty-eight hours would afford him all the time he needed.

"Craddock, be so good as to send next door to inquire if the Marquis of Vere is disposed to meet with me in my study within the hour. You may inform Norton that I require his presence directly in my chambers, and have Gaspard see what he can devise in the way of a cold collation to be sent up on a tray."

Taking the stairs two at a time, he vanished up the stairway, leaving Craddock to stare after him, a broad grin breaking across the butler's normally stolidly impassive features.

In the norm, Elfrida did not doubt she would have derived no little enjoyment from finding herself at Albermarle House after her six years' absence. She had always loved the sprawling Tudor mansion set on a wooded hill overlooking the rolling grounds. Certainly there was no denying Violet and Aunt Roanna were happy to have her in their company again after more than a se'nnight of being apart. Indeed, Elfrida was made to sustain a distinct sensation of guilt at the effusiveness with which she was received, once Lady Shields had partaken of tea, imparted a deal of no doubt worthy advice on Elfrida's prescribed behavior, and then, taking Lady Julia in tow, departed.

"Tell us it is not true!" squealed Violet, hardly before the withdrawing room door had closed behind their departing callers. "You were not really swept aloft in a balloon with the Earl of Shields! Faith, Elfrida, tell us everything. What was it like, soaring up in the sky like a bird?"

"It was perfectly dreadful, if you must know," Elfrida informed her. "It was odiously cold. And exceedingly exciting to the nerves. I feel sure you would have enjoyed it excessively under less trying circumstances. Nevertheless, I really cannot recommend it."

"No, of course you cannot. Far more importantly, what is the earl like?" demanded Aunt Roanna, pulling Elfrida down beside her on the dimity-covered sofa. "How did you come to be with him? You said you were going to watch his back. You did not say you were going to go flying off with him in some horrid balloon. What in heaven's name have you been up to these past several days?"

"I have not been up to anything much, my dearest Aunt Roanna," replied Elfrida, assuming an air of sublime innocence. "I have only saved his lordship from being run down by a runaway coach, stolen into his bedchamber and shot him with Valentine's pop gun—which, you will no doubt be interested to know, was when he was brought to kiss me for the very first time. I have been nearly trampled by a panicked mob, carried aloft in a balloon that was cut loose by a would-be assassin. I was literally frozen half to death before the wretched balloon finally was brought down in the branches of a gigantic oak tree, which I cannot regret, since it meant Shields was forced to set aside his scruples in order for us to achieve our karmic destiny. Only, now what must he do, but insist I must marry him in order to make an honest woman of me, and I cannot. Truly, I cannot."

"No, I daresay you cannot," agreed Aunt Roanna, who could have wished Elfrida had not been quite so confiding. "Never mind that Albermarle will undoubtedly cast the children and me into the streets when he finds out I have so far neglected my duties as to allow you to ruin yourself. And then what shall we do? Faith, I dare not think what *Vere* will do. No doubt he will begin by killing Shields in a duel, which will hardly make Albermarle any the happier. Elfrida, dearest, what the devil do you *mean* you cannot?"

"She means, Aunt Roanna," supplied Violet in reasonable tones, "that she cannot. I daresay it is written in the stars or some such thing, in which case there is absolutely no use in crying over what cannot be helped. And as for Albermarle flinging you out of the house, it would hardly signify, would it, since Elfrida will undoubtedly take you and the children to live with her in Mama's house in Bath. It *is* rightfully Elfrida's now, and there is nothing Grandfather can do about it. Does this mean, Elfrida, that we may now return home to Albermarle? I mean, if you are ruined, after all, there would hardly seem any purpose in my making my curtsey, would there?"

"Pray do not be absurd, Violet," replied Elfrida, who thought she had never been more fond of her sister and aunt than she was at that moment for so blithely relegating her ruination to the realm of the perfectly normal. "There is every reason for you to make your curtsey, and absolutely none why you should not. I, after all, have been wrapped in clean linen. Lady Shields has seen to that. And now, if the countess has her way, I shall be consigned to oblivion while Shields conducts his search for those who wish him dead, when he swore I should be allowed to help him. Really, it is the shabbiest thing."

"It is only if you do as the countess told you," Violet observed, sinking down on the floor at her sister's feet to gaze dreamily up at Elfrida. "Who is to say the countess must have her way?"

"*I* do," said Aunt Roanna, eying Violet in dawning horror. "I do most emphatically. Not that it will matter one way or the other what I say."

"But Violet is in the right of it!" exclaimed Elfrida, who could only suppose her wits had been dulled from excessive exposure to the countess's uninterrupted exposition on the vagaries of the modern generation which she had been made to endure all the way to the Campden Hill District. "I have every right to go anywhere I choose. After all, it is not as if I were not perfectly content to be a Fallen Woman. Especially as it was the criterion upon which Shields insisted before he would consider taking me as his mistress."

"His mistress! Good God, Elfrida," groaned Aunt Roanna, giving every appearance of one on the verge of a sharp decline. "What in heaven's name are you saying?"

"You know very well what I am saying," Elfrida asserted, patting her distraught kinswoman's hand held in hers. "It is all perfectly logical when you look at it rationally. Shields is, after all, my karmically predetermined, astrologically perfect mate, which means we are meant to be together. Unfortunately, a cruel twist of fate has decreed that I cannot be his wife on this plane of existence. Therefore, I am left with very little choice in the matter. Since I should not willingly choose to disavow my Twin Soul, the man I was born to love, I shall be content to be his mistress."

"You may be sure Albermarle will not be content with it. Nor Vere—good God," Aunt Roanna predicted with a shudder. "I daresay you will be consigning Shields or your brother or both to an untimely end on the field of honor."

"Aunt Roanna is right, Elfrida," spoke up Violet, her lovely eyes neither distant nor dreamy, but distinctly troubled. "Such a course would be courting disaster."

It was a point Elfrida had not previously considered. Possessed of an unshakable faith that somehow everything would come out right in the end, she had vaguely assumed her brother would simply understand her position and do the sensible thing by choosing not to interfere. He was a Scorpio, blessed with the power of insight into the motivations of others. Surely he would know how much Shields meant to her and spare her the anguish of engaging in a duel over what should not concern him. Shields had, after all, proposed marriage to her. It was hardly his fault if she could not accept his offer.

Gideon would understand. Gideon always understood.

"The truth of the matter," declared Vere, favoring Shields with his cold, unwavering stare, "is you were alone with my sister for the entire night. How, my lord, do you suggest I should receive that titillating tidbit of news?"

"With the knowledge that I am fully prepared to marry your sister with all due haste," replied the earl, calmly filling two glasses from a decanter of brandy. "Unfortunately, the lady has refused my offer."

"How very like Elfrida to behave contrary to expectations," observed Vere with chilling dispassion. Accepting a glass from his host, he languidly swirled the amber liquid, while continuing to study the earl's impassive features. "And now that you have satisfied the demands of honor, am I to presume you intend to let matters stand as they are between you? Is that why you have asked me here for this little tête-à-tête?"

"I think you know better than that, my lord," declared Shields, testing the aroma of the brandy in his glass. "I fully intend to marry your sister, if I have to cart her off to Gretna Green to do it. I require only a little time to try and overcome what she perceives as an insurmountable barrier to becoming my wife."

"Ah, a barrier," nodded Vere, smiling ever so gently. "I should have known, of course. And you, my lord, have been left in the dark as to the nature of this obstacle? Yes, I can see that you have. I did warn you, my friend. Elfrida is like no other female. Whether or not she is truly gifted with the Sight hardly matters so long as *she* believes it. It may be that not even you can break through the barrier she has envisioned between you. In which case, I feel obligated to ask, my lord. What will be your intentions should you fail in your task?''

"You are mistaken," replied Shields, meeting Vere's gaze unflinchingly. "The question is, what do *you* intend doing in the interim?''

A long look passed between the Scorpion and the Lion. Shields, an expert card player, was in the norm unsurpassed at reading the minds of his opponents. Silently, he cursed the young devil's whelp, even as he was moved to a reluctant admiration. Vere's cold-blooded stare was most damnably impenetrable.

The marquis's smile came, gently mocking. Deliberately, he lifted his glass to the earl. "I, my lord, shall remain a most interested observer. In the meantime, I wish you all good fortune in your worthy endeavor.''

Slowly, Shields let his muscles go lax. "To the Incomparable Elfrida," he said, matching Vere's gesture of salute.

"To Elfrida," concurred Vere, raising his glass to his lips. "May she not prove the Inconquerable." Then, meeting Shields's glance over the rim, "For both our sakes," he added gently, and drank.

Night had fallen when Shields stepped into his carriage and ordered Milburn to drive him to Lord Winterbrooke's. After an exceedingly enlightening session with Norton, his private secretary, the earl was hardly in the mood for one of Winterbrooke's mixed gatherings of bachelors and ladies of questionable reputation. Indeed, he undoubtedly would have cried off had it not been for the necessity to fulfill his obligation to nip any rumors in the bud concerning his conspicuous absence from Town in the wake of the balloon fiasco and riot. The certainty, in addition, that he would find his Cousin Albert in attendance had exerted no small influence on the earl's decision to accept Winterbrooke's written invitation, which Shields had found waiting for him on his return from Islington. Winterbrooke, he did not doubt, would be anticipating his old friend's arrival with a keenly honed curiosity.

Albert, on the other hand, might very well soon be wishing his cousin at Jericho, reflected Shields grimly, recalling to mind the look on Elfrida's face when he had come upon her, staring blankly into a spider's dew-beaded web.

Good God, his first thought, that the cumulative effects of her recent harrowing adventures in conjunction with the climactic event of their cosmically generated passion had served to unhinge her mind, had been enough to cause him to feel a cold vise clamp down on his vitals. Hardly less disconcerting had been the stark fear in her eyes when he had awakened her to his presence.

Upon retrospect, he had little difficulty determining a rational explanation for the dreamvision that had visited her—his mention of Nicodemus Pickering by name as the cent-per-cent who had got his claws into Hepplewaite must naturally have suggested the villainous character, not to mention the seedy setting, even as his observation that Albert promised fair to follow in the profligate steps of the young whelp's maternal grandfather must have triggered Albert in the role of the victim. And she *had* been staring into a spider's web, hence the spidery image of the bloodsucking money lender. Even so, Shields had still been unable to shake the uneasy premonition that Albert might indeed have got himself into deep waters.

It was, in fact, a feeling that he had entertained for no little time, only he had been too caught up in Hepplewaite's demise to heed the signs. Thanks to Elfrida's unnerving declaration, he had been brought to recall distinct peculiarities in Albert's behavior—his cousin's recent preoccupation with the seductively beautiful Mrs. Blakeley, which had led him to spend far too much of his time of late at her gaming establishment than was good for him, not to mention his newly developed penchant for excessive outbursts of gaiety whenever he found himself in Shields's proximity. Shields had, in addition, begun to suspect Albert had taken to dipping rather deeply of late; indeed, he did not doubt the young fool had already been bright in the eye upon the event of their encounter in Kensington Gardens, a circumstance that he had remarked at the time and then relegated to the back of his mind for later cogitation.

It would seem that time was now. If he could not bring himself to accept that Elfrida was possessed of the powers of prognostication, he nevertheless could not deny that she had thus far demonstrated a most damned uncanny knack for apprehending when trouble was at his doorstep.

Norton, with his customary efficiency, had had a deal to report on the subject Shields had given him to research in the wake of Mr. Tuttle's earlier visit, followed soon after by Shields's near fatal mishap on Bond Street. That Albert should have formed the most interesting part of Norton's findings was somehow not the surprise that it might otherwise have been.

Shields, entering Winterbrooke's four-story brown brick on Portman Square, checked his greatcoat, then made his way along the gallery overlooking the crowded ballroom below. Despite the fact that Winterbrooke's galas were not considered *de rigueur,* they never lacked in attendance. Though it was true no lady of fashion would have deigned to set foot across the threshold, there was not a dearth of gaily dressed females dancing or making eyes at the numerous gentlemen. For the most part they were the tainted beauties who lived on the fringes of fashionable society, the demimonde who depended upon the favors of wealthy gentlemen for their very existence. For the space of a heartbeat or two his glance fell and lingered on the slender figure of a gentleman, masked and draped in a black domino. The scion, no doubt, of a wealthy house who preferred to enjoy his forbidden pleasures incognito, Shields idly speculated, and allowed his gaze to move on in search of his cousin.

It was not long before he discovered Albert paying marked attention to a striking redhead, who, in her early thirties, was elegantly attired in the first stare of fashion. The lady, it was obvious, had her hooks in Albert. But then, that was hardly surprising. It was Shields's purpose in coming tonight to face Albert and the tart who had made him a tool for Shields's enemies.

"Shields, old man," came a familiar masculine voice from behind him. "I'd begun to believe you had chosen not to honor us with your presence tonight. No doubt you will pardon my curiosity. But what the devil happened to you yesterday?"

"Yes, what did happen to you—and the lady? Miss Rochelle, did you say, Oliver dearest?"

Shields, allowing the bored mask of the Corinthian to drop like a shutter over his handsome features, came about to meet his oldest friend—and Sylvia, his former mistress.

"Yesterday?" he queried, elevating a quizzical eyebrow. "Ah, yes—the regrettable incident of the riot at Kensington Gardens. I have yet to thank you,

Winterbrooke, for seeing my cattle were fetched home."

"As a matter of fact, you do," agreed Winterbrooke, eyeing his friend with appreciative amusement. "Not that you left me any choice in the matter. You never came back, old friend."

"Through no fault of my own, I assure you," replied Shields negligently. "We were carried away by the mob. It was only by the merest chance that I happened on a hackney. Naturally, my only concern was to see the lady safely home."

"How very distressing for Miss Rochelle," observed Lady Loring, fairly purring with malice. "I daresay I should have been forced to take to my bed in the wake of so frightful an experience."

"But of course you would, Sylvia, my pet," said Winterbrooke, dropping a kiss on one of her soft, white shoulders where it met the curve of her neck. "The devil, I'd have taken *me* to your bed."

The beautiful Sylvia's china-blue eyes above her fluttering fan met Shields's with malicious satisfaction.

"But not Miss Rochelle's, my lord Shields? How unlike you to dally with spinsters. I hear she is on the shelf."

"Whatever she is," replied Shields, soft-spoken and chillingly deliberate, "she is a lady—something I have come lately to appreciate." In the sudden ensuing silence, he inclined his head with negligent grace. "Winterbrooke. Madam. No doubt you will both excuse me. I see Alfred waiting to accost me."

Behind the earl's retreating back, Winterbrooke gave vent to a low whistle. "Not precisely what you were expecting, was it? My poor Sylvia, it would seem that, while your barb hit its mark, you were the one who was pierced—to the quick, I might add. But then, you should have known better than to cross swords with a man like Shields. I'm afraid, my dear, you simply are not up to his weight."

"No more than are you, Oliver, darling," returned Lady Loring with venomous displeasure. "I am not the first of his castaways with whom you have taken up. I wonder, Oliver, do you never grow weary of playing second fiddle to his lordship?"

"Weary, my beautiful Sylvia? Of Shields?" murmured Winterbrooke, his charming smile peculiarly devoid of its usual humor. "On the contrary, my dear, his conquests never cease to amuse me. I have made a study of his ladies—out of curiosity to know what he ever saw in them."

Lady Loring's head came up, her eyes flashing sparks of resentment.

"Quite so, my dear," Winterbrooke said ever so gently. "And now, the minuet is starting up. No doubt you would care to dance."

Shields, making his way around the press of dancers, was unaware of Winterbrooke's leading a considerably deflated Lady Loring out onto the dance floor.

In the course of his verbal exchange with the viscount and his former mistress, Shields had lost sight of Albert. That his cousin would appear to have exited the ballroom should not in the norm have occasioned the earl any misgivings. Albert might be anywhere—outside on the terrace or in one of the numerous card rooms or fetching a glass of punch from the alcove reserved for refreshments. Hell and the devil confound it, Shields cursed, chiding himself for a fool. The troublesome whelp might be involved in nothing more innocuous than relieving himself in the water closet. No doubt he could attribute to his divining Goddess of Beauty the peculiarity that he had taken of late to being plagued with sudden queasy sensations in the pit of his stomach which he had come to interpret as premonitions of an ominous nature, when very likely they owed themselves to nothing more extramundane than a digestive disturbance as a consequence of something he had eaten.

The fact remained, however, that he had experienced an immediate pang of uneasiness upon the discovery that his cousin was nowhere in sight, a sensation that had not been alleviated by the notable absence of the red-haired beauty over whom Albert had been fawning like a lovestruck mooncalf.

But then, Albert was in over his head. Worse, the young cub had not the smallest inkling of the coil he had got himself in.

Shields halted, debating where to begin his search.

"My lord," murmured a low, husky voice at his elbow. "He has gone upstairs to be alone with the lady. I think we must hurry. I feel he is in grave danger—indeed, I am sure of it."

Shields, sustaining a decided pang of premonition, came sharply about.

"The devil!" he cursed, regarding the slender form in the black domino and mask with something less than his usual sangfroid. "*Elfrida.* What in hell's name are you *doing* here!"

Chapter 12

It had come to Elfrida, as she disembarked from her hired coach, that perhaps she should have chosen a feminine costume for crashing the gates of Winterbrooke's gala. She did not doubt that, while a female garbed in mysterious attire would have been welcomed as an interesting diversion, the same could hardly be said for a masked gentleman draped in a domino. But then, she had wished to avoid the complications inherent in attracting a bevy of gentlemen admirers to her, which must surely have been inevitable had she come in the garb of a *femme fatale*. Still, she was not displeased with her appearance. She was tall for a woman, and with her hair subdued in a queue at the nape of her neck and most of her face covered with the black mask of a Harlequin, she might easily be taken for a young gentleman dressed to remain incognito.

No doubt she was fortunate to have arrived immediately after a pair of beauties, who did not hesitate to eye Elfrida's intriguing presence with unabashed interest. There was something exceedingly delectable about pretending to be something one was not, decided Elfrida, flinging herself wholeheartedly into the role of a gallant with a roving eye. Far from piercing her disguise, the two gave every evidence of being charmed by their supposed cavalier's adoption of the silent attributes of a mime, even going so far as to link arms with Elfrida, one on either side, and lead her gaily past the stone-faced butler standing guard at the door.

Once inside, she had amused herself with blending into the scenery while she looked for Shields to arrive. It was purely by happenstance that, while perched in a windowseat partially concealed by potted palms and damask drapes, she had been in the position to eavesdrop unintentionally on any number of private conversations. Indeed, she was quite certain Lady Edgecroft's ears must have been burning wherever and whoever she was. It seemed the whole world was perfectly aware that she was carrying on an illicit affair with her groundskeeper, and, indeed, who could blame her when her husband was forty-five years her senior and withered besides, while the groundskeeper was a strapping blond Welshman of three and twenty? Elfrida, unhappily reminded of Albermarle's proposed nuptials, came swiftly to the conclusion that *she* could blame the unknown Lady Edgecroft, who should have at least had the common decency to keep her young Welshman under wraps. She found her own ears were burning when more than one discussion turned to the subject of the mysterious couple who had apparently eloped in a balloon from Kensington Gardens. Speculation had ranged from the sublime to the ridiculous, although Elfrida's favorite held that the mysterious duo were French spies who, having run afoul of a pair of intrepid sergeants of the Coldstream Guards, had effected a daring escape by balloon.

Upon that amusing note, Elfrida, deciding she had been privy to more than enough of the gibble-gabble going the rounds, was just on the point of slipping away to a less popular spot when she was barred from leaving by the arrival of a blond beauty in the company of a young officer in scarlet regimentals with the blue facings and rich gold lace of the Life Guards.

Elfrida would, in any case, have been rooted to the spot.

"*Shields,* Freddy," hissed venomously from the lady. "My God, how I loathe that name. No more so than I despise the man, however. He is coming here tonight. Winterbrooke took great pains to see to that. I daresay he cannot wait to flaunt his latest acquisition in front of Shields. *Me,* Freddy, as if I were just so much bartered goods. Faith, how I loathe all of them. I would see Shields dead, if I could, and Winterbrooke with him."

"Not, I hope, before the viscount has been obliging enough to contribute a sizeable sum to our growing nest egg," blithely commented the young officer. Drawing forth an enameled snuffbox and extracting a pinch, he inhaled the stuff before continuing. "A pity you could not have kept the wool over Shields's eyes only a trifle longer. You know what they say: Two purses are better than one, and I did so have my heart set on Oxford Blues."

"Pray don't be a fool, Freddy. One bird in the hand is better than none, and it was only a matter of time before Winterbrooke boasted of his coup to Shields. I was glad to leave the earl's wretched house on Holles and take up permanent residence in Baker Street. You cannot know how tedious it was having to come up with excuses for why I was not home to one or the other. And at least the house on Baker Street is furnished in the Egyptian. Faith, how weary I was of Shields's fondness for Jacobean austerity!''

"Almost as weary as you were of Shields himself, I shouldn't wonder, considering the haste with which you vacated the place. Shields did say there was no hurry.''

"And wait to have him throw me out and be twice insulted by the same man? I think not. I should have been pleased to cut his heart out for him after the way he humiliated me. No man breaks it off with Sylvia, Lady Loring, and does so with impunity. I swear I shall make him pay for it if it is the last thing I do.''

"Perhaps, my dearest sister, you will not have to do anything,'' suggested Freddy in sly tones, which had the effect of causing Elfrida to clench her hands into fists at her sides. "Am I not mistaken, that is Albert Herrick in the company of Mrs. Blakeley. A formidable woman, Mrs. Blakeley. I have it from reliable sources she has made a sizeable fortune from luring inexperienced young gentlemen to play at Hazard in her gaming house in exchange for the promise of her favors. From the looks of him, I daresay Mrs. Blakeley will have young Herrick on the rocks to the tune of several thousands before she is through with him.''

"Freddy, dear,'' crooned Lady Loring, "you do have your moments. Herrick is Shields's heir, is he not?''

"He is until the earl should decide to set up his nursery.''

"Then I wish Mrs. Blakeley well of him,'' laughed Lady Loring, moving away from the window fronted by the potted palms, the leaves of which, curiously enough, appeared to be shaking from a nonexistent wind. "Indeed, I hope she may bleed them both dry.''

Elfrida, left trembling with unadulterated Arian fury, was hard-put not to fling herself after Lady Loring and her wholly despicable brother. Only the sight of Albert Herrick, being led across the ballroom floor by a woman, striking for her flaming red hair, not to mention her slink-hipped air of seduction, brought Elfrida to her senses.

Good God, what had Shields been thinking when he allowed his cousin to fall into the toils of an out-and-out vampire! Even if she had not just overheard what she had never been meant to hear, Elfrida would still have known Mrs. Blakeley for what she was. Surely, Shields, with all his worldly experience, could never be fooled by such a one. But then, Shields, she was immediately reminded, had been just a trifle busy of late. One could hardly blame Shields if he had failed to notice Albert was being lured into the spider's web when Shields himself was being stalked by a relentless assassin.

Surely, however, he would see it now, she thought, her heart leaping at sight of the tall, eminently arrogant figure peering down into the ballroom from the gallery above. She breathed a sigh of relief as she saw his gaze find Albert.

Her relief was to be exceedingly short-lived. Hard upon the thought that, having seen Albert's peril, he would immediately descend the stairs to extract his cousin from the vampire's unsavory sphere of influence, Elfrida knew that he would not.

It was curiously like being caught up in one of her dream-plays in which she was an observer able to perceive the whole while she herself remained strangely detached and unobserved: There was Winterbrooke, on the gallery in conversation with some of his guests; Shields, at the gallery wall, looking down into the ballroom at Albert in the throes of his first love; and Lady Loring, at the viscount's side, her eyes coming to rest on the tall, arrogant figure of her former lover.

Elfrida's breath caught. There was no mistaking the blond beauty's malevolent dislike as she let her gaze follow that of the earl's—or her malicious intent, as she directed Winterbrooke's attention to the presence of his oldest friend. She watched Shields turn, held her breath as he stood, curiously watchful despite his elegant pose of nonchalance, while he was engaged in conversation by Winterbrooke and the beautiful Lady Loring. And now, just when it would appear that Albert needed him the most, Shields had his back to him!

There really was little else that Elfrida could do but follow as Mrs. Blakeley lured Albert Herrick from the ballroom, up the curving staircase. How strange that they should pass so near where the three stood talking, oblivious to the drama being enacted only a few yards away! If only she dared call out, to alert Shields somehow to Albert's peril! Only the certainty that anything quite so brash as to call attention to herself in her indecent attire would serve little save to bring scandal down on all their heads kept her from it.

Elfrida, finding herself some little time later poised uncertainly in a hallway before a closed door, could only attribute her present circumstances to her Arian propensity for impulsive behavior, not to mention her inability to resist taking on a cause whenever it presented itself. Nevertheless, she did not require extra-ordinary powers of perception to know Mrs. Blakeley's intentions toward Albert Herrick were not to be trusted.

Turning, she made her way down to the gallery where last she had seen Shields. She was in time to see Winterbrooke escort Lady Loring down the stairs to the ballroom—and beyond them, Shields, working his way around the press of dancers obviously in search of Albert.

Swiftly, she went in pursuit of the earl.

"The devil!" cursed Shields some moments later. *"Elfrida.* What in hell's name are you *doing* here!"

"*Softly,* my lord!" admonished Elfrida, darting a quick glance about her. "You will have everyone know who I am."

"I shall do a deal more than that," Shields grimly predicted, "when I have you to myself directly. I thought we were agreed you would remain sight unseen for at least the next forty-eight hours."

"But I *am* unseen, for all practical purposes," the irrepressible Elfrida did not hesitate to point out. "Who but you would think to connect a gentleman domino with Albermarle's eldest granddaughter?"

"Perhaps, miss malapert, the gentleman who has just entered the ballroom," Shields replied, his eyes on a slim, elegant figure in black evening dress who was poised at the top of the curving stair.

"Dear! How *like* Vere to show up just when I might particularly have wished that he would not," uttered Elfrida as, following Shields's gaze, she melted instinctively into the shadows of a recess behind her. "I suggest, my lord, that we should be better served retreating upstairs to see to your cousin's welfare than waiting here for Gideon to spot us. One can never be quite certain what my brother will do in any given situation."

Shields, in no mood for a discussion on the unpredictability of the marquis, turned without comment and conducted Elfrida through the door at her back, which gave, as it happened, admittance to the service stairs. Nor was he content to stop there. Grabbing her hand, he led her up two flights before pausing to open a door off the landing and, after putting his head through to glance left and right, pulled her into a deserted hallway.

"Now, Miss Rochelle," he pronounced in dire accents, taking an ominous step toward her. "I shall not bother to ask how you knew to find me here. I daresay you will tell me you looked into your crystal ball . . ."

"Then, my lord, you would be greatly mistaken," retorted Elfrida, her temper flaring at his unwarranted assumption. Firmly standing her ground, she faced him with her hands on her hips, which caused the domino to part in front to reveal her slender form indecently attired in a gentleman's *habit à la française.* "As it happens, Lady Shields made the comment that she did not doubt you would be attending Winterbrooke's gala tonight. It seems that Albert let it slip that he could not serve as Julia's escort to Lady Hedley's soiree because he was already promised to Winterbrooke's. It was only *one* of the countess's innumerable examples of the baited traps that lie in wait to lure our misguided youth to abject lives of dissolution and vice."

Shields, who was given a fair image of just what his Goddess of Beauty had been made to suffer at the hands of his stepmama, had, perforce, to resist the unruly impulse to snatch Elfrida to his chest. Egad, dressed in skin-tight unmentionables, she was a cursedly delectable morsel. Indeed, the mere sight of her was enough to make him wish to take her right then and there in the hallway, and the proprieties be bloody well damned.

Grimly, he reminded himself of the dire nature of the errand that had brought them there and the calumny that would befall Elfrida if her identity were discovered.

"No doubt I regret that you were made to endure my stepmother's theories on the imminent decline and fall of the British Empire due to a growing lack of moral fiber," submitted Shields, who, indeed, would have spared his Goddess of Beauty that particular torture if only circumstances had not dictated otherwise. "At the moment, however, that is hardly to the point. You will kindly explain what the devil you hoped to accomplish with this ridiculous charade. Winterbrooke may be of the first ranks of Society, but his galas are nothing of the kind."

"Really, Shields," declared Elfrida, in no little disgust, "I do wish you will cease to think of me as a green girl just out of the schoolroom. I know perfectly well Winterbrooke's entertainments are not in the least *comme il faut.* Why do you think I should go to all the trouble to borrow evening attire from my brother's trunk of discards, not to mention a domino from my grandfather's attic?"

Shields, who did not doubt she had done it for the express purpose of driving him to the brink of wringing her pretty neck for her, could not but realize he had very little choice in the matter save to submit to have her lead him to his quarry. If Albert had indeed been foolish enough to allow himself to be lured into a room with a female who had nothing but ill designs for him, then there certainly was not the time to remove Miss Rochelle from the premises before he went to the young cub's rescue.

"Well?" demanded Elfrida. "Are you interested in saving Albert from the clutches of That Woman or not?"

"Very well, you will show me where he is, Miss Rochelle," Shields conceded with what Elfrida privately could not but think was exceedingly poor grace. "And then, my girl, you will refrain from doing anything that could possibly be construed as trying to protect me, is that understood? I will not have you flinging yourself into danger in the mistaken belief I am unable to defend myself."

"It occurs to me, my lord," Elfrida retorted, starting down the corridor, "that even a man as highly capable as yourself of coming to grips with every sort of peril, including causing bolting horses to come to a standstill and bringing runaway balloons safely back to earth, might find a woman of no little help when it comes to dealing with a villainous female—especially when that female is in a house filled with people and the man is restricted from certain actions by the impediment of a gentleman's code of honor."

Coming to a halt before a closed door near the end of the hallway, she glanced up at him out of eyes rendered even more spellbindingly lovely by the cut-out holes of the mask covering her face.

"I came up as far as the end of the hall in pursuit of them," she said simply. "I watched them go in here. Shields," she added, as the earl reached for the door handle, "pray be careful. I do not understand what is going on here, at least not precisely. I only followed them because I distrusted the intentions of that woman."

Shields's grim aspect softened ever so slightly. Yes, of course she had sensed the danger surrounding Albert. How not, when she possessed a heart more discerning than any demmed crystal ball? He did not doubt that therein lay her true power—the power of a generous, loving nature and a bright, courageous soul.

The devil, he thought. Elfrida was as different from the mean-spirited beauty who had thought to malign her as was the warmth of a summer's day from the frozen depths of a winter's night. What, then, did she see before her that was so dreadful she could not bear the thought of marrying him?

Grimly, he dismissed that troubling question for later contemplation and steeled himself for the coming confrontation with Albert and the young fool's inamorata.

His hand closed on the door handle. "You were quite right to mistrust her, Miss Rochelle," he said, wanting Elfrida to know. "As it happens, she is in league with the infamous Mr. Pickering. Together, they have been scheming to use Albert against me."

He pulled the door handle down and thrust the door open.

It occurred to Elfrida that bursting into a room occupied by a young man in the throes of a first, all-consuming love and the female who was the inspiration of his passion was not the surest way to win his heartfelt gratitude. Indeed, had it not been for Shields's utter conviction that Albert's well-being, perhaps even his life, was in dread peril beyond that oaken barrier, she did not doubt she would have strongly suggested they devise something rather less dramatic than flinging open the door to reveal Albert dressed in naught but a ridiculously slack grin, his arms and legs spread eagle, and his wrists and ankles bound to the corner bedposts.

Elfrida froze in the doorway, hardly knowing what they had stumbled upon. Of the strikingly attractive red-headed woman, there was not so much as a sign.

Shields, however, did not hesitate.

"The devil," he cursed, crossing in long, swift strides to the bedside. He leaned over the ominously still figure on the bed, his fingertips feeling for the pulse at the neck. A long breath escaped his lips. "He's alive," he pronounced. "We may be grateful for that much at least." Flinging a coverlet

over Albert's manly proportions, he straightened.
"Quick, my girl, we must get him untied."

"He lies so still," said Elfrida, working to unloose
the strips of binding. "Shields? What have they
done to him?"

"Drugged him with laudanum, no doubt. I daresay, aside from a thunderous headache, he should
recover well enough. The same, however, could
not be said for his reputation if Mrs. Blakeley's
plans had been brought to fruition."

"Her plans?" Elfrida queried, glancing quizzically up at Shields's chiseled expression. "I do not
understand."

No, of course she did not, thought Shields, feeling a cold rage burning deep in his belly at those
who had thought to ruin Albert for no other reason
save that he was the Earl of Shields's cousin and
the next in line to inherit. He had no illusions as
to what they had intended. Far more difficult to
apprehend was why they should have done it.

"Shields?" Elfrida prodded, when it seemed he
had no intention of answering her. "Pray tell me
what is going on here."

Shields's eyes, when he looked at her, caused a
tiny chill to creep into her heart.

"You do not imagine, do you, that Mrs. Blakeley
has only stepped out for a moment? You may be
sure that she is not coming back. On the other
hand, I doubt not we may expect momentarily the
arrival of any number of Winterbrooke's unsuspecting guests. What do you think should have
happened had we not been here to free Albert
from his less than dignified state?"

It was obvious he had painted a vivid enough
picture of what his enemies had intended. Elfrida
went pearly white with sudden, dawning comprehension.

Grimly, Shields turned from freeing Albert's

wrist. "Wait in the hall, Elfrida. You have done enough, and this is no place for a woman."

"Pray do not be absurd, Shields," Elfrida retorted. "A woman put him here. Besides," she added in an attempt to dispel some of the grimness of the moment, "it is not as if I have not seen a man before." She stilled at Shields's noticeable lack of amusement. "Really, Shields," she said then, quite soberly, "it is all right. Albert need never know a woman helped to dress him."

Silently, Shields cursed. No doubt his stepmama would have seen his present predicament as proof positive of her theories concerning the decline of the empire. Indeed, he did not doubt his moral values were noticeably slipping. And all thanks to a wholly improper miss without the smallest regard for what her selfless determination to help him at every turn might cost her. The devil, he thought, reaching for the discarded breeches on the floor. She would bloody well consent to become his wife. He was damned if he would wait much longer!

A low groan escaped Albert's lips as strong hands lifted him against Shields's chest. Elfrida slipped the white linen shirt over his head, and, together, she and Shields worked his limp arms through the sleeves. The waistcoat and coat were quickly to follow suit. It was finished. Albert was fully dressed.

Bending down, Shields caught Albert's inert form over his shoulder and lifted him.

"We will take him downstairs by the back way. Where is your coach?" he asked, as Elfrida, casting a glance up and down the corridor, let him out the door.

"I haven't a coach," Elfrida said, leading the way to the service stairs. "I came in a hackney. I rather thought you might give me a lift home. We are, after all, neighbors."

"The devil, Elfrida. Never say you intend to go

back to Godfrey's house! You might as well stay in mine as have the world discover you have been residing in the house next door to me.''

"Splendid," Elfrida did not hesitate to fling back at him. "I shall move in whenever you say the word, my lord. Although I rather had my heart set on your snug little love nest on Holles. From what I overheard tonight, Lady Loring has, after all, vacated the premises for a house on Baker Street. It seems it is far more conveniently placed for her newest interest. And you know it was growing so exceedingly tedious dividing her time between two gentlemen's households.''

"The devil!" uttered Shields, nearly dropping his burden at that sudden, unexpected revelation.

"My lord?" queried Elfrida with a sublime air of innocence. "Pray do not tell me you did not know.''

"Baggage," uttered his lordship, appreciatively aware that his Goddess of Beauty was deliberately testing his patience. She was, as she was so fond of reminding him, not so green as not to know that he had not lived a life of celibacy. Still, no doubt she could not resist punishing him just a trifle for not having preserved himself for his karmically predetermined Soul Mate.

Odd that he, on the other hand, had the uncanniest feeling that that was precisely what he had done.

Elfrida's voice came, a trifle gruff, out of the silence. "I do beg your pardon, Shields. I should not have given way to petty malice. I did warn you I have a terrible temper, and Lady Loring is odiously breathtaking. She is, in fact, just what I might have expected in one of your mistresses.''

Shields smiled grimly to himself in the dim light of the service stair. Lady Loring was precisely what one might have looked for in a mistress. But then, he had had his surfeit of mistresses. He was hardly surprised to learn where the lovely Sylvia had been keeping herself in his absence and even, it would seem, after his return from Shaftesbury. Winterbrooke had been at his old game again. Indeed, it was plain why the viscount had not been disposed to mourn overmuch over the loss of his divine Miss Slaton. He had already had his old friend Shields's mistress tucked away in his love nest on Baker Street. Equally certain was that the enterprising Lady Loring had made every effort to take full advantage of Shields's largesse before the game was finally up. No doubt she had been savoring the moment when she would give the Earl of Shields his walking papers. Only he had been before her, thus robbing her of the satisfaction. Perhaps she had not entirely made certain yet of Winterbrooke's continued support and was thrown into a cold panic at the prospect of losing Shields's purse before she had secured her immediate future. Certainly, finding herself in the role of a woman scorned had been enough to set her in a livid rage.

"Does it hurt very much?" asked Elfrida, peering up at him with troubled eyes. "Knowing your inamorata was playing fast and loose with your closest friend?"

"She was never my inamorata, *enfant*. She was my mistress, and Winterbrooke is more than welcome to her." Shields could not help but wonder if the viscount knew what he was getting.

Elfrida accepted that pronouncement in silence. It had never occurred to her that there was a difference between the two. But then, *inamorata*, by its very construct, must imply an intimacy of emotions, perhaps even love. A mistress, by default, was relegated, it would seem, to a purely physical realm. And yet, there was no denying that there were men who loved their mistresses. One had only to look to Nelson and his beloved Lady Hamilton or to

Prinnie, for that matter, and his Mrs. Fitzherbert. But then, it was the outside world who placed them in the category of "mistress," and then, having done so, heaped on them its scorn. And what of wives? she wondered. Under the law, a wife was a man's chattel, legally bound for life. Whether adored and lovingly protected or despised and basely abused, they were still wives with no clear distinction between them. Truly, it was only on the metaphysical plane of existence, where men and women were equals, that love could achieve its fullest expression, unfettered by codes and prejudices.

Still, she and Shields were on this plane, she reminded herself. And here, Shields had made it clear that he did not hold his mistresses in affection. She could not but feel immeasurable relief that the beautiful Lady Loring had not laid any claim on his heart. Faith, what had she not been made to suffer upon overhearing the blond beauty fling her poisoned barbs about Shields! Had not Albert and his red-haired *femme fatale* commanded her attention when they did, Elfrida was quite certain she would have given vent to the desire to scratch Lady Loring's beautiful chinablue eyes out.

If nothing else, Elfrida told herself, she would one day have the satisfaction of showing Lady Loring that Shields, far from being vulnerable to her poisoned darts, was no longer even aware of his former mistress's existence. He would, after all, have Lady Elfrida Rochelle on his arm. She did not doubt that would incite the blond beauty to a veritable fit of the spasms.

It was on that note and just as they stepped outside into the night, silvery with moonlight, that Elfrida was reminded of Lady Loring's vitriolic admission that she would gladly see Shields dead.

She had even gone so far as to declare she would happily have cut the earl's heart out. Perhaps they need look no farther than Shields's scorned mistress for the source of the two attempts on the earl's life. It was conceivable that, sensing Shields meant to cut her off from his generous purse and having found herself a new patron, she had decided to vent her spleen against her former lover by engaging someone to do away with him. If she had wished him dead before he had actually gone so far as to break it off with her, then how much greater must have been her motivation afterwards!

Nor was Lady Loring the only candidate for speculation in the shroud of mystery surrounding recent happenings. There was Niles Marston, whom Shields, long before the events at Kensington Gardens, had already had occasion to approach with a warning to abandon any thought of a further pursuit of Lady Julia. Just before she had been swept away by the panicked mob, Elfrida had not failed to make note of the hatred in Marston's eyes. Indeed, she did not doubt Mr. Marston's malice had only been deepened by having his nose literally bent out of shape by one of Shields's exceedingly handy pair of fives, not to mention the drubbing he must have sustained in the ranks of the Royal Fusiliers Military Band. Marston's resentment might very well have goaded him to sever the balloon's anchor cable. Certainly, he had been in the near vicinity and, consequently, could be presumed to have had opportunity as well as motivation. Further, he might very well have been moved to make the earlier attempt in Bond Street on Shields's life. There was no denying that, with Shields out of the way, Lady Julia would have been left a deal more vulnerable to Marston's ambitions to get himself an heiress by any means, even abduction.

And now there was the new twist to consider, involving the mysterious Mr. Pickering and his apparent cohort, Mrs. Blakeley, she thought, as she helped Shields settle Albert in the seat of the earl's coach. In all the hurry to remove Albert from the scene of his intended humiliation, she had not had the opportunity to question the earl further regarding his cryptic remarks to her in the hallway. But then, she had already been given a glimpse of Pickering's evil intentions the previous night when she had gazed into the crystalline depths of a dew drop.

"I believe I have been exceedingly patient, my lord," said Elfrida, pulling off her mask as the coach lurched into motion. "And as an Aries, I must warn you I am not in the least prone to forbearance. I really must know, Shields, what you meant when you said Mrs. Blakeley and Mr. Pickering have conspired to use Albert against you. Does it have anything to do with Mrs. Blakeley's custom of luring young gentlemen to lose money at her gaming tables by seeming to dangle before them the promise of her favors?"

"Good God, Elfrida," exclaimed Shields, who had been deep in his own ruminations concerning the web of intrigue that, like a thickening cloud, had seemingly sprung out of nowhere to suddenly encompass him and those near to him. "Where the devil did you garner that tidbit of information? Never say you saw that in a dew drop."

"As a matter of fact, I overheard it quite by accident at Winterbrooke's this evening," confessed Elfrida, lifting the earl's arm over her shoulders and snuggling into the warmth of his side. "From

Lady Loring's brother Freddy, who, if you must know, is plotting, along with his sister, to squeeze poor Winterbrooke for a sum large enough to finance their retirement. I fear you, too, were to have been made to donate handsomely to their nest egg. Unfortunately, you ruined everything by cutting line before they were through dipping into your purse. I do hope you will see fit to warn Winterbrooke not to deal too generously with his new mistress. I like him far too well to wish him a long association with a woman who is not only grasping, but who does not scruple to wish to see him dead. Which brings me to wonder if you have considered that your former mistress might very well have harbored similar ill feelings toward yourself, my lord. I believe she is a woman who has little affection for the men she manipulates to her own ends."

She was rewarded for that astute observation with a harsh bark of laughter from his lordship. "I should be exceedingly surprised if she did not wish to see me dead right alongside Winterbrooke and probably any number of others who were taken in by her facade of delicate femininity. If you are asking, however, if I think she is behind the recent attempts on my life, I should have to reply that she would not be my first choice for the role of Lady Macbeth. While the beautiful Lady Loring is not averse to attempts at verbal assassination, I seriously doubt she would lend herself to actual murder. It would involve a depth of imagination beyond that of which I believe she is capable."

"I, on the other hand, am reluctant to discard her," said Elfrida, who would not have been surprised by any despicable thing Lady Loring might have chosen to do. "If not your former mistress, however, then what about Niles Marston?"

"It is my considered opinion that Marston was in no case to sever the balloon's cable," replied

Shields, who, acutely aware of Elfrida's firm body pressed to his side, was inclined to shelve the discussion in favor of more pleasurable pursuits. "I believe he was, after all, considerably occupied at the time with the fife and drum sections of the Royal Fusiliers Military Band. On the other hand, my maddeningly single-minded Elfrida, I could not positively dismiss him. The fact of the matter is I have been of the opinion almost from the very beginning that our most likely candidate is Mr. Nicodemus Pickering. And the more I learn about him, the closer I come to being convinced he is the source of all our trouble. Unfortunately, while I am reasonably certain I know why he plotted to ruin Albert, I have yet to conceive of a possible motive that would lead him to wish me dead. One does not kill the goose that lays the golden egg, not if one wishes to turn a profit."

"You *know* why Albert was left trussed up like a lamb for the offering?" queried Elfrida, lifting her head to peer up into Shields's features obscured in the shadows of the coach. "I mean, aside from the obvious intent to make a laughingstock of him?"

Shields, finding Elfrida's lips an enticing few inches from his, felt the powerful tug of temptation. "How not, *enfant*?" he answered, lowering his head to hers. "It was obviously a message to *me*."

Elfrida, who could not but think the earl's answer, while it left a great deal to be explained, was most satisfactory in terms of the manner in which he appended it with a kiss, which had the peculiar effect of taking her mind off everything else.

Indeed, it was not until the coach came to a halt and the earl released her to give her a final kiss on the tip of her nose that she was made to realize they had not come to Grosvenor Square.

"My lord?" queried Elfrida, sitting up to peer in no little confusion at the tidy row of brown brick houses beyond the coach window. "No doubt you will pardon my curiosity, but I cannot but wonder. Where have you brought us?"

"To Holles Street, Miss Rochelle," pronounced his lordship, reaching to open the door. "I suggest you don your mask once more," he added, stepping down onto the curb. Then looking up at her, a quizzical glint in his eye, "You did say, did you not, that you preferred my love nest on Holles?"

She was perhaps fortunate that she was saved from having to come up with an answer by the intrusion at that moment of Albert's low groan and a distinct stirring of his considerably rumpled form.

"He is coming around, Shields," she announced, hastily reaching to cover her face with the mask.

"Yes, I'm afraid he is about to be sick," was Shields's grim observation. "Go straight into the house, *enfant*. I shall be along directly with Albert."

Albert was, indeed, sick. He was sick repeatedly for the next hour or so. So sick, in fact, that he could not even bring himself to question why there should be a slender boy helping Shields see to all of his needs—a boy whose face had seemed oddly familiar. And if it struck him, perhaps, that the fellow had a curiously soothing, gentle touch, he had not the strength to remark on it. In his wretched state, he could only be grateful for it—until at last he fell into an exhausted sleep.

"I believe we may be thankful that the worst is over," said Shields, who, long since having divested himself of his coat and waistcoat, not to mention his intricately tied neckcloth, stood in his shirtsleeves, staring down at Albert's pale face against the pillows. The devil, he thought, wearily unrolling his sleeves down his arms. It had been far worse than he had imagined it would be. He had begun to worry he had miscalculated in not sending for a doctor. The red-haired witch must have fed Albert more of the drug than was good for him. It had been fortunate, no doubt, that she had given it to him in champagne, a beverage that Albert had never been able to tolerate. The possibility that perhaps that was all that had saved Albert's life was like to haunt Shields for some time to come. Bloody hell! It had been far too much like that other time, that other, much younger boy. Only then there had been nothing he could do. The boy had died in spite of everything.

"Will he be all right, do you think?" asked Elfrida, who likewise had discarded her domino and man's cutaway coat in her efforts on Albert's behalf. Straightening from bathing Albert's face, she laid the cloth in the bowl of lavender water and stood, stretching the kinks from her back as she did so.

Shields's eyes were drawn to her—seeing the strength in her, the beautiful lines of her body. He reminded himself that she must be as weary as he felt.

"I'm sure of it," he said. Then, tersely, "You should go. Mrs. Pearson can see to him now."

Elfrida came around, hurt at his abruptness. At sight of him, the sharp retort on the tip of her tongue withered away, unspoken.

Wordlessly, she went to him. Taking his hand in hers, she led him firmly from the sickroom.

"Elfrida—"

Elfrida, closing the door, turned to him, her arms sliding up around the back of his neck. "Hush, my lord," she said, lifting her face to his.

Shields looked into eyes that compelled him to

forget everything, save his need for her, a need
that had little to do with lust, but a great deal to
do with a yearning he had not known he even
possessed. Ministering to the hurt that had lain
buried for so long deep within him, the hurt that
she must have seen moments before when she
looked into his face, Elfrida drew him down to her.
She was all womanly compassion and sweet fire,
was his divining Goddess of Beauty. With a groan,
Shields gave in to the sweet spell of her. Crushing
her lips beneath his, he bent down and swept her
up in his arms.

Forgotten was the impediment of a gentleman's
code of honor or even the vow he had made to
overcome her resistance to marrying him. There
was only Elfrida and his overpowering need to possess her. Releasing her lips, Shields carried her
down the corridor to his bedchamber.

Laying her on the bed, he covered her with kisses,
her eyes, her brow, her cheeks, her hair. With his
hands he caressed her, until she writhed beneath
him with a rising urgency. Only then did he move
to undress her, his fingers releasing the buttons
down her borrowed waistcoat, his hands tugging
at the fastenings at her waist. His lips and tongue
found the indentation of her navel, as he parted
the front of her breeches.

A keening sigh broke from Elfrida's lips. Faith,
she would never have dreamed the cosmic awakening of primordial passions could possibly be even
more potent the second time of arousal than it
had upon the first. But then, the first time Shields
had not been driven by a fierce, tender need quite
unlike anything she had ever sensed in him before.
Indeed, it was as if she had unwittingly tapped a
well of emotion in him, feelings which he had long
since learned to keep contained and hidden away
from the rest of the world behind an impenetrable

wall of Leonine arrogance. A wave of tenderness
welled up inside her at the realization that he was
sharing a part of himself which she knew instinctively he had never shared with anyone else before.

She suffered a swift pang of regret as he pulled
away to remove her boots and her stockings. Then
she was lifting herself, helping him to slip the
breeches down over her hips and legs, struggling
to rid herself of the ridiculous waistcoat and shirt.
Faith, she must die from wanting him, she thought,
as he turned from her to pull off his own boots
and stockings with hard swift hands, then, standing,
worked quickly to rid himself of his shirt and his
breeches.

A low gasp burst from Elfrida upon beholding
her karmically predetermined, astrologically perfect mate in the full sway of primordial passions. It
came to her that, truly, the astrological magnetism
between karmically predetermined Twin Souls was
possessed of the power to work marvels.

Then Shields was bending over her, and a sigh
burst from her depths as, forging a trail of kisses
up the inside of her leg, he found the moist warmth
between her thighs.

"My sweet, beautiful Elfrida," he uttered huskily
upon finding her flowing with the nectar of
arousal. Elfrida responded to his lovemaking with
a generosity like that of no other woman he had
ever known before her. But then, there *was* no
other woman like Elfrida. She had slipped through
the barriers of his resistance before he ever knew
what was happening and had not stopped until she
had penetrated into the protected realm of his
heart. He did not doubt that to have her remove
herself now would occasion him irreparable damage. Indeed, he could not foresee a future without
her. The devil, he thought, molding his lips to the
peaked bud of one of her nipples. When she had

confessed to being a scryer and a prognosticator, how could he have known then that she would have the power to see through all of his carefully maintained defences to his very soul?

Then Elfrida was pulling him down to her, and he forgot everything but her supple beauty moving beneath his caresses.

She was tinder to his touch, was the divining Goddess of Beauty, and he wanted her, needed her, more than he had ever needed anything in his life before. Inserting himself between her thighs, he drove himself into her.

Elfrida molded herself to his lean strength, met his longing with the full force of the love that had been growing steadily inside her. Faith, how she loved him! Had loved him through all the years since she had first looked up and beheld him in all his manly arrogance—his golden, magnificent pride—approaching her in the receiving line at her coming-out ball. She had loved him without knowing it; indeed, out of some little-understood karmic instinct, had saved herself for the day when she would be joined with him in body and soul to unleash a predetermined cosmic passion.

"*Shields,*" she keened, feeling herself on the verge of exploding with the wonder of what she had perceived.

Then Shields was drawing up and back. He plunged himself into her. Elfrida, arching to his manly strength, erupted in an explosion of cosmic release at the very moment Shields spilled his seed into her.

Chapter 13

It had never occurred to Elfrida that, when Twin Souls were destined to meet, there would be seemingly insurmountable barriers between them or that, indeed, having found one another, even going so far as to join in body and spirit in order to achieve the mystical heights of a karmically predetermined passion, they should descend to less exalted environs only to discover that one of them, at least, was possessed of personality quirks that could be exceedingly annoying.

A plague on Shields, she thought, turning testily away from the withdrawing room window overlooking the rolling Dukeries. Really, she would never have thought that in the wake of a passion that had been truly cosmic in its effects on them both, Shields would impose his will on her, even going so far as to carry her bodily out of the house on Holles Street and deposit her without ceremony in his carriage. Then, with an arrogant disregard of her feelings, not to mention his gentleman's word of honor that she would be his ally in tracking down those who would cut his stick for him, what had he done but drive her to Albermarle House and order her to stay there until he came for her! It was really too shabby of him, especially as she was perfectly aware he intended to call on Mr. Nicodemus Pickering that very afternoon. Further, she did not doubt that, being a wholly arrogantly fearless Leo, he would insist on going by himself.

The devil! she thought. It was not as if she had not made it abundantly clear that it was her karmic duty to do all in her power to protect him. He had admitted he understood well enough that she was dedicated to preserving his life. Well, what he had actually said, she conceded with a wry grimace to herself, was that there was nothing wrong with his understanding, thank you very much, that, indeed, he apprehended perfectly well that she was an impossibly headstrong, stubborn, not to mention meddling, female without an ounce of a proper sense of her own vulnerability. He did not doubt that she had been born utterly devoid of the first instinct for self-preservation and, further, could not imagine how she had succeeded thus far in surviving to womanhood.

He had ended by odiously pointing out that if it was her karmic duty to protect her karmically predetermined, astrologically perfect mate, then it equally devolved upon him to look after his, which meant that she would stay put at Albermarle House until he could return for her or he would not hesitate to put her over his knee when he had got his hands on her again and beat her—the *devil!*

Those were hardly the words she would have expected from him in light of earlier events, which had left them gloriously sated and as near to a mutual understanding of one another as they could ever have previously imagined to achieve. Indeed, it had come to her at the time as something of a revelation that the true joining of spirits must surely be manifested in the act of simply lying together in the wake of spent passions and talking quietly in the dark.

Elfrida could not recall ever having felt so close to anyone as she had felt that night, cradled in the circle of Shields's arms, listening as he told her things he had never told anyone before her. She had held herself still, afraid to move, lest she break the quiet fall of words in the night. He had needed to talk. And she had needed to listen. So much, after all, was being made clear to her about Shields, things that she had sensed, but never fully understood before. Not the least of these was why he should have taken it upon himself to befriend James Randall Ludgate, a boy several years his junior, who was to prove later in manhood as undeserving of the earl's aegis as he was lacking in moral principle.

But then, it was not Viscount Hepplewaite who occupied Shields's thoughts that night as he lay reliving with Elfrida events from his youth. It was of that other boy whom he talked, the memory of whom, long buried, but never forgotten, had been unearthed by the near loss of Shields's Cousin Albert. It was Neal Herrick, the son to whom Shields's mother had died giving birth, and whom Shields had taken under his wing almost from the time of the boy's breeching. But then, to a young Leo, it had been a sacred trust, and the youngster had looked up to him as boys do to an older, stronger boyish hero. How greatly it had hurt Shields to lose the boy who had showed such shining promise! He little doubted Neal Herrick would have grown into a man of whom even his estranged father might have been proud.

"I believe my father was never fully able to rid himself of the sense that he was responsible for the passing of my mother," he said, coming to the end of his story. "The doctors did warn him after the birth of a stillborn daughter that another pregnancy might prove the death of her. I cannot say what miscalculation led to the conception five years later of my younger brother. I know only that my mother made me promise long before her lying-in that, as the elder, I should always look after the child. Even at eight, I think I knew what she feared. Nevertheless, I was hardly prepared for my father to treat Neal with an aloofness that was made all the more conspicuous by the affection which he never denied to me."

"He must have loved your mother very much," Elfrida had observed, thinking Neal's mama could have chosen no better guardian for him than her young lion cub, whose natural inclination would be to fiercely protect one left in his keeping. But then, she must have had very little other choice in the matter. She had seen how it must be with the boys' father.

"I have no doubt," had replied Shields with chill dispassion. "No less than he loved the son she died bearing him. A pity he waited until it was too late to realize it. However, in the final analysis, I was the one who failed my brother. When Neal was stricken with the fever, I was powerless to do anything to help him. The devil, I was not even allowed near him when he lay dying. I watched from beyond the nursery window."

"It could hardly have been otherwise, Shields. You were little more than a boy yourself—fifteen, did you say? Naturally they could not chance that you might be taken with the fever, as well as your brother."

She had sensed his smile even in the darkness. "I might have known you would leap immediately to my defense," he said, lightly dropping a kiss on the top of her head. "You must not think I have been laboring all these years in the throes of a morbid preoccupation with something that happened a very long time ago."

"On the contrary, my lord," Elfrida had not refrained from retorting, "I am well aware that you are not of a morbid disposition. You yourself made sure to inform me of it."

"Impertinent little minx. Next you will be telling me it was my feeling of guilt that led me to take Hepplewaite under my wing. And no doubt you would be in the right of it. The truth of the matter is, however, I find it strange that I should have suddenly been visited with the memory of Neal after all these years. I suppose I did somehow blame myself for my brother's death. And seeing Albert in the throes of poison because of those who thought to get at me through him served to bring it all back again. The devil of it is I may be certain they will try again. If not with Albert, then with someone else. It is time, I think, I paid Mr. Pickering a visit."

"But why Pickering?" Elfrida demanded, reminded that Shields had yet to explain that particular from earlier in the evening. "You have yet to tell me his part in all of this. And Mrs. Blakeley. Who is she?"

"A conscienceless female who preys on unsuspecting young fools like Albert—and Hepplewaite, am I not mistaken."

He had told her all of it then, how Pickering and Mrs. Blakeley had joined forces to make a lucrative business of luring gentlemen to the siren's gaming house in which the odds were stacked against the gamesters by any number of nefarious means, including the use of marked cards and weighted dice. It was an old ploy to accept markers, which were then sold to Pickering, who tripled their profits through the practice of charging the usurious interest rates common to those engaged in the practice of money-lending. Hepplewaite was not the first to fall victim to the seductive Mrs. Blakeley, but he had promised to be the last, or so the two connivers must have reasoned, once Shields had demonstrated an apparent interest in the lady and her gaming house by the mere fact that he had deigned to step across her threshold. No doubt it had been a short leap to connect Shields's offer of a reward for the apprehension of Hepplewaite's murderers to the earl's unlikely appearance in the establishment that had conspired to bring about the viscount's ruin. Certainly, they had not hoped to conceal from a man of Shields's reputation the dishonest nature of their profitable winnings. They had, as a consequence, set upon Albert with the sole intention of sending Shields a message.

"But how exceedingly unwise of them!" Elfrida had not hesitated to point out. "What could they have possibly thought to gain by it? Surely, they did not truly believe they could intimidate the Earl of Shields with an act of coercion."

"Mr. Tuttle did warn me Pickering would stop at nothing to protect his interests, presumably not even at murder. No doubt, if nothing else, they thought to extract a sizeable sum from me for the redemption of Albert's gambling debts, which were already considerable and promised to accumulate a great deal more once they were transferred to Mr. Pickering. Which is where the line of reasoning appears to become muddled with seeming contradictions."

"You mean putting a period to the goose that lays the golden egg. But that is obvious, surely!" exclaimed Elfrida, who saw reluctantly that she might have to give up Lady Loring as her prime candidate for the cowardly attempts on Shields's life. "With you out of the way, Albert would inherit. Conceivably, they envisioned a golden goose on their platter, one whom they had already got their hooks in."

"I confess that had occurred to me," Shields said. "And no doubt it would have explained a great deal, had they not tried what they did tonight. After all, there would seem little point in hanging their prospective goose out to dry. No, it would hardly make sense to go to all the trouble to set Albert up to be publicly humiliated if they had hopes in future of milking him dry after he inherited the title and the far plumper purse that goes with it."

"I do see what you mean," mused Elfrida, perceptibly brightening. "In which case, I shall not give up on Lady Loring as the malevolent force behind the pall I glimpsed hanging over you. She did, after all, wittingly abet Mrs. Blakeley in her plot tonight against Albert. I was watching her from below. She deliberately engaged your attention in order to prevent you from seeing Mrs. Blakeley maneuver Albert to the room upstairs."

"I daresay it was only spite that motivated my former mistress," postulated Shields, who seemed to derive no little amusement from Elfrida's unconcealed dislike of the blond beauty. "And what must have presented itself as a golden opportunity. You may be sure she would never pass up a chance to spread thorns in my way, which is why I want your promise you will keep your distance from Lady Loring. If she thought she could hurt me through you, she would not hesitate to do so."

"But I haven't the least intention of placing myself in Lady Loring's way, Shields," Elfrida had returned sweetly. "On the other hand, she would do well to stay out of mine. In a cat fight, she would soon find I am more than able to hold my own.

Indeed, I do not hesitate to speculate she is not at all up to my weight."

Elfrida little doubted that was not the answer for which Shields had been looking. It had, in fact, immediately brought the barriers crashing down once more between them, with the result that Shields, in an unadulterated lionish peeve, had exiled her to Albermarle House with the expectation that she would stand tamely by while he proceeded without her to find and confront Nicodemus Pickering.

"A plague on him and his arrogance!" pronounced Elfrida, flinging herself down on the windowseat. "I'm sure I should not care less what Mr. Nicodemus Pickering does to him."

"Nor should I," declared a feminine voice from the doorway. "I am sure whatever happens to him, it will be too good for him. Who, by the way, are we talking about? And, equally to the point, who is Mr. Nicodemus Pickering?"

"You know very well whom I am talking about," grumbled Elfrida, glancing up to find Violet regarding her with sisterly affection. "And, as for Pickering, he is the grasping, mean-hearted villain who helped to send Hepplewaite to his early grave. More significantly, he is a cent-per-cent, who might very well be plotting at this very moment to knock Shields alongside the head and drop him in the Thames."

"And with good riddance, no doubt," appended Violet, her blue-violet eyes guileless.

"Oh, pooh!" exclaimed Elfrida, giving vent to a wry grimace. "You know very well I should die if anything happened to him. The devil, Violet, I cannot bear sitting around doing nothing while Shields is deliberately courting danger without me. I shall undoubtedly start flinging things before very much longer."

"Pray do begin with that wholly disgusting representation of a man being devoured by a tiger," suggested Violet, indicating a hideous silver epergne on the sideboard, which Albermarle's father had fetched home from one of his sojourns in India. "Or we might just go shopping in Bond Street. Aunt Roanna, who is wholly exhausted after an hour spent with the children at the Willingham twins' birthday party, has gone upstairs for a restorative nap. I daresay she would never miss us."

"And even if she did, she would only be relieved that she had not to feel guilty for putting off to another day taking you on the round of afternoon calls required for your introduction into Society."

"Naturally, we should not wish Aunt Roanna to be in any way discomfited, should we?" Violet grinned. "And I have yet, after all, to discover a bonnet to go with the new sprigged muslin Aunt Roanna has only just had made up for me."

Some little time later, Elfrida and Violet, stepping down from the carriage, made their way arm in arm along the shops lining Bond Street. Firmly, Elfrida told herself that if she were not to be allowed to help Shields, she should at least do her best to take her mind off worrying about him. Worrying, after all, had never helped anyone, least of all the one doing the fretting. Certainly there was no end of pleasant distractions to help her in her endeavor, not the least of which was Violet, who, until recently, had never set foot in Bond Street.

What had been intended to be an excursion of only an hour or two was by degrees stretched into three. Indeed, it was gradually borne in on Elfrida that her sister, who had previously seemed content with a wardrobe sufficient unto her means, had been harboring for some little time a craving for pretty things. Freed from constraint by Elfrida's assurances that Albermarle had given her carte blanche in the matter of the necessities for her sister's come-out, Violet was proving tireless in her pursuit of all the pretty, dainty things that had been so long denied her. With the result that, Elfrida, who had spent most of the previous night occupied with things other than sleeping and who, consequently, had been carried solely on nervous energy, found herself flagging long before Violet had sated herself with trying on hats and bonnets, examining endless examples of lacy scarves and dainty underthings, and purchasing any number of stockings, hair ribbons, and trinkets.

Telling herself the last thing she could wish was to cut short Violet's shopping spree, Elfrida resorted to luring her sister into Clevenger's Emporium, which was noted for the sheer volume and wide variety of any sort of goods imaginable. More than that, it had the distinction of offering the amenities of tea and cakes to its customers, not to mention a cozy array of chairs in which to enjoy one's refreshment.

Elfrida, pointing her sister in the direction of an exquisite display of the latest in reticules designed to complement the most discerning tastes in ladies' fashions, sank gratefully down in a red plush velvet wing chair with a high back, which was tucked away next to a screen separating women's haberdashery from household goods.

In spite of her best efforts to assume an interest in the various passersby, she could not quite stifle a yawn. Propping her elbow on the arm of the chair and dropping her chin onto her palm, she became aware of a gentleman's voice issuing from the other side of the screen and tried concentrating on the timbre, which would seem to strike a vague chord of memory. It was obvious the speaker was angry or displeased about something; indeed, he seemed particularly anxious at having misplaced someone who had been in evidence only moments earlier—a woman, his wife, no doubt, thought Elfrida, patting at a yawn with the palm of her free hand. Further, there was, tucked away somewhere—she jerked her head up, blinking the heaviness from her eyes—a what? A pearl? A girl?— which had got to be disposed of. Really, it would seem to make little sense, she thought, as, irresistibly, her eyelids drifted down over her eyes.

It came to Elfrida to wonder how it was that she should find herself standing on a corner in what gave every appearance of a new section of Town, which, even though it boasted the magnificent seven-story Imperial and Commercial Hotel among its many fine buildings, would seem to be peculiarly lacking in tenants. Glancing up, she was made aware of a street sign, which identified the thoroughfare as "Skinner Street." The designation meant little to her. But then, obviously the street and its buildings had not been there upon her last visit to London seven years before. Strange, then, that she should have a distinct sensation of uneasiness about the environs, which were to all appearances benign, even pleasant to look upon. No doubt it was the effect of the many gaping windows, the air of vacancy, the feeling that somewhere in the emptiness behind the walls, there was something—someone waiting for her.

Telling herself that she had never feared one of her dreams before and that she certainly did not intend to start now, Elfrida gave herself up to the thing that she sensed drawing her.

* * *

Shields, disembarking from his carriage before the less than prepossessing facade in Field's Lane, was moved to speculate that Mr. Nicodemus Pickering, whose weathered sign swung in disconsolate abandon over the door, must have had a tidy sum stashed away somewhere in a mattress. Certainly, the cent-per-cent who had availed himself of the greatest portion of Hepplewaite's erstwhile fortune had expended little or none of it on what might loosely have been called his counting house. But then, the soot-encrusted windows and weathered bricks would seem perfectly complemented by the accumulation of refuse littering the street.

The arrival of a gentleman's coach bearing a gilded coat of arms on the sides must inevitably attract notice in a neighborhood known to be an infamous rookery, a thieves' den, riddled with warrens and secret passages. Hardly more wholesome than the piles of filth rotting in the kennel were the dozen or so wretched creatures who stole near to stare at the oddity of a gentleman in Field's Lane.

No doubt the sight of Tom Milburn and the burly Tobias Whitley seated next to him on the driver's bench, a club clutched, ready, in one great fist, were sufficient to encourage the oglers to keep to a wide berth.

Instructing the groom to keep a sharp eye out, Shields opened the door and entered the murky environs of a stairway, which ended before a closed barrier notable for its peeling paint.

It was made immediately apparent that Shields's arrival in the street below had not gone unnoticed above. Before Shields could knock, the door swung open on creaking hinges to reveal a squat individual dressed in a poor example of the Jean de Bry coat with its distinctive padding at the shoulder seams and its coattails, short and scanty. Striped short trousers ended at the ankles to reveal scuffed shoes with lachets tied over protruding tongues, while a melon head sprouting lank, oily hair from a mottled pate sat in a high stand-fall collar to give the impression that the fellow was peculiarly lacking a neck.

"Mr. Pickering, I must presume," observed Shields, with the arch of a single arrogant eyebrow.

"The very one, my lord." Pickering bowed ingratiatingly, an arm sweeping in a grand gesture toward his humble dwelling. "Pray do come in. I believe I have been expecting you."

"Yes, I am sure of it." Shields, stepping past his unctuously grinning host, spared only the most cursory of glances at the room's interior, which was furnished with a large oak desk, incongruous in its seamy setting, two straight-backed chairs, and a tall cabinet, presumably locked, as would seem to be evidenced by a silver key hung about Mr. Pickering's nonexistent neck. "You were, after all, kind enough to leave me an invitation to call, were you not, Mr. Pickering?"

"An invitation. Yes,"—Mr. Pickering chuckled—"that was precisely what it was, and you, my lord, wasted little time in responding. As a man of business, you may be sure I appreciate promptness in a client."

Shields reached for the door key. "Of course you do. Time is money, and in your business, time is money trebled." Pickering's eyes narrowed at the grate of the key in the lock, but he said nothing, though perhaps he might wished to have done. "You will be glad to know that my cousin is recovering from his recent indisposition."

"Shall I, my lord?" queried Mr. Pickering, no doubt momentarily taken aback at the abruptness of what would seem a change of subject.

"Indeed, Mr. Pickering, you will," Shields replied, leaving little doubt that the one was connected with the other. "It is all that is keeping you alive. Furthermore, if you wish to continue in your present health, you will favor me with my cousin's markers—all of them. Now, Mr. Pickering. I am a man who dislikes having his time wasted."

"No less than am I, my lord," agreed Pickering, rubbing his ink-stained hands together in what must have been construed as a gesture of one in anticipation of concluding a lucrative business transaction. "The sum, taken with the accumulated interest, my lord, is considerable. I shall, of course, be willing to accept a letter of credit on your bank in lieu of pound notes, if that is more convenient for you."

"I have no doubt you would," agreed Shields, little amused. "On the other hand, I have no intention of giving you anything more than the merest possibility that you might come out of this alive—if you do precisely as you are told. The markers, Mr. Pickering. Without delay."

"Come, come, my lord Shields. You do not truly think I intend to just turn them over to you without my just compensation. You are a gentleman, and a gentleman pays his debts of honor."

Shields answered coldly, "I should not bring up mention of honor if I were you, Mr. Pickering. It is a concept beyond your comprehension. I will tell you that I have already taken steps to close down Mrs. Blakeley's gaming establishment. The Bow Street Runners were exceedingly interested in everything my cousin had to tell them. No doubt they will be even more interested to learn how you have twice tried to put a period to my existence."

For the first time Shields detected a flicker of hesitation in Pickering's demeanor. No doubt the slimy fellow had been used to dealing in back rooms and darkened stairwells with persons whose

last wish would be to have their business with Mr.
Pickering made known. It was obvious it had not
occurred to him that Shields would take resort to
the law. It lasted just for a second, and then Pickering had himself in hand again.

"You are a very fine card player, my lord," he
said, moving to place the desk between him and
his visitor. "I have heard that about you, but in this
instance I am well aware that you are not holding a
trump card in your hand. Your cousin would never
go to the Bow Street Runners with such a tale. You
and I both know it would be courting scandal. And,
as for entertaining so much as a thought of cutting
your stick for you, I assure you you misjudge me.
Why should I wish you dead, when I have every
expectation that you will come to your senses and
discharge your cousin's debt?"

"Perhaps, Mr. Pickering, because I am aware of
the part you played in the ruin of another of your
victims, one who was not so fortunate as my cousin.
In spite of what you think you know, you are mistaken in believing I should submit to giving you
so much as a cent for a debt that was incurred by
dishonest means. I will have my cousin's markers,
and you, do not doubt, will be receiving a call
momentarily from the Bow Street Runners."

"That would be very unfortunate, my lord," said
Pickering, appearing to reconsider. "Indeed, I
daresay it would not profit me at all to have the
Runners poking their noses into my business. But
then, I am a reasonable man. Perhaps we can still
come to an agreement of some benefit to us both."
Taking the key from his neck, Pickering proceeded
to unlock a drawer of the desk.

"I suggest," said Shields, as Pickering put his
hand in the drawer, "that you try nothing so foolish
as reaching for a gun." Pickering, glancing up,
froze, as he found himself staring down the bore

of a pistol trained on his chest. "I have not been so remiss as to come unprepared for just such an occurrence."

"Your cousin's markers, my lord," said Pickering, withdrawing a small stack of papers and setting them on the desk. "Look them over for yourself. Once again you have misjudged me. And now perhaps you are prepared to discuss business."

Shields, confirming that the scraps, consisting of half a dozen promissory notes to the sum of three thousand pounds, were what Pickering had claimed them to be, deliberately held them over the chimney lamp. Pickering, he noted with grim satisfaction, perceptibly blanched as what amounted to a small fortune ignited before his eyes. "On the contrary, Mr. Pickering," he said, watching the flame devour the writing on the papers. Dropping the charred remains to the floor, Shields deliberately ground them to ashes beneath his boot sole. "Save for the imminent arrival of the Bow Street Runners, I believe our business is concluded."

"Not quite, my lord."

It occurred to Shields, observing the man's oily smile, that either Pickering was exceedingly dense, or he knew something Shields did not. The latter possibility occasioned Shields to feel a sudden prickle at the nape of his neck.

He was turning, the pistol hammer thumbed back. Too late. A heavy weight smashed against the back of his skull and, glancing off, slammed between his shoulders. A searing pain exploded in his brain, and he was falling. The floor came up to meet him, and he lay paralyzed and helpless.

From somewhere beyond the descending darkness, he heard Pickering.

"You fool! You might have killed him, and then what use would he have been to us? He will pay handsomely for the girl, you may be sure of it. He is in love with her. Any fool could see that."

There came another voice, distorted in the roar of pain in his head.

"I have other plans for Miss Rochelle, and you do not play a part in them. Thanks to your bungling, you are become a liability I can ill afford."

The rest was lost in the enveloping blanket of darkness. Elfrida! stabbed through his brain, and then the blackness engulfed him.

It came to Shields through a heavy fog punctuated with a dull, throbbing pain in his skull, that *someone* would be made to pay for his present discomfort. He was conscious of lying on his stomach with the side of his face pressed down against a mattress covered with some less than immaculate sort of coverlet, and for some unknown reason his feet were bound and his hands were pinioned behind him.

Gathering his strength, he rolled himself over onto his back and was rewarded for his efforts with a sharp crescendo of pain in his head, which shot down through his shoulder blades.

"The devil," he cursed, feeling the sweat pour over his body. Drawing long, gasping breaths, he waited for the pounding in his head to subside before he sat up to take an assessment of his surroundings.

He was in a room peculiarly lacking in all of the amenities even to the dearth of curtains across the windows, which confirmed the fact that night had fallen and that, furthermore, he was confined somewhere in the City. Indeed, he could not mistake the distinct silhouette of a building across the way, not to mention the clatter of carriage wheels on a cobblestoned street perhaps three stories below. At least it would seem he had been moved to a better part of the City: the stench of rotting refuse was noticeably lacking.

The thought of refuse served to bring his memory of earlier events flooding back. Egad, he had been decked from behind like the veriest cull. It little helped his frame of mind to realize he should have been forewarned when Pickering used the key to unlock the drawer in the desk. Hellfire! He should have known to check the blasted cabinet! And then came the final memory. Elfrida!

Pickering, the slimy little rodent, had abducted Elfrida with the intent of demanding a ransom for her! There could hardly be any other explanation for those fragments of overheard conversation between Pickering and the felon who had been waiting in the cabinet to assault Shields from behind. Only the unknown attacker had had other plans for his captive. What—if not ransom?

Icy fingers of fear clutched at Shields's heart. It would hardly seem likely the felon intended simply to let Elfrida go. The only other possibility that came immediately to mind set Shields straining at his bonds until the cords cut into his wrists—to no avail. The bonds held with an annoying tenacity.

Bloody hell! He was trussed up like a bloody lamb for the slaughter. Why the devil was he still alive? Pickering and his damned accomplice had tried hard enough before to put a period to his existence. Why the bloody hell had they not finished the job when they had him bludgeoned and unconscious? Apparently they still had some other use in mind for him or perhaps they preferred to do away with him at their cursed leisure. Whatever the case, he was bloody well damned if he would wait tamely for them to come back to complete their business with him.

A glint of moonlight glancing off glass drew his

attention to a clutter of debris on the floor, evidence that someone had been living in the room—a circumstance for which Shields could only be grateful. Among the litter gleamed the broken remains of what gave every evidence of having been at one time a shaving glass.

Dropping to his knees on the floor, Shields reached for a glittering shard.

Ignoring the blood mingled with sweat that ran from his wrists down his hands, Shields worked until he felt the bonds give way. With grim satisfaction, he yanked his hands free, then, turning to the knots that bound his lower extremities, he made short work of them. Flinging the cords aside, he shoved himself to his feet—and froze, his senses strained in the dark to the silence around him.

Almost immediately, he heard it again—the distinct creak of a floorboard beyond the closed door, followed by the metallic grate of a key inserted into the lock.

Noiselessly, Shields stretched out on the bed and settled himself to wait.

He tensed, ready to spring, at the sound of the door swinging open, followed by an uncertain silence—at last steps approaching the bed. Again the silence. His nerves tingled, as he sensed someone leaning over him. He felt the trembling touch of fingers to his cheek.

He moved! His hand, darting up, clasped a slender wrist and dragged its owner down. Shields rolled, pinning the intruder beneath him.

"Shields, *no!*"

The earl went still, pierced through by a swift, hot stab of emotion.

"Good God," he uttered, dumfounded. *"Elfrida!"*

Then lowering his head, he savagely kissed her.

Chapter 14

Shields lifted himself up on his elbows to look down at Elfrida. He was ruefully aware of the pressure only just beginning to ease in his chest. Egad, she was *alive*, and she was here with him. Hellfire, he had come to within a hair's breadth of throttling her pretty neck for her!

"Elfrida! The devil, did I hurt you?"

Elfrida, reeling from the kiss she had received from Shields, not to mention the shock of relief she had experienced upon finding him living when he had lain so frightfully still as she approached through the gloom relieved only by moonlight, yet sensed something of what he was feeling. Smiling tremulously, she reached up to touch his face. "Shields, my dearest lord, I do wish you will cease to look at me in that way. I am all right, really I am. You did nothing more than startle me, which is no doubt what I deserve for not calling out to you. I'm afraid at the last moment I allowed myself to fall prey to doubt. Absurd, is it not? But I was dreadfully afraid you were going to turn out to be some poor soul without a home who had stolen in here in search of shelter."

"Nevertheless," said Shields, brushing a loose strand of hair from her face, "I should have known it would be you."

"Indeed, I daresay that you should," Elfrida retorted irrepressibly. "After all, who else should it have been? I have warned you repeatedly that it is my karmic duty to look after you, but you seem determined to thwart me at every turn. How dared you confine me to Albermarle House! For shame, my lord—you gave me your word I should be allowed to help you. I daresay if I were not a prognosticator and a scryer, I should have had a devil of a time finding you."

It was, perhaps, an unfortunate point to have brought up at that particular time and place, Elfrida was made instantly to realize.

"But you did find me," observed Shields ominously, reminded that she had been supposed to be safely tucked away in the duke's Town House until he, Shields, came for her. "Never mind that you were to remain at home or that Pickering and his unknown accomplice had plotted to abduct you in order to extract a king's ransom from whoever would be willing to pay for your return, their principal expectation being that *I* should pay it. Hell and the devil confound it, Elfrida! I was made to labor under the belief that you had already been taken and that, further, Pickering's accomplice had very possibly put a period to your existence, as he all but declared he intended to do."

"And very likely he would have done," submitted Elfrida, who could not but think it was exceedingly coming of Pickering and his unknown henchman to think to impose on Shields to pay a ransom for a woman who, far from laying any claim to his protection, was neither his kinswoman nor his wife.

"You were perfectly right to refuse to pay Mr. Pickering anything. Indeed, you must not think I hold it against you. Quite the contrary. No doubt you can imagine how I should have felt to discover you had paid out a fortune when I had been so disobliging as not to fall into Mr. Pickering's clutches. I daresay I should never have forgiven you."

"In such an event, I daresay you would have been perfectly justified in not doing so," conceded Shields, who could not but be much struck at that previously unconsidered possibility. Hellfire! In the wake of what he had been made to suffer in thinking he had irretrievably lost Elfrida, he did not doubt that he would have given a deal more than a mere fortune to have had her back again. "Which does not explain how it is that you are here where you have no business to be."

"But I have every business being here," Elfrida objected, thinking that quite possibly Lions were even more pigheadedly stubborn than Rams. "And, as for how I should be here, I already told you. I saw it in a dream, never mind that Violet insists I must have overheard the two gentlemen on the other side of the screen that separate ladies' fashions from household goods discussing something about Skinner Street and a woman whom they had misplaced though they were certain she had been in Clevenger's only moments before. I know I saw the street, the building, this room— and you, lying on this bed. Indeed, I can only wonder how it is that you are not bound, hand and foot, with cords. I am quite certain you were so in my dream."

"Your dream notwithstanding," said Shields, who, whether he believed in Elfrida's prognosticative dreams or not, was struck with the sudden queasy sensation that his Goddess of Beauty had been within a very few inches, little more than the width of a screen, in fact, of falling into the hands of Pickering's henchmen intent on abducting her for ransom, "I have a strong aversion to being forcibly restrained. I wasted little time in cutting myself free. Furthermore," Shields added, pushing himself up off the bed and extending a hand to Elfrida, "I suggest it is time we took ourselves away from here. As much as I should enjoy having my hands on the felon who put me here, I should prefer to choose my own time and place for it."

"As it happens, nothing would make me happier than to be quit of this room. There is something about it that I cannot like," said Elfrida. Then, laying her hand in his, she was startled into uttering a small exclamation of dismay mingled with horror. "The devil, Shields, what have you done? You are bleeding!"

"Never mind that for now," he said, pulling her to her feet. "It is nothing to signify. It has only just occurred to me why I might have been left alive when I should have expected something quite different from Pickering's unscrupulous accomplice. It is not inconceivable that it was done in the hope that you might do precisely what you did—set out to find me. How did you come here?"

"As it happens, I brought her," offered a compellingly familiar masculine voice from the doorway. "Though I daresay Elfrida would have come alone had I not been given a prognosticative premonition which led me to go to my grandfather's house to prevent just such an occurrence." Vere's slender form leisurely detached itself from the shadows. "It would seem I was not mistaken in thinking you might have need of some assistance, my lord. My carriage is just outside, while yours, I was curious to note, arrived at your home without you."

"I seem to be making a habit of becoming separated from it," dryly observed Shields, who could only be exceedingly grateful that Vere had apparently been on hand to witness Milburn's arrival home, an event that, in addition to being instrumental in sending Vere to intercept the impetuous Elfrida, he did not doubt had caused a deal of speculation among his retainers. "Did you, I wonder, have occasion to learn anything of interest from my groom when you saw him?"

"A great deal that was curious, but nothing which I doubt not can wait until we have you out of here," Vere replied, noting Shields weave on his feet. "I believe, my friend, that you are in need of some attention."

In spite of Shields's protest that he was suffering only a headache and a few cuts and bruises, he was soon glad enough to have the marquis's sustaining arm about his shoulders as they made their way through the murky corridor and down three flights of stairs. His skull was pounding abominably by the time he was helped to climb into Vere's coach, Elfrida sliding in anxiously beside him.

It was not until he allowed his head to sink back against the velvet squabs that it came to him that his abductors had seen fit to relieve him of his greatcoat, not to mention his pistol and his purse. It was soon to be made evident he was to sacrifice his neck scarf, as well, to Elfrida's insistence that the cuts on his wrists must be immediately bound to stem the bleeding. Shields did not doubt that Ellsworth, his exceedingly fastidious gentleman's gentleman, would have some comment to make on the depletion of his master's wardrobe. No doubt Shields could console himself, however, that Albert, unlike Hepplewaite, would not be made to pay the price of his error in falling for the lures of a conscienceless siren. The Bow Street Runners would already have seen that the doors to Mrs. Blakeley's gaming house were permanently closed, and the lady herself would be fortunate if she did not soon find herself on a boat to Botany Bay. At least *some* good had come from what he could only consider his failure to properly gauge his opponent.

Shields did not doubt that Pickering, along with his mysterious accomplice, would long since have vanished into the murky underworld of thieves' dens and rat warrens that infested the seamier parts of the City. In which case, it was most damnably unlikely that Hepplewaite's murderer would ever be brought to justice. More insidious, however, was that Shields could not be certain of Elfrida's continued safety. Even through the mists of pain, Shields had not failed to sense a malevolent purpose in the man who had assailed him from behind. Indeed, he could not dismiss from his mind the echo of the villain's words: "I have other plans for Miss Rochelle, and you do not play a part in them."

There had been something else as well, he realized, the memory causing him to jerk upright with a suddenness that set his skull to pounding all over again. Indeed, it was sufficient to earn him a word of reproach from his ministering Goddess of Beauty.

"Shields, pray do be still. I have almost got the bleeding stemmed, but you will ruin everything if you don't . . ." Elfrida stopped, sensing something singular in the way Shields was staring at Vere, sitting across from him.

The devil, she thought, aware of a premonitory tingling of the nerves at the nape of her neck. It had taken every ounce of her already frayed will power not to give in to a fit of the vapors at sight of the punishment to which Shields had submitted his wrists in his efforts to free himself. Further, she was quite certain from the telltale signs of blood on his coat and shirt that he had sustained a wound to the back of his head, which she did not doubt must have scrambled his brains. And now he had got that look in his eye of the lion preparing to leap once more into the fray. Really, it was too bad of him.

"Shields, what is it?" Elfrida demanded, frowning from one to the other of the two men. "You and Vere are staring at each other as if you had developed the power to communicate with one another by means of thought transference, which I do not hesitate to point out is rude in the extreme. I will not be left out, do you hear me? I will know what the two of you are thinking."

"Naturally we should never dream of being rude to a lady, even one who happens to be my sister," observed Vere, smiling ever so gently. "It has merely occurred to Shields to wonder why he should have been removed from the most notorious rookery in London to the far less seedy environs of Skinner Street. Skinner Street, as a matter of note, has the added distinction of being almost entirely untenanted, due to a miscalculation of the alderman of that name, who was instrumental in promoting its construction. The buildings, while inarguably fine, have failed to attract the interest that might have been expected."

"Which is how we have come to have a genteel neighborhood without the detraction of people to inhabit it," said Shields, his gaze never wavering from Vere's. It was obvious, having overheard the exchange between Shields and Elfrida in the recently vacated room that had served as Shields's prison and in possession of information of which Shields was as yet not fully aware, Vere had wasted little time in coming to certain conclusions at which Shields, himself, had only just recently arrived. "My mysterious assailant, it would seem, has a distaste for the seamier side of London, but, for his own reasons, prefers not to reside in a populous area.''

"Obviously, he was hiding out, Shields," Elfrida did not hesitate to point out. "I cannot think why else someone would choose to live in a perfectly fine house save for the fact that it is utterly lacking in all the conveniences."

"Yes, my dearest Elfrida," Shields agreed. "He was hiding out, and I daresay he is not of the skaff and raff. He is used to the finer things and cannot abide either the stench or the filth of a Field's Lane."

"He is a gentleman. That is what you are getting at, is it not?" queried Elfrida, who did not in the least like what Shields would seem to be leading up to. She, after all, had her own favorite choice for the role of villainy. "But there is only one gentleman on our list of candidates for the attempts to cut your stick for you. Or maybe two, if we include Freddy, the captain in the Life Guards, and I cannot think either of them would have reason to take up residence in an empty house on Skinner Street."

"Neither can I," agreed Shields, who liked what he was about to suggest even less than did Elfrida. "But then, I have come to suspect that the attempts on my life may have little or nothing to do with the reality of my abduction. Otherwise, I daresay I should not be sitting here now discussing it. I might even go so far as to say that I believed Pickering when he claimed he had never entertained the notion of wishing me dead. He was interested in my purse, which would most certainly have been lost to him in the event of my demise."

"But if it was not Pickering, then surely it must be his accomplice," Elfrida persisted, even though the line of logic would seem to be curving about at a ridiculous angle.

"I think we may be certain it was Pickering's accomplice who left me in the house on Skinner Street—in the room in which he had been hiding for some little time. Further, I am of the opinion that Pickering may be permanently removed from the list." Shields's gaze fixed once more on the marquis. "Tom Milburn has been with me almost since I left short coats. It was he who first put the ribbons and whip in my hands. I have no doubt that he did not leave Pickering's house in Field's Lane without first going upstairs to search for me. I should be interested to know what he found when he went into Pickering's rooms."

"I believe you know what he found," said Vere gently.

"Quite so," Shields agreed, feeling the cold grip of a vise on his vitals. "He found Pickering."

"Pickering with a seven-inch blade through his chest," Vere confirmed with singular cold-bloodedness.

"Good God," breathed Elfrida, clutching with icy hands at Shields's sleeve. "Pickering is dead?"

"While I, myself, cannot attest to it with any degree of certainty, Milburn was reasonably convinced of it," Vere replied with suspicious gravity.

"Really, Gideon," declared Elfrida in no little disgust. "This would hardly seem the time for levity."

"As a matter of fact, dearest sister, I could not agree with you more. If I am not mistaken, Pickering's death under suspicious circumstances would seem to present a certain sobering proposition."

Elfrida, who had been laboring for some little time under the growing suspicion that Shields and her brother were working up to something that they perceived as singularly consequential, not to mention fraught with dire potential, could not but feel a mounting annoyance at what she perceived as a wholly unnecessary male penchant for leaving her in the dark. "What proposition?" she demanded. "For heaven's sake, what is it that you are both reluctant to tell me?"

She was met with a wholly unrevealing shrug from her brother, the marquis, which led her to turn to Shields with a martial light in her eyes.

"You will tell me, Shields, before we go very much farther," she said with utter conviction. "I really must insist on knowing what you and Vere know that I do not."

"I believe you are left with little choice but to tell her," said Vere, who was well acquainted with his sister's Rammish determination to have her way when she had set her mind on a thing. "I daresay she has a right to know."

"Know *what?*" said Elfrida, as close as she had ever come to utterly losing her temper with either one or both of her two companions.

"Know, my girl," replied Shields, his grave aspect looking worn in the pale glow of a street light, "that it was never me Pickering's accomplice was after."

Elfrida, who was not sure what she had expected to hear, was most decidedly certain that it was not that. "Not you? But whatever do you mean? If it was never you, then who—?"

The answer came to her with blinding clarity just as Shields gave voice to it.

"Always and from the very beginning, our unknown assassin has been after you, Elfrida. The question now is why."

Elfrida, who did not have the answer to that significant question any more than she could have said who would wish her dead, yet could not but see everything that had happened would suddenly make incomprehensible sense. She, she recalled with vivid recollection, had just stepped off the curb when the runaway hackney appeared suddenly out of nowhere. She had been in the balloon that had been severed from its anchor and set adrift to an uncertain landing. And before that, there had been the unmistakable sensation that someone had deliberately pushed her into the path of the panicked mob seeking swift exit from the melee going forth behind them. Faith, it would, indeed, all seem to make perfect sense, save for one glaring exception.

"That night, Shields, when I shot you with Valentine's pearl-handled pop gun, I was certain I perceived an intruder fleeing the back of your house. Indeed, I was subsequently led to discover the back door to your house left ajar. Surely it would make little sense to suppose he was after me when it was *your* house into which he was trying to gain illicit admission."

"I have been thinking about that, too," confessed Shields, who would vastly have preferred to have had a different interpretation present itself for all the inconsistencies that would seem to be resolved only if Elfrida were the target of the unknown assassin rather than he, himself. "I'm afraid any number of possible explanations present themselves. The intruder might have been a simple burglar unconnected with the other events. Or he might have been led in the fog to confuse the back of my house with Godfrey's. It is fairly certain he had been observing you for some little time, in which case there is the possibility that he mistakenly believed you and I were involved in a romantic intrigue. Failing to realize that Godfrey had lent his house to Vere, he might have assumed you were living with me."

"It would all seem to make a great deal of sense," admitted Elfrida, averting her face in dismay from Shields and her brother. "The devil, I was afraid

you would come up with a plausible explanation.
Not that I am not relieved that you would not seem
to be the target of an assassin's bullet, Shields, for
I assure you I could not be more pleased to see
you off the hook. The thing is, if you are not the
target and I am, then it is clear that you were never
under a pall of danger until I imposed myself on
you in the misguided belief that you required me
to watch over you." At last she brought her head
around to look at him squarely in the eyes. "It is
all my fault, my lord. I most sincerely apologize for
any inconveniences that—"

"Elfrida—" said Shields, who did not require
the power of a prognosticator and a scryer to see
where Elfrida's logic was leading her. The devil,
he was bloody well damned if he would stand for
any Arian nonsense. She would not be allowed to
disregard everything that had happened between
them in order to gallantly sacrifice herself, not to
mention what he had not the slightest doubt was
his future happiness, out of the mistaken belief
that she was responsible for the malevolent deeds
wrought by evil men. "Elfrida," he said forcefully,
"you will listen to me."

It was at this juncture that Vere, in spite of the
fact that he would no doubt have derived a deal
of amusement out of allowing his two companions
to continue in their present vein, felt moved to
intervene.

"It would appear obvious that the two of you
have a great deal to discuss. Nevertheless, before
you do, I feel obligated to point out a few of what
I should consider to be pertinent observations. First
of all, while we have been indulging in a deal of
inarguably intriguing speculation, in the final analysis that is really all it is—speculation. We have yet
to discover the smallest proof to support any of
it. Secondly, it has occurred to me, purely as an

objective outsider, that it is still indeterminate who is the object of the alleged assassin's rancor—you, Elfrida, or Shields. The evidence would seem to point in either direction equally well. Further, we have yet to discover who would have reason to wish either one of you dead. Does it not occur to you that it is exceedingly odd that Elfrida, who has spent most of the last two years in seclusion at Albermarle, should manage to incur the enmity of one with an implacable lust to cut her stick for her? Equally curious is the fact that, while the odious Mr. Pickering would seem inordinately interested in your purse, Shields, the man who killed him would appear to have been content to leave you in circumstances from which an able-bodied man like yourself must inevitably achieve an escape."

Elfrida and the earl, who had been attending this recital with marked interest, were moved to a simultaneous burst of impatience engendered by Vere's sudden, inconclusive lapse into silence.

"And your *point?*" they demanded together, no doubt prompted to identical spontaneity by virtue of their astrologically predetermined perfect compatibility.

Settling back in his seat, Vere negligently shrugged. "I'm afraid I haven't the slightest notion what any of it means. I merely found it all very interesting."

"The devil you did," uttered Elfrida, eyeing her Scorpio brother with something less than her usual sisterly affection. "I daresay you are enjoying yourself immensely at our expense. Really, Vere, it is too bad of you."

"Nevertheless," interjected Shields, who was not fooled by the young devil's cub's elegant facade of indifference, "Vere is right on all counts. Until we find the answers to his undeniably intriguing questions, we can make no reliable assumptions.

It is possible that the plot involving Pickering and his associate is unrelated to earlier events. Still, I cannot be mistaken in believing that my assailant, whoever he is, entertains some evil design against Elfrida. I was not so far fallen into unconsciousness as not to overhear that much at least.''

"You are fortunate if you were not made to suffer a deal worse than a bump on your head," observed Elfrida, who, having returned to binding the earl's wounds, was reaching up to probe the back of his skull with her fingers. "How in heaven's name did you allow yourself to fall victim to a rear attack, when you must have known very well Pickering was not to be trusted? Really, Shields, I should have thought better of you.''

"No less than should I," uttered Shields, wincing as his indomitable Goddess of Beauty found the swelling beneath the crusted mat of hair and dried blood. "I was undeniably careless in failing to examine the cabinet in Pickering's unwholesome lair.''

Shields, exceedingly sensitive to Elfrida's touch as she tied off the final bandage on his wrist, related the details concerning the retrieval of Albert's markers and the manner in which he had come to be caught in Pickering's snare.

"At least we may be thankful we have not to worry about having those troublesome markers turn up somewhere," said Elfrida when he had finished. "How very clever of you to burn them. I daresay that did not set at all well with Mr. Pickering.''

Shields leaned his head back against the velvet squabs. His eyes closed, he heard his own voice seeming to drone on as though it were a thing separate from the weariness pressing, like a leaden weight, down upon him. "You may be sure, in light of what came after, that Pickering meant to take them off me. Which is only one more reason I should have suspected something. It was obvious that Pickering was taken aback when he saw what I was about. With him, it was always the chance for profit. What I cannot conceive is what his accomplice hopes to gain from all of this."

From somewhere far away Elfrida's voice impinged upon his consciousness. "Hush, my dearest. Tomorrow will be soon enough to contemplate it."

It was the last thing he remembered, until he awakened to the stream of sunlight through a lace-curtained window, the realization that he was lying in bed between silk sheets, and to the reality of Elfrida in one of Lady Loring's forgotten rose-colored night dresses. Curled up kitten-like in an easy chair by the bedside, she was asleep.

They were in the house on Holles Street. Of that much he was immediately certain. Of less certainty was where Vere was or how he, himself, had come to be in his present circumstances. In sudden suspicion, he lifted the bedclothes and peeked underneath them. Another bloody mystery—who the devil had undressed him? He dropped the covers and sent his glance about the room in search of his clothing. He was somewhat relieved to note that fresh apparel was laid out on a chair for him to don, which led him to speculate that Ellsworth, his valet, was somewhere on the premises. He could only be grateful that Albert, having recovered sufficiently to insist on returning to his bachelor quarters in St. James's Street, was not on hand to be witness to Elfrida's abandonment of all pretense of adhering to the proprieties. Indeed, he could only marvel that Vere had allowed such a glaring lapse.

But then, he reflected with a wry twist of his lips, even Vere might have found it difficult to dissuade Elfrida from something she had set her mind on doing. And there was no disputing that his Goddess of Beauty had been determined not to be separated from him in what she must have seen as his hour of need. Shields, after all, had before him indisputable evidence that Elfrida had spent the night, watching at his bedside. More than that, he was of the inalterable opinion that her natural generosity, coupled with a fiercely loving heart, would never allow her to abandon him before he was well enough to look after himself.

It was an aspect of her character for which Shields could not but be exceedingly grateful, since it had served to buy him time that might otherwise have been denied him. Shields did not doubt that, having convinced herself that she was the inadvertent cause of all of his recent troubles, Elfrida had made up her mind to leave him—and that he would not tolerate. In spite of her stubborn insistence on adhering to her karmic duty to protect her karmically predetermined, astrologically perfect mate, even going so far as to give him up to keep him safe, she *would* be brought to marry him. On that he was adamantly decided.

Having reaffirmed that much to himself, Shields was struck with the thought that he bloody well wished his Goddess of Beauty would bring herself to trust him!

It was at that point that the kitten stirred and, opening her eyes, beheld the earl regarding her with a fierce, lionish stare, which might have served to arouse her Arian temper had she not been so unutterably relieved to have him returned at last to full awareness.

"Shields, you are awake!" she exclaimed, scrambling to uncurl herself from the chair.

A low thud at her feet as she arose drew both Shields's and her attention. Elfrida froze for perhaps a heartbeat, her eyes coming up to meet his.

"A gun, Elfrida?" pronounced the earl in dire tones of inquiry.

"You needn't look at me as if I did not know perfectly well how to use it," declared Elfrida, bending down to retrieve the weapon, which, despite its dainty dimensions, was no less deadly looking. Certainly, Shields did not fail to note that it was not of the same caliber as the silver-plated, pearl-handled pop gun with which his Goddess of Beauty had first made her introduction to him. "Papa taught me, and he was an excellent shot."

"I've no doubt," agreed Shields, presented with the less than sanguine mental image of Elfrida standing armed guard over him while he slept. "I suggest, however, that, unless you intend to inflict worse injury than a cork to my forehead, you cease immediately to point it at me."

Elfrida, hastily setting the pistol on the table at his bedside, could not but think that Shields had awakened in a rare taking. But then, she did not doubt his head was hurting abominably. Indeed, she would have been exceedingly surprised if he had not been severely concussed from the blow to the back of his skull. When she, aided by Vere, had cleansed and bandaged the wound, Shields had lain so frightfully still! Indeed, he had remained unmoving and insensible for so long she had been brought to fear for the worst.

Certainly, Ellsworth's scandalized assurances that he was prepared to take excellent care of his master had not proven sufficient to persuade her to leave the earl's side. She could only be grateful that Vere, who had observed the proceedings with his usual dispassion, had chosen not to impose his will against hers.

Dearest Gideon! He had proven a tower of strength when she needed him most!

It had been Vere's suggestion to install Shields

in the house on Holles Street in order to avoid attention and the inevitability of wagging tongues among the earl's aristocratic neighbors. Elfrida did not doubt he had been thinking of her reputation. Indeed, he had known her too well to suppose she would consent to allow herself to be transported to Albermarle House, there to stand meekly by while she waited for news of Shields's condition. Really, it would have been too much to bear. It was Vere, too, who had seen Shields carried into the house and Vere who had helped Elfrida minister to the earl's wounds, and Vere who had gone to fetch Ellsworth to his master's side. Indeed, it had been Vere who, watching her with Shields, had finally taken the manservant aside and, with a few low-spoken words, had miraculously transformed Ellsworth's hostility into something curiously resembling deference.

Elfrida had not asked Vere what he said to Ellsworth. She had only been exceedingly grateful to be left alone to contemplate Shields's still face against the pillows. Nor had she objected when Vere, admonishing her to keep her wits about her, had pressed the pistol into her hand. He had left her then, presumably for Albermarle House to reassure Violet and Aunt Roanna of Elfrida's well-being. And, considering the manner in which she had rushed Violet out of Clevenger's Emporium with what Elfrida did not doubt had seemed to Violet to be a wholly irrational explanation concerning karmic destiny and the unfolding of cosmic events that demanded Elfrida's immediate attention, Vere would have need to exercise his considerable skill at instilling calm in the midst of feminine chaos.

At the moment, however, Elfrida's only thought was for the man who was shoving himself up in the bed.

"That is quite enough, my lord," she declared, firmly pressing him back against the pillows. "Do not suppose for one moment that you will be allowed to leave this bed before you are fully recovered. I have not worried over you all night to have you put yourself in peril by exerting yourself before you are ready. I mean it, Shields," she insisted, knowing she was foolishly running on and yet somehow unable to stop herself. "I may have had the misfortune to fall hopelessly in love with you, not only in this life, but very possibly in innumerable past lives, only to be compelled to have to give you up until we can achieve our karmically predetermined destiny in some future existence, but I will not allow you to hasten things by dying, Shields. Really, it would be too bad of you, and I simply could not bear—"

It was at this point that Shields, recognizing all the signs of a female on the ragged edge of her self-control, caught her wrist and dragged her down to him. "The devil, Elfrida," he uttered harshly, not stopping until he had rolled her over him onto her back on the bed beside him. "You are like to drive me mad." Leaning over her, he pierced her with his eyes, which were indeed lit with a fierce, burning light, quite unlike the cool, impenetrability with which they habitually viewed the world. "Say it again, my sweet, impossible girl. Tell me, Elfrida, before I lose all rationality."

Elfrida, who had spent the night torn between berating herself for having once again fallen into the unforgivable error of believing she could manipulate the future according to her interpretation of it and blaming herself for Shields's lying, pale and unmoving, in the bed with a probable concussion, not to mention all the other trouble she had caused him, was in no case to resist Shields in his present state of lionish imperiousness. To her horror, she felt tears well up in her eyes and spill over down the sides of her face.

"The devil," she gasped, brushing ineffectually at the disgustingly feminine things. "What would you h-have me tell you? That I l-love you w-with my whole h-heart and being? And indeed have done since you so a-arrogantly commanded me to take lessons in dep-portment, n-not to mention the m-minuet?" Drawing a deep, steadying breath, she lifted her hands to cradle his face. "Well, I do, Shields. I love you so much that, if Pickering's despicable accomplice had-had taken your life, I should have wished to die, too."

It was soon made apparent that that was precisely what Shields would have had her tell him.

"Hush, my sweet, beautiful Elfrida," he commanded, lowering his head to kiss the tears from her face. "I absolutely forbid you ever to do any such thing. You are mine, Elfrida, and I will not allow anything ever to take you from me. Nothing, do you hear me?"

It was on Elfrida's lips to reply that she heard him perfectly well, but that unfortunately it really changed nothing because, whether he willed it or not, she had no choice but to leave him—that, indeed, it was written in the stars. She was prevented from uttering it, however, by Shields, who, no doubt visited by his newly acquired power of premonition, covered her mouth with his.

He kissed her deeply, his mouth moving over hers with a fierce, aching tenderness that robbed Elfrida of any will to resist. And when he released her lips to kiss her eyes, first one and then the other, followed by her brow, her cheeks, her hair, she told herself it would not be wrong to allow herself this one last fleeting moment of happiness. He was her Twin Soul, her karmically predetermined love, and to save him, she would give him up. But not now, not when Shields needed her, not when she needed him with all of her heart and her being.

Reaching her arms around him, she surrendered herself to the all-consuming passion that Shields and Shields alone had the power to arouse in her.

Shields, fully aware that Elfrida's confession of love had come as a result of her having spent the entire night tormenting herself with the misguided notion that she was to blame for all the mishaps that had befallen them, could not bring himself to regret it. *Elfrida loved him!* Good God, he had begun to think he was never to hear those words from her, never mind that he had long since come to suspect that she had surrendered her heart to him along with her generous capacity for passion. Indeed, he would have sworn that no woman could have given herself to him with such sweet, wild abandon as she had without having her heart thoroughly involved. Nevertheless, he had been equally aware that his infuriatingly stubborn Goddess of Beauty, even with her affections fully, if unknowingly, engaged, was perfectly capable of walking out of his life forever out of the absurd notion it was for his own good—egad! Now, having come to know her own heart, she would not find it so easy to leave him. Even so, he meant to make sure of it.

It was time Elfrida learned she could not drop uninvited into his life, take up permanent residence in his heart, and then simply leave him to an existence robbed of any real meaning.

Carried on the heady sense of power of knowing Elfrida could not escape him now, Shields aroused her with a savagely tender passion. His lips teased and tormented her, while his hands worked the hem of her gown up over her long, slender legs.

Elfrida helped him, lifting herself to be freed of

the confining fabric. It came to her with a rending pang that even so had Shields stripped the gown from his former mistress in this room, here, in this bed. Faith, how she had hated having the gown, *her* gown, next to her skin! In truth she would have preferred to have kept to her own dress soiled with Shields's blood had she not known it would have distressed him to see her so. In her tormented fancy, she wondered if Shields would take the beautiful Lady Loring back again when Elfrida Rochelle was no longer a troublesome thorn in his side. Then his hands were molding themselves to her, stroking and caressing her, trailing tantalizing flames of arousal over her breasts, her nipples peaked with desire, down the slender length of her torso to the hidden treasure between her thighs, and she forgot everything but Shields and the aching wonder of Twin Souls carried on a cresting wave of primordial passion.

Elfrida arched to him, her fingers digging into the flesh of his shoulders. "Shields, hurry! I cannot bear it!"

Shields quickly spread her thighs and, inserting himself between them, fitted the head of his manhood to the swollen lips of her body. It was the moment for which he had been waiting, husbanding his will and his strength. Elfrida wanted him. Elfrida needed him. She would soon find that, even between karmically predetermined perfect lovers, the Ram was no match for the Lion. Slowly, carefully, he moved himself into her.

Elfrida, feeling herself filled with him, clung to him, willing him to carry them to the threshold of completion. Faith, she was like to die of wanting him. "Shields?" She opened her eyes to find him posed over her, his eyes smoldering with primordial fire.

"Tell me, Elfrida," he said, his every muscle

strained to contain his need to finish what he had started. "Swear you don't intend to walk away from me."

"The devil, Shields," she gasped, as his thumb moved most distractingly over the taut bud of her nipple. "I swear I shall die if you do not cease to torment me." A low groan burst from her as he pressed his lips to the throb of her pulse at the base of her neck. "No doubt it is only what I deserve," she breathed, her hands moving over him as if they had a will of their own—touching him, glorying in the magnificent male strength of him. "I have caused you nothing but trouble from the first moment I imposed myself on you."

It was not the answer he wanted from her. With infinite care, he moved inside her, teasing her with long, slow forays, even as his lips brushed hers with infinite tenderness. Lost in the feel of him, she reached to him, returned his kiss on a low, keening sigh. "You love me, Elfrida," he whispered insidiously near her ear.

Elfrida moved her head aimlessly back and forth against the pillow, lost in an agony of glorious torment. "Yes, Shields, always, from the very beginning and forever. Faith, I cannot help myself."

"Then trust me to know what I want," uttered Shields mercilessly. "I want you, Elfrida. I will have you as my wife."

It was too much for her. Indeed, she could not bear it. Shields wanted her in spite of everything— not for honor, but for her alone. Really, it was too bad of him.

Her heart breaking, Elfrida cradled his face between her palms. "I will never leave you, Shields. How could I? It would be like leaving myself."

It was not the promise he had wanted from her, but it was enough.

"Elfrida," he groaned, harsh with triumph. De-

vouring her lips with his, he thrust himself into
her with a feverish need. And when at length he
carried them both to a karmic explosion of release,
which left them both trembling and weak, it came
at last to Elfrida, lying in his arms, that he had said
he wanted her, not that he loved her.

Chapter 15

Elfrida stared into the crystalline depths of the shew stone and willed the mists of vision to come to her. It was no use. The visions came of their own, or they came not at all. She knew that and still she had tried, wanting more than anything to see beyond the blindness of what she did not doubt was her own besieged heart.

The devil, she thought, thrusting herself away from the table and rising to prowl restlessly about her bedchamber overlooking the wooded hills of the Dukeries. For once she had not protested upon being ordered home to Albermarle House, a circumstance which had undoubtedly caused Shields no little concern. Indeed, she had been keenly aware of his probing looks in the carriage as she pretended a gay insouciance she was far from feeling.

Shields, she did not doubt, had seen past her pretence, just as, once before, he had seen through to her heart and, knowing she had intended leaving as soon as his strength was recovered, had broken the barriers of her resistance. The devil take him, she thought petulantly, flinging herself across the four-poster bed draped in a rosebud-embroidered counterpane. She was glad to be home where she might have solitude in which to think, she told herself, and knew it was a lie. More than anything she would have wished her false dream of happiness to continue on forever.

Tucked away from the world in the house on Holles Street, she had been given five glorious days and nights in which to learn what it might have been like to be with Shields, her Twin Soul, the only man she would ever love. How odd that time had seemed somehow inconsequential. There had been only Shields and herself and the pretence that beyond the walls of their little haven the world had not waited to claim them back again. She had almost forgotten that it must inevitably come to an end.

By tacit agreement, they never spoke again of Pickering's violent demise or of the mysterious henchman who was undoubtedly the cause of it. It was as if for those few days the pall of danger which Elfrida had unknowingly brought upon them had simply ceased to exist. Only the gun hidden away in the drawer of the bedside table had served as a grim reminder that, even in the tiny corner of their make-believe paradise, reality waited to shatter the illusion. And, indeed, despite Shields's determined efforts to present a cheerful front, Elfrida had known he chafed at the weakness that kept him bound to his bed.

He was up now, however, and, despite her protests, determined to behave as if he were fully returned to his former health, when she knew very well that he was not. And now it must all begin over again—the dread uncertainty of not knowing where he was or what he was doing in his resolve to discover the man who wanted her dead. Or, as Vere had so aptly pointed out, it could be Shields who was marked by an assassin for death. Either way, she did not doubt Shields would not stop until he was brought face-to-face with a desperate villain who was undoubtedly responsible for the cold-blooded murder of one man and perhaps another. Really, it was too bad of Shields.

It did not help in the least that, just when Shields was set on flinging himself once more into danger, she would seem curiously powerless to do anything to help him. She had been visited with any number of dreams while blissfully installed in the house on Holles Street—all of them incredibly sweet scenes of domestic tranquility centered around Shields, even to the extent of representing Shields dandling a child on his knee, a boy who, save for his raven curls, must surely have been another such a one as his beloved Neal. Indeed, she did not doubt that Shields's reminiscences of his lost boyhood companion had been at the source of the vision.

Really, it was too absurd that she should have so immersed herself in the false dream of happiness that she would now seem utterly incapable of anything of a prognosticative nature. And now the shew stone, too, would seem peculiarly closed to her, just when she would most wish to avail herself of its divining powers.

Shields had asked her a question, and soon she must arrive at an answer.

He had taken her wholly unprepared and just when she was at her most vulnerable—lying, sated, in his arms in the wake of their lovemaking. No doubt he had planned it that way. Certainly, she should have seen it coming. That she had not, she could only attribute to her singular loss of all prognosticative powers, not to mention the fact that she had been adrift at the time in a blissful state of contentment that hardly lent itself to contemplation of practical matters.

"Elfrida," he had said, odiously breaking in on her train of thought, which had been occupied with tracing the life line across his strong, shapely palm, which deeply etched, left little doubt that he was possessed of great energy, forcefulness, and determination. But then, as a Leo, he could hardly have been otherwise. "Elfrida, it is time we talked."

Faith, he could have found no surer way of shattering her contentment. But then, his head line, traveling straight across his palm, underscored what she had known all along. Her lionish love would not be content for long to put off contemplation of more serious worldly matters. "No, must we?" she had countered, wrinkling her nose at him. "It has been my experience that when people say it is time to talk, it is invariably the prelude to some wholly disagreeable subject."

Her observation had engendered one of his endearingly crooked smiles, which had ever had the unsettling effect of making her heart lurch ridiculously. "It would seem, infant, that this instance is not to prove the exception. As much as I should like to continue in our present circumstances, you know as well as I that we cannot."

"You are leaving," she said, her eyes fixed, unseeing, on the foot of the bed.

"*We* are leaving, Elfrida. You are returning to Albermarle House. Today."

"Yes, I daresay I am," said Elfrida, summoning a facsimile of a smile. It was, after all, already what she had decided—to remove herself as far from Shields's presence as she could without breaking her promise to him. She supposed Albermarle House was as good as anyplace, at least until she could see her way to something rather more permanent. She had just thought to have another day, perhaps two, alone with him. "Are you sure you are up to it, Shields? You have only just left your bed."

"I have put it off longer than was strictly necessary, Elfrida. You may be sure there is already a deal of speculation concerning my absence. I have no intention of adding to it. I must go back. That, however, was not what I wished to talk about."

No, of course it was not. There had never been any doubt what subject he had wished to discuss. His heart line, ending abruptly halfway across his palm, would seem indication enough, even if she had not already known what it was. Wrapping a shawl around her, she had left the bed, saying that if they were going, she must bathe and dress. And later, in the carriage, she had not given him the opportunity to bring it up again. Nevertheless, the question had been asked, never mind that it had not been voiced.

He had been exceedingly patient with her. He was not, however, disposed to wait forever. She would marry him. He was quite Lionishly set on that. It waited only for her to say when, never mind that she had already made it abundantly plain that she would do no such thing. And truly, if she had been convinced before that marrying him would be the death of him, how much more certain was she now, knowing that she was the source of the danger she had seen hanging over him. And then, to make matters worse, he had tricked her into swearing she would not leave him!

The devil take him! She had not the slightest notion how to answer him or how she was to resolve the dilemma in which she found herself. She had spent a sleepless night battling her pillows when, by all rights, she should have been having some sort of prognosticative dream. She had awakened feeling rather less than her usual self and had then proven it by failing to summon so much as the faintest tendril of mist in her great-grandmother Lucasta's uncooperative shew stone. And now she supposed she had little choice but to go down to breakfast, never mind that she had not the least appetite or that she really did not feel up to morning conversation with the family members who were no doubt gathered in anticipation of hearing all about her most recent adventures.

Still, she supposed a morning spent with Violet and Aunt Roanna, discussing the progress of Violet's come-out, which had finally been launched in the form of a small impromptu musicale at Lady Ashcroft's the previous evening, would be better than being left to her own unrewarding thoughts, which had thus far availed her nothing better than what promised soon to be a headache.

She was wholly unprepared upon her approach to the breakfast room to hear what was unmistakably a baritone laugh, followed by what gave every evidence of being a lively exchange of conversation among any number of people. No doubt she should have been heartened to be visited with an instant, powerful premonition.

"Here she is now," pronounced Aunt Roanna, looking up to see Elfrida, standing in no little amazement in the open doorway. "I was just suggesting we should send up for you, but Shields would not hear of it. He was most strongly set on not disturbing your beauty sleep. Do come in, dear, now that you are here, and say good morning to everyone. I believe you know Lord Winterbrooke. And Lady Shields, of course, who has been kind enough to bring Lady Julia. Even Vere has condescended to join us. And how not on what can only be described as an exceedingly special occasion? I was never so happy about anything, I promise. And you may be sure Albermarle will be pleased as well.

Really, Elfrida, I can only wonder why you did not think to tell us yesterday.''

It was on Elfrida's lips to declare that she did not think to tell them because she had not the smallest notion what the devil her aunt was talking about, when she was prevented from doing so by Shields, who, crossing to her, proceeded to slip his arm about her waist.

''I believe it is safe to say she was in hopes of keeping it a secret until we should be able to tell you together,'' smoothly suggested his lordship. ''Is that not it, my dearest?''

''I should say that was it precisely,'' agreed Elfrida, made instantly aware of the earl's hand applying a distinct pressure to her side. ''Indeed, I can only wonder—'dearest,' '' she added, favoring him with a less than humorous glance brimful, nonetheless, of expectancy. ''How is it that you have apparently gone ahead without me?''

''You must not blame Shields, my dear,'' spoke up Lady Shields, positively beaming in the earl's defence. ''You may be sure he was as closemouthed as ever you could wish. Naturally, he could not have anticipated that we should all read it in the morning *Gazette* before he had the opportunity to make his little announcement.''

Good God, thought Elfrida, who could little imagine what had appeared in the morning paper to make everyone so absurdly pleased—even Lord Winterbrooke, who had stepped forward to give Shields what gave every appearance of being a hearty handshake along with the thump of the side of a fist to the earl's shoulder—though, on retrospect, she had no doubt she should have done.

''You have *all* read it?'' she ventured, thinking that by now nearly the entirety of London must be aware of something of which she knew naught.

''Everyone, my dearest Elfrida,'' observed Vere,

who, she little doubted from his unreadable smile, handed her the copy of the morning paper out of brotherly pity. "Save you, it would seem."

No doubt it was due to the unexpected revival of her prognosticative abilities that Elflrida, before her eyes were drawn to a small item happily circled in ink, knew what it was that everyone was so abominably delighted about.

The Earl of Shields, it would seem, was pleased to announce his intended nuptials to Lady Elfrida Frederica Rochelle, the daughter of the late Marquis and Marchioness of Vere and the granddaughter of none other than the Duke of Albermarle, who resided in the south of Devon.

"Shields, how *could* you?" demanded Elfrida some ten minutes later, coming around to face him in the relative privacy of her grandfather's bookroom, to which the happy couple had presumably withdrawn with Vere in order to discuss the proposed marriage settlements.

"I'm afraid, Elfrida, you gave me little choice but to have done," Shields pointed out with insufferable, lionish arrogance. "Simply as a matter of record, I should perhaps point out that I did try to broach the subject. You, however, refused to even discuss it."

"No, did you, Elfrida?" drawled Vere, settling himself on the edge of the great mahogany desk, his long legs crossed at the ankles, stretched out before him.

"That is because you already *knew* what my answer was," declared Elfrida, ignoring her brother, who was observing the scene before him with obvious amusement. "I had already told you any number of times that I must reject your suit. And now *look* what you have done. It is not enough that I have nearly been the death of you, not once, but four times that I know of. I will not make it five, Shields. I *swear* I will not."

Elfrida, who had been pacing in her agitation, was made suddenly to come up against an immovable obstacle.

"Elfrida, *enough,*" declared his lordship, moved to grasp her firmly by the arms and shake her. "Whoever is responsible for the incidents which nearly resulted in tragic consequences, it is hardly you or your demmed prognosticative abilities. Or shall you now say you were wrong in believing we are karmically predetermined Twin Souls, Elfrida, for, if you bring one aspect of your vision into doubt, then you inevitably do so for the other."

It was a point that she had not previously considered before, and one that would seem fraught with significant implications.

"I know, if you do not," continued Shields when Elfrida went suddenly still in his clasp, "that you could never willingly harm anyone, Elfrida, least of all me. It would seem patently illogical to suppose that I should perceive your visions and dreams, which stem from you, as agents of my own destruction. Does it not occur to you, in fact, that whatever it was you envisioned in your great-grandmother Lucasta's shew stone and however it was made to come about in reality, all of it and everything that has happened—it was simply meant to be?"

Elfrida stared up at him, her eyes huge in the sudden pallor of her face as she wrested with what he was trying to say to her. Always and from the very beginning, they had been caught up in the fabric of karmic destiny. Given her own Arian propensity to take up a cause and pursue it with single-minded Rammish determination, there was little doubt that she would have chosen to do precisely what she had done. Indeed, even now, after all that

had come from it, she could not visualize herself
electing to remain at home at Albermarle Castle
to be torn with doubt and self-recrimination for
not having acted on her impulse to protect her
karmically predetermined love. She did not doubt
she must inevitably have withered away into some
dried-up eccentric creature, unfulfilled and perpet-
ually waiting for something that would never come
to her because she had missed it. And now she was
faced with yet another decision, whether to cast
doubt to the wind and snatch at happiness with
Shields, even at the risk of losing him, or to
renounce all claims to bliss and leave him now,
before she brought him to the fate she had foreseen for the man she wed. Really, it was all very
complicated. In truth, she knew not whether to
follow her heart or her head.

"I don't know, Shields," she said, her eyes troubled on his dearly loved face. "Honestly I do not."

Shields, who *did* know and who had no intention
of losing her now that he sensed her on the point
of wavering from her resolve, was sorely tempted
to shake her until her teeth rattled and she had
finally got some sense into her head. Only the sure
knowledge that it would be utterly fruitless to rush
his fences with his maddeningly stubborn Goddess
of Beauty—that indeed it might very well serve only
to make her dig her heels into the ground—kept
him from it. Breathing a heavy sigh, he dropped
his hands from her.

"Very well, Elfrida," he said, a shutter descending like a mask over his handsome features, "I shall
strive to be patient for a while longer—until we
have resolved the matter of Pickering's unknown
accomplice, but no longer. In the meantime, do
not ask me to retract the announcement of our
coming nuptials, for that I will not do."

"Speaking of Pickering's elusive associate,"

drawled Vere, who had remained an interested if silent witness to the scene that had just been enacted before him, "it occurs to me to wonder what your Bow Street Runner has been about all this time—Tuttle, did you say his name was?"

"No less than I have been wondering about it," replied Shields, relieved at the diversion, which he did not doubt Vere had intentionally tossed his way. "No one, not even his superiors, seems to know where the devil he has gotten himself off to. I am told he is undoubtedly following the trail of clues he has unearthed and that he will show himself when the time is ripe. In the meantime, I am damned if I know where to turn next. Thus far it would seem that no one knows anything about Pickering's gentleman associate. Even the alluring Mrs. Blakeley has managed somehow to slip into obscurity. The Runners found her house bolted up and the lady fled. It would seem we are no closer to uncovering Pickering's murderer than the Runners are to finding who killed Hepplewaite, though I should be exceedingly surprised if the two are not somehow connected."

"No more than should I," agreed Vere, reaching behind him for a decanter of brandy and two glasses set out on a grog tray on the desk. "Perhaps your Bow Street Runners should solicit Elfrida's super-ordinary abilities to resolve the riddle of the viscount's unfortunate passing. A seance, perhaps," Vere suggested with sardonic appreciation. "I daresay Elfrida could ask Hepplewaite himself who did him in."

"Really, Gideon," declared Elfrida in no little disgust, "you know very well I am neither a necromancer nor a pythoness. I have never communicated with the dead." She paused, her expression reflective. "Perhaps if I were allowed to hold something of the murder victim's in my hand, however, I might . . ."

"Indeed you might," Shields agreed hastily. "Fortunately, however, Hepplewaite's regrettably untimely demise is not our concern at the moment. Pickering's is." Strangely enough, Shields, too, paused, a peculiar gleam in his eyes as he accepted a brandy from Vere only to hold it absently, as if he were not aware it was there. "On the other hand," he said, "Vere's suggestion might have some merit. Has it occurred to either one of you that our mysterious assassin has thus far demonstrated an uncanny ability to show up wherever Elfrida and I happen to find ourselves?"

"It would seem odd, Shields," nodded Elfrida, wondering what Shields was getting at. "Presumably, however, he has spies watching us."

"Precisely," Shields applauded, swirling the amber liquid in his glass as he allowed the germ of an idea that Vere had implanted to take hold. "I should not be surprised if he had someone outside the house watching for us now. It is conceivable he has even bribed some of the servants now and again for tidbits of information."

"I shouldn't doubt it," shrugged Vere, his hooded gaze unreadable. "Certainly, Godfrey's household would have little compunction in letting slip a thing or two for a trifle. Their loyalty is hardly to me or Elfrida."

Elfrida, who was beginning to suspect she might have developed the same capacity for thought transference as that seemingly demonstrated earlier by the earl and the marquis, sat up, her attention fully caught. "You think we might use that knowledge somehow to our advantage." Her pulse quickened as she began to see precisely where Shields's thinking would seem to be leading. "If we cannot find Pickering's accomplice, then you intend trying to lure him to us, is that it? But how?"

She knew before Shields said it.

"With a seance, my divining Goddess of Beauty," declared Shields, smiling as he lifted his glass. "A greatly publicized seance."

It was to occur to Shields over the next several days that he had no doubt completely lost command of his senses ever to have come up with the wholly preposterous notion of staging a seance to catch a felon—especially with Elfrida set up to be the bait.

It was not as if the idea had not caught on, Shields reflected dourly as he waited for Ellsworth to finish fussing over the set of his coat. Hardly had the word gone out, along with a select number of invitations, than the seance to be held by the Duke of Albermarle's eldest granddaughter was literally the talk of the Town.

No doubt Lady Shields could be credited a great deal for that and for the fact that Elfrida's reputation as a prognosticator and a seer of no little renown was being broadcast in every fashionable salon in Town. Somehow, moreover, it had begun to be touted that Elfrida was undoubtedly her great-grandmother Lucasta reincarnate, as was evidenced by the curious coincidence that the spirit of the previous Duchess of Albermarle had passed from her body at the precise moment that Elfrida had been born into the world. It was a little-known tidbit of family history that Elfrida had shared with him as they had lain talking together in the wake of having been visited by a whirlwind of karmic primordial passions. Shields had kept it to himself, in which instance he did not doubt that either Violet or Aunt Roanna had seen fit to publish it.

Whatever the case, it had not taken long for someone to resurrect Lucasta Albermarle's former reputation as the woman who had foreseen not only
the emergence of the first cuckoo clocks in the
Black Forest, but the memorable event of Genevieve Hayden's daring plot to steal the Albermarle
betrothal ring, which had resulted in her becoming
the next duchess.

As for Elfrida herself, Shields mused, smiling
grimly to himself, she, naturally, had taken to her
part with an enthusiasm surpassed only by her
brother's free play of imagination. It had been Vere
who suggested the persona of Zorganna, a made-
up entity who was possessed of the power to see
all, presumably from her vantage point on the
Other Side, and whom Elfrida was prepared to
summon in order to reveal the answers to any number of pertinent questions. Not the least, it was
hinted, was the question of who was behind the
recent horrendous death of Viscount Hepplewaite.

Shields found it not a little curious, not to mention bizarre, that a wide number of individuals
confessed privately to him that they were perfectly
acquainted with the fascinating Zorganna, who, it
seemed, was a Persian princess from the time of
Zoroaster.

No doubt, he told himself as he made his way
downstairs to Albermarle's ballroom, which was to
be the scene of the summoning, Princess Zorganna, as she was now known to be, could be
expected to feel right at home among so many of
her familiars. With any luck, whoever was behind
the recent attempts at murder would be among
them, drawn by the opportunity to have Elfrida
and the Earl of Shields displayed like wooden ducks
in a small pond.

The scene was set, carefully arranged under his
direction and Vere's earlier that afternoon, and

the players, with the notable exceptions of Violet,
Elfrida, and himself, were all present. Before he
summoned Elfrida to her starring role at center
stage, there remained only to confer with Vere and
Winterbrooke concerning their surveillance of the
fifty or so invited guests for anyone who was
unknown to the two noblemen.

"Are you quite sure you should go through with
this, Elfrida?" queried Violet, watching as Meggie
Wheeler arranged the folds of Elfrida's gown, a
strikingly beautiful creation of scarlet satin with an
underdress of Valenciennes lace dyed to match.
Made in the Empire style with an almost indecently
low scooped neck, high waist, and short puffed
sleeves which left her arms bare, the gown was
highly improper for a single female almost on the
shelf. Which was, of course, why Elfrida had chosen
it, Violet wryly reflected. Elfrida would wish to make
certain the evil man they were hoping to lure into
the net could not possibly miss her. The realization
gave Violet a queasy sensation in the pit of her
stomach, which made her wish to implore her sister
to cry off from making a target of herself, never
mind that she herself had insisted on making up
one of the nine participants in the supposed
seance.

"I can hardly *not* go through with it," replied
Elfrida, who was occupied with reading over her
notes one last time before she descended to take
her place on center stage. "Not now, when everyone has gathered in the ballroom to witness the
summoning of Princess Zorganna. Faith, I should
be utterly disgraced if I failed to show up. I only
hope I do not fall utterly on my face. With the
exception of the plays we used to act out as children, I have never really performed before a live

audience. I confess my stomach is riddled with butterflies at the moment."

"You will do fine," said Shields, entering the small alcove which, concealed at present behind damask drapes, would normally have been occupied by the musicians hired to play for the dancing in the ballroom. He stood back to allow Violet to slip past him on her way to join the others already at their places.

Abruptly, he halted at sight of Elfrida, his sharply indrawn breath belying the stern impassivity of his features. Save for a profusion of short curls framing her face, Meggie had left her mistress's hair to fall in a mass of ebony curls down her back. The dress spoke for itself. His future bride presented a wholly improper appearance. Egad, she had never looked more beautiful!

Elfrida, turning with a swirl of satin and lace skirts, awarded the earl a darkling look. "The devil, Shields. Where have you been? I have been waiting on pins and needles."

"No doubt I beg your pardon, infant," replied Shields, crossing to take her by the arms. "I was with Vere and Winterbrooke. Everything, it would seem, is ready."

The devil, thought Elfrida. Even in black evening dress, Shields's tall, imposing figure presented a magnificent target. She did not doubt the white ruffled expanse of his silk shirt above his grey marcella waistcoat had been perfectly designed to draw attention to the area over his heart.

Suddenly afraid for Shields, she leaned into him, her face turned anxiously up to his.

"You will be careful, Shields," she said, knowing how absurd it sounded, and yet unable to keep the words from tumbling out. Of course he would not be careful, she thought. He had designed everything to draw attention away from her to himself—

the mirrors, the darkened stage with but a single candle, himself standing over her while everyone else would be sitting. Really, it was too bad of him.

"You may be certain of it, *enfant*," Shields answered, going over everything once more in his head, afraid that he might have overlooked something that could have been done to protect Elfrida and the others on the stage.

They had been hampered by the necessity of forming a circle of hands about the round table lit with a single candle. Elfrida had thought of the mirrors, the black velvet drapes, and the screen. He himself had seen to the placing of armed men throughout the ballroom in the disguise of pages. It would seem that everything had been done that could be done, and yet he could not quite still a small voice of doubt. No plan could ever be foolproof.

"Remember, my girl," he said, heartily wishing it were all over, "no heroics. Not this time. At the first sign of trouble, you will drop to the floor and remain there until everything is finished. Promise me, Elfrida."

"Very well, I promise." Then, as he made to turn away to set the play in motion, "Shields?"

"Yes—?" Her arm about his neck, she pulled him down to her, her lips seeking his.

Wordlessly, he clasped her to him, his mouth moving over hers.

"That," she said a moment later, her voice sounding breathless even in her own ears as she released him, "is to remind you that I shall never forgive you if—"

He silenced her with a kiss. "When this is over, Elfrida—"

He did not finish it. Indeed, he did not have to have done. Turning, he slipped through the curtains.

* * *

It was to occur to Elfrida that she had never experienced anything quite so queer as finding herself sitting on that elevated stage, one hand clasped tightly in Violet's on one side and the other gripping Roanna's on the other side, while, directly across from her, staring at her with varying expressions of sardonic disbelief, were Lady Loring, Capt. Freddy Wilkes, and Mr. Niles Marston. Indeed, she could only wonder what pressure had been brought to bear to win the cooperation of the three persons who might least wish Elfrida and Shields well. No doubt Winterbrooke could well be thanked for the presence, at least, of the beautiful Sylvia, who sat next to him, and her brother. As for Marston, perhaps he had been enticed by Lady Julia's participation in the drama, despite the glowering immanence of her mama seated next to her, not to mention the immediacy of Shields's imposing stature seeming to tower over Elfrida.

Drawing a deep breath to calm her nerves, Elfrida turned her gaze on her great-grandmama Lucasta's shew stone, which she had placed on the table next to the lighted candle purely for moral support. She began to intone the words from the memorized script she had composed several days before, which, consisting of a good deal of nonsense concerning the desire of those persons gathered in the circle of transcommunication to commune with the spirit of Princess Zorganna for the purpose of contacting the souls of certain of the dead, served to inspire a hushed silence from what gave every evidence of being a spellbound audience.

Curiously enough, it would seem to have quite a different effect on Elfrida. She, despite her numerous recent failures to entice anything of a prognosticative nature out of her great-grand-mama Lucasta's shew stone, was vaguely aware of an odd sense of detachment stealing over her as she gazed fixedly into the erubescent heart of the crystal.

The room faded and receded, even as a black fog descended over her, and suddenly she was aware of a voice, which was not her own, speaking.

It was rather like one of her dream-plays and yet markedly different, Elfrida decided, hearing the name Thaddeus Scrimshaw waft through the crystalline darkness. There was something else about "a terrible truth" about to be revealed in conjunction with James Randall Ludgate, Viscount Hepplewaite, and she found herself straining to hear what might come next. Then, suddenly, the candle went out as if touched by a chill wind. From somewhere a woman screamed. The very next instant a shot rang out. There was the sound of glass shattering, and Elfrida was struck a heavy blow that sent her, sprawling, out of her chair.

For the space of several heartbeats, she lay, stunned by the sounds of pandemonium. A stentorian shout rang out that compelled an almost preternatural silence. Then someone had the presence of mind to light a lamp.

"Elfrida! The devil, are you all right?"

It was Vere, bending over her, his face for once sharp with concern. Elfrida, shaking her head, waved him away as she searched for a tall, familiar, arrogant figure.

"He's over here. He is unharmed, I assure you." Vere, grasping her elbow, was pulling her to her feet.

And then she saw them—Shields, miraculously unharmed, and, pinned beneath his kneeling figure, another man, strangely familiar.

With a sense of mounting confusion, Elfrida

beheld an odd creature, peculiarly dressed in a wrinkled overcoat opened to reveal a crumpled yellow coat of inferior cut and paisley unmentionables that gave the impression that their owner seldom if ever took them off, saunter purposefully toward the earl and his prisoner, whom Shields was just reaching to drag up to his feet.

"Splendid, your lordship," congratulated the rumpled newcomer. "I see that you got him. He's led me a merry chase, he has, but you won't be running anymore now, will you, my bonnie lad? We got you all tight and proper, we have."

"Tuttle," pronounced the earl in tones heavily laced with irony. "It would seem you are possessed with an excellent sense of timing. How the devil do you come to be here?"

"Given up on me, had you, milord?" said Tuttle, extracting a pair of manacles from the voluminous pocket of his nondescript olive green overcoat with oversized brass buttons, one of which was conspicuously missing. "I was never very far away, as it were, following the twistings and the turnings of the trail that led to and away from Ludgate Hall. Unhappily, it was always two steps behind this enterprising young gentl'man. May I say, milord, that I'm that glad to see he didn't do so great an injury to you as he did to Mr. Nicodemus Pickering. I did try and warn you what Pickering was, milord. I daresay he'll not be missed. But even he doesn't compare to the likes of this gentl'man here. A proper bad 'un, he turned out to be."

Elfrida, who could not have agreed more with the Bow Street Runner, was yet mystified by something she sensed in the rigid cast of Shields's shoulders. Even with his back to her, she could feel the emotion in him, held sharply in check.

"But then, I guess you'd know that better'n anyone," said Tuttle, finishing the job of clapping the prisoner in irons. "I'm sorry it had to turn out this way."

"No doubt I am grateful for your concern," rejoined Shields with a singular lack of emotion, which should have warned Elfrida, but strangely did not. Indeed, there was a mystery here that she sensed, but could not explain, as she watched Shields's erect figure turn away from the sagging prisoner. "However, far from requiring your sympathy, I am moved by nothing more than relief to be done with what in the end has proved little more than an aggravation I shall no doubt do better without. I should be obliged, Mr. Tuttle, if you would do me the favor of getting him out of my sight."

"I understand, milord," Tuttle said, clamping a hand on one of the prisoner's arms. "It will be my pleasure to escort Lord Hepplewaite to gaol where he belongs."

"Hepplewaite?" Elfrida, wondering if she were caught up yet somehow in the vision of darkness that had incredibly appeared to her in the depths of the shew stone, stared with disbelieving eyes at the prisoner's back. "But it cannot be, surely."

"That it is, Miss," declared Tuttle, turning his head toward Elfrida. "Here, see for yourself."

Elfrida, however, did not have to see the handsome, dissolute features to know it was in truth Hepplewaite, seedier than she remembered him, and a deal more wretched, it was true, but James Randal Ludgate, Viscount Hepplewaite, nonetheless.

"I believe, Mr. Tuttle," she said, thinking the gallows would be too good for the miserable creature who had basely betrayed the one man who had ever stood his friend. Her eyes met Shields's across the intervening distance and held. "His lordship requested that you remove Lord Hepplewaite from our presence. I pray that you will do so at once."

Then she was walking up to Shields, who was waiting to put his arms around her. It was over, she thought, laying her cheek against the earl's chest. The mystery surrounding Lord Hepplewaite's exceedingly untimely demise and the body found, buried, in the charred remains of Ludgate Hall had yet to be explained, but Mr. Pickering's unknown accomplice had been identified and captured. Surely, that was enough for the present. Indeed, as Shields, holding her to his side, turned to lead her away from the noise and all the curious stares to someplace where they could be alone together and quiet, she did not doubt explanations could wait until the morning.

Chapter 16

It was rather late in the morning, and the breakfast table at Albermarle House in the Dukeries buzzed with talk of the previous night's climactic events. Upon Aunt Roanna's insistence that her nerves were shattered and that, further, she could not possibly face a night without the assurance of a masculine presence in the house, both Shields and Vere had been prevailed upon to spend the night along with Lady Shields and Lady Julia to lend countenance to the arrangement. Even Winterbrooke, professing to be curious to know how it was that Hepplewaite should have turned up alive when he had supposedly been burnt to a crisp, presented himself at Albermarle House in time to partake of a late breakfast, his second, he did not forbear from confessing.

Hepplewaite and his unexpected reincarnation as Pickering's mysterious accomplice, not to mention Shields and Elfrida's elusive would-be assassin, had, not unnaturally, occupied the greatest part of the conversation.

"To think, all along it was Heppelwaite who was stalking the two of you," declared Aunt Roanna, shaking her head over the vagaries of human nature. "And he killed that poor soldier—what was his name?"

"Thaddeus Scrimshaw, Aunt Roanna," Violet answered, as she obligingly passed the cream to Viscount Winterbrooke, who sat to her left. "I shall never forget how you appeared, Elfrida, when you seemed suddenly to fall into some sort of a trance. At the time, I was amazed to think how well you had contrived it. That, however, was as nothing when compared to hearing you suddenly start to speak in that strange gravelly voice, not to mention with a Cockney accent! I was quite moved to admiration."

"No more so than was I," affirmed Lady Julia, who had been sitting almost next to Elfrida at the time. "It never occurred to me it was not all an act, not even when you professed to have been deliberately murdered and left to burn to a charred mass. And to think it was all because Lord Hepplewaite could not bring himself to do the honorable thing in the face of financial ruination."

"Really, my dear," Lady Shields could not forbear from mentioning, never mind that she had been every bit as thrilled at having been a part of what could only be presumed, in the lack of any more rational explanation, to have been a successful summoning of a murdered soul from the dead, "one should not speak of charred bodies at the breakfast table."

"Well, I think it was dreadfully unfair that that poor man should have been foully done in merely because he had the misfortune to stop at Ludgate Hall in the hopes of obtaining gainful employment just at the very moment Lord Hepplewaite discovered he could not put an end to himself," Lady

Julia persisted. "And then for Hepplewaite to plot, further, to deliberately murder Elfrida, simply because he happened to overhear her mention something in an inn about an overcooked goose rising from the flames of its own destruction. It positively gives me gooseflesh at the thought."

"Actually, I believe it was Vere who suggested the burnt goose must pertain to poor Hepplewaite's demise from overcooking," Elfrida emended, setting her cup of coffee into its saucer on the table. "I merely agreed that, as my dreams very often are of a prophetic nature, I did not doubt Hepplewaite had indeed risen from the scene of destruction and had very likely already taken on a new persona."

"A pity he was unaware you were thinking in terms of reincarnation," said Violet. "It would have saved everyone a great deal of trouble. But then, obviously he was more than a trifle unbalanced to begin with or he would never have been hanging about the posting inn at Shaftesbury in the guise of an old man, when he should have been well on his way out of the country."

"As to that," said Shields, setting his napkin aside, "I believe we may have Tuttle to thank for it. As Tuttle himself said, he was never more than a step or two behind Hepplewaite, who, at one point, having made his way to Portsmouth with the intention of booking passage on a ship bound for the East Indies, only just missed being captured by the port authorities. Tuttle, it seems, having anticipated just such a move, had sent ahead to warn them."

"How strange it is to think he must have been working his way back to London in the hopes of finding transport away from England when he had the misfortune to encounter us at the posting inn in Shaftesbury just in time to overhear us discussing my prognosticative dream," mused Elfrida, who could not but marvel at the intricate workings of karmic destiny. "And all along, Mr. Tuttle was behind him, following his 'twistings and turnings' with a tenacity that poor Hepplewaite must have found daunting in the extreme."

"The man is a veritable hound on the trail," agreed Shields, who little shared in Elfrida's sympathy for Hepplewaite. "Having become convinced that it was not Hepplewaite who perished in the fire, it was only a matter of time before he tracked Hepplewaite down. But then, Jamey was never very good at paying attention to details. Had he been, he would never have made the mistake of placing his signet ring on the little finger of Scrimshaw's hand. I daresay the problem lay in the probability that Scrimshaw's fingers were those of a man who had been born to a life of hard labor."

"Damme!" exclaimed Winterbrooke, a gleam of unholy amusement in his eyes. "He was unable to fit the bloody ring on the blighter's index finger."

"It was, I confess, a particular that I overlooked, no doubt because I was not given to see the body before it was removed from the ruins left by the fire. It required Tuttle's bloodhound instincts to question the servants who found the body. You may be sure he inquired into the minutest of details."

"It would seem exceedingly ironic that Hepplewaite, having staged his own death, should find himself in league with the man who had driven him to that extreme," observed Vere, with dispassionate humor. "No doubt it was Hepplewaite's misfortune to have been duped by a woman. I daresay, when he went to the enchanting Mrs. Blakeley in search of a safe haven in which to elude his trackers, he was ill-prepared to discover she was hand in glove with the man who had ruined him. How clever of him to think of offering Elfrida and young Albert up as a means of recouping his losses and holding

Pickering at bay until he had made sure to silence Elfrida."

"I suggest, my dearest, best beloved brother," smiled Elfrida, "that you should let that be a lesson to you. Our grandmother Genevieve, notwithstanding, I daresay one should be careful about playing about with women with flaming red hair. One might get burned, just as Hepplewaite did."

"I must presume you are referring to the charming Estelle," said Vere, smiling ever so gently. "You will no doubt be relieved to learn that Lady Barstowe and I have already reached an agreement. She is undoubtedly a fortune hunter possessed of a conniving heart, an observation which I did not fail to share with the duke. Unfortunately, he was not disposed to accept what he did not hesitate to term my 'bloody demmed impertinence' in interfering in matters that did not concern me. I was charged to remove myself forthwith from his sight."

"Faith, no wonder you so readily agreed to accompany us to London!" declared Violet, giving way to a gale of laughter. "Dearest Albermarle. You may be sure he is perfectly capable of seeing through Lady Barstowe for himself. I should not be at all surprised if he were not, in the meantime, enjoying himself immensely and, indeed, why should he not? He is, after all, the duke. If he wishes to marry a woman less than half his age, who happens to bear a slight physical resemblance to his dearest departed Genevieve, then let him. He will anyway if that is what he has made his mind up to do."

Elfrida, who could not deny the truth of that final declaration from her Pisces sibling, could still not but wish the topic of conversation had not turned to marriage. She was acutely aware that a pair of gimlet eyes were regarding her from across the table with a set purpose in mind.

"On that note," Shields said, rising to his considerable height, "it is time Elfrida and I asked you to excuse us. I believe we have certain matters of importance to discuss."

It was on Elfrida's lips to protest that she was not finished eating yet, never mind that she had hardly touched a morsel on her plate and had very little wish to have done, but a single look into Shields's glittering eyes was enough to change her mind. Reluctantly rising, she excused herself and departed the breakfast room with the earl, who guided her with grim purpose up the stairs to the nearest unoccupied bedchamber.

Consequently, Elfrida failed to hear Aunt Roanna confess to a small sin of omission.

"I believe the subject of the duke's marriage is moot at best," submitted Aunt Roanna. "I have it from the most reliable of sources that Lady Barstowe was seen leaving Devon. In all the excitement I forgot to mention it, save to Shields, who expressed an interest in the duke's marriage plans."

"And now, my divining Miss Rochelle," declared Shields, closing and locking the door behind them. "Pickering's mysterious accomplice is happily in gaol."

"A circumstance for which I can only be grateful," agreed Elfrida, thinking Shields had never looked more lionishly forbidding than he did at that moment as he took a deliberate step toward her. "Although I cannot but regret that it should have turned out to be who it was. I daresay you feel dreadfully betrayed, Shields. I cannot help but point out, however, that Hepplewaite did not cut your stick for you when he had you knocked out and helpless. I daresay, when it came right down to it, he could not bring himself to do it."

"Then I fear you would be mistaken," said Shields, who was in no mood to discuss Hepplewaite's descent into infamy. "You may be sure he would have stopped at nothing—even putting a period to my existence when he had no further use of me—either as a tool to draw you into his snare or as a possible source of funds to finance his escape from England." He took another step toward her. "Even if there were an ounce of good left in Hepplewaite, I should not hesitate to consign him to the devil for what he tried to do to you." He had been steadily closing the distance between them, until now he appeared to tower over Elfrida. His eyes bleak in a face that appeared carved from stone, he clasped her by the shoulders. "If he had succeeded last night in harming you, Elfrida—"

Elfrida, unable to bear the look in his eyes, flung herself against his chest, her arms clasped about his waist. "Shields, pray do not look at me in that way. Nothing happened. I am fine."

Shields folded her in his arms, his gaze grim as he held her to him. "Do not doubt, Elfrida," he said with measured coldness, "Hepplewaite would not be alive today had he so much as touched a hair on your head."

"But he did not, my dearest Shields," breathed Elfrida, wishing to erase the bleakness from his beloved features. "And Hepplewaite will never harm anyone else again. You made sure of that."

"Thanks to you, *enfant*," said Shields, pressing his lips to the top of her head. "You and your prognosticative vision of a pall of danger hanging over my head. Had you not come to warn me, my dearest, most provocative prognosticator, I should never have been on hand to save Julia from abduction and Albert from falling deeper into Mrs. Blakeley's unsavory sphere of influence. I daresay Hepplewaite might very well have succeeded in

escaping justice had it not been for you and your
timely vision of Thaddeus Scrimshaw."

"Perhaps," said Elfrida soberly, thinking of
another of her dreams, one which, in light of the
previous night's discoveries, would seem even more
possibly prophetic. "Still, I cannot dismiss my own
failure to recognize the true meaning of my vision.
I should have read the signs aright, but I was so
absorbed in the premonition that a pall of danger
was about to descend over you that I could think
of nothing but reaching you. And now it seems
that that was the very thing that brought the peril
upon you. The runaway hackney coach, our near
demise in that dreadful hot-air balloon, your being
rendered unconscious and abducted—all of it was
my fault. If only I had stayed away, none of it need
ever have happened."

"A hideous prospect!" observed Shields, determined not to be distracted either by Elfrida's
trembling lips or by her wandering fingers undoing
the buttons of his waistcoat. "Not to mention foolish beyond permission. Need I remind you we were
destined to meet under astrologically predetermined circumstances, which mere mortals are powerless to change or avoid. You told me so yourself.
Had you not taken it upon yourself to come to my
rescue, we quite possibly should never have met,
and that, my little peagoose, I should never tolerate. Clearly, you did just as you had ought. And
now, to make sure I shall never lose you, I really
must insist that you do me the honor of marrying
me. I warn you I am prepared to go to extreme
lengths to have my way in this, Elfrida. Indeed, I
will not take no for an answer."

"Oh, but I cannot marry you—indeed, it would
not be in the least wise," Elfrida insisted, moved
by irresistible impulse to run her hands up under
Shields's shirt and over the wholly magnificent mat

of hair on his chest. "For if you must know, I was visited with a dream one night on the way here to London."

"Ah, but of course you were, my most adorable of divining females," murmured Shields, who had some time before come to the suspicion that something of the sort must lie behind his darling's reluctance to wed him. "I daresay it was a dream fraught with dire portents of disaster."

"Pray do be serious, Shields," objected Elfrida, her lips puckering in a wholly alluring frown. "It was, in fact, a dream pregnant with meaning. A lord and a lady were playing at Pall Mall. Nine times the lady struck the ball through a golden hoop and nine times the hoop shattered as the ball shot through it. There can be no mistaking the symbolism or the warning. Clearly, the nine strokes through the golden hoop represent the age-old custom of divining a maiden's chances of marrying by passing a piece of wedding cake through a golden wedding band. Everyone knows that, if the wedding band shatters, it portends the certain death of the groom. Well, I will not have it, Shields. I love you far too much to chance losing you by wedding you."

"And I love you far too much to allow a dream, which you will admit is obscure at best, to dictate my future happiness. You may be sure I have no intention of cutting my stick before I have fathered a houseful of raven-haired, blue-eyed Herricks. Besides, my beautiful little soothsayer, have you considered the possibility that it was not *our* wedding that you envisioned, but the nuptials of someone else close to you?"

"No, why should I?" demanded Elfrida, clearly discarding such a farfetched possibility. "I can think of no one close to me who is even remotely contemplating matrimony—save, of course for . . ."

Elfrida's lovely eyes widened with sudden startled understanding.

"Precisely, my dearest," smiled Shields. "I daresay you have not been informed of Albermarle's most recent misfortune. It seems the duke, in attempting to lift his bride over the petting stone as they left the church, suffered a dislocation in his back, necessitating his complete immobilization in bed. Lady Barstowe, apparently having second thoughts, eloped, during what was meant to be her wedding night, with her late husband's fencing master. It is Vere's considered opinion that the duke will pay handsomely for the return of the Albermarle betrothal ring, which will suffice to set the newlyweds up in the grand style to which Lady Barstowe is accustomed."

"Dear me, poor Albermarle," choked Elfrida, her eyes shimmering with mingled pity and mirth. "How galling it must be for the duke to acknowledge Vere was right all along about the divine Estelle! She was in truth a fortune hunter with a conniving soul."

"And you, my dear Elfrida, are a fortune-teller with a divining heart, which must surely tell you I really cannot contemplate a future without you. I love you, Elfrida, as I never thought to love any woman. Say you will marry me as soon as I can obtain a special license. While I predict we shall have a long and happy life together, I am unwilling to wait longer than three days to claim you as my wife."

It came to Elfrida that she had been exceedingly mistaken ever to have believed her powers of prognostication had left her. *Shields loved her!* Surely, he had loved her even in the halcyon days spent in the house on Holles Street. The dreams that had visited her there had not been idle after all. Indeed, she did not doubt the future she had glimpsed of domestic bliss was every bit as true as had been the vision that appeared to her in her great-grandmama Lucasta's shew stone, the vision of her karmically predetermined, astrologically perfect mate beneath a descending pall of danger.

"But of course I will marry you, Shields," breathed Elfrida, lifting her face to his. "How should I not, now that I see the future clearly? We are, after all, astrologically predetermined mates—Twin Souls who are meant to be joined in body and spirit in order to achieve spiritual wholeness. You are the one man I was born to love. I should be a fool to think I might change that which has been ordained by the stars."

ABOUT THE AUTHOR

Sara Blayne lives with her family in New Mexico. She is the author of nine traditional Regency romances and four historical romances set in the Regency period. Sara is currently working on her next historical romance set in the Regency period—look for it in 2002. Sara loves to hear from readers and you may write to her c/o Zebra Books. Please include a self-addressed stamped envelope if you wish a reply.

BOOK YOUR PLACE ON OUR WEBSITE AND MAKE THE READING CONNECTION!

We've created a customized website just for our very special readers, where you can get the inside scoop on everything that's going on with Zebra, Pinnacle and Kensington books.

When you come online, you'll have the exciting opportunity to:

- View covers of upcoming books

- Read sample chapters

- Learn about our future publishing schedule (listed by publication month *and author*)

- Find out when your favorite authors will be visiting a city near you

- Search for and order backlist books from our online catalog

- Check out author bios and background information

- Send e-mail to your favorite authors

- Meet the Kensington staff online

- Join us in weekly chats with authors, readers and other guests

- Get writing guidelines

- AND MUCH MORE!

**Visit our website at
http://www.zebrabooks.com**